FOUL IS FAIR

FOUL IS FAIR

A NOVEL ABOUT THE GREATEST UNSUNG
BRITISH HEROES OF THE SECOND WORLD WAR

ROBERT O SCOTT

Matador
9 De Montfort Mews
Leicester LE1 7FW, UK
Tel: (+44) 116 255 9311 / 9312
Email: books@troubador.co.uk
Web: www.troubador.co.uk/matador

This is a work of fiction. Names, characters, places and incidents are either the
product of the author's imagination or, if real, are used fictitiously.

ISBN 978-1848760-172

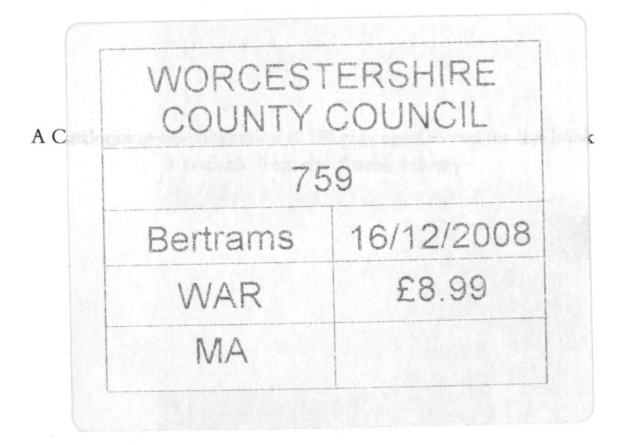

A C

Typeset in 11.5pt Bembo by Troubador Publishing Ltd, Leicester, UK
Printed in the UK by TJ International Ltd, Padstow, Cornwall

Matador is an imprint of Troubador Publishing Ltd

This book is dedicated to all those, remarkably few, very brave men who served in the S.B.S. (Special Boat Section) of the Royal Navy during the Second World War. These few men are the greatest unsung British heroes of that war. All their wartime activities were kept strictly secret, but surely now, more than sixty years later, their truly outstanding exploits deserve to be belatedly recognised.

I especially dedicate this novel to one of these exceptional men - Joseph Corry. From 1942 until the end of the war Joe successfully carried out many important and dangerous S.B.S. missions in German-occupied Western Europe.

'Fair is foul, and foul is fair,
Hover through the fog and filthy air.'
The three witches in 'Macbeth'

'Not by strength, by guile'
Motto of the S.B.S.

Chapter One

'These are your targets, gentlemen. These are the two men you must kill.'

Commander Richardson, the Royal Navy intelligence officer in charge of planning this vitally important clandestine operation, silently pointed for some moments at the enlarged black and white photographs pinned on the board beside him, then continued his briefing. 'Yes, these are the men you must kill, but this time your targets are not Germans.'

Aware that he had his audience's alert attention, he emphatically repeated, 'No, your targets are not Germans. They are – if that is possible – even worse than the diabolical Huns. They are two Dutch traitors who are whole-heartedly working with the Germans.'

Steadily staring at the five young sailors sitting silently in front of him, the Commander forcefully reiterated, 'I repeat, you must kill these two traitors. It is absolutely imperative that you do!'

There was no visible reaction from the five young sailors. Had any one of them involuntarily betrayed the least sign of doubt, dismay or fear on hearing that emphatic statement he would not be here … . would not be a member of that élite team of the Royal Navy's Special Boat Section.

Commander Richardson's gaze met the resolutely steady gaze of each man in turn. Again he was impressed by the aura of self-assured determination, the keen honed experienced discipline of all members of that specially picked team, consisting of one lieutenant, one petty officer and three leading-seamen. He was sure that if these extremely tough and resolute S.B.S men – some of the very best men in what was certainly the best of all British Special Forces – could not successfully complete this dangerous and vital mission then no one else could.

1

The balding, middle-aged Commander smothered a sigh. These men made him feel old. They were all so young, so superbly fit, so outstandingly tough.

Insistently he once more drove the point home: 'Yes, gentlemen, at all costs you must kill these two Dutch traitors.' He paused, glanced at his notes, then continued, 'I know how well you have trained and worked together. Your team is undoubtedly one of the best in the Special Boat Section.' He gave a quick, bright smile, 'It may very well be the best team in the entire S.B.S.'

His calculated (but sincere) flattery was greeted with flashing smiles and modestly agreeing nods.

Commander Richardson now drew a gold-plated cigarette case from one jacket pocket and a gold lighter from another. Before lighting up, he said, 'You may smoke, gentleman.'

He waited patiently until all the fumblings, the withdrawing of packets of cigarettes and the striking of matches was over and his audience were smoking in attentive silence, before resuming. 'I know of all the times each one of you, working in various teams, have most successfully operated in German-occupied Western Europe. You all have truly impressive records.'

He clearly remembered details of some of those hazardous operations, all meticulously recorded in each S.B.S. sailor's confidential file.

During the darkest times of the Royal Navy's desperate battle against formidable German U-boat packs in the North Atlantic, when the numbers of merchant ships being torpedoed and sunk in most convoys were rising so horrendously that they seriously threatened Britain's ability to continue the war, S.B.S. teams had sneaked in flimsy canoes into some of the largest German U-boat pens in occupied France. The roofs of those impressively massive concrete structures were so thick that they were impervious to the heaviest bombs dropped on them by the R.A.F. But some U-boats berthed in what seemed the complete security of these concrete pens fell victim to limpet mines daringly fixed to them by brave S.B.S. men.

Many of these men were later landed by Lysander aircraft or parachuted into France to help organise and supply arms to various French Resistance groups. Unfortunately all too many of those Frenchmen seemed more keen on fighting rival Resistance Fighters than killing Germans. One S.B.S. team had become embroiled in this rivalry; had even – reluctantly obeying imperative orders from London – eliminated suspected traitors in one Resistance Group.

That team had also landed in Holland, and this time with no reluctance, but with great daring, perhaps even with a touch of bravadic enthusiasm, had killed a high-ranking Luftwaffe officer, one of that Air Force's foremost experts on radar.

These S.B.S teams often operated as highly skilled frogman close under the barrels of enemy guns. They daringly obtained details of German coastal defences at numerous French beaches. At great risk to themselves they minutely examined the German's underwater obstacles. These rows of steel tripods were linked with coils of barbed wire; each rusty but viciously sharp barb threatened to rip their rubber suits. Some obstacles were festooned not only with deadly anti - landing craft mines, but also with extremely ingenious, lethal booby-traps. The information they gathered enabled counter-measures to be developed to neutralise many of those hazards.

They brought back samples of sand and mud, gravel and pebbles from many beaches. All this vital information helped British intelligence officers decide where the planned Allied invasion of Europe would take place. Commander Richardson knew only about two hundred sailors were in the S.B.S. He was also well aware that the value of these few men's contribution to Britain's war effort was vastly out of all proportion to their modest number. In his opinion they were by far this country's greatest unsung heroes.

The Commander now continued, 'All those important operations you most bravely and brilliantly carried out pale – completely pale – before the importance of the operation you are now about to undertake. At the danger of becoming a bore, I repeat, this operation is vital... is absolutely vital! And, I don't try to pretend otherwise, it is also quite hazardous.' He gently smiled, 'But you gentlemen are well accustomed to hazardous situations, aren't you?'

The smiles he received in reply seemed somewhat forced.

The Commander immediately became contritely serious. Those brave sailors wanted no bullshit. Those tough, experienced, determined men silently demanded, and surely deserved, the plain, unvarnished truth. Weren't they entitled to know why, once again, they were going to unhesitently risk their lives on yet another hazardous mission?

Commander Richardson decided that on this very special, this supremely important operation, he would explain to them much more then he usually did why their task was so vital. He stubbed out his cigarette in the glass ashtray on the lectern in front of him and glanced at his detailed notes. He risked another smile, 'Please bear with me, gentlemen, while I give you a short history lesson... I will try not to be too boring.

'As you all know, at this stage of the war, well into September of 1943, it seems a foregone conclusion that we, the Allies, must in due course win it. The Soviet army is smashing the German army; it is relentlessly driving the hated Huns out of Russia. It seems the Germans can do nothing to halt the truly awesome might of the advancing Russia army.

'After a long and desperately savage struggle we, the Royal Navy, (with some little belated help from our American Allies) have got the upper-hand in the Atlantic. The German U-boat packs are being decisively defeated.

'And it is no secret that vast British and Americans armies are assembling in Southern England in preparation for invading and liberating France and the rest of Germany-occupied Western Europe.

'There is no possible way that the Germans can now win the war... or so it seems.

'But Hitler keeps assuring his people that the great, the unique, secret weapons his scientists are developing will yet win the war for them. That seems impossible. But if there is one thing this war has taught us it is never to underestimate these Germans. We know that some of their best engineers are experimenting with new types of aircraft – jet-propelled ones, and also with pilotless planes, or "flying bombs". They are also trying to develop large, long range rockets. If successfully developed, these new weapons would pose quite alarming threats to us... but they should hardly be decisive. They should not win the war for Hitler.'

Commander Richardson again glanced at his notes, again gave a quick grin, 'And -although I hate to admit it – the R.A.F. bomber boys are doing a first class job of disrupting and delaying the production of all those secret weapons of Hitler's.'

This time the five sailors sitting in front of him smiled with genuine amusement; but they smiled more *at* the Commander, rather than *with* him. To them, mere wartime conscripts, he was a perfect example of a regular Royal Navy officer (and gentleman) who displayed all the Senior Service's disdain for, jealously of, and almost unashamedly outright hostility to that upstart junior (very junior) service – the Royal Air Force.

Although they smiled with a concealed touch of good humoured mockery, these conscript sailors had been in the Royal Navy long enough to have been indoctrinated with a deep pride in their 'Senior Service'. They too had developed a touch of contemptuous disdain for all 'lesser' services... especially for the 'Brylcream Boys' of the R.A.F.

The Commander turned a page of his notes. He raised his head and once again his steady gaze met the unflinching gaze of each man in turn. He let a dramatic silence build up. Then, with solemn seriousness, he stated, 'But, gentlemen, there *is* one secret weapon which could win the war for Hitler! This is where you come in. You must help prevent him getting that weapon. That is what your vitally important mission is.'

Again he paused, then explained, 'I am not a scientist, I do not fully understand this possible new and terrifying secret weapon, but I am assured by our own scientists – our best backroom boffins – that some of Hitler's most brilliant scientists are urgently working on an entirely new type of bomb, one which, theoretically at least, should, by splitting and releasing the titanic power of atoms, yet win the war for him.

'If those dedicated German physicists are successful, seemingly just one single bomb could destroy an entire city and kill most of its inhabitants.'

This time there was a reaction from his tough, war-hardened audience. They gasped audibly, they moved uneasily on their hard wooden seats then settled into a profound silence. All stared at the officer in what seemed dismayed disbelief. They solemnly waited for him to continue.

Commander Richardson knew exactly how these men felt. They were reacting as he had reacted on first being told this awesome secret – were dismayed by the almost unimaginable implications of this hideous new weapon. He felt a touch of relief at being able to share this heavy burden with these five sailors. Despite their initial dismay, he knew they all possessed more than enough disciplined strength and resolute determination to bear the weight of this terrible knowledge. And, hopefully, these brave men could do something to help ensure that Hitler did not get this appalling new, war-winning secret weapon.

'I hardly need to spell it out for you, do I? All of you can imagine the disaster if Hitler exploded such a bomb – an atom bomb – over Moscow, over the Kremlin; it would instantly knock Russia out of the war. And it doesn't bear thinking about such a bomb exploding over the heart of London, does it? ... nor over New York. Nor over our huge armies assembled in the South of England. The Allies would be forced to make peace with Hitler; would have to leave him undisputed ruler of almost all Europe.

'Such an unmitigated disaster must not happen! You, the five best, most experienced men, the greatest élite team in the S.B.S. are going to help prevent it happening!'

A surge of immense pride flooded through Commander Richardson as he saw the expressions of grim determination on the faces of all the sailors sitting before him take on an even stronger expression of unpretentiously brave resolution. Obviously he had their wholehearted agreement on the absolute necessity of them taking any risks, accepting any dangers to help prevent Hitler getting his war-winning atom bomb.

He expected nothing less from these brave, resolute men ... still he was moved; he murmured, 'Thank you, gentlemen, thank you.'

He quickly distributed a bundle of photographs, giving two to each man. 'These are photos of both the Dutch traitors. Accurately remember these faces so that there is no shadow of doubt over recognising them when you meet them in the flesh. Also memorise all the details on the back of each photo; then each one of you will return these photos to me on the day before you leave this base on your vital mission.'

For a few minutes the Commander let the five sailors study the photos while he in turn unobtrusively studied these men. He was not surprised that each man's reaction as he turned from the top photo to the second one exactly mirrored what his own reaction had been.

The first photo was of Professor Johannes de Waal. That Dutch nuclear physicist conformed perfectly to the popular image of what a prominent scientist should look like. He was tall, was abnormally thin, his gaunt face was dominated by a massively overhanging forehead.

Untidy grey hairs straggled to his shoulders. His large head seemed much too heavy for his scrawnily thin neck to support. He suggested wild eccentricity.

The second photo was of Professor Willem Maurik. This Dutch atomic scientist looked nothing like the popular conception of a 'mad professor'. He was smallish, was rotund; his chubby cheeks were framed by a bushy white beard. This beard combined with a curly mass of snowy hair to give him a really jolly Father Christmas image.

Commander Richardson was acutely conscious that even those toughest, most experienced of S.B.S. sailors intensely studying that enlarged photo might well have uneasy qualms about killing a man with such a benign, innocent looking appearance. All their savagely tough intensive training plus the experience of many extemely dangerous situations had transformed those five young men from naively untested civilians into war-hardened resolute fighters, and – when the occasion demanded it – into absolutely ruthless killers. But even such relentlessly moulded formidable killers were still human, still had all too human feelings.

The Commander spoke out loudly and authoritatively, 'Now, gentlemen, I know how you feel. I felt exactly the same when I first saw that photo of Professor Maurik, but I assure you that you need have no qualms about killing him. His benign, Santa Claus appearance is completely deceptive. You must not be fooled by it. He is an out and out Nazi supporter and is wholeheartedly working with the Germans in their attempt to develop a war-winning atom bomb. My information is that he is a brilliant scientist; is one of Europe's leading nuclear physicists and has some theories which he is developing and which – if they work in practise – could be a definite breakthrough, could provide a real shortcut to the making of the German atom bomb.

'So, I repeat, you must not be misled by his Father Christmas appearance. You must have absolutely no compunction about killing him. Is that clearly understood, gentlemen?'

Replies of, 'Yes, sir,' and solemn agreeing nods came from all the sailors. They were thankful to have this assurance that the ruthless killing of that treacherous Dutch boffin was completely justified.

Commander Richardson turned over a page of his notes then said, 'The code name for this vital mission is … "Operation Waterloo".'

Smiling to himself he recalled how it had been given that code name. A Rear-Admiral in Naval Intelligence (an officer noted for his peculiar sense of humour) had decided on that word not only because we British would surely meet our own Waterloo if we failed to prevent Hitler getting his atom bomb, but also because it gave that Admiral the opportunity to paraphrase the Duke of Wellington's famous order at the Battle of Waterloo ....'Up, Guards, and at 'em'! to ....'Up S.B.S. lads, and atom!'

'Now, gentlemen, I'll get down to what you're all patiently waiting for – the full gen on "Operation Waterloo".'

Chapter Two

As the conning tower of the Royal Navy submarine emerged from the unusually calm waters of the North Sea it erupted a boiling cauldron of sparkling phosphorescence.

A brilliant sheen of glittering water cascaded from the squat grey shape as it rose higher. The vivid brightness of that pouring water made the surrounding dark sea appear much darker.

Even before the narrow hull of the submarine had fully emerged the captain appeared on the conning tower. He was immediately followed by two sailors on look-out duty. Each took up his appointed place. All alertly searched through night-vision binoculars. First one, then the other lookout reported, 'All clear, sir.'

The captain grunted acknowledgements as he continued staring through his binoculars and slowly swept them round in a complete circle, painstakingly searching the entire sea. Satisfied that no enemy vessels were anywhere near, he now concentrated his gaze on the low coastline of Holland dimly stretching out ten miles away. Like all war-ravaged Europe, that land was blacked-out, but, aware that he was five miles north of the Hook of Holland, the experienced young captain knew that the weak glow further to the north must be from the dimmed capital city, The Hague, while the more widespread subdued glow to the south east could only come from the huge, untidy sprawl that was Rotterdam. Confirmation of this came from the numerous flaring flashes of welder's oxy-acetylene torches at that city's many shipyards. Even from this distance these torches flared amazingly brightly.

The captain gave a satisfied smile as he made out the tall shape of an unlit lighthouse on a jutting spit of land directly ahead of him. That was the prominent landmark he had been briefed to look for. He hinged up the watertight brass cover on the voicepipe in front of him and ordered, 'Send Lieutenant Smith to the conning tower, please.'

He wondered if 'Smith' was that S.B.S. lieutenant's real name, or was it, for greater security, a cover name? He doubted if he would ever know for sure. This was the fourth time his submarine had landed small groups of Special Service Units on the coasts of German-occupied Europe, and on three of these occasions the officer in charge was named 'Lt. Smith'; the fourth lieutenant had been called 'Brown'. Wryly he thought, 'I suppose it is just possible that those were the real names of all four officers, but somehow I doubt it … I very much doubt it.'

The darkly bulky figure of Lt. Smith appeared and silently moved to the side of the captain. The lieutenant was not a man to waste words: he merely murmured, 'Thank you,' as the captain eagerly pointed out the dim shape of the Dutch lighthouse.

With intense concentration Lt. Smith minutely searched the entire coastline through his powerful night-vision binoculars. He then concentrated his search on the vaguer line of extreme darkness which he knew was a thick belt of pine trees to the south of the lighthouse. After seven minutes of silent scrutiny he was satisfied. Quietly, but authoritatively, he said, 'Let's go in towards that lighthouse now, captain.'

The senior officer bent to the voicepipe and obediently gave the order, 'Slow ahead.'

There was hardly a word from any of the four anxiously alert sailors grouped closely together on the small conning tower during all the time the surfaced submarine steadily, almost silently, and it seemed stealthily slid through the darkness towards the apparently peaceful, but potentially dangerous coast of German controlled Holland.

Two miles offshore the captain ordered, 'Stop engine.'

As the submarine lost momentum it gently rolled in the dark sea's slight swell. More orders were given: were silently and efficiently obeyed. A hatch on the forward deck was opened. A large black rubber dinghy was hauled out and rapidly unfolded. There were stifled curses from seamen and angry frowns from officers as a compressed-air cylinder clattered on to the submarine's steel deck. That clattering clang swept hideously loudly out over the dark and silent sea. Then the hiss of compressed-air as it inflated the dinghy also sounded alarmingly loud in the tense darkness.

All five men of the special boat section team expertly prepared the rubber dinghy. As he looked down from the conning tower at these silently moving shadowy figures all dressed in black, with dark woollen hats pulled low over heads, with a sub-machine gun strapped to each back, an automatic pistol holstered at waist, a commando knife scabbarded at each belt and with webbing pouches bulging with hand–grenades and spare ammunition, the captain was immensely impressed by their deadly sinister appearance. He was thankful to have such fearless, ruthless men as allies ... he would hate to have them as enemies.

As the S.B.S. team got into the dinghy and pushed off from the submarine no good luck wishes were given, There was a strictly enforced superstition that to openly wish good luck was liable to attract bad luck. The crew of the submarine did not know what dangerous mission these brave men were engaged on, but they silently wished them complete success and a safe return.

For a couple of minutes the captain watched the dinghy paddle off into the darkness then gave the first of the orders which directed his submarine back out to the deeper waters where they would submerge and lie on the sandy seabed until the following night, when – if all went as planned – they would return to the rendezvous position and pick up that S.B.S. team.

Chapter Three

Half a mile from the dim shore Lt. Smith ordered his team to stop paddling. He glanced at the luminous dial of his watch then again searched the shore through his night-vision binoculars. Despite the awkwardness of searching from the unstable dinghy he quickly located the isolated boat-shed where two members of the Dutch Resistance should be waiting in readiness to guide them to their targets.

For three long, anxious minutes the men in the dinghy sat in complete silence with all eyes, all ears alertly straining. Nowhere on that blacked-out Dutch coastline were friendly lights to be seen. The night seemed unnaturally silent. The only sound was the murmur of waves gently surging up the deserted shingle beach, then their solemn sighing retreat back down the trembling pebbles.

Suddenly – right on time – a pre-arranged number of long and short blinks of torchlight flickered out through the darkness. These flashes came from deep within the boat shed. They could only be seen by anyone direct in line with its wide open, sea-facing doors. The windowless wooden walls concealed that flashing signal from any unfriendly watchers at the three isolated houses in one direction and from the small fishing village five miles along the shore in the other direction.

The sailors silently waiting in the drifting dinghy exchanged quick, tension relieving grins then eagerly paddled for the shore. With startling suddenness the three quarter full moon appeared in a gap amongst the darkly overcast sky. The entire scene was immediately transformed to glowing, glimmering, brightly revealing moonlight. The S.B.S. men silently cursed. As they urgently paddled they felt like defenceless 'sitting ducks' vividly exposed by that moonlight. It was easy to fear betrayal; all too easy to imagine those friendly torch flashes suddenly replaced by deadly accurate flashing bursts of German machine-gun fire.

With relief they leapt ashore as the dinghy grounded. With well practised precision they spread out and rapidly advanced up the beach with Sten-guns at the ready. Lt. Smith called out, 'Waterloo!... Waterloo!'

The correct reply immediately rang out from within the boat-shed, 'Blenheim!.... Blenheim!'

Two figures emerged from the building's darkness. As the two Dutchmen approached, one exclaimed, 'Ah, it is Lt. Smith again, is it not?'

'Yes, it is... it is! And its damned good to see you again, Erik!' Their outstretched hands met and gripped in a strong handshake. 'And it's damned good to meet you, too, Peter!' said the lieutenant, turning to the second Dutchman with his hand again outstretched.

This was the third time those outstandingly brave and trustworthy Dutch Resistance Fighters and that élite S.B.S. team had worked together on hazardous missions.

Quickly, eagerly, but with no over-demonstrative excess, all these men greeted one another. All felt united in a bond of tremendously strong camaraderie – a bond such as can only be forged between men who share the dangers of war together, who have complete trust in one another, who willingly put their lives at risk for each other.

After the brief burst of greetings, Lt. Smith asked, 'Is everything as planned?... No new developments, are there?'

'No, no new developments. All is the same,' replied Erik.

'Good!...Good! Well, let's get cracking.'

As silently as the shifting pebbles allowed, they carried the dinghy up the beach and hid it in the boatshed. Erik locked the double doors. Every man carefully noted the exact position of the flat stone where he hid the key.

Lt. Smith said, 'All right, Erik, you lead and we'll follow.' He gave a quick grin, 'Lead on Macduff!'

Erik returned the grin, 'Ah ya, again I be Macduff!' Then, proud of his English and his knowledge of the strange intriguing British humour, he chuckled, 'I be Macduff ... or be a plum-duff, eh?'

The seven men arranged themselves in two parties. Erik led the first group, with Lt. Smith and leading-seamen Mathieson and Lucas closely following him. Peter led the next group consisting of Petty Officer Williams and leading-seaman Armstrong. If sudden disaster befell the first group the – hopefully still intact – second group would attempt to complete this vital mission by themselves.

For three hours both parties moved like silent menacing shadows through the dark, deserted Dutch countryside. Ironically, the German's strictly enforced curfew forbidding the local population to move about late at night, helped these men travel quickly along the traffic-less narrow roads and country lanes. Some parts of this flat landscape were quite heavily wooded. They took immediate advantage of this on the two occasions when they saw the subdued headlights of German army vehicles approaching them. The intense dark under the roadside fir trees securely concealed them while the enemy trucks trundled past.

They were well aware that the black fir trees which so conveniently hid them could just as easily conceal any number of alert Germans. They frequently prayed that they did not – so far their prayers had been answered.

All felt the threat of a greater menace each time their route went along a straight stretch of treeless road with wide, stagnant ditches and bare, featureless fields stretching on either side. There was no place for concealment in this bleak environment. When these stretches of precariously open road were unavoidable all seven men, feeling terribly vulnerable, especially in the increasingly frequent periods of bright moonlight, jogged along 'at the double'. They were lucky, they met no German vehicles or patrols at these dangerous places.

They bypassed many scattered villages. All the farmhouses they were forced to pass were deeply shrouded in silent darkness. Only once was their – as they thought – completely silent passage challenged ... was furiously challenged by the angry barks of an alert farm dog. How terribly loudly, how hideously alarmingly these barks reverberated over the sleepy, curfewed, dismally blacked out Dutch countryside.

The seven men hurrying away from that frightful noise were annoyed by this sudden, unexpected, possibly dangerous incident. At a safe distance they stopped and looked back. They were relieved to hear or see no sign of any alarmed, enquiring humans. Probably the disturbed inhabitants of that isolated farmhouse had wisely decided it was much safer in these desperately hazardous times not to enquire too deeply into what had alarmed their dog at this sinister dark hour.

14

Shortly afterwards, the light of the three quarter full moon again flooded down from a gap in the clouds. It instantly transformed the wide expanse of sluggishly solemn water in front of them into a thing of beauty .... a silvery mirror brilliantly reflecting the moonlight's glittering gleams.

Erik halted and pointed, 'That is the lower estuary below Rotterdam. Our target is just five kilometres away now.' He grinned, his teeth gleamed in the moonlight, 'About two English miles, eh?'

Chapter Four

All seven men lay in a neat row along the gentle sloping side of a deep ditch. They were ten yards from the perimeter fence enclosing their target. The high, chain-link wire fence topped with a roll of barbed wire glimmered metallically coldly against the moonlit sky.

'The sentries should pass here soon,' Erik whispered.

'Good,' Lt. Smith murmured in reply, 'the sooner the better.'

The two carelessly unwary German sentries were heard long before they were seen. To those keenly listening hidden British and Dutch, their faces now lowered to the damp grass, the hateful Teutonic voices coming so clearly to them through the tense dimness sounded even more arrogantly harsh and domineering than usual as they rose in loud, impassioned arguments.

Once those sentries had walked well away down the narrow road on the other side of the fence, the seven faces rose from the grass. Erik and Peter grinned at one another; then, turning to Lt. Smith, Erik asked, 'You understood what these Krauts say?'

'Yes, I think so. My German's not so great, but they seemed to be arguing about football, weren't they?'

Peter answered, 'Yes, they discuss the ... the merits? ... ya, the merits of two great football teams in Berlin.'

Petty Officer Bill Williams chuckled, 'Yeah, they sure sounded real het up in their argument.' He pointed at Leading -Seaman Neil Mathieson who lay near him, 'They sounded just like Jock here when he's arguing with another Glaswegian about the merits of Rangers and Celtic.'

Neil Mathieson grunted an obscure, perhaps obscene, cheery rejoinder and flashed a wide, good natured grin.

Lt. Smith now ordered, 'Right, let's get through the fence.'

In their two groups they silently hurried to the high fence. With eager haste Erik began snipping through the chain-link fencing with his wire-cutters. A few yards to his left Petty Officer Williams displayed a more methodical expertise as he plied his cutters; he had much more experience at cutting through enemy fences. Once he had cut through one horizontal and two vertical stretches of wire, Erik started to hinge the loosened section forward. Lt. Smith stopped him, saying, 'No, Erik, hinge the fence this way, outwards towards us.'

Although puzzled, Erik immediately obeyed.

'You see, Erik, we might have to come back through that gap in a great hurry. It's much easier to dive against and slide through the wire if it hinges up and away from us. It might only make a few seconds difference, but those seconds can make all the difference between life and death.'

Once both groups slid through the neat gaps the wire was left hanging loose. Darkness would hide these two mutilated pieces of fence for most of the time, and even in daylight they would not be too conspicuous.

Guided by the two Dutchmen, both groups stealthily made their way towards the target area. They followed along the narrow gap between the fence and a dark belt of fir trees. In places the trees were thickly planted and hid the narrow road running parallel to the fence; in other places the road could be indistinctly seen.

After ten minutes they halted and Erik pointed, 'Your target is exactly opposite us, beyond the trees.'

Lt. Smith nodded, 'Good!...Good!' He had already noted the large pond glimmering outside the fence; it was this marshy pond and the extensive stretch of treacherously soft quagmire surrounding it which had necessitated them entering at some distance from their target. He was pleased to see that pond; it confirmed the accuracy of the maps he, and all his team had so intensively studied in England. He said, 'We've plenty of time before dawn, but let's get through those trees and into position to wait for our two targets to arrive.'

Crouching, they silently advanced into the belt of fir trees. To the S.B.S. team this slow and cautious advance, with an upraised hand protecting eyes from stabbing branches, was pleasantly different from the many times when, in violent training or on actual operations, they had rushed at desperate speed through fir plantations and had thin branches sadistically whip their sweating faces and agonisingly sting their watering eyes.

Near the edge of the trees they lay in the spongy comfort of the layer of dead pine needles which lushly carpeted the ground and, concealed in the firs deep darkness familiarized themselves with the scene dimly revealed in the fitful moonlight.

Erik again pointed, 'That is your target … that building there. Professor Maurik's office is in that window on the right. Professor De Waal's office is in the left window.'

All the team keenly scrutinized that squat, red-roofed brick building. It seemed innocently asleep in the silent, blacked-out pre-dawn dimness. They noted with satisfaction that the building, with its eight stone steps leading up to the closed green door, and with the office windows on each side, conformed exactly with the plans they had studied in England and with the replica wooden building where they had practised this vitally important operation.

That building was only a small part of an extensive complex of offices and laboratories taken over by the German Navy. Pre-war it had been an annexe of Rotterdam University, mainly devoted to Marine Biology. A small part of it was still used for that peaceable purpose. It was there that Erik and Peter worked. Both were marine biologists. It was their suspicions and warnings which had first alerted British Intelligence Services to the dangers – the potentially disastrous dangers – of the research the two pro-German Dutch nuclear physicists were carrying out here.

Lt. Smith consulted his watch. 'Just one and a half hours till our targets are due to arrive. Are they always punctual? … and are they always on bicycles?'

'Oh ya, they are always on time,' Erik replied, 'and ya, always on bicycle.'

'Ya,' confirmed Peter, 'they are most punctual. They are like those … those awful Krauts they work for and so admire; most punctual, most efficient.'

Petty Officer Williams grinned, 'Well, let's hope their love of Teutonic punctuality helps make this operation go off like clockwork.'

All the others nodded in agreement.

Remembering their detailed briefings, Lt. Smith asked, 'What about the two Dutch charwomen who clean these offices before our targets arrive; are they always punctual, too? Are they always finished and well away before the two scientists arrive?'

'Oh ya, they also are punctual. They are away long before the professors arrive,' Erik replied. Peter nodded his agreement, then, grinning, whispered rapidly in Dutch with Erik.

Also grinning, Erik reverted to English. 'That is correct, they are two "Mrs Mops"!' He turned to Lt. Smith: 'In England such office cleaners are called "Mrs Mops", are they not? We hear them on B.B.C. They are most funny. We love to listen to them.'

The S.B.S. men smiled as Lt. Smith said, 'Oh, you mean Mrs Mop on the B.B.C. comedy show, "Itma". Yes, that charwoman is very funny. Whenever we can, we listen to that great programme.'

In this respect they were like everyone else in Britain: practically every British wireless set was tuned in on Friday evenings to hear "Itma". Mrs Mop was one of the funniest and most popular characters in that brilliant, morale boosting comedy show.

Petty Officer Williams said, 'I didn't know you listened to "Itma" here in Holland, Erik. I don't suppose the Jerries approve of that, do they?'

'Oh, no, of course not. We listen in secret. The Krauts try to blank out the B.B.C., but we still hear it. It is great to hear something real funny in this terrible serious war, is it not?'

'Aye, it is,' Leading-seaman Neil Mathieson readily agreed, then grinning broadly, quoted, ' "It's being so cheerful as keeps us going!" '

All, especially the two Dutchmen, heartily chuckled over this saying of Mrs Mop's which she used every week; used after having just spent five minutes dolefully moaning about all the miseries of the war: the nightly air-raids, the endless queues, the meagre rations, the dreary blackout. This saying of hers was now a widely used British catch-phrase.

Lt. Smith smiled at Peter and Erik, 'Yes, you certainly deserve something cheerful to help keep you going. You do a really brave job here in German-occupied Holland. Much of our work would be impossible without your gallant efforts.'

The four other members of the S.B.S. team murmured their whole-hearted agreement.

Deeply moved by this sincere appreciation of their patriotic efforts, the Dutchmen modestly muttered, 'Thank you ... Thank you. It is most good of you Englishmen – oh sorry – you British men (Erik grinned at Jock Mathieson as he corrected himself) ... you also most brave men, to say so.'

Leading-seaman John Armstrong chuckled, 'We're beginning to sound like members of a mutual admiration society!'

Those experienced men well knew the benefit of indulging in some tension-easing humour in the long inactive wait before going into violent action. But even during the most relaxed seeming of their whispered banter not for one moment did any man cease to be alertly watchful.

Now Lt. Smith asked, 'Do those Mrs Mops lock that door when they leave?'

'Oh ya, they always do. German naval officers have other keys; they open it and start work there half an hour before the two scientists arrive.'

Lt. Smith nodded: this confirmed the information they had been given at their briefing. 'And, Erik, the Mrs Mops never see any scientific documents lying on the scientist's desks, do they?'

'Oh no, never! All documents are locked in the safe in each professor's office before he leaves at night.'

Again the lieutenant nodded; again this confirmed their briefings. They would give the Dutch scientists time to open their safes and withdraw the secret documents connected with their development of a German atom-bomb before they eliminated these two traitors. British nuclear physicists were extremely anxious to see those important – perhaps vital – top-secret scientific papers.

Lt. Smith glanced at his watch then said, 'Well, Erik ... well, Peter, you've guided us perfectly. You've done all you can to ensure this mission's success. Thank you both very much. Now, as arranged, you must go back and wait outside the perimeter fence. If all goes to plan we will join you there soon after we've eliminated our two targets.'

Obediently, though with real reluctance, the Dutch Patriots left the élite S.B.S. team to silently, patiently and alertly wait for dawn.

Chapter Five

This alert, motionless, silent waiting was the worst part of such an operation – it always was. Waiting, endless seeming tensely waiting for violent and dangerous action to begin; action which could all too easily result in death. All five men, to a greater or lesser degree, secretly felt the icy touch of fear – fear of the cold ugliness of death; fear of the agonising shock of terrible wounds. This inactive waiting gave imagination ample scope for vivid play. These men in that élite team were not mere common 'cannon-fodder' with little or no imagination. They were tough, resourceful, hand-picked individuals who had often used quick-thinking imaginative initiative to get out of extremely dangerous situations when, usually with dramatic suddenness, their carefully rehearsed plans were blown apart.

But, no matter what horrors imagination might conjure, not one man showed the least sign of fear. To display any fear would be a betrayal of yourself; be a betrayal of your strong male pride, and – worst of all – would be to let down your bravely resolute, trusting and trustworthy comrades.

Eventually these hidden men heard the sound they were expecting – distant Dutch voices. They were soon recognisable as two loud, shrill and cheery female voices. As, punctually on time, the owners of these animated sounds appeared in the pre-dawn dimness the hidden watchers exchanged quick grins; these two Dutch charwomen were true 'Mrs Mops'. Both carried a zinc pail in one hand and a long mop in the other.

The tinny clatter of a pail reverberated loudly as a charwoman dropped it on the stone platform at the door of the shadowy building opposite the keen watchers. She fumbled to get the key in the lock, then opened the door. Both entered.

Half an hour later they emerged, re-locked the door and – still vivaciously chattering in what was to the keenly observing British sailors truly 'Double Dutch' – walked away, mops at the ready, towards the next building they were to 'do'.

As night finally gave way to dawn, the five S.B.S. men silently slithered backwards deeper into the concealing darkness of the fir trees. They made a final check that all their weapons were loaded and ready. Lt. Smith and Leading-seaman John Armstrong, the two most deadly accurate marksmen in that team of expert marksmen, again checked that the long, ungainly silencers were securely screwed on to their .45 calibre Colt automatic pistols and that their specially improved, more reliable, more accurate, mark two Sten submachine-guns were firmly strapped on their backs. The other three team members held their Sten-guns ready for immediate use.

Suddenly the early morning silence was disturbed by the faint, but unmistakable, sound of rhythmically marching men. The hidden British sailors tensed.

The orderly tramp of heavy German jackboots on tarmac drew inexorably nearer. To the alertly anxious hidden sailors there was something terribly menacing in the sound of those steadily approaching jackboots; their firm, disciplined, steady beat seemed to defiantly declare the arrogantly boastful self-assurance that, in only a few fateful years had thudded the all-conquering Hun hordes over all Europe.

Soon a steadily marching squad of twelve German Navy Marines appeared. Those dark clad enemy marines were in full battle order: all wore steel bucket helmets, all carried rifles or sub-machine guns.

With profound relief the hidden S.B.S. team watched them march past and continue down the narrow road and out of sight. Their relief was short lived. Those German marines had barely vanished before the sound of another group of marching men was heard. This second group soon revealed itself as twenty soldiers of the Wermach – the formidable German army. They too were heavily armed and in full battle order. To the dismay of the concealed British watchers, the corporal in charge bellowed an order and the German soldiers thudded to a halt on the road immediately in front of them.

The tensed British sailors exchanged apprehensive glances. They feared that those German soldiers were going to guard that building opposite them and make it impossible for them to complete their vitally important mission. The arrival of those Germans was completely unexpected. Their briefings in England, confirmed by Erik and Peter, made them expect only two enemy sentries going round the boundary of this research complex once every three hours.

These experienced S.B.S. men knew they should always expect the unexpected. Often in previous operations they had successfully overcome the sudden, dangerous, challenges of the unexpected – would they this time?... it seemed unlikely, not if these German soldiers stayed between them and their targets.

And why had that large, well armed German patrol arrived at just this vital time? Each British sailor was tormented by the same insistent unspoken thought: could this top-secret operation possibly have been betrayed?... been betrayed by someone in England or Holland? This was most unlikely. Only a very few knew of this clandestine operation, and surely those few were absolutely trustworthy?

For the present Lt. Smith determinedly put the thought of possible betrayal out of his mind. He concentrated instead on the problems posed by those German soldiers. Facing down the road in the direction they had been marching, they stood at ease. Obviously they were completely unaware of the British sailors hidden in the dark fir trees. They certainly would not be standing at such relaxed ease if they had any inkling of those deadly enemies being so near them. The Germans seemed to be waiting for something, or for someone. What would they do next? If they fanned out and guarded that building opposite the S.B.S. team, that would turn this operation into an infinitely more difficult, an infinitely more dangerous one.

Lt. Smith knew that one of the treacherous Dutch scientists usually arrived a few minutes before the other one. From where he was hidden it should be possible for him to shoot and kill that first traitor as he dismounted from his bicycle.

After that all hell would break loose! The German sentries would violently react. His S.B.S. team would expertly kill some of those sentries, but it would be very difficult for them to escape from this place intact. That party of German marines would join in the fight ..... they might have discovered the cuts in the fence; they could already be making their way along between the fence and the trees in search of them. Lt. Smith and Petty Officer Williams exchanged worried glances; they − like every member of the team − were trying to accurately and unemotionally calculate their chances of survival if, despite those German soldiers guarding that building, they pressed on with their imperative duty to eliminate at least one of the Dutch scientists. They did not rate their chances highly. The presence of these Germans turned this hazardous operation into an almost suicidal one.

The attention of every British sailor switched to a couple of rapidly approaching figures. One was a German Army captain, the other was a bulky sergeant. Side by side they strode purposefully down the road.

The waiting German soldiers sprang to attention. After an exchange of salutes the officer gave an order and the entire group marched away.

The British sailors gave a collective sigh of relief, Now, hopefully, this operation might go ahead as planned. All prayed that none of those enemy soldiers or marines would return.

Now, in twos and threes, and then in larger, untidily straggly groups, Dutch civilian workers came cycling down the road. They cycled past the concealed watchers and continued out of sight.

Soon after the last of those civilians disappeared from view two German naval officers came smartly striding down the road. The intently watching S.B.S. men noted that, judging from the amount of gold braid boastfully gleaming on the sleeves of his jacket and the generous serving of 'scrambled egg' heaped on the skip of his cap, one of these officers must be − or must be damned close to being a full admiral. The other officer's more modest display of glittery gold braid revealed his more junior rank.

The British sailors had been briefed to expect the arrival of those two German naval officers, but actually seeing them made their trigger-fingers itch. They longed to kill them. How easy it would be to 'take out' those enemy officers, those legitimate targets, from here. But their orders were strict; the eliminating of the two treacherous Dutch scientists had absolute priority; that was their supreme task; the successful completion of it overrode all other considerations. Once that vital mission was completed then, if an opportunity presented itself, they had full permission to kill those enemy officers as well.

Both the German naval officers carried a bulging attaché case. They climbed the stone steps together, unlocked the door and entered the building across from the hidden S.B.S. team. Those officers were highly skilled technocrats, were experts in the ever more demanding complex technical aspects of German naval developments. British Naval Intelligence suspected they were working not directly on the nuclear heart of the German atom bomb – that was the two Dutch scientists area of expertise – but on some of the elaborate technicalities surrounding the bomb's core, each one of which would have to function reliably if the bomb was to explode exactly as planned.

Even the most enthusiastic Nazi nuclear physicists, the ones who were certain that, given sufficient time and resources, they could create an atom bomb for The Führer, were forced to admit that they had little idea how large that bomb would turn out to be. They feared it might be too large and heavy to be carried by even the largest aircraft the Luftwaffe possessed.

Those two German naval officers secretly hoped that those fears would prove correct, for then not the Luftwaffe, but the German Navy would have the 'honour' of delivering that large atom bomb to its target.

What none of the British or American Intelligence Services knew was that those German naval experts were working on well advanced top-secret plans to adapt at least three of the new, larger and faster class of submarines that were already under construction, to enable each of them to carry an atom bomb. The first of those U-boats would transport its bomb across the Atlantic, would sneak into New York harbour and then explode it. That atomic explosion amongst Manhattan's towering mass of densely packed skyscrapers would cause un-imaginable devastation.

Those German naval officers ideal scenario was to have three U-boats explode three atom bombs simultaneously ... one in New York harbour; one in the Thames near London; one at Leningrad harbour. They vividly imagined the terrible devastation and the utter panic this would cause. They gloatingly pictured America, Britain and Russia dejectedly begging for peace ... peace at any price from the Ever Victorious German Fatherland.

They fervently prayed that their scientists would produce the atom bombs in time. They would have no qualms about using them. Their only regret was that the German Navy would be unable to explode one of these atom bombs on Moscow.

Chapter Six

The narrow road in front of the hidden British sailors was now silently empty. Soon the two Dutch traitors should appear. Soon the long spell of inactive waiting should end.

They tensed, and a slight tremor of anticipatory excitement coursed through every man as a solitary cyclist appeared.

This should be one of the traitors ... the first of their two targets.

As the desperately pedalling cyclist drew near he was revealed as a stout, bald, middle-aged Dutchman. Gasping loudly he quickly passed the concealed men. They exchanged amused, tension-relieving grins. Obviously that laggard was late for work. They thought he deserved a good bollocking for his lateness and for unwittingly misleading them.

All eyes swivelled back up the road as another solitary cyclist appeared. This time there was no mistake. All recognised that cyclist. It was Professor Johannes de Waal. He dismounted and carefully fitted his bicycle into the rack near the steps of the building opposite the keenly watching hidden men. As he bent his lean, lanky body to remove his cycle-clips it seemed as though the enormous weight of his huge, ungainly head might snap his scrawny thin neck.

Once the now unlocked door closed behind the treacherous Dutch professor, Lt. Smith and Leading-seaman Armstrong exchanged confirming nods. John Armstrong's target was correctly in place; now they had only to wait for the lieutenant's target to arrive.

They did not wait long. There was no mistaking Professor Willem Maurik. His small, rotund body seemed in some discomfort as it perched high and his short fat legs stretched to labour at the pedals of his sturdily solid bicycle.

With intense concentration Lt. Smith studied his target. With his tubby figure, his white beard and hair, his glowing cheeks, he − even more than his photo – was a real Father Christmas figure. Surely he should be comfortably ensconced in a reindeer-powered sleigh, rather than being so uncomfortably perched on that all too solid bicycle?

Frowning with grim determination the young lieutenant forced himself to remember all the briefings he had received in England; all the repeated warnings not to be misled by the benign appearance of his target; the reiterated assurances that his target was a great admirer of Hitler, was eagerly devoting all his immense scientific knowledge in an unremitting effort to help present The Führer with an atom bomb.

As he watched that Father Christmas look-alike wheezily labour up the stone steps, Lt. Smith resolutely steeled himself to the absolute necessity of cold-bloodedly killing him.

He glanced at his watch then whispered, 'Ten minutes.'

The four men lying beside him nodded their understanding. They would give those two traitors ten minutes to open the office safes, remove their top-secret contents and pile these scientific documents on their desks. If all went as planned, British scientists would soon be eagerly studying these documents. The information gleaned from them might hasten the development of a British and American atom bomb, and the deaths of the two Dutch physicists should delay the development of a German one.

As the increasingly tense last minutes slowly ticked away adrenalin began to flow and constrained tenseness transformed to real impatience to get going, to get the violent and ruthless action over and done with.

Chapter Seven

Lt. Smith gave a final quick scrutiny up and down the road. It was deserted. He exclaimed, 'Right, lads, let's go!'

Simultaneously the five men scrambled out from under the trees, effortlessly leapt the deep ditch, sprinted across the road and bounded up the eight stone steps.

As arranged, Leading-seaman Lucas stayed at the doorway on lookout duty. He crouched with cocked Sten-gun held ready while the other four silently entered the building.

Lt. Smith, with Leading-seaman Jock Mathieson close behind him, paused outside Professors Maurik's office door. Leading-seaman John Armstrong, with Petty Officer Bill Williams at his back, halted outside Professor de Waal's office door.

The lieutenant nodded and exclaimed, 'Go, John, go!'

Both doors loudly slammed open.

With silenced automatic pistol held in front of him, John Armstrong burst into Professor de Waal's office. The professor sat behind a large, paper littered desk. His heavy head jerked up, amazed eyes snapped wide. They stared in incomprehending shock and fear.

For a couple of seconds John stared steadily at the petrified professor. Satisfied beyond all doubt that this was his correct target, he steadied the heavy automatic with both hands, carefully aimed, then gently squeezes the trigger twice.

The efficiently subdued belches of the silenced shots were immediately followed by a terrifically loud clatter as the professor jerked back under the impact of the two bullets thudding into his chest, and, taking the large swivel chair with him, hurtled violently backwards onto the wooden floor.

John bent and examined Professor de Waal. He needed to be sure both bullets had smashed through that traitor's heart. They had. His eyes were dulling into the hideous blank stare of death.

With lightning reaction John swivelled and aimed his automatic at a figure which suddenly appeared in the office doorway.

He relaxed and lowered his pistol as Lt. Smith hurried in and urgently asked, 'Did you get your target? ... Is he dead?'

'Oh yes, I got him. He's dead!.... He's stone dead!'

The lieutenant glanced at the dead body behind the desk and at the bulging waterproof bag Petty Officer Williams was securely zipping up and which contained all the documents he had swept from that dead professor's desk, then said. 'Good work, both of you!'

P.O. Williams asked, 'Did you get your target, too?'

'No, damn it, I didn't! He wasn't in his office. His safe hadn't even been opened. There are no papers on his desk.' Lt. Smith was silent for a moment then said, 'I'll see if he's in the lavatory. From the plans we studied there should be a lavatory along the corridor.'

'Aye, that's correct. The second door on the left.' Leading-seaman Jock Mathieson confirmed.

Leaving Jock on guard outside the toilet door Lt. Smith entered the brightly tiled room. No one was at the urinals. There were two cubicles; the door of one was wide open, the other was almost fully closed. Holding his silenced automatic ready he kicked the door open.

'Damn it.' he cursed, 'empty, bloody well empty!'

He re-joined the others in the corridor. Angered at not having fulfilled his part of this vitally important mission, he gasped, 'Where the hell is my damned target? Where's that bastard got to?'

He quickly reviewed the situation. That treacherous Dutch scientist was not in his office, was not in that lavatory and he had not left this building. He must have gone through that heavy, fireproof metal door at the far end of the corridor. From his intensive briefings he knew there were a further two offices, usually occupied by the German naval officers, and a large, well equipped laboratory used by them and by the Dutch professors. That strong door was the only entrance to those rooms; it was kept securely locked. The senior German officer and both professors had keys.

Lt. Smith decided he would go in after his target in that laboratory. He would kill both German officers as well. Professor de Waal's key for that formidable door should be in one of his pockets. He hurried towards the dead professor's office. An urgent warning shout from Leading-seaman Lucas halted him in mid-stride. The clattering clamour of a Sten gun immediately followed that shout.

The Sten was answered by deeper, louder barks from German submachine-guns, then by a ragged volley of rifle fire.

The lieutenant huddled in the corridor with his team. Leading-seaman Lucas lay inside the wide open front door. He was severely wounded. Two of his comrades dragged him into Professor's De Waal's office. A broad streak of blood marked the route of the dying British sailor. Wide eyed, he urgently gasped for breath then vomited a torrent of scarlet arterial blood. His body convulsively shuddered. He died.

The situation of the remaining members of the S.B.S. team was desperate. One , or perhaps both, patrols of German soldiers and marines must be deployed outside this building; must be lying in wait for them to appear and be shot down or to ignominiously surrender.

There seemed little possibility of them escaping from here alive, but there was absolutely no question of them surrendering. All these S.B.S. sailors were acutely aware of what would happen to them if they became prisoners of the Germans. They would not be treated like 'normal' British sailors and spend the remainder of the war in a prisoner-of-war camp. Hitler had issued an order that all captured British Special Service Forces were to be handed over to the Gestapo for interrogation, and, after as much information as possible was tortured from them, to be executed. This command direct from The Führer was eagerly obeyed by Gestapo sadists.

All were resolutely united in deep, unspoken agreement. They would not surrender. Much better to face a quick, fighting death than to be taken captive.

Lt. Smith decided their tactics. Turning to Petty Officer Williams he said, 'You throw two grenades blindly out to the left of the doorway, Bill. I'll throw another two out to the right. Then we'll all rush for the cover of the trees, all right?'

The three men grimly nodded their agreement. The lieutenant and the petty officer laid their Sten-guns on the floor, withdrew two hand-grenades from webbing pouches, carefully removed the safety-pins then cautiously moved to the doorway. Simultaneously they threw the four grenades.

Snatching up their submachine-guns they tensely waited for the mingled explosions – waited a few more seconds until all the jagged shrapnel should have ceased flying, then, led by Lt. Smith, all leapt down the stone steps.

They dashed across the narrow road and were leaping the deep ditch before some of the Germans reacted. Loud bursts of submachine-gun fire drowned out the more erratic rifle fire.

Leading-seaman Jock Mathieson collapsed at the edge of the ditch and died.

As Leading-seaman John Armstrong leapt, Petty Officer Bill Williams violently collided into him. John had a vivid image of Bill's bulging bag containing the secret scientific documents flying past him as both of them fell awkwardly into the deep ditch.

Bill Williams had been caught by a burst of submachine-gun fire. One glance at his savagely torn throat and upper chest showed John that he was beyond help. Lying beside that choking, gulping body as it drowned in its own blood, John urgently concentrated on his own desperate situation. For the moment he was safe in this deep ditch. If he moved from it he too would die, but if he stayed in it too long the Germans would find him and kill him here.

Lt. Smith violently threw himself under the shelter of the dark fir trees. He was amazed to have reached this concealing cover unscathed. He was the only one who had. While all his S.B.S. training ordered him to rationally think of a way out of this desperately dangerous situation, other feelings – wildly undisciplined feelings of savage hatred of those Germans – urged him to kill some of them, do something to avenge his killed comrades.

Yes, he decided, he would kill some of those bloody bastard Huns before he tried to escape from here.

His passionate love of cricket, the many hours he had spent eagerly practising his bowling, now stood him in good stead as he half rose, and, crouching awkwardly under the dense fir trees, lobbed a hand-grenade underhand over the ditch towards some advancing German soldiers

As the accurately bowled grenade rolled towards the Germans a brave corporal took a desperate step forward and kicked it away from his patrol.

As he flung himself down to join the soldiers on the ground the grenade exploded.

31

There was a tense silence after the shock of the grenade's stunning explosion, then the Germans rose and, wildly firing into the trees, continued their advance.

Lt. Smith opened up at them with accurate bursts of Sten-gun fire.

The Germans again dropped to the ground. One lay dead or silently dying. The agonised screams of another proclaimed his hideously wounded condition.

Tensely crouching in the deep ditch, John Armstrong waited until the Sten-gun bullets ceased flying over him then urgently clawed and scrambled up the ditch's steep side. He rushed to the fir trees and threw himself down beside Lt. Smith. Urgently re-loading his Sten-gun, the lieutenant gasped, 'Thank God you made it, John! I thought I was on my own.'

As bullets whistled through the trees above their heads, he exclaimed, 'Let's get the hell out of here!'

After firing wild bursts towards the Germans, they rose together, turned, and crouching under the obstructing fir branches, desperately ran. As they reached the high perimeter fence Lt. Smith screamed and collapsed. Two bullets had thudded into his left thigh. The bone was smashed. A rapidly spreading ooze of blood darkly stained his trousers.

John fired a burst of Sten-gun fire at three German marines approaching along the narrow gap between the trees and the fence. One German fell face down and lay still. The others vanished into the trees.

John knelt beside Lt. Smith, whose face was ghastly grey, but who managed to gasp, 'Where's my Sten?'

John could not see the lost gun. He threw away the empty magazine of his own Sten-gun, slammed home a fresh magazine of 32 rounds and handed the submachine-gun to the brave officer who now lay with his back propped against the fence. Despite being in a state of numbed shock, the agonising pain would come later – if he lived long enough – he, with a tremendous effort, whispered, 'You go, John. I... I'll kill more Hun bastards!'

As John hesitated, Lt. Smith almost angrily ordered, 'Go, John, go!'

Although reluctant to leave him, John hesitated no longer. There was nothing more he could do for the heroic officer, and if he stayed he too would die. If he ran there was a chance – a slight chance – that he might escape, might live to fight another day.

He gave the lieutenant's hand a quick, firm commiserative farewell grasp then rose and hurried away.

Chapter Eight

With his left hand shielding his eyes from thin branches and automatic pistol firmly gripped in the right, John ran along the narrow gap between the high fence and the dark fir trees. He urgently headed away from where the German soldiers and marines were infiltrating through the trees towards Lt. Smith.

This route took him further and further from the return route they would have taken if things had gone as planned. He was going directly away from where Erik and Peter were waiting outside the perimeter fence. Despite concern for his own safety, John managed a quick thought for those two patriotic Dutchmen. After hearing the grenade explosions and all the shooting they must be most anxious; must be fervently hoping that at least some of the S.B.S. team would join up with them before they were forced to withdraw once the reinforced Germans discovered the cut fence then extended their search beyond it.

As he hurried away, John heard the distinctive sharp, stuttering clatter of a Sten-gun. There were a number of short bursts as once more Lt. Smith gallantly took on the cautiously advancing Germans. Then for a brief time there was an unnatural silence. The thumps of exploding German grenades, followed by the savagery of concentrated machine-gun and rifle fire ended that silence .... it also bloodily ended the life of Lt. Smith.

Now a more definite silence descended. The only sounds occasionally heard were the harsh ugliness of German orders being loudly shouted.

John increased his pace. He cursed the thin branches which seemed to take a sadistic delight in tormenting him; but even if these branches annoyingly hindered his progress, at least the dense fir trees effectively hid him from the searching Germans.

After a few more minutes he noted with profound relief that those menacing German voices were getting less distinct and more distant. He slightly eased his pace. His hopes rose. He might yet escape from the confinement of this high fence at his side. But might he escape from the frying-pan into the fire?

A vast expanse of flat Dutch landscape stretched calmly, silently, invitingly beyond the fence, but John was well aware of just how dangerously deceptive that attractive silent calmness could be, From previous missions in Holland he had first-hand knowledge of how efficiently that country was controlled by thousands of German soldiers and by the Gestapo, who's sinister menace was all-pervading. Perhaps even more menacing for him were the regrettably large number of Dutch collaborators who whole-heartedly worked with the occupying Germans. These traitors would un-hesitatingly turn him over to the Gestapo if they got their hands on him. Until he got in touch with absolutely trustworthy Dutch Patriots it was extremely difficult to know who you could trust and who might betray you. He would be one Englishman on his own against those many thousands of enemies.

His S.B.S. team had been briefed on a contingency plan to follow if their operation went wrong and they were unable to rendezvous with the waiting Royal Navy submarine. He would determinedly follow these instructions which should lead him to brave Dutch Resistance Fighters who would arrange for his eventual return to Britain.

John halted and stood listening. Reassuringly there was no sound of searching Germans labouring through the fir trees, nor of heavy jackboots thudding on the tarmac of the narrow road beyond the trees, and the shouted Teutonic commands were getting fewer and from further away. Calmly – as calmly as his vulnerable situation allowed – he reviewed his position and decided what immediate action to take. His intensive S.B.S. training now stood him in good stead. He was pleased, was not surprised, at how clearly and logically he thought things out.

Remembering the detailed plans he had diligently studied in England, he knew that this fence should soon take a right angle turn, go through the trees, then emerge at the road. There, blocking that road, should be a gate and, beside it, a small hut manned by two

German sentries. To escape from this place he would have to deal with these sentries. That should present no great problem. Utilising the cover of the trees he would get close to them unseen and take them by complete surprise. He would have absolutely no compunction about killing them ... their deaths would, in some small measure, avenge the deaths of his S.B.S. comrades.

Suddenly, with vivid intensity, he pictured those four brave men – those grand comrades. Now he was the only one left alive in what had been a really great, a truly élite team. For him their deaths were a profoundly searing tragedy; but at this time, in this place, he could not allow himself the indulgence of wallowing in grief for his killed comrades. Perhaps he would indulge in that enervating dark luxury sometime in the future ... provided, of course, that he did have a future, that he was not fated to soon meet as sudden, as savagely violent a death as had befallen all his comrades.

For a moment John thought of the bravery of Lt. Smith who, despite the severity of his wounds, had valiantly taken on those searching German soldiers and by delaying them helped ensure his escape. He vowed that if he did succeed in returning to England he would glowingly report Lt. Smith's bravery to Commander Richardson, would emphatically suggest that the officer's gallant conduct deserved posthumous recognition by the award of a medal. He was well aware that a belatedly awarded medal would be of no use to the dead lieutenant, but it might help his grieving parents reconcile themselves to their son's death by assuring them that he had died a hero's death while helping one of his men to escape. And perhaps the other three dead members of Lt. Smith's team would acquire some reflected glory from that medal..Didn't they deserve some recognition of their bravery as well? Of necessity, all the extremely dangerous clandestine operations the S.B.S. teams successfully carried out went unsung and unacknowledged in public. Only a few privileged to know the full extent of their vital operations realised just how outstanding was the skill and bravery of every member of every S.B.S. team

These thoughts only took a few moments to surge through John's mind as he continued to stand and alertly listen. Now, silently moving on again, he concentrated on the tasks immediately facing him – the killing of those German sentries and then escaping from the constricting confinement of this high perimeter fence at his side. He ruefully reflected on how much simpler it would have been to escape from here if only he too had been issued with wire-cutters.

Soon, as expected, the fence turned at a right angle. Now he heard what sounded like two German voices. They came indistinctly from beyond the thick belt of fir trees. They must be the sentries at the gate.

John was pleased to have this confirmation of the accuracy of the maps he had studied and of the information he had been given; it boosted his confidence in the reliability of the contingency plan he was following.

He did not know what the two sentries were saying, but they did not sound too alarmed. He guessed they were speculating on what all the noise of exploding grenades and gun-fire had been about; perhaps they wondered if it had been an unannounced training exercise.

John quickly checked that the silencer was still firmly screwed to the muzzle of his automatic pistol and that a bullet was ready in the breech before he lay down and started silently crawling under the dark trees towards the German sentries.

The thick layer of dead pine needles were spongily soft, they made it easy to crawl soundlessly, but he had constantly to look out for, and cautiously shift out of his way the many small, dead branches littering the ground. The careless snap of one of those brittle branches would alert the sentries. Stealthily he inched forward. Peering out from under the trees, John could now clearly see the Germans.

These two soldiers, a corporal and a private, were standing outside the sentry hut. They were about thirty feet from him. They steadily stared down the empty road towards where all that noise had suddenly erupted. All was calm enough now. They both appeared fairly relaxed, standing with rifle hanging at shoulder, quietly talking together.

John steadily pointed his silenced automatic at them. They were within easy range ... they were dead ducks! There was only one snag. Those Germans were standing side-on to him, it would be impossible to get heart-shots. John slowly reached over and lifted a short, thick, brittle branch. He threw it on to the road between himself and the sentries.

Startled by the sudden sound, both Germans swung round. Now, face on, they were perfect targets. John squeezed the trigger twice. The corporal collapsed backwards. As the confused and scared young private unslung his rifle, John shot him twice in the chest.

Almost before the second body thudded to the ground, John was up, leapt the deep ditch and dashed through the gap between the sentry hut and the large gate.

Running down the narrow road, he thought it unlikely that any other Germans had heard these four effectively muffled shots. Hopefully it might be quite a while before the dead sentries were discovered. He should be well clear of this place by then.

All The Netherlands stretched before him ... surely somewhere out there he would find a safe place to hide?

Chapter Nine

John anxiously glanced around him as he rapidly continued down the straight road. No chance of hiding anywhere here. Dismally flat and featureless fields stretched endlessly on both sides of this road, and anyway he must put more distance between himself and the German soldiers who would almost certainly eventually come searching for him.

He slowed as he neared a junction. He knew that the road on the right led to a small town about two miles away. That was where most of the Dutch workers had cycled from. He also knew that German soldiers and sailors were based there near the main entrance to the large research complex he had just escaped from. He would keep well clear of that town. With great caution he passed the junction then increased his speed down the narrow minor road which led ever deeper into the flat, silent countryside.

Three miles further on a group of hawthorn bushes straggled between the road and a wide, stagnant ditch. John hid amongst those gaunt thorny shrubs. He sat and commanded himself to clearly review his situation.

Before clear logic got into gear, keen honed militisticly trained senses took over. They rang urgent alarm bells. They severely reprimanded. They accused him of inexcusably neglecting something vital.

Guiltily, he remembered that he had fired six shots and that the magazine in his automatic was almost empty. With haste, but with unflurried disciplined skill he removed the old magazine then slapped a full one into the butt of the pistol. Once more he was ready to deal with German soldiers in the way they deserved to be dealt with. Smiling grimly he hoped that no German soldiers would manage to deal with him in the way they no doubt thought a British soldier – or in his case sailor – deserved to be dealt with. And those bloody Jerries outnumbered him by many thousands to one.

John drew out and unfolded his map. One glance confirmed what he remembered from his study of it back in England. There was an isolated hamlet of about twenty houses one mile ahead of him. He would have to risk going through it. There was no real alternative. There would be no advantage in detouring across the flat, wide open fields, most of which had recently been, or were being, ploughed and were muddily uninviting. To labouriously ploughter through those fields would only delay him and make him glaringly conspicuous to the numerous heavy-footed plodding farm-labourers working there.

The map also revealed a more varied, a more wooded landscape a reasonable distance beyond the hamlet. That was where he must head for: it should offer better scope for concealment.

John unscrewed the silencer from his pistol and put it in one of his webbing pouches. If he had to fire while running it would be much easier and more accurate without the cumbersome awkwardness of the long silencer. And his passage through the hamlet would hardly be inconspicuous, would hardly require the subtle discretion of a silenced shot.

He came out from the hawthorn bushes, glanced up and down the deserted road then started jogging towards the hamlet. He increased his speed as he resolutely entered it.

Fortunately this tidily neat Dutch hamlet seemed to be peacefully asleep. Only the columns of grey smoke lazily yawning up from bright red chimneys proved that the silent cottages were inhabited.

The only humans John saw as he hurried into the heart of the sleepy small village were an old, stooped, stick supported Dutch couple haltingly making for the only shop. The deliberate slowness of their progress seemed all the more snail-like in comparison with the urgent speed of John's passage. Startled, staggering precariously, they creakingly turned and speechlessly stared open-mouthed after him.

At the far end of the hamlet two housewives, one on each side of the narrow road, were vigorously beating rugs. Their staring eyes swivelled after John as, mystified, they watched him run past them and continue on down the road. While they silently stared they mechanically continued beating their rugs – it took much more than the passage of a strange, wildly hurrying armed man to stop those house-proud Dutch women from performing their sacrosanct household chores.

A mile further on John caught up with a horse and cart slowly trundling in the same direction as him. The cart was heavily laden with large, purple turnips. The wizened old man driving the cart gasped and gazed in wondering silence and his steadily plodding horse gave a frightened start as that strange man suddenly ran past them.

For another hour John hurried along that almost deserted road. Groups of trees and straggly bushes were now conveniently scattered about the roadside, so that on the one occasion when German army vehicles appeared he was well hidden before they passed him. Twice he hid for much longer to allow slow moving farm carts to trundle past. It was much safer not to allow himself to be seen by the drivers of these carts. What they did not see they could not reveal. These Dutchmen might be completely trustworthy. Perhaps they would be only too eager to help him. Perhaps they would be only too eager to report him to the Germans. It was impossible to know.

As he reached the edge of a large fir forest, John decided he had put sufficient distance between himself and any searching German soldiers. He would hide in the depth of this forest for the rest of the day; would revert to the normal S.B.S. routine in German-occupied countries of hiding by day and moving by night.

Deep in the woods he discovered a large clearing. This open space was an oasis of bright green lushness, its brightness all the more vivid in contrast to the sterile darkness of the surrounding fir trees. Two tall, stately beech trees graced the clearing. A third beech had fallen. The hollow under its mass of upturned roots made a dry, snug, sandy den.

Before comfortably settling into this inviting den, John admiringly noted how, despite two-thirds of its roots being airily exposed to the elements, the tree's remaining hidden roots tenaciously clung to life. These roots kept the fallen tree alive, they even sent fresh branches vigorously shooting upwards at right-angles to the horizontal trunk. He was heartened by the stricken tree's tenacious determination to survive against all the odds ... hopefully he too would survive despite the formidable weight of odds stacked against him.

He sat with legs stretched out and back snugly resting against the tree's upturned roots. He neatly tucked his automatic under a webbing strap at his chest, the butt exposed and conveniently at hand ready for immediate withdrawal and use.

Now, for the present, there was nothing he could do except to husband his energy by resting, snoozing, and, as much as possible, calmly relaxing. Fortunately he could also keep up his strength by judicially and sparingly – but enjoyably – eating. He felt youthfully, healthily hungry. His last meal had been in the Royal Navy submarine ... that seemed aeons ago.

He had one large, solidly compressed nutritious slab of Kendal mint-cake, one thick bar of dark chocolate, a few pemmican biscuits and some barley-sugar. All this highly concentrated, extra strength food was a quick source of energy, was made specifically for British Special Service Forces. As he heartily chewed he thought over his unenviable situation.

Unenviable? .... that harsh word jarred. It suggested a touch of self-pity. Oh, of course it would be all too easy to feel sorry for himself; all too easy to give way to dismay at being alone, being one English sailor on his own in this German-occupied country. Then his tough, intensive, character-forming S.B.S. training came to his aid. He smiled as he lay comfortably at ease in this dry, snug, hidden forest den and thought, 'This is real luxury compared to some of the places I've been holed-up in before.'

He vividly remembered the tough courses he had successfully completed at the Commando base at Achnacarry Castle, near Fort William. From that ancient stronghold of Cameron of Lochiel he had been sent on many training exercises in various parts of the vast wet wilderness that was Scotland's Western highlands. He, like every man who became a member of the Special Boat Section's quietly proud élite team, had proved his physical and mental toughness, his great resourcefulness and firm determination in that harsh environment.

Often, for nights and days, he had lived in soaking clothes, was denied the comfort of a dry shelter or the luxury of a heating or cooking fire. His food consisted of what he could find for himself on soggy peat moors and bleak, rain-battered hillsides. At the insistence of, and following the example of his instructors he even forced himself to swallow some of the abundant large black slugs which these fabulously tough Commando sergeants assured him were extremely rich in protein. Amazingly, as he had also been assured would be the case, after the initial horrendous gagging revulsion he got the first ugly slug over the back of his tongue and down his throat, the next one went down with comparative ease.

After that experience with these black slugs, the scrounging for food along the seashore was quite a picnic. The raw seagulls eggs and mussels and whelks seemed delicious, were, as the gloating instructors said, "food to delight even the most fancy pansy gourmet!"

Taking another bite of mint-cake, John thought, 'Yes, this food truly is glorious compared to those repulsive large black slugs. Yes, my situation here does have some compensations.'

Again he thought sadly of his four great , brave comrades who had shared those severely testing training exercises with him; had shared some of the even more testing and dangerous missions in German-occupied countries with him. Their circumstances really were unenviable – they were all dead! No matter how hazardous his present situation, it was positively enviable compared to theirs!

Chapter Ten

Lying resting and relaxing as much as possible while all his senses remained acutely alert for any hint of dangers, John calmly and methodically reviewed his present predicament.

He knew that the captain of the Royal Navy submarine would report to Commander Richardson the failure of any of the S.B.S. team to arrive at the appointed rendezvous. He also knew that Erik and Peter would get a radio message to London informing the commander that something had gone badly wrong with 'Operation Waterloo'. They would report hearing gun-fire and grenade explosions and the non-arrival of any of the S.B.S. men outside the perimeter fence. They would convey their fears that every member of that team must have been killed. They would alert the commander to the un-palatable possibility of 'Operation Waterloo' having in some way been betrayed.

But the more John thought it over the less likely any betrayal seemed. If that operation *had* been betrayed surely the Germans would not have risked these two immensely important Dutch nuclear scientists being killed? Surely they would have been kept well away from their offices, and German soldiers would have waited in ambush to ruthlessly deal with the unsuspecting British team. He came to the conclusion that these extra German patrols had been there, and had bumped into the S.B.S. team, by mere chance. He had sufficient experience of hazardous clandestine operations to know how suddenly and dramatically pure chance could upset the most painstakingly planned operation.

John knew that Commander Richardson would be deeply disappointed once the Dutch Patriots got news to him that only Professor de Waal had been killed and that Professor Maurik, by far the most vital target, was still alive, was still free to continue his work on developing the Germans atomic bomb.

If that scientist continued working in the same office and laboratory, that building would from now on be constantly guarded by alert German sentries.

The thought of those alert Germans freed John from any sense of guilt at not attempting to return to that research complex he had just escaped from and endeavouring to – even at the cost of his own life – successfully completing 'Operation Waterloo' by killing Professor Maurik.

John was brave; he had often willingly faced great dangers when carrying out his S.B.S. duties – but there was a limit.

Suddenly another thought, a much more selfishly personal one, came to him: if Commander Richardson believed that all five of that élite S.B.S. team had been killed, how long would it be before the Admiralty informed their next of kin? They might delay for some time in hope of getting more definite information about these lost sailors, then the "missing in action; feared dead" telegrams would be sent out.

John vividly imagined the telegram-boy setting out from the main post-office in Keswick; saw housewives stare with breath-held dread as that small messenger of death cycled towards them, heard their gasping relief as he passed their door. He pictured the shyly self-important boy determinedly peddle up the slope to his mother's house; saw her apprehensively accept the dreaded yellow envelope. He saw his sister trying to console her mother with the thought that John was only "missing", that he might not be dead.

But for a distraught mother, perhaps the terrible uncertainty of not knowing if her only son was alive or dead was even worse than the definite knowledge that he was dead. Through countless sleepless nights she must wonder was her son lying somewhere severely wounded?.... would he survive?.... would he eventually return to her?

Had he been last seen adrift on wreckage from his sunken warship?..... might he yet be rescued by a passing ship?.... or was he already an ugly bloated corpse carelessly afloat on the coldly indifferent North Atlantic?

No doubt his mother and sister would pray that he had been taken prisoner by the Germans; would live in hope of sooner or later receiving confirmation of this. They had absolutely no idea of the terrible fate he would meet if he was captured; the excruciating torture he would have to endure at the hands of the Gestapo, then the summary execution as a member of the greatly feared and savagely hated British Special Forces.

This knowledge of what awaited those outstandingly brave, those truly special British servicemen if captured was kept a deep secret from all their next of kin. Those parents, those wives, had sufficient reason to worry about the dangers their sons or husbands constantly faced without having the almost unbearable weight of the extra burden of this terrifying knowledge imposed on them.

In reflex action, John's index finger gently touched the cyanide pill firmly held hidden by flesh-coloured tape behind his right ear. That small, square, white suicide pill was his last desperate guarantee of release if sadistic Gestapo interrogation became unendurable. As he issued these pills the Royal Navy doctor had assured the S.B.S. men that their effects were painless and practically instantaneous. John fervently prayed that he would never have to put that assurance to the test.

He forcefully thrust thoughts of possible capture, torture and execution out of his mind. He would resolutely do his damnedest to stay out of the clutch of the Gestapo. He would stay alive and, sooner or later, return home to Keswick and be re-united with his mother and sister. Once again he would rejoicingly climb his favourite mountain, Skiddaw, which rose so familiarly, so invitingly, so welcomingly at the back of his home.

John unfolded his large-scale map of this part of Holland. In case this map fell into enemy hands, no revealing marks had been put on it. From memory he accurately traced the escape route he would follow. By following this contingency plan he would arrive at a certain building about nineteen miles from here. He should meet a Dutch Patriot there, one who had been alerted to the possibility of some British Special Forces arriving and requiring help.

After some minutes of re-familiarising scrutiny he was completely confident of having accurately memorised the exact location of the distinctive Dutch building which was now his rendezvous point. He should have no difficulty in following the obvious route to that building in the dark tonight – as long as he did not bump into any bloody Huns.

Comfortably settled in his cosily dry forest den, John patiently resigned himself to the long wait for autumnal dusk to descend. He ate a little more food. As he chewed he suddenly – perhaps very foolishly – felt supremely confident that things would go well for him, that with the indispensable help of resolute Dutch Patriots he would succeed in getting out of Holland and somehow or other get safely back to England.

Chapter Eleven

John's almost euphoric feeling of confidence in the likelihood of him getting back to Britain was suddenly shattered. Something set his keen-honed senses violently thrilling. His nerves tingled as with a slight electric shock. Although not knowing exactly what his senses were warning him of, he immediately reacted.

He silently withdrew his automatic pistol. Carefully making no metallic click, he gently thumbed off the safety-catch. With a bullet already in the breech, he held it ready for instant use.

Listening intently he heard a very faint, but very definite noise. What seemed a furtive, rustling sound came from the lush grass behind the fallen tree. The thick curtain of upturned tree roots hid the source of these sounds from him.

Moving infinitely slowly and silently he eased himself up from the ground. He crouched with his body tensed ready to stand rock firm while he aimed and fired.

Fired at what? Was a cautiously searching German soldier likely to make as little noise as that? It seemed unlikely … but just possible, and those very faint rustling sounds were undoubtedly getting nearer. Soon whatever was making them should come into view.

John steadily pointed his pistol in that direction. With every nerve tensed his finger was poised on the trigger ready to instantly squeeze.

The source of those faint sounds suddenly stood revealed. John grinned with relief. His finger left the trigger, his grip on the pistol eased, his entire body relaxed. He saw not a German soldier, but a pair of roe deer.

Those beautiful small deer were completely unaware of John's presence as he continued crouching absolutely silent and motionless. The slight breeze carried his strong, vile, human scent away from the deer. He stared enthralled as these charming creatures daintily grazed and gracefully moved through the lushness of the forest clearing.

Suddenly the doe stopped grazing. An intuitive sixth sense alerted her to danger. Probably that mysterious sense felt the intensity of John's fixed stare. Obviously puzzled, she stared wide-eyed directly at him.

Holding that un-deviating questioning stare she vigorously stamped an anxious, uncertain front hoof. Alerted by his mate's action, the buck stretched up his modestly antlered head and he too stared unerringly at that strange, indistinct motionless thing lurking in the shade of those familiar upturned tree roots.

Now, as unmoving as fossilized stone, deer and man silently stared at each other. All held that stare for timeless, breathless moments, then the buck gave one sharp, terrier-like bark then both deer turned and ran.

John was delighted at having had such a perfect view of those beautiful creatures so daintily going about their innocent lives. It was heartening that in the midst of this foul war he should be privileged to witness such a fair scene. He also felt it salutarily humbling to realise that – ignoring all the devastation, the carnage, the hideous degrading brutality that this most foul war was loading on the mad human species – for most of Earth's other species' normal life went on much as usual.

Once more settled down behind the upturned tree roots, John lay comfortably, but never un-alertly at ease. He had ample leisure to think and to remember. He fondly remembered the last time he, a gangling youth, had been expertly guided by his father to breathlessly observe undisturbed roe deer. These deer – a proudly maternal doe and her eagerly suckling and unsteady tottering tiny twin fawns – were even more beautiful than the adult pair of roe he had just seen. His forester father had taken him birdwatching in the woods where he worked near Lake Derwentwater. The roe deer were a joyous extra bonus.

His father eagerly passed something of his deep love of the glorious Cumberland landscape and of its wildlife on to his keenly receptive son. For the sensually and spiritually awakening youth these emotional feelings mingled with his strange, new and urgent physical sensations in a powerfully confusing but wonderfully intoxicating cocktail.

Under his father's guidance John read Wordsworth's greatest Nature poems. With ever increasing wonder he discovered that the poet's profound mystic insight expressed what he himself confusedly felt but could not articulate.

With tragically perverse irony it was one of his admired old, stately, but decaying beech trees which, falling awkwardly while being felled, had killed his father six years ago. John clearly remembered how terrible, how overwhelming the shock of that sudden tragic death had been. It was incomprehensible that his father – who had always been so warmly aglow with eager love of life – should lie so still in that coffin; should be so hideously waxed in the abysmal coldness of death.

That legacy of love for the Lake District he had inherited from his father still pulsed strong in John. Each time he travelled home on leave from the navy the eager anticipation of being with his mother and sister again (and of the mouth-watering delights of their excellent homely cooking and fabulous baking) was at least equalled by the eagerness with which he anticipated the pleasures of once more striding out on the familiar grassy fells and exhilaratingly scrambling about on the challenging rocky crags of his marvellous ancestral homeland. These outings were pleasurably easy exercises for his superbly fit body, were profoundly relaxing peaceful delights for his tense, war-geared mind. It was wonderful to walk and climb entirely for physical pleasure and aesthetic delight and not to have the killing of enemies, or the avoidance of being killed by enemies, as the purpose of these strenuous activities.

Suddenly John's militaristicly trained mind asserted itself. It reprimanded him for indulging in all those memories sparked by seeing the two roe deer. From the military point of view there was only one fact – a vitally important fact – to be realized from the behaviour of the deer. The confident way they had grazed in the undisturbed security of this clearing in the woods was proof that no searching German soldiers were anywhere near. That was all he should be concerned with.

Subconsciously he had already registered the obvious reassuring lesson of the deer's behaviour, but he welcomed this upbraiding reminder by his war-honed conscious brain. His survival, one Englishman on his own in this dangerously alien Dutch environment, depended on his conscious and subconscious – his reasoning logic and his intuitive instincts – constantly working together at the peak of their powers.

The remainder of that long day passed uneventfully. Occasionally he scouted around his hiding place to confirm that no danger threatened, but for most of the time he lay and rested. Consciously, as he had been trained to do, he conserved his energy: stored it at maximum power, held ready to instantly react to any sudden desperate call on his physical and mental resources.

He did not allow himself the luxury of deep sleep. He willed himself to indulge in nothing more than shallow cat-naps during which his senses remained alert for danger. This denial of real sleep was one more penalty of being on his own. On previous missions in German-occupied countries four members of his five man S.B.S. team could sleep soundly, secure in the knowledge that their fifth comrade was taking turn to alertly guard them.

Eventually, with what seemed infinitely slow and weary reluctance, the autumnal dusk descended. John patiently waited and watched until the dismal fir trees dissolved into shadowy darkness. While welcoming evening's concealment, he also felt vaguely menaced by the stealthily shrouding dimness. He warily reflected that the darkness which concealed him could also conceal his vastly outnumbering enemies.

Chapter Twelve

It was good to be moving again.

After this morning's experience of having to move through the Dutch countryside in the full glare of daylight, John greatly appreciated the more familiar and much more secure method of travelling by night. It was reassuring to be correctly following the standard S.B.S. routine while in enemy-held territory of hiding and sleeping by day then furtively moving by night. The mad abnormalities of war transmuted this erratic behaviour into the normal.

As the silent miles and the tense hours uneventfully passed, John was heartened by the thought that each passing mile brought him nearer to the place where, if things continued to go so well, he should soon meet up with, and be whole-heartedly helped by a brave Dutch Patriot. It would be a great relief to no longer be on his own in this dark countryside where every dim shadow suggested hidden menace and where every blacked out building he cautiously passed might conceal alert German soldiers or betraying Dutch collaborators.

Walking silently and alertly along narrow, dark and curfew deserted minor country roads he had no difficulty in following the route accurately memorised from his map.

The steady drone of rapidly approaching aircraft halted John. Standing in the darkness he gazed skyward through gaps in the low clouds. He could see none of the R.A.F. heavy bombers now noisily passing high above him in a continuous stream. There seemed to be hundreds of them; their deep-throated steady roar endlessly vibrated through the trembling night sky and smothered all lesser nocturnal sounds.

Following the sound of these planes and visualizing a map of Western Europe, John confidently (and correctly) surmised that they were heading for the Ruhr – that homeland of German heavy industry, that vital heart of the Third Reich's war production. Night after night the R.A.F. bombed Dusseldorf, Cologne or Dortmund. They paid special attention to Krupp's huge sprawl of armaments factories at Essen which produced many of the tanks and artillery and much of the vast amounts of ammunition needed to keep Hitler's army fighting. So regular were these raids on the Ruhr that the resolute R.A.F. aircrews had, with perhaps a touch of gallows-humour facetiousness, nicknamed them ; 'The Milk-Run'.

John silently wished these brave airmen the best of luck. He heard only a small amount of flak being sporadically fired at them, but he knew that once they met the Luftwaffe's alerted night-fighters and then came within range of the formidable batteries of flak guns desperately defending the Ruhr, they would need all the luck they could get as they once more delivered not bottles of milk but tons of bombs to Ruhrland doorsteps.

As he listened to those bombers steadily wing between clouds and stars, John could not help envying those airmen the speedy ease with which they, or most of them – the lucky ones – would in a few hours be back in the safety of England. He wryly wondered how long it would be before he got safely back to England .... if ever?

Perhaps his chances of returning to Britain were not all that great. He would have a better idea of his chances once he met up with the Dutch Patriot at the appointed place. From then on he would have to trust his life to brave, patriotic Dutch men and women. He fervently hoped, and confidently expected, that they would all prove as absolutely reliable and trustworthy as Erik and Peter had proved to be.

As he once more reviewed his present situation, John suddenly felt much more positive about his chance of getting back to Blighty. Surely it was quite possible that once the Dutch Patriots got word to London that he was still alive, was the only one of the élite S.B.S. who had survived, Commander Richardson – anxious to learn the full details of the part success/part failure of 'Operation Waterloo' – might pull a few strings to get him quickly whisked back to England for extensive de-briefing. That Royal Navy intelligence officer would be especially keen to interview him if there were real suspicions that this secret operation had been betrayed in some way.

One hour later John was pleased to see moonlight reflected from a sizable stretch of water straight ahead of him. Although he had complete confidence in the reliability of his map-reading and route-finding skills, he welcomed this further proof of the accuracy of these vital skills. That lake had revealed itself exactly where he was expecting it.

Slow moving clouds once more hid the moon. Darkness obscured the lake. That darkness vaguely revealed the subdued glow of the dimmed street lights of a blacked-out town. John knew that this must be the town of Gouda, a few miles north of the lake. The main road from The Hague to Utrecht and Arnhem and on into Germany passed through there. Being an important supply route for the occupying German army it was strongly guarded and regularly patrolled ... a place for him to keep well clear of.

At the south end of the lake John searched for, and soon discovered a narrow road – little more than a farm lane – leading towards the west. With eager keenness he hurried along that lonely road for six long, dark miles to the village which was his destination for tonight.

With stealthy caution John thoroughly reconnoitred the blacked-out, mist shrouded silent village, most of whose houses companionably huddled together around the rough cobbled market square. He noted the position of the small stone bridge which crossed a narrow canal at the southern edge of the village.

Satisfied, he returned to the focal point of his reconnaissance – the village church. He had inspected it earlier, but now he more minutely examined it and its environs. He again noted how solidly the squat square tower heaved up its modest height from the south end of the solemn church's dim greyness. The surrounding churchyard was shadowy bordered with tall elms. An ancient yew tree cast its deep gloom over the corner where the oldest, the most sadly awry gravestones mourned. A wide gravel path led from the village to the church. A narrow path angled from the church door straight to an imposingly large parsonage.

Satisfied that the churchyard was deserted, John settled himself comfortably on the dustily dry ground at the foot of the large yew. He was well sheltered and well hidden in the dense darkness under the tree's thick canopy of sweeping branches. Peering out from here he would have a clear view of the church and of the parsonage once dawn brightened the scene. According to the contingency escape plan that path was the place, and dawn was the time when he should meet with the alerted Dutch Patriot.

★ ★ ★

Dawn was nothing but a pale yellowish smudge of light above the eastern horizon when John heard the noisy crunch of heavy feet on gravel. Holding his automatic pistol ready, he silently sat up and peered out from his snug den.

A tall, bulky man was slowly walking from the parsonage. Despite his slow pace, each heavy tread of his large boots on the path's gravel was surprisingly loud. He was muffled in a long, dark overcoat and a black homburg hat sheltered his head from the fine, misty drizzle. His slight stoop and cautiously deliberate movements suggested old age, but the keenly alert glances with which he scrutinised the mistily dismal churchyard belied any suggestion of age's senility.

Waiting until that man had almost reached the church door, John scrambled out from his concealing shelter and hurriedly approached him.

The man swung round as he heard the scrunch of boots on gravel. John exclaimed, 'Waterloo!...Waterloo!'

With relief the Dutchman eagerly gave the correct reply, 'Blenheim!...Blenheim!'

John put his automatic away then thrust out his right hand.

As their out stretched hands met and firmly gripped, the smiling Dutchman asked, 'You are special English soldier?'

John grinned his answer, 'Yes, I am a special – a very special – English soldier! And you are a Dutch Pastor? ....This is your church?'

'Ya, ya, I am Protestant Pastor, and ya, this is my church.' He pointed to the parsonage, 'And that is my house. That is where you will hide.' After searchingly looking around the churchyard the pastor enquired, 'Are there other English soldiers hiding?'

'No, I am alone.'

'Oh, I see.' The Dutchman asked nothing more. John volunteered nothing more. Both experienced men knew that the less they knew about one another the less they could disclose if captured and tortured by the Gestapo.

55

The pastor smiled, 'You are hungry, yes?'

'Yes, very hungry!'

'Ah, when I was your age I was always hungry, too. Come with me, my wife will have breakfast ready soon.'

As he ushered John into the parsonage's large, spotless, brightly gleaming kitchen, the pastor said, 'This is my wife. Hilda, this is…is?'

'John.'

'Hilda, this is brave English soldier, John.'

The stout, grey-haired Dutchwoman moved from the huge, hot, cooking range, wiped her hands on her clean apron then heartily shook John's hand. 'You are most welcome in our house.' She beamed, 'You arrive at good time. We eat food soon.' She turned to her husband, 'Johannes, you show John his hiding place, then I will have our…our?'

'Our breakfast.'

'Ya, ya, our breakfast ready.'

'Thank you,' John politely murmured. He grinned, 'The food on your stove smells really great!'

The pastor led John upstairs. Passing the first floor's bedrooms they climbed steeper, narrow stairs to the next floor. Obviously some of this more austere, carpetless area had once been servants quarters. They entered a room near the end of a long corridor. The pastor smiled, 'You like this place to hide, John?'

John glanced around. This had been a servant's bedroom, but was now a cluttered lumber-room. It was crowded with dark, dusty, massively solid old furniture. He could hardly see enough clear space for him to lie and sleep on the bare wooden floor. He looked rather doubtfully at the pastor.

Smiling, the Dutchman pulled open the door of a huge, ornate mahogany wardrobe. There was barely room for the door to fully open. Pushing aside musty and antiquated dark clothes he squeezed into the wardrobe and opened a door concealed at its back. He passed through into a hidden room. John followed.

'This is better, John, is it not?'

'Yes, much, much better.' John happily inspected the secret bedroom. 'This is real luxury compared to some of the places I've been holed-up in before.'

One double mattress and two single ones lay along a wall. An old fashioned marble-topped washstand complete with blue and white china basin and jug stood against another wall. Beside it were two pails: one was full of fresh water, the other was for dirty water. There was one comfortable looking easychair. Three straight-backed chairs were grouped around a well scrubbed kitchen table. A heap of books, mostly in English, graced one corner.

The pastor pointed to the door of a roomy cupboard, 'There is a chemical toilet in there.' He went to the window, 'And this is the emergency exit.'

John expertly examined the rope neatly coiled on, and securely bolted to the floor beneath the window. Every four feet a knot was tied in the rope. Opening the window, he looked out. He accurately judged the rope to be the correct length to almost reach the gravel path fifty feet below. A dense jungle of rhododendrons rioted beyond the path. Behind these dark shrubs rose a clump of fir trees all vague and insubstantial, all solemnly shrouded in dawn's misty drizzle. These shrubs and trees should provide perfect cover after any escape via the rope.

'If you need to, you will manage down the rope?' the pastor asked.

'Yes, of course ... a piece of cake!'

'What? ... What cake? ... What do you mean?'

John laughed, '"A piece of cake" means something very easy.' Climbing down – or up – that knotted rope would be easy; would be nothing compared to the many hazardous rock-climbing and abseiling training exercises he had completed on spray-drenched sea-cliffs and on intimidatingly high and sheer mountain faces.

'Ah, I understand,' the pastor said. He laughed, 'Now we go and get not a "piece of cake", but a piece of breakfast, yes?'

'Yes, please.'

They returned to the warmth of the kitchen where two electric lights brightly glowed and were cheerfully reflected on blue and white tiles and on the massed ranks of brilliantly gleaming copper pots and pans. The heavy, dark green curtains hiding the windows effectively prevented any of the brightness escaping out into dawn's blacked-out dimness. They also hid the room from any unfriendly prying eyes.

As he sat down opposite the pastor at the kitchen table, John noticed that only two places were set. He asked, 'Is your wife not having breakfast with us?'

'No, she is not. Hilda has had her breakfast already.'

Setting a bowl of steaming porridge before each man, Hilda said, 'I will have a glass of milk with you when I give you the ... the samble ... eggs.'

'Scrambled eggs,' her husband corrected.

'Oh ya, Johannes, the scrambled eggs.'

Johannes smiled fondly at his wife, 'You see, John, there is good reason Hilda does not have breakfast with us. If any Krauts come here suddenly you could run upstairs and hide in the secret room before they see you in the kitchen, but they might see three places set at table and, knowing only two live here, demand to know who third place set for.'

John nodded understandingly. For a few moments he gazed at the white-haired pastor and his grey-haired wife. Glaringly revealed in the kitchen's unflattering brightness and seen through the equally unflattering clearness of his young eyes they looked a really old couple. With deep sincerity he said, 'It is very brave of you both to be active Dutch Patriots at your age.'

'Oh, but you are brave, too, John,' Johannes declared.

John grinned, 'Yes, but its easier for me, I'm young ... you're old.'

Husband and wife laughed. Johannes exclaimed, 'Oh, John, we are not all that old! I am only sixty one, and Hilda is a good bit younger.'

Sixty one seemed quite ancient to twenty two year old John. He apologised, 'I'm very sorry. I only meant that it is easy to be brave at my age, but it must take outstanding courage to be brave at your age.'

Johannes gave Hilda an anxious glance then solemnly said, 'Oh, but you see we have strong incentives to be brave against the hated Krauts. Our daughter, her husband and their two young children were killed in Rotterdam when the Krauts bombed it in 1940.'

John murmured, 'Oh, I understand. I'm sorry. It must have been terrible for you.' He had read of that bombing in May, 1940. The invading Germans had given the Dutch government an ultimatum — they must surrender by a certain time. Two hours before that time expired the Luftwaffe ruthlessly bombed and devastated much of central Rotterdam. About one thousand Dutch civilians died and thousands more were wounded.

Tearfully, Hilda said, 'Oh yes, it was terrible .... terrible! And how the conquering Krauts arrogantly gloated! Now every time we hear your brave R.A.F. bombers passing over on way to Germany we ... we applaud, we wish them well.'

John nodded, 'Yes, it was all right for those Germans when they were bombing others , but now that they're getting a taste of their own medicine they don't like it. When bombs land on them they call it "Terror Bombing" – as if all their Luftwaffe's bombings had been fair and pleasant bombing.'

Johannes mournfully nodded, 'Ya, it is all very, very sad. I know as true Christians we should forgive our enemies, but oh it is difficult. It is near impossible not to hate those .... those hateful Krauts.'

When the porridge was finished, John did full justice to the scrambled eggs then to Hilda's home-baked bread thickly spread with luscious honey from Johanne's bee-hives.

Chapter Thirteen

For two uneventful days and two nights of undisturbed sleep John stayed hidden in the parsonage.

The pastor cycled around his rural parish visiting old and infirm parishioners. Under cover of these legitimate journeys he got in touch with trustworthy Dutch Patriots, one of whom wirelessed a coded message to London with news that one British sailor taking part in 'Operation Waterloo' had survived; was hidden awaiting instructions for his return to England.

Shortly after breakfast on the third day of John's inactive hiding, the morning's calm silence was disturbed by the noise of many motor vehicles. Johannes and John went out into the garden. They stood and listened for a few moments then forced their way through the dense rhododendrons. From there they cautiously made their way to the concealment of a clump of fir trees. From this vantage point they could see the stone bridge across a narrow canal at the edge of the village. A grey motor-cycle and sidecar were parked near the bridge and two German military police were directing a stream of army traffic over it and into large fields and a sparsely wooded heathery heath beyond.

Both keen watchers methodically noted the details of that seemingly endless flow of German military traffic. There were many tanks, most looking factory-fresh, on large transporters. A few of these tanks were huge, were by far the largest tanks either man had ever seen. They correctly guessed they must be the formidable new 'Tiger' tanks now coming into service in Hitler's best, his most feared Panzer Divisions. There were many lorries, some laden with grey-clad soldiers, others crowded with the élite of the Wehrmacht, the dark uniformed Panzer crews. Other trucks, their canvas covers tied down, must be loaded with stores and ammunition. Many of that ubiquitous, that most versatile of German artillery pieces, the 88 MM gun, were towed over the bridge and trundled into the grassy fields where very soon they would be ready for use in one of their many roles – as flak guns.

'Have you seen as many Germans here before?' John asked.

'No, not so many. Other times they use these fields, but never so many; never so much tanks and guns.'

They continued watching for a while then returned to the parsonage.

Johannes set out on his bicycle to visit a severely ill parishioner in the village and to try to find out why all these Germans had arrived.

He returned two hours later.

Hilda asked, 'How is Margareta?'

'Oh, she's much the same.' He explained to John, 'Margareta Langerak is old widow. She is 93 years old. She was very ill last December. The doctor was certain she would not last out the winter, but she is still tenaciously holding on. I visit her every day. She likes me to pray with her.' The pastor smiled, 'She is in no hurry to enter the Kingdom of Heaven, which I assure her is waiting to gloriously welcome her.'

Johannes had failed to discover the reason for the arrival of all these Huns. During the afternoon the intermittent rumble of military traffic announced the arrival of yet more Germans.

Later – as usual- Hilda went out to feed her hens then lock them in their shed. A few moments after leaving the kitchen she returned. She was wildly agitated. She trembled, her cheeks were pale. She urgently gasped out something in Dutch.

Johannes instantly translated, 'Two German soldiers come up path! Hide, John, hurry, hide upstair.'

John pounded upstairs. Gaining the sanctuary of the secret room he drew his automatic from its holster, thumbed off the safety catch and slid a bullet into the breech. He then screwed the silencer onto the muzzle. If he had to use this pistol in the house the silenced shots should not be heard by any other nearby Germans.

He opened the window and cautiously looked out. From here at the back of the house he could not see the gravel path the Germans had approached by. He left the window open. It would only take a moment to throw the knotted rope out then escape down it. He was confident that, utilising his fine honed S.B.S. expertise and having the great advantage of the 'element of surprise', he should have little difficulty in killing those two Germans. Then it would be easy to escape. He should be all right, but what about Hilda and Johannes … what would happen to them?

Other German soldiers would come searching for their missing comrades. They would find the dead bodies and almost certainly also find the secret room. The brave Dutch couple would be sadistically interrogated by the Gestapo. If not executed, they would be sent to a more cruel, a more protracted death in a German Concentration Camp.

John determined he would do his utmost to prevent this happening. As long as he stayed hidden in this secret room, and provided those Germans failed to discover it, he would be safe, as – with the Huns finding no evidence against them – should be Hilda and Johannes.

But of course if those Germans did discover this secret room with him in it he would have to kill them. Then not only he but also Johannes and Hilda would have to flee this 'blown' safe-house. Hopefully it might be a while before the dead soldiers were missed by other Germans; this breathing space plus the rapid onset of evening's darkness should help them escape.

John quickly made his preparations. Reaching up he unscrewed the bulb from the light in the centre of the room's low ceiling. He silently moved the large heavy armchair. If a searching German opened the door in the back of the wardrobe he would be silhouetted against the light in the lumber room. He would be a perfect target for John crouching in the dimness behind the armchair. But what about the second German soldier …. where would he be? If he was searching another part of the parsonage John would have to go after him – go searching for the searcher. Not having seen those two enemy soldiers, John was at the disadvantage that he did not know how they were armed. If both had rifles his task should be easier. Rifles were clumsily awkward weapons to use indoors: but if they had sub-machine-guns the killing of them could prove much more difficult – and much more dangerous.

His preparations complete, John stood tensely waiting and keenly listening. He heard no sound from downstairs. Silently he opened, and left open, the doors into and out of the wardrobe. He cautiously eased the lumber-room door a few inches ajar. The sound of indistinct male voices and the opening and closing of doors come to him. These noises seemed to come from the bedrooms on the floor below.

Now he distinctly heard the clatter of boots on the uncarpeted wooden stairs leading up to this floor. Quickly, and silently closing the doors he retreated to the secret room.

Crouching behind the armchair he faced the closed door leading into the back of the wardrobe. He held his silenced automatic ready for instant use.

Noisy footsteps rapidly moved along the corridor. Door after door was opened then closed. The door into the lumber-room squeakily opened. Someone noisily entered the cluttered room. Something was said in German, then, slamming the door behind him the Hun soldier left.

John gave a sigh of relief. He slightly relaxed. He heard the muffled noise of German voices and the thud of jackboots on the bare boards grow fainter. Moving to the open window, he stood listening. After some minutes he heard the unmistakable crunch of more than one pair of boots striding on the gravel. Hopefully that was the last of those Germans – for the present at least.

Fifteen minutes later Johannes knocked at the wardrobe door and called out, 'You can come downstairs now, John, the Krauts have gone.'

Hilda, Johannes and John sat around the kitchen table. Each had a glass of milk. Hilda apologised, 'I am sorry we have nothing better. Of course we have no English tea and what is sold as ersatz coffee tastes like ... like muddy sawdust.'

Johannes smiled. 'Ya, and we do not have any brandy or Dutch gin. And we could all do with something stronger than milk to wash away the taste of the bad news those arrogant Krauts brought us.'

John grinned, 'Yes, if the news is all that bad it's a pity we don't have a dram of "Dutch Courage" to fortify us.' He paused then asked, 'Well, Johannes, just how bad is this bad news? Were those Germans searching for me? Are they suspicious that you might be hiding British fugitives?'

'Oh no, no they do not suspect that. It is not as bad as that, not quite. Those Krauts, a captain and a lieutenant, are in charge of finding suitable billets for their officers. They search through our house and, finding three good bedrooms empty, are billeting four officers here. We cannot prevent it. If we protest too much they will turn us out and commandeer the entire house. As it is we still live here and the Krauts will only be here at night to sleep. So, although it will be terrible having them sleeping here, it could be worse; at least we should not see them during the day. And they do not eat with us, they feed at their own army mess.'

'They offer to give us extra rations for ourselves if I cook for them,' Hilda indignantly exclaimed. 'But I refuse to be bribed. I tell them if I cook for Kraut officers I put rat-poison in their food!'

Her husband smiled fondly and admiringly at his Amazonian wife then grinned at John, 'Ya, and I believe she would, too!'

With tears flooding her eyes, Hilda agitatedly asked; 'Oh, how can you be so calm, Johannes? It will be terrible having Krauts staying in our house. And what about John? How will he manage? What if they find him?'

'Ya, that is real problem. It will not be safe for you to stay, John. But I have solution. You will hide in other place .... in my church. You will be safe there.'

John nodded his agreement. 'I am completely in your hands. I agree to whatever you think best. I would hate to get caught in your house, Johannes.' He paused and stared with real affection at the brave, elderly Dutch couple then suddenly smiled, 'Actually I would hate to get caught anywhere by the damned Krauts; but I would hate even more to think of the terrible consequences for Hilda and you if I was discovered in your house.'

Johannes solemnly nodded, he glanced at Hilda ... for a few moments fear misted his eyes as he pictured her being tortured by the Gestapo. He blinked those fears away and said, 'The Krauts are moving in later this evening, so you better hide in the church now.'

'Yes, of course. Did you find out anything about why all these Germans are here?'

'I think they are part of Panzer Division who are exhausted after much fighting in Russia. They come here to rest and re-equip with new tanks.'

'How long will they stay for?'

'Oh, I do not know. A few weeks?....A few months? But with all those Krauts about it will be dangerous for you. I try to arrange to get you away from here very soon.'

'Yes, the sooner the better!' John said, then smiled apologetically at Hilda, 'Oh, I am sorry. That sounds terribly impolite to you after all your wonderful hospitality and kindness to me'

Hilda gave him a warmly maternal smile. Reaching over the table she placed her hand over his and gently squeezed. Somewhat tearfully she gulped. 'We are happy to have you here, are happy to help you. You are ... are almost like a son to us.'

Chapter Fourteen

One hour later, after gulping the hastily prepared meal provided by Hilda, John was guided by Johannes to the large crypt under his church.

After passing dark and gloomy recess's which the uncertain light of their solitary candle vaguely revealed to be lined with antique stone coffins, they reached a remote recess which had been partitioned off to form a small, low-ceilinged, windowless room.

As he lit a candle on a dusty shelf in this secret place, Johannes said, 'I am sorry this room is not very cheery. It is like a prison cell .'

John glanced around then grinned, 'Oh, it's not too bad. At least its much more cheery than a Gestapo cell!'

As he left, Johannes promised, 'I bring you breakfast early tomorrow.'

Now on his own in this dismal and rather eerie crypt, John resolutely set about inspecting his hiding place. There were two mattresses and a heap of rough woollen blankets; there was a pail of water and a toilet bucket .(This last item cheered him: it reminded him of the rude saying, 'He crept into the crypt and crapped.'). On a shelf were two bibles, one in English, one in Dutch. A box of matches lay beside the stump of a spare candle. The amount of molten wax glaciered around the base of the lit candle suggested its life was more than half over. He knew that candles – like so many items in German-occupied countries at this stage of the war – were becoming increasingly scarce.

Only removing his boots, his webbing belts and pouches, and placing his loaded automatic ready to hand, he crawled on to a mattress and heaped many blankets over himself. He blew out the precious candle. He pulled his black woollen hat low over ears and forehead.

Despite the crypt's clammily earthy coolness and the dampness of its thick old walls, he soon felt as snugly and comfortably settled as a hibernating hedgehog, and – eventually – he slept almost as deeply as one.

★★★

At dawn next day Johannes kept his promise. He brought food. Watching John eagerly breakfast by the light of the candle, he said, 'I have good news. You move away from here tonight. It is all arranged.'

'Oh, that really is good news. It'll be great to be moving again.'

'Do you know what day this is, John?'

'If I've not lost track, I think it should be Sunday.'

'Ya, it is the Sabbath. At ten-thirty I hold service in this church. You will hear my sermon.' Smiling broadly, the Dutch pastor quoted an amusing phrase which John was fond of using, 'But I am afraid my sermon will be 'Double Dutch' to you.'

'Yes,' John laughed, 'I'm afraid it will be. Perhaps I'll recognise some of your hymns, though. I might even join in your congregation's singing.'

'Oh ya, as long as you do not sing too loud. But definitely do not sing when you hear hymns after twelve-noon.'

'Oh, why not? .... Who will be singing at that time?'

'Kraut soldiers will be singing!' Johannes aggrievidly explained, 'A German army padre came to see me. He did not request permission to use my church. He arrogantly informed me he would use it promptly at noon. I was ordered to make sure my Dutch congregation was well away by then.'

So, a few hours later, as John lay on his back and stared through the crypt's dimness towards the vagueness of the dark oak planking which was both the ceiling of his cell and the stout floor of the church, he heard mingled male and female Dutch voices rising in hopeful, soulful praise of their Protestant God. He recognised one hymn, but thought it safer not to join in the singing.

Shortly after the last straggling noises of the departing Dutch congregation faded away the more regimented thudding of heavy jackboots on the floorboards above his head warned John of the arrival of the German soldiers.

Again he recognised a familiar hymn – the same one the Dutch had sung, but there was a vast difference in the way it was now sung. The aggressively male German congregation sang it with much louder, more forceful and masterful gusto. As he, a secret captive audience, unwillingly listened to those macho German soldiers standing so unsuspectedly close above his head, it seemed to his (perhaps somewhat biased) judgement that they raised their domineering Teutonic voices not so much to praise their Protestant God, but rather to send orders to Him.

As the service ended and the Germans began to leave, John again tightly close his eyes to protect them from the fine dust the thudding jackboots sent drifting down from the old floorboards. His highly trained, easily controlled body obediently lay in restful relaxed ease, but it was not so easy to control the activities of his imagination. It was all too easy to image those German jackboots thudding not only on to floorboards, but also viciously smashing into his captured, defenceless, agonised body. In automatic reaction to that vivid image his index finger once again gently touched the cyanide pill (that extreme release from unbearable torture) taped behind his right ear.

Now, the dark crypt's profound silence disturbed by nothing but his frequent, half-stifled, dust triggered sneezes, John had nothing to do but lie and, patiently waiting, conserve his physical energy for whatever demands he made on it tonight when, thankfully, he should be on the move again. The trouble with all this inactive waiting was that it gave him much to much time to think and to remember. He thought of that recognised hymn he had heard sung twice today; he remembered singing it two weeks ago at a church parade in England. The Royal Navy chaplain had blessed the British sailors and prayed for their safety. With fervour and absolute certainty he assured them that their Protestant God would bring a righteous Allied victory.

Likewise in this Dutch church the German army padre had blessed the German soldiers, had prayed for their safety, and with even greater fervour and confidence assured them that their Protestant God would bring a righteous German victory.

With perhaps foolish eager optimism John tried to think out some way to reconcile these apparently irreconcilable Christian promises. He soon gave up the futile attempt. Sadly frustrated, he exhaled what seemed a rather cynical sigh. That feeling of cynicism unavoidably increased as he thought of all the British and American priests assuring their avid congregations of the certainty of Allied victory, while other priests in the same Roman Catholic church were assuring eagerly believing Italian and German worshippers of the inevitability of their victory. How could that church which claimed to the one true church speak with so many confusingly contradictory voices?

Once more he sadly sighed. Then with a resolute effort of will he refused to despairingly give in to the arid negativeness of bleak cynicism. He fondly remember the warm, loving, unquestioning Methodist faith of his mother. How cosily and reassuringly she had wrapped his sister's and own childhood in her evangelical faith. He vividly recalled how his father, while willingly attending most of the Sabbath services with them, seemed to get much greater and more glorious spiritual uplift from the wild hills of his beloved Lakeland than from anything he got within the confinement of the church. As he grew to manhood John continued to believe in his mother's Methodist faith, but, rather confusingly, as he discovered ever more of the fantastic beauty surrounding his Lakeland home he was increasingly captivated by what seemed the almost Pagan Pantheism his father had obviously felt. More than ever he deeply regretted his father's untimely death; he – the only one John had known with such feelings – would have helped guide him through his spiritual confusions.

Now, although at heart he still did believe in his Christian faith, he no longer believed unquestioningly. The horrors of this terrible war forced him to question much that had seemed plain, undeniable truths before. At times the war made it almost impossible to have any absolutely certain convictions at all.

His too active mind in his too inactive body forcefully reminded him of some of the foul sights he had seen in this war and some of the vile things it had forced him to do.

He clearly remembered the appalling helplessness with which he looked on as six British merchant-seamen agonisingly died on the deck of his convoy escorting corvette. They had pulled those oil-coated sailors from the North Atlantic after their ship was torpedoed by a German U-boat. There was nothing of any real value they could do for them as they desperately tried to cough up and spit out the thick oil they had swallowed. As their gasping efforts grew weaker the agonized eyes of those dying men bulged larger and glared whiter in their oily black faces. Desperately, pleadingly, accusingly, those glaring eyes refused to believe the compassionately attending Royal Navy sailors kneeing around could no nothing more to help them as the thick black oil coating their mouths and throats and clogging their lungs inexorably suffocated them one after the other.

That helpless, pitying, inactive waiting and watching had been distressfully harrowing.

Suddenly – all too vividly – his memory insistently conjured up another harrowing scene; a scene his conscious mind vainly tried to suppress. He accurately relived every detail of that nerve-wracking time. The one and only time (so far) when he had silently slit the throat of a German Sentry.

The moonless, darkly overcast night had been well chosen for that hazardous mission. Even the westerly breeze helped as it moaned around a shadowy group of bulky elms and gustily fluttered their oval leaves,. This fluttery rustling would effectively drown any slight noise he might make as he slowly crawled through lush damp grass towards the solitary German sentry.

As he stealthily inched forward with well practise skill, he remembered the motto of the S.B.S: 'not by strength, by guile'. Once more he trusted his painstakingly acquired expertise at moving and operating in the darkness of night and using the most deadly guile to bring him success.

Suddenly the sentry turned and took a few steps in his direction. John froze. While he lay motionless his heart violently pounded. The German soldier could not see him in the darkness, but had he heard something suspicious? Surely not! But why was he now standing facing in this direction? John relaxed and smiled with relief as he saw the answer. The sentry, silhouetted against the night sky, fumbled with his fly-buttons then he too obtained relief as a stream of urine gracefully arced then noisily splashed on to the grass. Finished, he turned and faced away.

With perhaps a cruel touch of black humour, John thought: 'Now that his bladder's empty at least that Jerry won't piss himself as he dies!'

Again he silently bellied forward. Those last few yards were extremely hazardous. And this sentry posed an extra hazard. German sentries were usually armed with rifles, but this one had a sub-machine gun. He held it alertly cradled over his right arm. If his reactions were swift he might manage to swing round and fire a deadly burst when he heard John rising behind him.

Now lying only five feet from the German, John urgently nerved himself to make the spilt-second, life or death, final decisive move. He made it! In one continuous movement he leapt up and sprang at the sentry. He grabbed and snapped back his helmeted head. Viciously, but with expert skill, he slashed open his helplessly exposed throat.

Blood gushed torrentially from the German's severed jugular vein. How quickly, how terribly easily that one slashing stroke of the razor-edged Commando knife transformed that enemy soldier from a strong, fierce struggling human to a limply sagging lifeless puppet.

The silent death of that sentry was essential to ensure the success of the important S.B.S. mission and to allow the team to escape safety. They had neither the time, nor the desire, to indulge in emotional remorse over that savage killing. The one, the only, violent emotion John felt was deep satisfaction at a dangerous, an unpleasant but vitally necessary action successfully completed.

He had once more proved his absolute reliability to his absolutely reliable S.B.S comrades.

Now, three months later, lying so inactively hidden in this Dutch church's dim crypt, he had far too much time to remember, to think, to feel.

The worst thing about that ugly deed had been the realization of just how terribly easy it was to turn a warm living human body into a cold motionless corpse. It needed no great courage, it need cause no great emotion to kill remotely by bomb, by shell, by bullet. But to use a knife to slit a throat was entirely different. Looking back he hated the necessity that had forced him to do it. He slightly shuddered, for, despite his true revulsion at that deed, he felt some faint inking of being able to understand how some (fortunately only a very few) men could get addicted to such stealthy callous killing – could get a fierce perverted thrill from it. And as long as those men killed 'correctly' in war they got a medal hung on them for doing what in peace would get the hangman's noose hung on them.

How many times have such, and much worse, foul deeds been perpetrated in this most foul war? Again John slightly shuddered. To think of these ongoing horrors made it difficult to retain belief in a all powerful, an all loving God. Yet if he lost the reassuring promise of that belief what was left? Atheism?... He could not live with nothing but atheism's bleak negativeness; could not live without some – even if uncertain – higher hope.

He was tired of having nothing to do but lie here by himself and think of such things. Too much of this introspective remembering and questioning could all too easily lead to bleak despair, to depression, even to madness.

With a resolute effort of will, John forced such thoughts out of his conscious mind. He sat up and groped for the box of matches on the shelf above him. He lit a candle. Unfolding his map, he held it in the candlelight and studied it. Tonight, thankfully, he should be on the move again. Guided by a Dutch Patriot he would travel through some of that Dutch countryside clearly detailed on this large-scale map. He had no idea what route they would follow. He did not care – all he cared about was to be moving once more on the next stage of his return journey to England.

The following hour passed usefully as he painstakingly studied and memorised that map. If for any reason he got separated from his guide tonight, the knowledge gleaned from it should increase the chances of him surviving safety in the dark Dutch countryside.

It was a great relief to be so thoroughly engrossed in doing something practical.

Chapter Fifteen

At six-thirty Johannes arrived with food for John. In less than fifteen minutes he finished the welcome meal then they both left the gloomy crypt.

'Your guide is waiting over there at the far side of the graveyard.'

'Good! ... Good!' John eagerly gulped deep lungfuls of cool, invigorating autumn air. 'Its's great to be out in the open air again. It'll be even greater to be on the move again.'

'Ya, ya, you have been cooped up quite a time. You have been most good, most patient. You have had good rest?'

'Yes, a great rest, with great food thanks to Hilda and you. I will never be able to repay you both for all your kindness and hospitality'

Johannes placed a fatherly hand on John's shoulder. 'Oh, John, you *are* repaying us by bravely fighting to free our poor country from the.... the tyranny of the horrible Krauts.'

As they passed out of the graveyard into a narrow lane a figure materialized out of a thick, dark hedge.

'Ah, here is your guide. John, this is Wims.'

As Wims approached with outstretched hand, John scrutinised him as best he could in the evening's darkness. He was surprised and somewhat apprehensive at how young he appeared to be. He looked little more than a boy – fifteen years at most. His body was short and very thin. They warmly shook hands. Perhaps sensing John's unease, Johannes enthusiastically declared, 'Wims has acted as guide before. He knows this countryside really well. In daytime he cycles about bird-watching, he is quite an expert. He also does German-watching! He notes all German troop movements; any new arrivals, any new equipment or unusual activity is reported to our Resistance Fighters. Any real important news they wireless to London.'

John's unease vanished. He grinned at Wims, 'It's great you do such important work for your brave Freedom Fighters. I'm impressed. I have complete trust that you'll expertly guide me.'

Standing in the darkness John sensed rather than saw a flush of proud pleasure glow the youth's face as he replied in excellent English, 'I am most pleased to help our own Dutch patriots. And it is extra good to help you British soldiers bravely helping us in the Netherlands.'

Johannes said, 'You better go now' Suddenly he smiled, 'Oh John, I forget to ask you: can you ride a bicycle?

'Yes, of course. I have a cycle at home.'

'Good!....Wims has a bicycle hidden for you. Now go John ... and God go with you.'

They quickly shook hands then Johannes turned and left them.

John accompanied the Dutch youth to the two bicycles hidden further along the hedge. With Wims leading the way they cycled down the narrow lane and away from the church and village.

Mile after mile they silently cycled through the blacked-out Dutch countryside. Most of the time thick black clouds added an extra gloom to the September night. The dismal darkness and the lampless state of their bicycles forced them to travel slowly and cautiously It would be all too easy to tumble into a deep ditch.

They were not quite sure if they welcomed the occasional spells of bright moonlight. While the brightness allowed them to travel faster, it also made them feel terribly exposed to any watching enemy eyes.

John noted and greatly admired the skill with which Wims, by keeping to farms lanes and minor country roads, avoided going through any villages. John now had complete confidence in Wim's reliability as a guide. As they halted at a wooden stile and cautiously peered into the dim field beyond he said, 'You certainly know this countryside really well, Wims. I would be blundering through villages and farms if I did not have you to so expertly guide me.'

Again John sensed rather than saw the Dutch youth's smooth, razor-innocent face blush with pride and pleasure. Then he modestly replied, 'Oh, it is nothing much I do. I want to fight with our Resistance Fighter's. I want to kill Krauts. But my parents say I am too young.'

John smiled in the darkness. He remembered when war was declared in 1939 how eagerly he, when only a few years older than Wims, had longed to join in the exciting adventure of fighting and killing Huns.

Wims ruefully continued, 'Oh, the war might be over before I am old enough to kill Krauts and to help free my country.' He paused, and through the darkness John could almost see — could definitely feel — the aura of hero-worship with which Wims intently stared at him as he asked, 'You have killed Krauts, John?... Many Krauts?'

John instantly thought of that German sentry with his gashed, blood gushing throat. He suppressed a sigh. He had no wish to encourage the Dutch youth in his inexperienced blood-thirsty longings. Nor yet did he want to discourage him from his understandable, his praiseworthy, eagerness to help free his country from the tyranny of the vile Germans. He quietly said, 'Yes Wims , I have killed Huns. Quite a few.' He discouragingly continued, 'Yes, I have killed them, but, you know it is not a nice thing to do.'

Sensing the uncomprehending disillusionment of the patriotic Dutch youngster, John immediately, almost guiltily relented. He spoke up more firmly and loudly,' No, Wims, it is not a nice thing to do. But is a thing that must be done. It is brave of you to want to fight the Huns.' He smiled, 'Now let's get moving again: "Lead on Macduff."'

After crossing a wide field they reached another minor road. A few miles along it they approached a thick clump of elms. Standing on both sides of the narrow road the trees reached out bulky branches to form a gloomy canopy over it.

John tensed as they entered the leafy darkness. All his training, his experience, his senses, warned him that this place was ideal for an ambush. He imagined German soldiers alertly lying in wait. He could almost feel enemy guns trained on him. He was about to warn Wims to be extra cautious, when suddenly he made out a dark figure on the road ahead of them. His reactions were immediate. Hissing a warning to Wims, he dismounted, dropped his bicycle, slid down the slight slope at the edge of the road and drew out his automatic. He thumbed off the safety catch and aimed at the vague dark figure standing on the road.

Wims untrained reactions were much slower. He stood holding his bicycle. John urgently hissed at him, 'Get down Wims! Lie down behind me.'

He obeyed. Togther they stared through the dimness towards the dark figure who seemed to be staring at them. Suddenly, a rather quavery high-pitched voice shouted out a Dutch word. It was repeated twice more.

Wims laughed with relief . Scrambling to his feet he eagerly shouted that same word three times.

Thoughts of possible betrayed surged through John's mind. Angrily he demand, 'What's going on?.... Who's that Wims?'

Breathlessly Wims explained, 'Its Theo. He's my friend. We go bird-watching togther. He also helps our Freedom Fighters. He shouted our secret password, "Skylark" three times.'

'Tell him to slowly walk down the middle of the road towards us with his hands up.'

Puzzled, Wims hesitated, 'But why?... He's my friend. You can trust him, too.'

Keeping his eyes and his automatic steadily pointing at the slowly and uncertainly advancing figure, John angrily snarled, 'Do what I say, Wims!'

Surprised and upset by John's anger, Wims obeyed.

As if also rather puzzled, the dark figure hesitantly obeyed the shouted order. As he drew nearer it became obvious that he was no bucket-helmeted German soldier. He too appeared to be little more than a boy.

Now standing with hands above his head, a blink of moonlight revealed him to be a youth of about the same age as Wims. He was slightly taller and quite a bit plumper. Still rather sulkily upset by John's anger, Wims triumphantly exclaimed, 'See, John, I told you! He is my friend, Theo.'

Rising to his feet, holstering his automatic, John tolerantly smiled, 'All right, Wims, I'm sorry I snarled at you, but in any uncertain situation one person has to be in command and his orders must be immediately obeyed. My greater experience makes me the natural commander, okay?'

All trace of sulky annoyance vanished as Wims grinned and said, 'Sure, John, that's okay.'

With great excitement Theo now poured out a stream of Dutch. Wims quickly translated, 'Theo was waiting to tell us not to go to the house I was taking you to. There are now Krauts sentries at a canal bridge five kilometres from here. We were going to cross that bridge tonight. But now we cannot.'

'What are going to do, then?' John asked.

After another torrent of Dutch, Wims again translated, 'We must stay tonight at Theo's parents farm. It is not too far from here. You will be safe there.' His voice rose louder as he proudly exclaimed, 'All Theo's family, like my own family, are true Dutch Patriots who hate the Krauts.'

They retraced some of their route then Theo led them across a series of fields to his home. John and Wims put their bicycles in a shed then waited until Theo confirmed it was safe for them to enter the farmhouse.

After travelling for hours in the night's blacked-out darkness, the gleaming brightness of the farm kitchen dazzled John and Wims, and seeing so many people crowded into the snugly warm room momentarily bemused them.

Wims quickly recovered and eagerly introduced John to Theo's parents and grand-parents. Theo's two younger sisters shyly hid behind a settee and refused to come out to meet the strange 'Englander.' As soon as amused attention shifted from them, the girls wide inquisitive eyes peered out and greedily drank in every detail of the stranger.

Now seeing John fully revealed in the brightness of the kitchen, Theo also keenly observed every exciting detail of the brave Englander. The black clothes he wore were sinisterly different from the usual khaki British army uniform and they were much darker than the pale blue uniforms of downed R.A.F. airmen Wims and he had helped guide to safety. And how excitingly he was armed. The menacingly large automatic pistol bulgingly holstered at his right hip was balanced by an even more menacingly sinister large Commando knife conveniently scabbarded at his left hip. And what other exciting dangerous weapons might be hidden in the bulging webbing pouches strapped about his body?

With lively eyes sparkling in his glowing face, Theo animatedly drew Wims attention to these awesome weapons. He wildly speculated on how many Krauts John had killed with them.

His mother authoritatively spoke up, 'Oh Theo, don't be so silly and so noisy. Sit down and be quiet.'

His father, awkwardly limping and supported by a strong stick, agreed, 'Ya, do what your mother says, Theo.' Then, reaching out and fondly ruffling his son's unruly hair, he warmly smiled down and said, 'You did well tonight warning Wims and John about those Krauts. I'm proud of you, son. Proud of you doing what this prevents me doing.' Grimacing, he bent and slapped his artificial leg.

Soon all were seated around the kitchen table. John hungrily obeyed the hospitable demands that he eat up. Lavishly and honestly he praised the fresh baked bread and scones and the home-made butter and cheese.

Supper over, Theo's father poured a little schnapps into three glasses. As he handed a glass to John, Wims translated, 'He apologises for there being so little schnapps. It is not easy to get it, or gin or brandy here now. The Krauts take it all!'

The white-haired, white-bearded tall old grandfather stood up and lifted his glass. He gave an impassioned toast. John hardly needed it translated – 'Victory over the foul Krauts!'

The two sleepy girls obediently, though reluctantly, went to bed. Soon afterwards their mother and grandmother also retired to their bedrooms.

The five males remained sitting around the kitchen table. They held a council of war. Theo was proudly delighted to be allowed to join in their deliberations. Although better at hiding his excitement, Wims was perhaps even more delighted, and he had good reason to be truly proud of his vital translating skills. He was the only one who could accurately translate their Dutch to English.

They quickly agreed it would not be safe for John to travel at night now that, for some unknown reason, many more German patrols were on the local roads, and now with sentries guarding the canal bridge it would be impossible for him to slip unseen across it. And yet he had to cross that bridge to get to the safe hiding place arranged for him.

With impressive, quietly firm deliberation the grandfather explained his simple, his hopefully foolproof plan for getting John across that bridge in broad daylight. With excited eagerness Wims translated. John was impressed. He immediately agreed to the plan. He had no option. With hope, with trust, with emotion, they all shook hands.

Theo and Wims led John to the hay loft where he was to sleep. The cattle in the byre drowsily stirred and turned peevishly questing, lugubrious eyes towards the disturbing humans who now climbed the steep wooden steps to the large loft running the entire length of the byre and stable.

Standing in the deep darkness, Wims pointed at the greyer darkness that was a row of skylights above them. 'You can have no light here, John, the Krauts would see it.'

John grinned, 'I need no light. All I need is to get my head down in that inviting hay. But first, is there any other entrance to this loft?'

'Ya, there is door along there where the hay is put in.'

'Good! Let's go and inspect it.'

They groped along the gap between the piled hay and the back wall. John unbolted the door and peered down. Satisfied, he closed and bolted the door. Grinning in the darkness, he asked, 'You know why I do that?'

'No...no, I do not,' Wims replied.

'Should searching Huns come in at the byre door, I might manage to escape out that back door. It is not high, I could easily jump down from it.'

Wims nodded understandingly. He quickly translated for Theo. John continued, 'If you ever have to hide from the Huns always try to pick somewhere with more than one entrance and exit. You'll both remember that, won't you?'

John smiled understandingly at the youthful enthusiasm with which they faithfully promised they would remember. Obviously in their still essentially innocent and inexperienced boyish minds this war was an exciting game. A game they desperately hoped would not be over before they were old enough to take a much more active part in. John, his few extra years of age allied to his vast experience of the raw and ugly realities of war, hoped and prayed it would be over before then. He said, 'You better get back to the farm now.'

Wims glanced round the dark loft. He thought it a very gloomy place to spend the night by yourself. With anxious compassion he asked, 'Will you be all right here, John?'

'Yes, of course I will. This heaped dry hay is real luxury compared to many places I've slept. I'll be okay!'

Giving a sudden impish grin, Theo chortled, 'I'll be okay-doky!'

Helpless with unrestrained laughter Theo and Wims clattered down the steep steps and ran to the farmhouse.

Lying fully clothed in the springy comfort of the cosily cocooning hay, John indulgently savoured its subtly sweet scent – so voluptuously, almost erotically suggestive of sunny summer meadows. The cosiness of the heaped hay combined with the warmth rising from the cattle in the byre below to form one of the oldest, and best forms of central heating. It lured him into pleasantly relaxing drowsiness He smiled with tolerant amusement each time his drowsily blissful state was violently disturbed by one or other of the two horses stabled next to the cattle. The loud, rude, windy explosions they frequently gave vent to seemed obvious proof of their equally blissfully well fed state.

Before dropping into profound sleep he once more thought over the plan arranged for tomorrow which should boldly take him past the German sentries at the canal bridge in the full glare of daylight. He fervently hoped it would succeed. The old, white-bearded patriotic Dutch grandfather was confident it would. John had to trust him; trust his life to him. He did – wholeheartedly!

If things went badly wrong John might lose his life, but the brave old Dutchman risked losing much more than merely his own life. The lives of his entire family were also at risk, for the usual German punishment for anyone discovered helping escaping Allied servicemen was to be sent to concentration camps. This ruthless punishment was inflicted on entire families – men, women... and children.

Chapter Sixteen

A sudden loud noise woke John. Although startled and momentarily disorientated, his right hand immediately closed on the butt of the automatic holstered at his waist. Lying motionless in his bed of hay he listened intently.

In early morning's misty darkness someone had opened the byre door below the hay loft. He now heard it being firmly closed. Vague, yellowish, moving light gleamed up the steps from the byre. There was a loud clank and clatter of pails on cobbles. Milk pails! John relaxed. Soon a female voice gently crooning a Dutch milking-song, then the soothing noise of milk rhythmically flowing into a pail confirmed that one of the women from the farm had started the morning's milking.

Not only the cows were drowsily lulled by the crooning. John indulgently lay in pleasantly relaxing ease until the pails were full and the song was finished.

As he sat with that entire Dutch family silently crowded around the breakfast laden kitchen table and waited for the grandmother to finish saying morning prayers, John fervently prayed with her – prayed that all would go well today. It was unbearable to think of the possibility of that complete family – even those two young girls shyly peeping at him through half-closed eyes – perishing in a German concentration camp merely for the 'crime' of helping him. A lump choked his throat. Perhaps their quiet, steadily resolute bravery was of a higher order than his. He usually only came into German -occupied Holland for a short time, completed his mission, then returned to Britain. They, for almost four long miserable years had lived under the constant menace of Gestapo torture.

Soon after breakfast the two sisters left for school. They halted at the farm gate and laughed and gaily waved at the waving Englander, then, cheerily chattering, cycled away.

John turned and went with the two Dutchmen and young Wims and Theo to start preparations for his hazardous journey.

A sturdy, oldish, grey horse was quickly harnessed to the shafts of a high-sided cart. It was backed into the open door of a large shed. John climbed into the cart, lay down and fitted a stong strutted wooden box over himself. Stretching from head to knees, this box protected him from, and allowed him to breath under the weight of many large purple turnips dumped into the cart. As soon as a sufficient depth of turnips covered John the old Dutch grandfather clambered onto the cart and urged thr grey mare into indolent action

Deliberately keeping to the mare's steady plodding pace, they moved innocently inconspicuously through the misty grey drabness of the autumnal Dutch countryside.

Coffined in the dimness of his vegetative tomb, John saw nothing of the passing scene. To compensate for this lack of sight he kept his hearing sensitively alert to pick up any scrap of knowledge of what was going on. He wished his sense of smell was not quite so acute; it was almost overwhelmed by the pungent scent being insistently thrust upon it. Until now he had never realised just how powerfully turnips smelt; of course until now he had never had quite such intimate acquaintance with these humble vegetables.

Mile after mile, or kilometre after kilometre (John gently rebuked himself for not thinking in European measurements) the grey mare steadily plodded along. So far all seemed to be going well, but the real test would come soon. They must be nearing the canal bridge guarded by Germans sentries. How conscientious would those Huns be? Would they be fooled by the mellow innocence of the white-bearded Dutch grandfather? Would they thrust probing bayonets deep amongst the turnips? John's life, the life of the old Dutchman and of his family could depend on the answers to those questions.

Now these questions were about to be answered as John clearly heard a German voice issue a loud command. Obediently the grandfather halted his horse. There were more words in German. They were replied to in Dutch. Now there seemed to be Germans talking amongst themselves. Listening intently, John thought there were only two Huns. Standing at the cart, they were only a few feet away from him.

Now there were noisy movements amongst the top layer of turnips. Were those sentries searching through the turnips?...Were they using their bayonets? John's grip tightened on his automatic held ready under the shielding box. If necessary, probably he could 'take-out' those two Huns. But were there more Germans at the other end of the bridge?

John's tension eased as he heard the Germans move away. One gave what seemed a rather jeering command, then the old Dutchman coaxed the mare into plodding action.

John correctly surmised that those Huns had helped themselves to some turnips – a small price to pay for him getting past them undetected.

As once more the kilometres slowly passed, John drifted into a pleasantly reminiscent mood. Encouraged by the ease with which they had fooled those Germans sentries, he conjured up schoolboy memories. He clearly remembered the excitement of reading 'A Tale of Two Cities' and 'The Scarlet Pimpernel'. His impressionable young mind had been thrilled by the adventures of the characters in these novels as they used many ingenious subterfuges to escape the guillotine. And not only fictitious characters had fooled sentries and escaped the excesses of 'The Reign of Terror' by hiding under vegetables in farm carts.

Now exactly 150 years after that 'Terror', here he was escaping another – an even more vile 'Terror' – by hiding under vegetables in a farm cart.

It seemed history did repeat itself. John did not know it, but there was another historic link to the earlier 'Terror', for in the early days of their concentration camps the Germans also used the guillotine; used it until they perfected their much more efficient gas-chambers to dispose of 'undesirables'.

These thoughts were suddenly blanked from his mind by the violent roar of aircraft. Cursing his inability to see what was going on, he counted about five or six planes roaring past. By their speed and noise he guessed them to be either British or American fighters taking part in one of their frequent low level sweeps over Holland, looking for, and shooting-up any moving German military vehicles.

That noise quickly died away and once more he heard nothing but the rumble of the cart's wheels and the steady clop of the mare's hoofs. Ten minutes later another mechanical sound disturbed him – the less violent, but more menacing throb of a rapidly approaching motor-cycle...more menacing as practically the only people in Holland who had petrol to run motor-cycles were members of the German Military Police. As it neared the horse and cart it's engine was throttled down to a gentle purr. The motor-cycle stopped and a loud, authoritative German voice bellowed out. The Dutch grandfather reigned the mare to a halt. More German was violently shouted. John heard the old farmer wheezily climb down from the cart. There was a slight bump as he guided the horse and cart off the road onto the grassy verge. Horse and man stood silently waiting, the mare eagerly snatching mouth-fulls of grass, while the motor-cycle accelerated away.

Lying keenly listening in the motionless cart John soon heard the noise his analysis of the situation alerted him to expect – the approach of German army lorries. He counted them as they passed. They were well spaced out and driven at speed; obviously their drivers were anxiously aware of, and did not want to be caught by any searching R.A.F. planes. He too hoped they would not be caught and shot-up by these planes – at least not here!

He imagined the horror of lying helplessly immobile under the load of turnips while R.A.F. fighters swooped and strafed those German trucks as they passed the horse and cart. All too vividly he imagined a deadly line of cannon-shells and machine-gun bullets tearing up the road, smashing through a German truck and through the poor old mare, then turning the load of turnips – and him – into a messy pulp. The constant threat of death at the hands of the enemy was menace enough without the additional threat of being killed by our own R.A.F. aircraft!

Soon after the eleventh, and last, truck passed, there came the sound of another motor-cycle. It slowed. The German military policeman shouted something at the white-bearded Dutchman, then accelerated away. That old farmer had been standing at his horse's head, gently patting and calmly reassuring her while all the vehicles noisily rumbled past. He now led her back onto the road, mounted the cart and continued their interrupted journey.

There were no further alarms. They met and passed another horse and cart going in the opposite direction. The approaching farm horses neighingly greeted one another in what to John seemed a much more sincerely friendly manner than that in which the two farmers gruntingly acknowledged one another. He correctly surmised that the patriotic old grandfather knew the other farmer; knew him to be a treacherous collaborator. Had that farmer been a trustworthy patriot surely both men would have stopped and enjoyed a few minutes friendly talk.

The grey mare continued at her slow, steady , plodding pace. Eventually horse and cart turned sharply off the road into a narrow lane. John guessed by that sharp turn and by the muddily muffled sounds of hoofs and wheels that they were approaching a farm. He hoped they were almost at journey's end. He longed to stand up, to move about, to get free of the smells of turnips, which with each passing hour seemed to be getting overwhelmingly stronger.

The challenging barks of a dog, the welcoming neighing of horses, and – determined not to be left out – the inquisitive mooing of cattle, confirmed that they were now at a farm. John happily listened to a male and a female Dutch voice join in warmly welcoming the old grandfather as he drove into their farmyard.

 Horse and cart halted. The old driver clambered down. There were renewed greetings. From the side of the cart a deep male voice asked in English, 'Are you all right in there?'

'Yes, yes, I'm fine,' John replied. 'I stink of turnips, that's all!'

'Good! ....We will soon get you out from under them.' The unseen Dutchman climbed into the cart and rapidly shifted the turnips away from John, who eagerly heaved the sheltering wooden box off and staggered to his feet. He helped the Dutchman neatly re-arrange the turnips, then together they climbed out.

The tall, slim, middle-aged Dutchman brightly smiled as he held out his hand, 'I am Frans. You are English soldier? ....Your name is John?'

'Yes, I'm an English soldier. Yes, my name's John.'

Frans introduced the buxom, rosy-cheeked, middle-aged Dutch woman at his side, 'This is my wife, Blanche.'

Broadly beaming, she eagerly shook hands with John; the grip of her large, red, toil hardened hand was at least as strong as her husband's. She greeted him in faltering English, 'Welcome.... welcome, John.' Then, turning to the smiling old grandfather and thankfully reverting to Dutch, she ushered both of them into the hospitable warmth and gleaming comfort of the farmhouse's impressively large kitchen.

Frans apologised, 'I am afraid Blanche does not speak much English.' He fondly smiled at the young woman who quietly entered the kitchen from another door; 'But Anna does. Her English is excellent.' He grinned disparagingly, 'She even speaks it better than I do.'

With what to John seemed most attractive modest shyness mingled with genuine affection, she gently replied, 'Oh, Uncle Frans, please be quiet, you know you speak it much better than me.'

Frans laughed, 'Oh well, we will agree that we have an equally good command of English.' He made a formal introduction. 'This is my niece, Anna ... Anna this is brave British soldier, John.'

With hand outstretched, John eagerly moved to where she stood motionless at the doorway.

She politely raised her hand to John's. There was little response to his firmly eager grip. She gave a momentary smile then quickly withdrew her hand.

John did not show his disappointment at her lacklustre response. He did not detect any unfriendliness in it. All he detected was a nervously withdrawn caution mingled with a diffident shyness which combined to add a mysteriously elusive attractiveness to her physical charms. And she certainly was physically attractive. She seemed much the same age as himself, and was about the same height. Her well formed figure was crowned with fairish, not quite blond hair which swept back from her forehead, covered her ears, then most attractively cascaded to her shoulders. Her tanned face was smoothly unlined, but its rather drawn and haggard look displayed what seemed clear signs of strain.

John guessed she was suffering from memories of some harrowing experiences. Often at the end of a particularly savage North Atlantic convoy, with many merchant ships and some escorting warships torpedoed and sunk, his Royal Navy shipmates wore a similar, or an even more gaunt and drawn exhausted appearance.

As Anna helped her aunt at the large cooking range she thought of John. He was not the first escaping British soldier or airman to be given hospitable sanctuary here while the next part of his hazardous return journey to Britain was being arranged, but she sensed something strangely different about him. Although she could not see him as she stood at the kitchen range with her back to him, she felt strangely excited by the knowledge of his near presence.

In those few moments when she had gently touched his hand her shy glance had taken in every detail of his appearance. Yes, there certainly was something strangely – something disturbingly – different about him. For one thing he was dressed differently from all the other British servicemen she had seen. Those unusual black clothes, those bulging webbing pouches and that large gun and evil looking knife at his belt gave him a sinister appearance. She had the same thought as the R.N. submarine captain had had: she was pleased to have him as an ally ... would hate to have him as an enemy. His only being of medium height in no way detracted from the aura of resourceful, self-reliant controlled power which she had felt emanate from John. She felt sure he was highly skilled and well experienced in the praiseworthy art of ruthlessly killing Germans.

But the friendliness of the smile with which he had greeted her, and the way that smile was repeated in his beaming eyes surely revealed another side of his character. Her instinctive feminine intuition reliably assured her that behind John's extremely tough, strong and resolute outer persona there lurked a warmly humane and kindly personality.

Anna felt strongly – but shyly and confusedly – attracted to John. She silently prayed that he would stay hidden at this farm long enough for her to get to know the real John.

Sitting at the kitchen table with the two Dutchmen, John kept unobtrusively glancing at Anna. He felt strangely strongly attracted to her. Yet surely not strangely attracted? .... she was the only other young person in the room; wasn't it natural that their lively, healthy, male and female hormones should attract one another? He hoped he would be ordered to stay hiding at this farm for some time – long enough for him to get to know Anna much better.

Chapter Seventeen

An hour later, after some welcome food and milk, the old Dutch grandfather re-mounted his turnip laden cart and slowly drove away. Frans had explained to John that he was going to a nearby small town where he would stay overnight then sell the turnips the following morning at the weekly market. With Frans translating, John had sincerely thanked the patriotic old Dutchman for so ingeniously getting him undetected passed those German sentries at the bridge. It was unlikely that John and he would meet again.

As soon as horse and cart had trundled out of sight the aunt and niece went to continue their interrupted work in the extensive vegetable and fruit gardens behind the impressively large, red bricked, pink tiled old farmhouse. Frans smiled and said in English, ' I'll just show John his hiding place then I'll come and help you in the vegetable garden'.

Giving a pleasant chuckle, Anna replied, 'Yes uncle, be sure you do come and help us soon... we are well aware how much – or rather, how little – your enjoy working at the vegetables.'

Frans laughed and walked away. John went with him; he was secretly elated by the memory of how that sudden chuckle of Anna's had transformed her face, had replaced its rather careworn expression with one much brighter, one infinitely more pleasantly attractive.

He followed Frans into the empty stable and up the steep steps into the hayloft where the fresh hay's summer-sweet scent instantly reminded him of last night's similar sleeping place. But this time the hay was not to be his bed. Frans led him to the wall that seemed the far end of the loft, but was in reality merely a wooden partition. A narrow door was well hidden by plaid patterned horse-blankets, black oilskin coats and tangles of leather reins hanging from pegs above it.

Pushing these encumbrances aside, Frans led John through the concealed door into a secret room. He grinned, 'How do you like this place, John?'

'Its excellent!' For a moment he paused, overcome by a strong feeling of déjà vu; ' It's very like the secret room I slept in at the pa-.' He stopped in time before saying "pastor's house". He smiled, 'At one of the places I slept in before.'

Frans returned his smile; pleased with John's caution he said, 'Obviously you have some experience of hiding in secret Dutch rooms.'

'Yes, I have... and not only in Dutch ones.' Passing the heaped mattresses and blankets, the table and two chairs, John swiftly went to the loft's stone gable wall where there was a small window. Opening the window he satisfied himself that it was just large enough for him to struggle through; and conveniently below it was the tin roof of a lean-to shed and from there to the ground was only a six foot drop. Closing the window, he turned and smiled, 'I'm delighted to see your secret room has such a good emergency exit.'

Frans was impressed by John's experienced thoroughness; it gave him confidence that he would do nothing foolish; would do nothing that might endanger the security of this place and put at risk the lives of all the Dutch patriots at the farm. He smiled in turn, 'I am pleased it meets with your approval – your obviously expert approval. This will be your safe house.... your secret home until I can arrange for your return to England.'

John knew better than to ask how long that was likely to take. From previous experiences he was well aware of how uncertain, how hazardous, how liable to be changed or cancelled were all escape plans. 'Oh, I'm sure I'll be very well looked after here. This room really is very comfortable.' He grinned at Frans, 'I'll start increasing my comfort by taking off this gear.' He unfastened his webbing belt then rapidly struggled out of his laden pouches, holster and scabbard. He carefully arranged all this webbing gear over the back of one of the wooden chairs in such way to ensure it could be quickly slipped back on.

Again Frans was impressed by John's thoroughness. He keenly observed him as he rummaged in one of the commodious pouches... was he going to reveal another example of his skilled thoroughness? But no, he was pleased to see John reveal a more human side as he lifted out a flat tin of cigarettes, tore the waterproof sealing tape from the lid and held them out towards him, asking 'Do you smoke?... Do you want a British cigarette?'

'Oh yes please,' Frans accepted with alacrity. As they eagerly lit up, John grinned, 'It should be perfectly safe to smoke them here; there are no Huns anywhere near to smell them, are there?' Although he made this remark light-heartedly it contained a serious message, as he explained, 'While working in France with Resistance Fighters we quickly learned just how distinctly different the smoke of British cigarettes smelt from the strong, harsh smell of French cigarettes. We never smoked our British fags any place where there was the least risk of Germans or treacherous Froggy collaborators smelling them.'

Frans nodded his understanding, except for one word; he asked, 'What does "Froggy" mean?'

John laughed, 'A "Froggy" is a Frenchman. "The Froggies" is our impolite, our rather disparaging British slang name for the frog-eating French people.'

Frans laughed, 'Ah, I see. That is most funny. Did you eat any frogs with these "Froggies", John?'

'No, I didn't. The frogs were not in season when I was in France. But I've eaten much worse than frogs, I assure you!' He grinned but did not elaborate.

Frans suddenly turned serious, 'Were these French Resistance Fighters good, brave, patriotic people to work with? 'Even as he spoke Frans guiltily knew he was asking a question he should not have asked.

John knew that Frans had realised his mistake. Both men were acutely aware of the "need to know principle" – the principle that the less they knew the less they could disclose if captured and tortured by the Gestapo. For a few moments he silently thought then decided on this occasion to give Frans some information, give him some well deserved encouraging praise for the dangerous work he was patriotically carrying out and also show that he completely trusted him. 'Yes, Frans, many of those Froggy Freedom Fighters are good, brave and patriotic, but unfortunately there are many others who seem much more interested in fighting and betraying rival Resistance Groups than fighting the Germans. My experience amongst them is that it is often quite difficult to know exactly which group was completely trustworthy.'

John paused and smiled at Frans, ' My experience with Dutch Resistance Fighters is different – I have found all of them are like you, are absolutely trustworthy!'

Frans was delighted with John's sincere praise, he reached out and firmly shook his hand. 'Thank you John, thank you. It is most good of you to say so; it is encouraging to have all our efforts appreciated ….appreciated by an obviously well experienced British soldier like you.' He paused then solemnly said, 'But I am afraid not all Dutch people support our Resistance Fighters; it is a sad fact that all too many of our people willingly collaborate with the Germans.'

John nodded 'Yes, I know, Frans, I know. But surely that explains why all your Dutch Freedom Fighters are so completely trustworthy? They have valiantly determined to make up for the vileness of the many collaborators. The steadfast bravery of your Freedom Fighters more than compensates for the cowardly collaboration of your quislings.'

Frans smiled his silent agreement and sincere thanks. Once again he was greatly impressed by John; was moved and encouraged by the depth of his sympathetic understanding, his profound appreciation of the motives which drove him and all Dutch Freedom Fighters to willingly face many dangers in their struggle to help free their country from the oppressive tyranny of the German occupation. Yes, he thought, our brave struggle does compensate for even the most despicable of our traitors – those many young Dutchmen, all fanatic Nazis, who have voluntarily joined the Netherlands S.S. Legion and are fighting with the Germans army against the Russians.

The Germans boastfully claimed there were 100,000 of those Dutchmen fighting the Soviet menace. That figure was grossly exaggerated for Nazis propaganda purpose, but even if the true numbers were less than half that claim, they were still disgracefully high, were a shameful blot on the Dutch nation.

Frans voiced none of these thoughts. His cigarette was smoked out, he crushed the stub in an ashtray, glanced at his watch and said, 'I better put you in the picture, John, before I go as promised and help Blanche and Anna in the vegetable garden.'

John grinned, 'You don't seem too keen on that work.'

Frans returned his grin, 'No, I'm not! I can think of many more interesting things to do instead.'

Although that Dutchman and that Englishmen had met for the first time only a little more than an hour ago, both felt completely relaxed in one another's company; they felt as if they had known each other a long time. This was quite a common experience ... often one hour of shared wartime hazards forged relationships of a far deeper, far warmer, far more trusting camaraderie than many years of peace could forge. John secretly wondered if – and fervently hoped that – some similar deep wartime bond would quickly bring Anna and him together in warn, intimate, fraternal closeness. Bring them together just how warmly and closely? ..... just how intimately?

Frans repeated, 'Yes, I will put you in the picture, John. What is your English military word for that process?'

'The word is "brief" – you will brief me.'

'Ah yes, I will brief you on the situation at this farm and on those living in it. I will tell you things you better know, but nothing that you are best not knowing, all right?'

John readily agreed to this further wise example of the "need to know principle". He did not know, and probably would never learn the surnames of Frans and his relations and therefore – even under the most hideous Gestapo torture – would be unable to reveal their names. Likewise, these Dutch Patriots might never get to know his surname.

'Well, John, I must tell you that only three of us live at this farm: my wife, Blanche, my niece, Anna, and myself.' Frans grinned, 'And I assure you we are all absolutely trustworthy patriots. We have helped many British airmen travel back to England, and we will do the same for you. I do not know how long it will take to arrange your escape to England, but if only a few days or some weeks, you will be well hidden from the Germans here. And you are most welcome to share our meals with us.'

'Thank you Frans, thank you. But I'll feel rather guilty about eating your precious, scare, strictly rationed food. I hope I won't impose on you too long.' Although he expressed this hope in all sincerity, John could not help again having that deep secret hope that he might be here more than a mere ' few days'; might stay long enough to get to know Anna much better. Although giving his full attention to what Frans was telling him, he could not put the though of Anna entirely out of his mind. A picture of her rather strained, careworn face being brightly transformed by that sudden pleasant chuckle she had given her uncle remained vividly clear in his mind.

'Oh John, you need not feel any guilt about eating our food. We are fortunate living in the country. It is only in Rotterdam and other large Dutch cities that there are bad food shortages and real hardships.

'We grow our own vegetables and fruit on this farm; we have hens and eggs; our cows provide ample milk and Blanche expertly turns much of it into excellent butter and cheese. She is also excellent baker and makes our own bread. We have to sell most of our food in the markets – much of which, unfortunately, finds its way to Germany – but we still have enough for ourselves. So you must not feel guilty about sharing our meals, John. All of us, Blanche, Anna and myself are pleased?... no, are more than pleased, are delighted to share our food with you, John, you who risk your life fighting and killing Germans.'

Frans's voice rose passionately , his eyes blazed fervent patriotism, ' Working together with the likes of you, John, we Dutch Patriots will – sooner or later – drive the hated Krauts out of poor, sadly oppressed Holland.'

Moved by the Dutchman's sincere deep emotion, John warmly declared, 'Yes, Frans, we will, together we will, and let's hope it happens sooner rather than later!'

For some silent emotional moments the two men stared at one another, then Frans grinned, 'Oh, I suppose I should go, as promised, and help Blanche and Anna in the vegetable garden.'

John laughed and again said, 'You don't seem too keen on that work! ... Here, have another British fag instead.'

After they lit up, John asked, 'Do just the three of you run your farm?'

'Oh no, a neighbouring couple help us. They live in a smallholding with their two young children just a few fields away. You will meet them. They too, are completely trustworthy Dutch Patriots. The husband does most of the ploughing and other heavy farm work. His wife mainly helps Blanche with the milking and butter and cheese making. Anna looks after the hens, and she and I help when needed, especially at harvesting.' Frans ruefully grinned, 'And also at the... the interminable damned weeding.'

John laughed, 'You don't sound like a real keen farmer, Frans.'

'No, I'm not. I'm not really a farmer at all. Actually I am a school teacher, as is – or -was – Anna. Only Blanche is of real farming stock. Her parents had a large dairy farm. Even when only a girl she became a great milker and later became an expert butter and cheese maker. She still loves dairy work; she gets much more milk from her cows than anyone else does and her butter and cheeses are truly of exceptional quality. And she is also a really great cook and baker.'

Frans disarmingly smiled at his perhaps somewhat excessive praise of his wife's remarkable qualities. He then modestly added, 'But you will be able to judge for yourself, John, when you share our meals.'

'I certainly look forward to that. All your praise of Blanche's food has fair got my mouth watering.' He warmly admired the genuine pride with which Frans had praised his wife. He felt a touch of envy for that middle-aged Dutch couple who seemed so comfortably and lovingly settled. He ruefully wondered if he (an unattached young bachelor) would ever achieve such a happily settled state?.... Perhaps a more pertinent question in his present situation was – was he likely to survive to reach middle-age?... And if he did meet a loving, lovable, young woman would it be fair to make her his wife in the midst of this foul war, when the chances of him continuing to survive to the end of it must be rather slim?

As he asked these questions a picture of Anna flashed into his mind. He had not consciously summoned up that picture, but it now shone vividly bright in his consciousness. Had it been summoned by healthy young manhood's soaring optimism and boundless virile eagerness?

Smiling to himself as that picture of Anna pulsed bright in his mind, John self-mockingly wondered, 'Could this be a case of Love at First Sight?' He did not really believe in such a thing; he thought it merely a vapid, romantically poetic notion. He had never been helplessly swept away and almost drowned in the violent passion of deep love. Could this vision of Anna be a portent of something strong, pure and deep?... Or was it merely a natural touch of healthy male lust?

Fran's explanation of much more practical matters brought John's thoughts bumping back down to earth. 'You are mistaken, John, when you speak about "our" farm. This farm is not ours – not Blanche's, Anna's or mine. We do not own it. It belongs to my older brother ... Anna's father. He allows us to live in and run his farm.'

'Oh, I see. He does not live here, though?'

'No. He lives in Rotterdam and teaches at the university there. We do not see much of him. Only very occasionally does he come to see

Anna. He usually only stays one night at a weekend.' Frans paused then rather hesitantly added, 'Which probably is just as well for all concerned!'

In answer to John's enquiring look, Frans continued, 'Oh, you know what families are! Neither Blanche nor I get on well with my brother, and Anna only tolerates him because he is her father. But you will not meet him, John. If he should come for a weekend while you are here you will have to stay hidden from him.'

With some apprehension John again looked enquiringly at Frans. He seemed reluctant to say more about his brother, but John needed to know more. 'Is your brother not to be trusted, then? ... Might he betray me to the Huns if he saw me?'

'Oh no ... no, he's not as bad as that.' Frans paused, frowned, then rather doubtfully added, 'Not as far as I know! ... Oh no, no, he could not be so bad! And of course if he did betray you that betrayal would involve all of us here who were helping you: Anna, Blanche and me – his own daughter, his younger brother and his sister-in-law. Oh no, no, he would not do that!'

'No, I should hope not. I should damned well hope not! But if you three were not involved, if I was on my own, might he then betray me?'

Again Frans hesitated, again deeply frowned before replying in an anguished voice, 'Oh God, John, I don't honestly know! ... I don't really think he would do such a terrible treacherous thing, but ... but I cannot be certain!'

For some moments there was a tense, thoughtful silence, then Frans (deciding in fairness to John that he had now to put him more in the picture) solemnly continued, 'Before the war my brother visited Germany a number of times. He was most impressed by the strictly disciplined hard working Germans. He thought them a great example for the Dutch to follow. He became .... became, how do you say it in English? – right-wing? ... Yes very right-wing. I was very left-wing then. As you can imagine, John, my brother and I had many violent and impassioned arguments. After he got appointed as a professor at Rotterdam University and I became a school teacher at a small, remote Dutch town, we never saw one another for some years.

'I don't really know how the occupation of The Netherlands by the Germans has affected my brother. Does he still admire their strict discipline, or – seeing that discipline savagely applied to his sad country – is he now less keen on it? ... Has it made him, openly or secretly, hate the occupying Germans? .... Or does he openly or secretly collaborate with them? ... I just don't know.

'On the rare occasions when he does visit Anna, all of us, but him especially, carefully keep clear of discussing the war, politics, and all such controversial subjects.' A sudden smile replaced Frans's solemn frowns, 'It is more peaceful that way, but as you can again imagine, John, it is quite a strain. So, as I said, it is just as well for all concerned that he does not come here often and does not stay long. Hopefully you will be well away from here before he makes his next visit.'

John returned Frans's smile, 'I hope so... I sincerely hope so.' He thoughtfully paused then asked, 'Your brother does not know about you being a patriotic Resistance Fighter, then?'

'Oh no, he knows nothing of us being Patriots who help the likes of you, John, to escape back to England. The knowledge of what we do is kept a strict secret, is known only by a few other completely trustworthy Patriots.'

Frans rose to his feet, stretched and sighed, 'Oh, I suppose I better go as promised and help Anna and Blanche with the weeding. You stay and rest here, John. I will collect you in a few hours when dinner is ready.'

Obeying Frans's instruction and his S.B.S. training, John lay on a mattress, relaxed, and conserved his energy in readiness for any sudden unexpected demands that might be made on it.

While his body quickly settled into restful ease his mind remained actively alert. With clear calm logic he reviewed his situation. Reassuringly he summed it up as really being not too bad .... Quite good, in fact, compared to some of the extremely 'hairy' situations he had found himself in on previous missions in German-occupied countries. He was absolutely confident of the complete trustworthiness and experienced reliability of the Dutch Patriots at this farm. He had no doubt they would do their utmost to get him safely back to Britain. His only cause for concern was the uncertainty over the possible untrustworthiness of Fran's older brother, who was also Anna's father. Frans had described him as being "very right-wing". John wondered just how far right he actually was – far enough to still admire, possibly collaborate with, the occupying Huns?

From personal experience with various nervously suspicious rival groups of Resistance Fighters in France, John knew what a desperate strain it was when there were doubts about the trustworthiness not only of some of your own comrades, but of all members of other Resistance Groups who – in theory – were allies in fighting the Huns. How terrible were the suspicions, how hateful the accusations when families were savagely and fanatically divided.

On one memorable occasion his S.B.S. team had been deeply embroiled in an especially ugly tangled web of deceit, vile lies and foul deeds. Reluctantly obeying urgent orders, that British team had dramatically and decisively intervened between rival groups. With ruthless skill had eliminated some suspected traitors. Only after that unpleasant task had been completed did they learn that one of the traitors – the leader of a Gaullist group – had been denounced by one of his sons – the leader of a Communist group.

After all these anguished decisions, these foul (but fair?) deeds, John had felt something like relief at getting back to "normal" killing as he again went on sea-going duties on a convoy-escorting destroyer. Although fierce and savagely ruthless, at least the endless war in the North Atlantic was straightforward. Each side – the deadly predatory German U-boat wolf-packs, and the urgently hunting British warships – knew exactly who their enemy was; knew with no touch of doubt how to deal with these enemies.

John sympathetically wondered if Anna's nervous manner and her rather stressed, careworn face were at least partly caused by the strain of worrying over the terrible nagging doubt about whether her father was or was not trustworthy.

After a while as he dropped into sleep, John had a vivid vision of Anna's face – her transformed, happy, carefree smiling face. Dreaming tender, semi-erotic visions he shallowly slept.

Chapter Eighteen

Three hours later, having been collected by Frans, having with a healthy young man's hungry eagerness shared in what he thought (in the depth of Holland's severe war-time shortages) a surprisingly abundant, but un-surprisingly delicious dinner of thick vegetable soup and even thicker, even more filling mutton casserole, John was now leisurely and most enjoyably finishing off that meal with a generous wedge of cheese, thickly buttered home-baked bread and a refilled glass of fresh, creamily thick milk.

Smiling across the large, well-scrubbed, well-laden pine kitchen table, he loudly and sincerely enthused, 'Oh, Blanche, your cheese, your butter and milk and your fresh-baked bread are really great! They are even more excellent than Frans said they were. They finish off this perfect meal perfectly! Thank you .... thank you very much.'

Although she did not fully understand John's English, Blanche had no difficulty in understanding that he was deeply sincerely praising her food. With no foolish false modesty she beamingly basked in his honest praise. With her husband helping to translate her Dutch thoughts into English words, she disjointedly stammered out, 'I am...am delighted to do something... something real good to.... to help, to really help you brave English soldier who fights the ... the horrid? ...Yes the terrible horrid Krauts.'

Once he finished translating, Frans silently smiled at his flushed, benignly beaming wife with gentle loving affection. He then added his equally heartfelt praise to John's.

As Anna enthusiastically joined in this paean of praise she rewarded John with a quick bright smile which thanked him for so sincerely praising her nobly patriotic aunt's outstanding dairy and cookery skills. With another smile which lit up her face, she quietly, a touch shyly, apologised, 'Blanche, Frans and I are sorry we have no coffee or you English people's favourite drink – tea, to finish the dinner off with, John.'

He secretly felt foolish elated at hearing her use his name for the first time. During most of dinner she had been a silent alertly attentive listener while Frans and he did most of the talking. He guessed her silence to be partly caused by a constraining shyness, that shyness augmented by the strains and constrains of some old, lingering sadness which still weighed heavily on her. He was delighted to see her smile, to hear her brightly comment on the great English love of tea. Beaming a joyous smile at her, he lifted his glass of milk and said, 'Oh, Anna, this rich, creamy milk of Blanche's' – he grinned, 'or rather of Blanche's cows – is great is certainly greater than coffee.' Again he grinned, 'is almost as great as our famous, fabulous British char!'

With instant amiable eagerness Anna returned his grin and asked, 'Char... Char? What exactly is char, John?'

Again he felt a strange surge of delight at hearing her use his name again; use it more confidently and with what seemed a suggestion of friendly familiarity. He was moved by a stronger elation than he had felt before as he sensed her shyly constrained reserve begin to melt. Daring to hope that this might be a first step towards them getting much better acquainted, he cheerily explained that "char" was an affectionate British slang word for our beloved national beverage – tea.

Anna smiled, 'Oh, I see . Well, John, I am sorry we have no "char" to give you.'

Frans also smiled, 'It is strange that I do not remember ever having heard that word "char" when I was in England. Is it a vulgar word?'

'Oh no, not at all. It's an innocent nickname used with cosily warm affection. It's mainly used by British soldiers and other servicemen.'

'Oh, I understand. That must be why I did not hear it.'

'It would be before the war that you were in England, Frans?'

'Yes... yes, long before this war, but just a short time after another war – the First World War. I studied for three years in England. I greatly improved my command of English language.'

Blanche stood, lifted some of the empty plates and glasses and carried them over to the sink. Anna immediately followed her example. Frans and John also got to their feet. Smiling, Frans said, 'We will leave the ladies to get on with the washing-up, John. Come through to the next room and we will have a smoke.'

Also smiling, John willingly obeyed. As he closed the kitchen door Frans explained, 'The ladies – especially Blanche – like to be left by themselves to wash the dishes etc. Blanche says that any men in the kitchen when she's working only get in her way. Often she is not too keen even to have Anna helping her.' He mischievously grinned, ' No, it is usually not good to have two women working in the same kitchen, is it? It is like your English saying: "Too many cooks spoil the soup", eh? It is even more true here where neither woman actually owns the kitchen and therefore there is no definite undisputed boss. Although when it comes to the actual cooking then Blanche definitely is the boss. She is a great cook. Anna is not. She is not really interested in cooking, so, wisely, she willingly leaves Blanche to get on with it.'

As he ushered John into the large sitting room Frans pointed at a leather armchair and hospitably urged him to make himself comfortable. Before doing so, John observantly looked around the rather sombre room. It was almost overwhelmingly crowded with solidly substantial dark furniture. The darkly stained wooden floor added to the dullness, as did the thick, heavily brocaded curtains of purplish plum colour which, in compliance with the strict black-out regulations, completely shrouded the window. Although the room gave an impression of antiquated drabness, everything was spotlessly clean. All the sombrely gleaming wood gave out the distinctive scent of beeswax furniture polish.

The bright, blue and white tiles of the room's neat fireplace were a brilliant contrast to the surrounding drabness. So too were the rows of books crowding a shelved alcove at one side of the fireplace.

Running his eyes along the books, John was pleasantly surprised to see that many were printed in English. Great English novels shared shelves with Shakespeare, Byron, and Wordsworth. There were even a number of brightly coloured Penguin paperbacks. With delight he recognised some of the titles he treasured in his bookcase at home. Costing only sixpence, these books had been a real godsend to impoverished readers in pre-war Britain. Obviously they were also greatly appreciated by some Dutch readers.

Seeing John magnetically drawn to those crammed shelves, Frans smiled, 'You like reading, John? There are ample English books for you to borrow while you are hiding here.'

'Yes, but I would need to hide here a good few years to read through that magnificent lot. Are they all yours, Frans?'

'Oh no. The collection of English books are Anna's. I have read some of them, but she has read them all. She studied English language and literature at university and then taught English. She is much more interested in artistic aesthetic thing than me.' Grinning, Frans pointed to the massed lower shelves of books which – being mostly in Dutch and German and looking forbiddingly dull – John had ignored. 'Those are my books. They are about subjects I studied at university and now teach.... science, chemistry, biology.'

'Oh, I see.'

'You do not find these subjects so interesting?'

John smiled apologetically, 'Oh, I'm sorry, Frans, of course these are interesting, vitally important subjects; it is just that I am not really scientifically minded, that's all.' He grinned, 'Although in the last few years I've had to study and expertly master some scientific subjects too – the dangerous, often unstable, chemical properties of various types of lethal explosives and how to safely hand them. I've had to study some biology too – have acquired enough knowledge of human anatomy to enable me to skilfully and stealthily silently kill certain people... usually German sentries. Useful scientific subjects to learn, eh Frans?'

Ruefully grinning, Frans conceded , 'Oh, of course it is terrible that war should so pervert science, but it is necessary if we are ever going to win this ghastly war, is it not?' He paused then grimly added, 'One of the most terrible things, one of the greatest dangers, is how many first-class scientists the Germans have.'

John silently nodded. He wondered if Frans had any inkling of the terrible, war-wining, new weapon some of the best scientific brains in Germany were desperately try to develop – the atom-bomb. Had he heard any whispered rumours about there being two Dutchmen – brilliant scientists, but despicable traitors – working for the Germans on this project? If he had, those rumours were now incorrect, for there was now only one of these traitors assisting in this project. John had killed the second one, Professor de Waal. Thinking of Professor Maurik the remaining traitor, John again deeply regretted that he had evaded the same fate planned for him in 'Operation Waterloo.' To make up for the loss of his assistant, was that scientist even more eagerly, ever more urgently collaboration with the Germans on developing their atom-bomb?

101

Switching his thoughts to Anna (a much more pleasant subject) John asked, 'Does Anna still teach English?'

'Oh no. She had a nervous breakdown which forced her to stop teaching. Anyway the Germans have banned the teaching of English in Holland, as in every other country they have conquered. So she could not teach it even if she wanted to, which I am sure is just as well for her and all connected with her.'

Frans stood thoughtfully silent. So did John, then he handed Frans a British cigarette. They lit up then got comfortably settled in armchairs on either side of the neatly set, but unlit, fireplace. Both were well aware of the wisdom of the 'need-to-know' principle; yet in conflict with this awareness of the need for discreet secrecy was the, at times, almost irresistible necessity to show complete confidence in your trustworthy brave comrade by disclosing a little more than you strictly should. So, in answer to John's silently enquiring steady gaze, Frans explained. 'You see, John, although the Krauts would not allow Anna to teach English, they do allow me to teach my universal subjects: science, chemistry and biology. I teach three days per week at the senior school in a small town ten kilometres from here.' He paused, he smiled, 'I cycle to and from that school. It is good exercise. It keeps me fit.'

John grinned, 'It keeps you fighting fit to fight the Krauts, eh Frans?'

'Yes, exactly,' Frans delightedly exclaimed. 'And at the school I meet other teachers who are also completely trustworthy Dutch Patriots.' Wisely, he revealed no details about these Patriots. He kept secret the fact that he was the leader of the local Dutch Resistance Group and that one teacher was his clandestine wireless operator who kept him in touch with London and that another teacher was his expert forger of fake identity and travel documents.

He would instruct both of them tomorrow. One would prepare faked documents for John. The other would encode then transmit a wireless signal to England. That transmission would go direct to S.O.E (Special Operations Executive) in London and – if the correct procedures were followed (they weren't always) – that message would be passed on to Commander Richardson at Royal Navy Intelligence. He would receive the restricted information John had given Frans earlier: the fact that he, Leading-seaman John Armstrong, had successfully completed his part of 'Operation Waterloo' – his 'target' was dead! But, regrettably, the other, the even more important target was not! He had not been in his office. All other members of John's S.B.S. team were dead. He was being hidden by Dutch Patriots. He waited instructions for his return to Britain.

Frans had been intrigued to hear for the first time a little – a very little – about 'Operation Waterloo'. He secretly speculated about who the two 'targets' of that operation were. Obviously they must have been of real importance for a special British clandestine team to be sent into Holland to kill them, And as only John's 'target' had been killed, was the other 'target' still at loose somewhere in Holland? He knew better than to ask John about this. He knew that John would only disclose this sensitive secret information to him if there was an imperative need for him to be told.

He had also been intrigued to learn that John was not, as he had thought, an English soldier, but was a sailor in the British Navy. He had asked, 'What is the S.B.S you are in, John?.... is it like the great, brave, British Commandos?'

John had replied, 'Yes, Frans, the S.B.S. – the Special Boat Section – are something like the Commandos. Only we are much greater, much tougher, much more resolutely versatile and very much more secret than the Commandos.

'The S.B.S. are not only by far the best, the true élite, of not only all British Special Forces, but of all Special Forces anywhere in the world!'

Frans smiled as he remembered the broad grin with which John had boastfully declared, 'Yes, the S.B.S. are truly unique. Being part of the Senior Service, with its legendary boast "that nothing is impossible to the Royal Navy", we can do anything. Of all Special Forces we are the only ones who can actually walk on water!'

Once his cigarette was smoked out Frans started the pleasantly familiar procedure of methodically half filling his large meerschaum pipe's commodious bowl with desperately scarce, ever more precious thick black tobacco.

Delaying the keenly anticipated delight of his pipe's subtly soothing, deeply satisfying smoking pleasure, Frans sat with a box of matches in one hand and the primed pipe in the other. Deeply sighing, he sorrowfully continued, 'But unfortunately, John, not all teachers at my school are Patriots. Some are terrible traitors who wholeheartedly collaborate with the Krauts. As you can imagine, it is quite a strain having to work with them. We Patriots have to keep our true feelings well hidden or these traitors would denounce us to the Nazis. It is a strain we older, more experienced, more cautiously careful Patriots manage to cope with, but which poor young Anna would find impossible to deal with. She could never keep her true feelings hidden. Her deep hatred of the Krauts and her even deeper hatred of all collaborating Dutch traitors would burst out. She would be arrested by the Gestapo. They would search this farm. When they discovered the secret room above the stable all of us – Anna, Blanche and I would be sent to a German Concentration Camp and either be, quickly, ruthlessly killed in the gas chambers or forced into Slave Labour until our health gave out and then be sadistically disposed of.

'So it certainly is a good thing that the Krauts forbid her to teach English, eh?'

John nodded, 'Yes, obviously it's much better for all concerned that Anna stays safely out of the way here, away down on the farm. Is she reconciled to not teaching now? Of course I don't really know her yet, but I get the impression that, although showing some signs of strain, she seems reasonably content here... Is she really?'

Noting how eagerly John asked that question, Frans thoughtfully paused then struck a match and lit his pipe. Once the tobacco was well alight he slowly jetted out the first of many long delightful streams of smoke, smiled and replied with another question, 'Are you very interested in Anna, John?'

With hidden amusement John also paused thoughtfully before replying. He thought that Frans seemed like an alarmed Victorian father anxiously enquiring if a young man's intentions towards his attractive daughter were strictly honourable. 'Oh of course I am interested in Anna; that is perfectly normal and entirely natural, isn't it?' He smiled, 'But Frans, I give you my solemn assurance that my interest in her and my intentions towards her are entirely honourable!'

It was obvious that Frans had also read some Victorian novels as, grinning, he asked, 'Do you give me your word as an English officer and gentleman on that?'

John laughed, 'Oh of course I give you my word on it .... my word as not quite an English officer and not quite an English gentleman!'

Frans joined in John's laughter, then, turning serious, explained. 'You see, John, I – Blanche and I – feel almost like anxious parents towards Anna She is like a daughter we never had. She's been through some grievous experiences. She had a nervous breakdown. We would hate her to suffer any more terrible upsets. You understand, John?'

'Yes,' John solemnly nodded. 'Of course I understand. I assure you I will do nothing to upset her. I would hate to add any more marks of careworn strain to the ones already writ on her face.'

'Ah, so you notice that .... well, John, I will give you some of Anna's history. It will help you to understand her better; help you patiently sympathise if she is at times rather strangely constrained and withdrawn.

'Anna was only two months married when the Germans invaded Holland in May, 1940...'

'Married?.... Anna's married?' John involuntarily gasped with foolishly irrational dismay.

'Yes, she was married in March, 1940. Then her husband was killed two months later bravely fighting the ruthless invading Krauts. A few days later her brother was also killed heroically resisting the overwhelming Kraut hordes. Anna was devastated by these grievous blows. She had a ... a nervous breakdown.

'Although heart-broken by the death of her son; terribly distressed by her son-in-laws death; and constantly worried about the unknown fate of her second son who was serving in the Dutch Navy and who was thought to have escaped to Britain and might be continuing the gallant fight from there against the hideous Krauts, Anna's mother nobly subdued her own grief in her desperate struggle to nurse her daughter back to mental and physical health. Slowly, wearily slowly, she succeeded.

'Then when her mother fell seriously ill, Anna tenderly and lovingly nursed her for almost a year until she died.'

Frans paused then gently smiled, 'So you can now better understand the reasons for Anna's careworn face and why she so hates the Krauts and so eagerly helps our Resistance Fighters and brave British soldiers – or sailors, like you, John.'

'Thank you for explaining Anna's background to me, Frans. I again assure you I will do nothing to upset her. It would be cruel to load any more troubles on to the ones she's already endured.'

Chapter Nineteen

There was a gentle knock at the door, it opened and Anna entered.

For a few moments there was a constrained silence.

Intuitively knowing that Frans and John had been talking about her, Anna's face vividly flushed and she started turning to leave the room.

Frans hurried to her, grasped her arm and gently guided her to the armchair he had vacated. He grinned, 'Sit down and rest, Anna. Have you finished the washing-up or has Blanche insisted on being left in peace to have the kitchen to herself?'

'Oh yes, as usual she wants to be left as undisputed boss of "her" kitchen!' The disarming smile accompanying this emphatic statement robbed it of any suggestion of too nasty a cattiness. Somewhat shyly she glanced at John. 'Blanche made the excuse that I should come here and practise my English on you, John.'

'I'm delighted that you have left the kitchen; delighted that you've come in here; will be truly delighted to have you practise your English on me, although surely it needs no practise. It seems perfect to me.'

John's gallantly sincere praise made Anna's face once more brightly flush.

John keenly noted and deeply admired the way the attractive blushes and modest smiles combined to wash away all signs of strain from Anna's features. They transformed them to glowing beauty. Instinctively he spontaneously responded to her pulse-stirring blushing charm. He warmly smiled. His face happily beamed.

With discreetly silent tolerant amusement Frans smiled down on those two young people sitting gazing at one another. It was good to see the burden of vividly remembered old tragedies temporarily lifted from Anna. It was pleasant to observe John in this quietly natural relaxed mood which surely further confirmed the warm good nature that – seemingly effortlessly – co-existed with the war-toughened, strong, resolute, ruthless, Kraut-killing side of his character.

Suddenly becoming self-consciously aware of his gaze being too steadily fixed on Anna for too long – as if he was adoringly gazing like a soppy, pimply, immature youth – John dragged his eyes away. He glanced at Frans; almost apologetically he uncertainly grinned. Returning his gaze to Anna and pointing to the gloriously crowded bookshelves, he said, 'Frans was telling me that most of those books printed in English are yours, Anna'

These words instantly had a profound and magically wonderful effect. Anna's shyness vanished. She rose. She lightly and lovingly ran her fingers along some of her books. Alight with the eagerness of a real book-lover she brightly smiled and passionately declared, 'Not just most of these books are mine – all of them are!' Lifting her smile to her uncle she gayly continued, 'At least, all the books that are worth reading are mine. Those drearily dull volumes on the lower shelves are Uncle Frans's. They are all about science and chemistry.'

Beaming with good humour, Frans slowly, silently, disparagingly, shook his head.

Obviously this feud between science and art was a long-standing friendly dispute between uncle and niece.

John gently shook with restrained, but sincerely joyous laughter. Frans, then Anna, joined in.

John felt elated. It was wonderful to be so trustingly and so companionably included within the deep bond of kinship and friendship which so strongly existed between niece and uncle. He felt as completely relaxed as if he was in the company of old friends; it seemed impossible that they had met for the first time only this morning. Now, standing beside Anna, he too reached out and touched some of her books. For a few moments their fingers lightly, unintentionally touched.

Instantly, and foolishly thrillingly, Anna experienced a tingling shock of keen pleasure as if John and she had secretly indulged in a wonderful act of sensual intimacy.

Blithely unaware of the powerful surge of feelings his casual fingers had innocently triggered, John said, 'I see you've got some of the greatest English poets here. I'm impressed! Have you read them all?'

'Yes, oh yes! I've read and studied them all. They are marvellous! English poetry contains some of the greatest art ever produced by mankind .... especially Shakespeare, of course!' Feeling her face glowing brightly, fearing that perhaps she had been too gushingly eager, she forced herself to more calmly ask. 'Do you like Shakespeare, John?'

'I'm afraid I don't really know Shakespeare. What little of him we were taught at school was so drearily unimaginatively battered into us as to put us off him for life.' Thinking of how to openly express − or even hint at − a liking for any poetry to one of his shipmates in the lower ranks of the Royal Navy, and especially in the fabulously tough S.B.S., would be like confessing to a shameful vice ... to something suspiciously cissy, if not downright pansy, John hesitated then , as if loath to admit it, said, 'But there is one poet I do really like; one I know well − William Wordsworth.'

As the touch of his fingers had done, these words of John's thrilled Anna as with a galvanic shock. Her face flamed. She beamingly smiled. She excitedly gasped, 'Oh John, that's amazing! Wordsworth is one of my favourite poets too!' With an effort she collected her delighted thoughts. 'Oh, of course, Wordsworth is nothing like as great a poet as Shakespeare − no one is- but he certainly is one of the greatest English poets. The greatest after Shakespeare!' She gave another beaming smile and less emphatically added, 'At least I think so. Do you, John?'

'Yes, I think so too. But obviously you are a much better judge than me. You have studied English poetry. I haven't. Wordsworth is the only poet I really know. At school I, like almost every British child, had to learn, memorize, then mechanically parrot 'The Daffodils'. That was practically the only Wordsworth poem we were taught. It was only later, as an older schoolboy, when − under my father's guidance − I started discovering my wonderful Lakeland homeland and tentatively began to appreciate something of its glorious beauty that − again under my father's guidance − I also began to excitedly, but not fully comprehendingly, appreciate something of the greatness (the unique mystic greatness) of Wordsworth's Lakeland poetry.'

Again beaming with amazed delight, Anna gasped, 'You live in the English Lake District, John?'

Surprised by her delighted surprise, he joyfully smiled, 'Yes, I do.' He paused, he again thought of the 'need- to- know' principle. He decided it could do no harm, would betray no great British state secret, if he revealed details of where he lived. 'Yes, I was born and brought up in the English Lake District. That's where my home is.' He grinned, 'That is where my heart is!... That's where my family live.'

Mixing a shyly mischievous sideways glance with a rather apprehensive grin, Anna asked, 'Your family, John? ... Your wife, your children?'

Delighted by how often, how familiarly, she was now using his name, he eagerly returned her grin. 'No, not my wife and children. I am not married. Now that my father is dead, only my mother and sister now live there.'

Giving a relieved smile, Anna said, 'Oh, I see. Where about in the Lake District do they live?'

'In the small town of Keswick.'

A tremulous shock once more galvanised Anna. Again she brightly flushed. Again she delightedly beamed . 'Oh, that's amazing John! Keswick is where I stayed with a party of students from Rotterdam University in 1938. We were all studying English language and literature. After a week at Stratford-on-Avon, seeing some Shakespeare plays, we spent the next week at Keswick. We were taught about, and were taken to see, some of the wonderful mountainous landscape that inspired Wordsworth and the other Lakeland poets.'

Frans laughingly intervened, 'She fell in love with those lakes and mountains. Blanche and I got tired of her constantly extolling the glorious wonder of that inspiring rugged landscape. We also got weary of her never endingly complaining about the drearily monotonous pancake flatness of our poor old Holland.'

Anna gave a gentle apologetic smile, 'Oh, uncle, I was young then.... was young and foolish. Was merely a confused, inexperienced teenage girl. Was confusedly full of all the wildly emotive uncertainties and endless unreasonable complaining that was normal at that time of life. I am a bit older – and hopefully- a bit wiser now.' She paused then solemnly added, 'Yes although only five years older in calendar time, I am now much, much older in experience... in harsh experience of life.'

Frans reached out and sympathetically touched her hand, 'I know, Anna, I know life has not been easy for you.'

Moved by this guarded reference to her war-inflicted miseries, John with compassionate kindness guided her back to the innocently happier time when she had discovered his deeply loved homeland. 'Did you climb any mountains when you were in the Lake District, Anna?'

Reminiscent joy brightened her face and animated her voice, 'Oh yes, John, we climbed two mountains. I still lovingly remember the first one – the first mountain I ever climbed – the one that thrusts up its huge solid bulk near Keswick – Skiddaw. Being accustomed to the flatness of Holland, the climbing was really exhausting, but when eventually we reached the summit the reward was well worth the effort. Being a day of playful breeze, swift moving white clouds and glorious sunshine, the views were wonderful and were ever changing under the effects of the brilliant light and racing shade. It was truly unforgettable... I was wonderously exhilarated.' Nostalgically Anna smiled at John, 'You have climbed Skiddaw too, John?'

'Yes I have, and more – much more – than once. I climb it every time I am home on leave at Keswick. Like you, Anna, Skiddaw was the first mountain I ever climbed. My father took me up it when I was a boy. Again like you, I found it an unforgettable experience.'

For some moments they silently and happily stared at one another. Both felt strangely wonderfully united by those experiences they had in common. Anna, especially, was profoundly moved. John was so different from all the other British soldiers and airmen who had briefly hidden here while making their way back to Britain. Only he came from, and deeply loved, the English Lake District; only he had climbed Skiddaw; only he knew and loved Wordsworth's glorious Lakeland poetry. She found it really amazing and truly wonderful that they had shared interests. It was great that she felt so genuinely, so easefully relaxed with him. Surely their coming together was not merely a chance occurrence!.... Surely not just the blind chances of war had haphazardly brought them together! Hadn't Fate – some brighter destiny – definitely played a decisive part? .... She was certain it had!

With her face glowing she brightly smiled, 'Oh, John, how fortunate you are to be able to climb Skiddaw when you are home on leave.' Abruptly her smile faded, her face shadowed, she sadly sighed. 'I intended to climb it again in the summer of 1939, but because of the threat of war looming over Europe, Rotterdam University cancelled our holiday in England. Oh, John, how eagerly I look forward to climbing it again once this terrible war is over. The image of me once more staring around from the summit of Skiddaw is an ecstatic vision forever hovering before me. It is a vivid dream that helps me struggle through this endless war with all its dreadful, ceaseless vileness.'

John stared his profound understanding sympathy. He, much more than Anna, was all to well, all too intimately, acquainted with the vileness of this terrible war. But, regrettably, only by people like him carrying out foul (foul, but in the broader context, fair) deeds would this war ever be brought to a successful conclusion. He, too, sadly sighed. Then he felt uplifted by other feelings – fine, happy, romantic feelings which were, he was well aware, strongly touched with other definitely more basic, more fleshy feeling. Brightly smiling he confidently promised, 'As soon as this damn was is over we will meet up again, you and I, Anna, and we will climb Skiddaw together. You agree?.... It that a deal?'

'Yes, Oh yes, John!.... it's a deal!... It's a promise, a wonderful, wonderful promise!'

Benignly looking on, Frans smiled and murmured, 'Yes, let's hope and pray that we all survive this war and see that promise kept.'

Suddenly the door opened and Blanche entered. She got sedately settled and almost immediately her knitting needles were a blur of industrious motion. While, seemingly of their own volition , her fingers continued their amazingly intricate non-stop performance, she stared at Anna and spoke a few words in Dutch.

Anna shrugged, gave a monosyllabic reply in that language, then turned and withdraw a few books from their crowded shelves.

John (correctly) surmised that Anna was not as fond of knitting as her aunt was. She handed three of the books to him. They were illustrated guides to the English Lake District and a collection of some of the greatest of Wordsworth's poems. Eagerly and happily animatedly Anna discussed these treasure with him in English while Blanche and Frans, like the typical sedate, married, middle–aged couple they were, occasionally chatted in a desultory way with one another in Dutch.

Surprisingly quickly the hours passed. Then promptly at ten-fifteen Blanche stopped knitting and got to her feet. Frans also rose and smilingly apologised to John, 'We all go to bed early here. Blanche has to get up very early to milk the cows. Anna also rises before dawn to get our breakfasts ready.'

After bidding the ladies good night, John followed Frans through the front door. In the cloudy darkness Frans guided him across the farmyard to the stable. By the shaded dim light of his torch John cautiously made his way up the steep steps to the hay loft and then groped to his concealed hiding place and his lonely bed.

For a few minutes Frans stood by himself outside the farmhouse door and smoked his pipe. Staring up at the low, heavy dark clouds from which a few drops of rain were starting to fall, he listened to the indistinct, cloud smothered, angry growl of heavy R.A.F bombers on their almost nightly, almost routine predatory hunt for German industrial cities, for Krupps vast armaments factories and for rail marshalling-yards crowded with military traffic. Once more he wished these brave British airmen good luck on their hazardous flights. Since the fall of France in 1940 this night-time British bombing, and the American daylight bombing, were the only possible way these allies could take the war to the Germans and disrupt their formidable military production. And this would remain true until their allied armies invaded and liberated Western Europe. Frans, like many, many other patriots in German-occupied countries had, fired with ardent eagerness, fervently hoped the invasion might have happened this year (1943). But now, with the first autumn gales foreshadowing winter's storms, it must surely be too late.

Keeping his disappointment hidden, he had now resignedly steeled himself to face yet another long, dreary, dangerous winter before he could realistically expect the allied invasion. He kept his morale up with the confident expectation that it would be successfully launched next Spring or early Summer. Surely Holland would be liberated from the hideous tyranny of the obnoxious Krauts by this time next year?

As he knocked the dead ashes from his pipe, Frans glanced at the dimness of the hayloft which sheltered John's lonely bed. His glance then swivelled to the blacked-out farmhouse window behind which was Anna's lonely bed. He could not help rather anxiously wondering if these two beds would remain chastely solitarily lonely.

It was obvious that Anna and John were strongly attracted to one another. That was natural. It would be most unnatural if they were not. With caring apprehension mingling with tolerant understanding Frans secretly smiled in the overcast darkness. It required no profound knowledge of biology and psychology to understand why those two young, healthy, normal people were so strongly attracted by each other, and allied to those strong natural attractions were those joyfully discovered common interests they shared.

He was almost certain that Anna, since the tragic death of her husband in 1940, had, leading a life of resolute austere celibacy – refused to satisfy her natural sexual instincts with any other man. For a time after getting over the worst of her nervous breakdown caused by her husband's and then her brother's deaths, she seemed reasonably calm and settled, but during the last six months she was definitely showing renewed signs of nervous tension. This was revealed in her uncharacteristic crabbed irritability and increasingly frequent acrimonious disputes with Blanche.

As with secret sympathetic understanding he unobtrusively observed her, Frans became convinced that these nervous outbursts were symptoms of a deep, unhealthy frustration brought about by her unnatural long repression of her sexual instincts.

Yes, it was glaringly obvious that Anna must find John – a healthily strong and tough, but not insensitive male (and surely also a virile one) –irresistibly attractive.

And what of John?... Although confident that John would keep his promise, would not intentionally do anything to upset Anna, Frans felt almost certain that if they spent too much time together almost inevitably they would become lovers.

Were they likely to be together for long? That was an unanswerable question. All previously escaping British fugitives had only spent a night or two hidden here before continuing their hazardous journey back to Britain. John might be different. Burdened with the secret knowledge he had acquired during the last few weeks, Frans had deep misgivings that it might now prove exceptionally difficult to get John safely returned to England.

Frans fatalistically sighed. Hopefully things would become clearer tomorrow. His wireless operator would send a coded message to London and should receive instructions about John's return to England. What would those instructions be?..... how soon or how long would it be before John left here?

Once more Frans gave a rather weary fatalistic sigh then went indoors to his cosily inviting, Blanche warmed bed.

Chapter Twenty

After having spent most of the following day hidden, resting and reading in his secret room in the hay loft, John hurried down the steep stairs and eagerly greeted Frans as, returning from his day's teaching at the local school, he put his cycle away in an empty stall of the stable.

Once the greetings were over John expectantly stood staring at Frans. He knew better than to ask questions. He was well aware that Frans would give him as much information as he thought wise; would put him as much in the picture as possible without betraying the strict 'need to know' principle.

'We have been in touch with London, John, but we haven't been given definite instructions about getting you back to England. This is Tuesday, the S.O.E. in London do not think they will be able to arrange anything this week. Possibly they will manage something next week. You are to stay hidden here in the meantime.'

John ruefully grinned, 'Not cooped up in the hayloft all day every day surely?'

Frans smiled, 'No, I knew you would not want that. I've made arrangements.' Pulling documents from a pocket he handed them to John. 'Those are your new identity papers complete with the photo of you I took yesterday. Those documents show that you are a Norwegian; a sailor in the Norwegian merchant navy. Your ship is being refitted in a Rotterdam shipyard and instead of dissolutely wasting your time, health and energy in dockside bars and brothels, you are voluntarily working on this farm. The Germans have approved a genuine scheme for temporarily out of work merchant seamen to help out on Dutch farms, so with these documents you can safely help us harvest our turnips and potatoes.' His eyes merrily twinkled,, 'I am sure Anna, especially, will be delighted to have you working beside us.'

'Yes, I hope so. It will be delightful to work beside her – beside you all.'

'Before you go out to the fields tomorrow you must memorise your Norwegian name, your home address in Norway and the name of your ship in Rotterdam. Should you be questioned by any Krauts or collaborating Dutch police remember you only speak Norwegian and some English. You have an official letter there in both Dutch and German authorising you to work on a Dutch farm. However, hopefully, you will not be questioned here.'

John laughed, 'Let's hope I don't meet any Krauts soldiers who were stationed in Norway and learned Norwegian!' After studying and being greatly impressed by the skilfully forged documents he anxiously asked, 'What about this special black British uniform I'm wearing, Frans, it would hardly pass as belonging to a Norwegian civilian sailor, would it?'

'Don't worry, John, I've thought of that. We will soon get you well disguised in Dutch clothes which you have donned to work in the fields. That they are borrowed will explain why they may be a bit ill-fitting. Come with me.' Frans led him to the large, sprawling old farmhouse. They passed a single storied extension containing two bedrooms, one of them Anna's. They passed the higher main house then entered a second extension. At a bedroom door Frans remarked, 'That is where we sleep, Blanche and I.' He unlocked a second door. 'This is more than just a spare bedroom, John.' He opened two massive old wardrobes. 'This is my special drapers shop; my hoard of clothes to disguise the likes of you, John. I'll soon fit you out like a real Dutchman – or Norwegian.'

With well practised skill Frans selected clothes to fit John. Heaping the load on him, he instructed, 'Take these to your secret room. Strip off every stitch of your British clothes; your uniform, your underwear, your boots and stockings ... everything. Leave them in that room. Dress in, and get accustomed to these Dutch clothes. Should the worst ever happen and you are strip searched by Gestapo thugs, they must find no incriminating British clothes on you. Is that clearly understood, John?'

'Yes, oh yes, that's perfectly clear. Thank you Frans.' As he turned to leave the room Frans halted him. 'Of course you realise the deadly danger you face if the Krauts ever discover your English nationality while you're wearing these civilian clothes, don't you?'

John wryly grinned, 'Yes, I do. They would execute me as a British spy.'

'I admire your courage, John. This extra danger does not daunt you?'

He grinned even more wryly, 'Actually it makes no difference if I'm in my British uniform or Dutch civilian clothes. As a member of the S.B.S. I would be shot anyway in strict compliance with Hitler's order that all captured British Special Forces were not to be treated as normal prisoners of war, but were to be executed.'

'Oh John, I did not know that.' Frans gazed silently at him for a few moments. 'Oh John, I admire your courage more than ever!'

'Oh well, this knowledge of what would happen to us gives us in the S.B.S. a great incentive to never allow ourselves to be captured by the Krauts.' Gently touching the cyanide suicide pill taped behind his right ear, John grimaced. 'If the worst ever comes to the worst, I've got this drastic ... this all too final escape ready to hand.'

'Oh, I see. I did not know that either.'

'You Dutch Patriots do not have any suicide pills?'

'No. None of us have them.'

'Well in that case I think your courage is even greater than mine!'

'Thank you John. Thank you very much. Now go, get completely changed. Get accustomed to your civilian Dutch clothes and spend the time before dinner memorising your Norwegian details, all right? Oh, and also practise talking in basic English. It's just a pity you don't speak Norwegian.' Frans grinned, 'You don't, do you?'

John replied in a very broad Cumberland dialect: Then he laughed, 'Does that sound Norwegian enough?'

Frans echoed his laughter, 'Ya, it sounds real Norse to me. It should fool the Krauts.'

Two hours later John, in his unfamiliar civilian clothes, presented himself at the farmhouse kitchen. Sweeping off his cloth cap he stood smiling. 'Well, what do you think of my disguise? Do I pass muster as a Norwegian sailor working on this Dutch farm?'

Anna and Frans laughed. Blanche turned and stared. While staring at John she never once ceased methodically stirring the contents of a large copper cooking pot which gave out a delicious mouth-watering aroma.

When Frans translated John's questions, Blanche smiled and

merrily answered. Frans explained, 'She says you look like a real Dutch farmer with your baggy blue dungarees, shapeless jacket, big boots and weather-beaten face. She asks are you as good as she is at milking cows?'

Soon all were seated around the large kitchen table. Soon the steaming hot rabbit casserole heaped on each plate lived up to the promise given out by the assiduously tended cooking pot.

The after dinner hours passed as similarly, as quietly contentedly, as had yesterday evening. Again promptly at ten-fifteen Blanche stopped knitting and retired to bed.

Anna and Frans accompanied John to the moon-bathed farmyard. Standing in front of the stable Anna exclaimed, 'Oh what a beautiful almost full moon.' All gazed up at the cloudless, bright night sky. 'I don't feel in the least sleepy. I think I'll take a leisurely stroll around the fields.' She glanced at her uncle. 'Do you fancy coming with me?'

Silently, and apprehensively, John waited for Frans's reply.

Slowly removing his pipe, Frans smiled with understanding, 'I'll just stay here and smoke my pipe out then go to bed. Don't stay out too late, will you?'

Anna promised she wouldn't. Smiling modestly, but – John thought – also warmly invitingly, she asked him, 'Would you like to accompany me?'

Concealing just how eager he was, he smiled, 'I would love to, Anna.' He laughingly turned to Frans, 'Anyway, after being cooped up in the hayloft all day I should take a walk in the line of duty; get some much needed exercise and test out how well my new Dutch boots fit me.'

As most paths along by the deep ditches were not wide enough for two people to walk side by side, Anna led the way and John closely followed.

After a while Anna stopped and cautiously leant against the rather rickety rail of a narrow plank bridge. John leant beside her. Gazing into that face, so close to hers, so glowingly revealed in the bright moonlight, she murmured, 'The full moon's romantic magic turns even this normally dull dark stagnant ditch into a picture of gleaming beauty, doesn't it?'

Gently sliding his arm round her waist, drawing her to him, staring into her alluringly bright, moon-glittering eyes, John whispered, 'The ditch isn't the only thing of beauty the moon's romantic magic reveals!'

Their mouths met. The one as eager as the other, they passionately kissed. Their bodies eagerly melted closer together. The insecure rail alarmingly creaked and shakily moved. Startled they jumped apart. John laughed, 'We better get off this wee bridge before we end up in the ditch. That would fair dampen our ardour, eh?'

They moved to the shadowy seclusion of a large elm tree. Leaning against it their lips again eagerly met. Their arms again hugged their tremulous bodies together.

Timeless time passed gloriously un-noticed.

Gradually their enraptured senses became aware of the steady roar of approaching aircraft. The sound rapidly grew nearer and louder. Reluctantly they drew apart and, craning their necks, stared almost vertically up into the moonlit sky. Suddenly they saw the noisy plane, saw it briefly, a distinct black silhouette against the moon's glowing brilliance. John instantly recognised that large aircraft. 'It's a R.A.F. Lancaster bomber.' He judged it to be only about five thousand feet high. Staring intently they saw a glow of flames at one of its four engines, then watched a thin trail of smoke draw an ugly black scar across the moon's innocent face.

Anna compassionately murmured, 'Oh, John, I hope those brave British airmen make it back to England safely.'

Hoping to reassure her, John confidently declared, 'As they've made it as far as this from Germany, I'm sure they have a really good chance of making it the rest of the way to England.'

This fresh reminder of war returned him to its harsh, inescapable reality and its heavy responsibilities. 'Oh, Anna, it's getting late. We better head home.'

Giving a sad wry smile she reluctantly agreed.

Murmurously self-engrossed, they arrived at the door of the farm's jutting extension which housed Anna's bedroom. As they again eagerly kissed, both were all too vividly aware of her awaiting, temptingly inviting empty bed so near them. Their re-awakened flesh urged them to share that bed.

Noble – or foolishly – they resisted.

John forced his moral strength to override his fleshy urges.

While Anna's fevered senses wanted John to share her bed, her many years of sexual abstinence imposed strange, illogical, severely inhibiting constrains on these same senses.

Sadly, almost dejectedly, but resolutely determined, they parted ... made for their sad, lonely, respective beds.

★★★

After breakfast next day John prepared to help the others harvest autumn's vegetables from muddy fields. No matter how wearisome and back-torturingly cruel this unaccustomed farm work might prove to be, it would be preferable to being cooped up by himself hour after hour, day after day in that secret hiding place in the hayloft.

He was introduced to the near neighbours who regularly helped on this farm. Roelant and Alie were husband and wife; were both about forty years old; they had two young children. That couple were completely trustworthy Dutch Patriots. Roelant was one of the keenest of the local team of seven Patriots who were organised and commanded by Frans.

While Alie helped Blanche expertly transmute creamily rich milk into excellent butter and cheese, Roelant harnessed the farm's sturdy horse to a high-sided cart.

More quickly than usual, Anna hurried through the inescapable, unvarying morning housework. In Blanche's opinion the correct performance of these daily chores was an indispensable necessity. Although she – usually – uncomplainingly complied with Blanche's dogma, Anna was far from convinced of the absolute indispensability of these chores – surely the world would not end (as Blanche seemed to think) if they were occasionally neglected.

Housework thankfully completed, she eagerly hurried to help the others labouring in the fields ... or perhaps it was only John she was so eager to meet up with and work with?

Certainly as John and she industriously laboured side by side, somehow the back-aching stooping labour of lifting heavy turnips, slashing off their soggy green foliage before throwing them into large baskets then carrying the full baskets to, and heaving them into, the waiting cart, seemed almost like play instead of work.

But after four steady hours of this labour even they were feeling it most definitely was work – and damned hard work at that! And once this lot of turnips were lifted, the cart filled and the load removed there were large fields of potatoes to start on.

All were delighted when it came to lunch-time's hour of well earned ease. All did full justice to Blanche's and Alie's delicious fresh bread thickly spread with equally fresh, perhaps even more delicious butter and generously thick slices of cheese.

As the men, long after the women, finally came to the end of their meal, Frans said, 'Thank you Blanche, that was great.' He then turned to John and, reverting to English, said, 'A wonderful meal like that makes me feel almost guilty when I think of the severe rationing and the terrible food shortages the inhabitants of Rotterdam and other Dutch cities are suffering.'

John nodded in sympathetic agreement, 'Yes, I feel the same. Even in Britain the food rationing is really quite severe now.' He smiled at Blanche and Alie, 'I haven't tasted real fresh butter since before the war. I've never ever tasted butter or cheese or thick creamy milk that is anywhere near as great as this!'

Frans translated and Blanche and Alie openly, and honestly, beamingly basked in his sincere praise.

All afternoon, row after endless row of muddy potatoes were labouriously forked up, lifted and heaved into the waiting cart. A cool, gusty breeze had swept away dank morning's misty drizzle and left the wide Dutch sky one vast cloudless dome of pale blue.

The lazy drone of distant aircraft provided a welcome excuse for these weary potato-lifters to cease their labour. As one they straightened up, stretched, and with hands massaging the small of backs, exchanged sympathetic smiles. They then gazed into the cloudless sky with grubby damp hands shading searching eyes.

The drone of steadily approaching planes grew insistently louder as many vapour trails chalkily scrawled their distinctive straight white marks high over the huge sky and revealed the exact position of each, as yet unseen, aircraft.

Soon the keen watchers made out many high planes – an impressive flight of bright silvery arrow-heads accurately, steadily, and it seemed almost sedately aiming straight for the welcome security and cosseting comfort of their English airfields. Sunshine occasionally flashed brilliantly from aluminium surfaces as if sending out obscurely coded morse signals.

The planes passed and their noise lessened.

Individual vapour trails drifted and merged and drew their delicate gossamer veil across the immense empty sky.

'Those were American bombers, weren't they, John' asked Frans. 'What is their name in English?... I have forgotten.'

'They are Flying Fortress's.' Remembering some of the vivid images of these formidable bombers he had seen in Movietone News films at cinemas in Britain, John enthusiastically elaborated. 'These American planes are well named. Flying tightly packed in close formation, each plane bristling with heavy machine-guns, they truly are flying fortress's which fight through packs of savagely attacking Luftwaffe fighters to deliver their bombs on strategically important targets deep in Germany.'

'Ay, yes. Flying Fortress's ... now I remember. They are becoming quite a frequent sight in our daytime Dutch skies, but not nearly as frequent as the familiar noise of R.A.F. bombers in our dark night sky. We wish them well. It is good the Krauts get bombed − they deserve it!'

'Yes, they deserve all they get!'

'Ya. What their Luftwaffe did to Warsaw, Rotterdam and London the R.A.F. and U.S. Air Force now do to Berlin, Hamburg and Cologne. It is just! What is the English saying for this? I have forgotten it also.'

'They are getting a taste of their own medicine.'

'Ay yes. They get taste of own medicine − good, good!'

Anna translated this exchange into Dutch and the others vigorously nodded and eagerly expressed their wholehearted agreement.

By this time the noise of these aircraft had faded away and their white vapour trails were slowly, dispersing. No longer having any excuse to stand and idly stare, the potato-lifters again stooped to their toilsome task.

Chapter Twenty One

John's life now settled into a uneventful routine of daily physical toil in the farm's extensive potato fields, varied by frequently helping Roelant muck out the byre and stable, and – a much easier task – assisting Anna feed the hens and collect eggs.

These daytime labours were followed by what had become an eagerly anticipated, pleasantly familiar pattern of relaxing after-dinner and ease in the solidly substantial ornate comfort of the farmhouse's sitting room. The first period of each evening's restful relaxation John shared with Frans; then – her company most keenly looked forward to – also with Anna. Eventually, her washing-up and kitchen tidying finished, Blanche completed the easeful company quietly relaxing in the rather sombre room's somnolent comfort. But there was never the least hint of somnolence in the effortless, eye-defying speed of the knitting needles she immediately brought into action once she was comfortably settled.

Sitting cosily close beside John, Anna used this opportunity to practise some of her frustrated teaching skills on him. Unable to teach English language and literature to Dutch children, she eagerly grasped this unique chance to revel in sharing something of her great love of English poetry with him. She became his happily animated personal tutor, while he most willingly became her keenly receptive delighted pupil.

With her great, knowledgeable love of Shakespeare now augmented by her glorious new love for John, Anna's teaching was illuminated by passionately felt vivid new insights.

John, like most British schoolchildren, had had some Shakespeare unenlightingly battered at him when much too young to understand it or appreciate its greatness, so that until this love-inspired enlightenment by Anna he had self-deprecatingly regarded Shakespeare as being far too high-brow for the likes of him.

Now he was amazed as something of the wonder, the beauty, the searing timeless truths of Shakespeare's genius were clearly revealed to him.

After some evenings almost entirely devoted to 'The Bard,' Anna deliberately, with definite ulterior intention, shifted to Wordsworth. She knew he was the one poet John knew better than she did and that he shared Wordsworth's profound love for their common Cumberland homeland. Her one short, pre-war visit to that marvellous English Lakeland helped her understand these feelings; helped her, to a lesser extent, join in these feelings. She delighted in discovering more of this side of John's character, so different from the quietly brave, firmly resolute war-toughened side of him. With bright eyed loving eagerness, with tremulously nervous sympathetic understanding she listened to his hesitant, unpractised struggles to articulate something of what he deeply felt about the greatest of Wordsworth's nature poems and about their shared hills and lakes.

Silently gazing with sincere empathy, with glowing inner excitement, she knew she deeply and truly loved John. The more she knew of him the more she loved him. She amorously imagined them – married, the war over – spending their honeymoon in John's beloved Lake District. Oh, was that a gloriously attainable realistic vision, or was it hopelessly impossible ... a starry-eyed lover's foolish pipe dream?

Frans was secretly amused at the chaperoning role his presence in this pleasant, after dinner sitting room forced on him. While discreetly appearing to be completely immersed in his book, he could not fail to be aware of Anna and John sitting so intimately together near him. Inwardly smiling with tolerant understanding he was conscious of being completely (but not unkindly) ignored by both those self engrossed young people. He was delighted to see Anna so relaxed in this mutual happiness she so openly shared with John ... shared with her lover, John?

There seemed no doubt that they were deeply in love, but Frans did not think they were sexual lovers. Nor did Blanche. They had apprehensively discussed this in the snuggly familiar intimacy of their conjugal bed. Blanche's alert, keenly observant senses, reinforced by the trustworthy guidance of her feminine intuition, assured her that although Anna and John were most obviously, most sincerely deeply in love they were not sexually active.

But would they remain chaste? Sitting surreptitiously observing them, Frans could not help rather anxiously asking himself that question. They seemed so young – Anna appeared to have shed years of stressful worry – seemed so wondrously innocent sitting so intimately engrossed in one another with their heads almost touching over their poetry books. But if John remained here much longer would they continue to successfully resist what must surely be the increasingly insistent, the ever more urgent, demands of their passionately aroused, but unnaturally constrained and frustrated healthy young flesh?

Frans trusted John ... trusted him not to cruelly and selfishly 'take advantage' of Anna; was fully confident that he would do his utmost to spare her anything that might be too traumatically upsetting, but he knew there were limits to the constrains that sorely tempted virile young flesh could endure. And in the midst of this terrible war when any one of them might be killed at anytime, the pressures to satisfy their profound sexual urges while they still had the chance must at times be almost irresistible.

Blanche and Frans were also worried over how Anna would react when, as must surely happen soon, John was ordered back to England.

How would she cope with him leaving? How would she manage knowing that there was almost no chance of her hearing from him, or even learning if he was alive or dead until this hideous war finally ended? Might the strain of the parting, followed by the threat of perhaps years of not knowing, of constant worrying, of endless waiting, plunge her into another nervous breakdown?

As he discretely observed John and Anna, Frans permitted himself a wry, self-mocking smile. There seemed no need of the sensitive, unobtrusive caution with which he watched them, for these two young lovers were all in all to one another, were so blissfully self engrossed as to seem entirely unaware of his chaperoning presence. With a suppressed sigh he pictured these two as a reincarnation of those ill-fated young lovers, Romeo and Juliet.

The happiness of these enraptured modern lovers was threatened not merely by senseless warring families but by the much vaster, more savagely cruel dangers, hazards and chances of senseless warring nations. What would the fate of these star-crossed, war-tossed lovers be? Were the odds against them too great to allow the triumph of their love? Would their story end as tragically as the tale of Shakespeare's young lovers? Frans fervently hoped not.

Each pleasant restful evening in that solidly comfortable Dutch sitting room drew to its invariable end when, punctually at ten-fifteen, Blanche got to her feet, put her knitting tidily away, then retired to bed. Frans sat on for a while longer, then, taking pity on the young lovers, rose and with a gentle smile trustingly relinquished his chaperoning role and headed for bed

As soon as Frans firmly closed the door and left Anna and John in possession of the room they wasted no time. Their arms encircled one another and drew their bodies tightly together. Their lips met in urgent, passionately eager kisses. Wondrous timeless minutes passed in a vivid glow of fervent, tender love.

Resolutely bringing the utmost strength of his self-control into action, John denied his virile flesh what it so urgently, lustfully demanded. He determinedly eased himself away from Anna.

She tried to hold him tight, gave a heartfelt sorrowful sigh then with an acquiescent smile reluctantly accepted his help as the two of them struggled to their feet.

Once again they went on what was now their well established, eagerly anticipated late evening stroll.

As – in defiance of the Germans night time curfew – they leisurely strolled with arms entwined, with murmuring mouth ticklishly touching eagerly receptive ear, they not only welcomed the cosy intimate concealment that all courting lovers welcome, but also appreciated the vital knowledge that night's concealing darkness also hid them from any collaborating and betraying Dutch eyes or any dangerously alert German eyes.

They revelled in the luxury of being so wondrously together, revelled in the silent beauty of the mild windless night. They marvelled at how amazingly peaceful everything was tonight . There was none of the usual growling drone of high, unseen, passing R.A.F planes, no distant indistinct rumble of exploding bombs; no sight of far flares nor of anxiously probing fingers of searchlight beams; no angry challenging barks of German flak guns.

The strictly enforced blackout dimmed the entire Dutch landscape and helped dark night reveal its myriad display of stars. Awed by the fantastic glory of the star filled sky they stared up in dreamy silent wonder. They were moved by something that seemed profoundly, but obscurely, deeply spiritual. Anna's love-gleaming, star-reflecting eyes smiled into John's bright eyes. Their souls tenderly merged in a fantastic galaxy of love. They held one another even more tightly. They seemed to merge into some timeless, limitless universal wonder.

Eventually John gently brought them back to something like reality. Slowly, dreamily, they made their way along the familiar path that led back to the farmhouse.

Once again they stopped outside Anna's bedroom. Once again they kissed and fervently re-avowed their love. Hesitantly and with shyly uncertain smiles Anna told John of that wonderful picture she had visualized earlier this evening.... that dream of the war over, then married and spending their honeymoon in his beloved Lake District. Her body shivered, her voice trembled, her throat choked with emotion as she anxiously asked, 'Oh John... John, will my dream ever come true?.... Will we both survive this war, this terrible war?.......Will we really meet up and marry once this war finally ends?..... Oh John, I sometimes despair that it will never end!'

Hugging her shivering body tightly, John firmly stated, 'Of course it will end. It will almost certainly end next year once vast British and American armies land in France and swiftly liberate all Western Europe. And of course we will both survive; of course we'll meet up again and get married.' Giving an extra hug and a reassuring roguish grin, he promised, 'We'll have the time of our lives on our honeymoon. We'll make up for this.... this foolish wasted chaste time, won't we? Amidst the hills and lakes of my homeland we'll put the war behind us, we'll forget it and together for ever we'll have a much brighter, much better life!'

John put more assurance, more certainty, into these optimistic statements than he really felt. He – unlike Anna – was all too well aware of the very real risk of him being killed once he returned to duty in the Royal Navy and again took part in extremely hazardous S.B.S missions.

Anna stopped shivering. Trusting and reassured she smiled and dreamily revelled in picturing the glorious future John and she were going to have once this hideous war was over.

Standing passionately hugging and kissing in the concealing darkness outside the farmhouse, both of them were once again temptingly aware of the nearness of Anna's empty bedroom. But once more they heroically resisted the almost irresistible temptation of her seductively inviting bed.

Lying frustratedly sleepless in that solitary bed, Anna restlessly visualized John and her united in post-war marriage, united in love, united in passionate sex.

John, too, lay restless and sleepless on his lonely bed in the secret room above the stable. He tried to image a time of peace; a time of love with Anna; a time when, at long last, he was finished with the need to carry out ruthless killings. His imagination painted a bright glowing picture of Anna and him on their honeymoon in his beautiful homeland. As he pictured them passionately consummating their love his erotically aroused body mockingly thrust aside his overwhelmed mind's foolish attempts at sex-denying self-censorship.

Later, lying at sweaty ease, he drowsily relaxed in the welcome calm. He thought of this most unusual, long period of pleasant calm he was enjoying at this Dutch farm. How much longer could this wonderful peaceful interlude continue?

With each day that peacefully passed he felt increasingly certain that this was the calm before the storm. He feared this peace would end with dramatic suddenness.... would soon be thunderously engulfed by war's hideous savagery.

He hid these strong forebodings from Anna. She worried enough about him and about their future as it was.

Chapter Twenty-two

John's forebodings were realized the following day. Once more he was caught up in the horrors of war.

The morning started and continued in its ususal pleasantly familiar way. After breakfast Frans cycled off to teach at his school. Blanche and Alie busied themselves in the dairy transmuting some of this morning's milk to delicious butter and cheese. Anna resignedly hurried through her inescapable daily household chores. John assisted Roelant with harvesting ever more of the endless seeming fields of vegetables.

After lunch Blanche and Anna also helped in the fields while Alie returned to her nearby home to get on with the housework and prepare dinner for her husband, Roelant, and their two boys.

Later in the afternoon Blanche and Anna returned to the farmhouse kitchen, leaving Roelant and John to finish off the day's work in the fields. As soon as they unloaded the last cartful of vegetables Roelant set out along the path leading to his home, his industrious wife, and his two sons.

After their exhilaratingly fast cycle ride from school each boy's healthily flushed cheeks glowed almost as brightly as their mother's hot kitchen-stove flushed face. Leaving the wondrously alluring mouth-watering scents escaping from the stove's simmering cooking pots, the boys, as usual, ran to meet their father and hurry his homeward progress. As soon as he saw his running sons, Roelant, again as usual, gave a teasing grin and deliberately slowed his pace.

The boys impatiently, but obediently waited until their father – with relenting cheerful swiftness – had washed, then the entire family got eagerly settled around the well-laden kitchen table. As the first spoonfuls of thick vegetable soup were being appreciatively swallowed, the old, tediously scything pendulous clock high on the wall ponderously declared the time to be exactly five o'clock. Alie beamed a happy contented smile at her quietly relaxed husband. The boys cheerily grinned at one another; they knew that their father liked to be sitting relaxing at dinner each day as that clock chimed five.

★★★

John had just finished throwing armful's of hay to the stabled mare when Frans returned from his day of teaching chemistry and biology. After wheeling his bicycle into an empty stall he turned and met John's routine questioning stare. He smiled and answered that unspoken question with his usual negative shake of the head. Still no instructions from London about John's return to Britain.

With some concern, John again wondered if he had been forgotten by Special Operations Executive and by Royal Navy Intelligence. Could the message transmitted by Frans's wireless operator informing London of his survival and requesting orders for his return to England have gone astray somewhere in one or other of these Intelligence Agencies? Might the message be inadvertently filed away in some obscure bureaucratic file? Or could it deliberately have been put aside as needing no immediate action? Surely not! Surely Commander Richardson must be anxious to learn full details of what went as planned with 'Operation Waterloo' and what went badly wrong with it? And only he, John, could supply these details.

Might the S.O.E. (For some deep, obscure reason of its own) not have informed Naval Intelligence of his survival? From his extensive S.B.S. experience of both the S.O.E. and Royal Navy Intelligence he had learned something about the strength of the jealous rivalry that existed between these and between other even more shadowy secret Intelligence Agencies. And he was well aware that he was only one very tiny cog obscurely operating in these vastly complex Intelligence Machines.

There might be some definite reason for him being left so long in the peaceful comfort of this Dutch farm... a reason he might never get to know, but which he could not help speculating about. However he was not complaining about his protracted stay in this cushy billet; no, he most certainly had no complaints about being kept here with Anna.

John revealed none of his speculative thoughts to Frans.

Frans, in turn, disclosed none of his much more apprehensive thoughts to John. He, too, secretly wondered over how long it was taking London to arrange for John's return to England. And he had more reason to worry over this than John had. He had information that John hadn't. He knew just how unusual it was for a British fugitive to be kept here for such a length of time. He had expected to have received instructions to pass John along to another Dutch Resistance group long before now, or to have had him picked up by a R.A.F. Lysander aircraft from one of the fields they had used on other occasions. This inexplicable delay was one more worry added to his many other undisclosed worries.

He had secret knowledge that one nearby Resistance Group had 'disappeared;' had almost certainly been betrayed, been captured then executed by the Krauts. And there were many more most disturbing hints and unconfirmed rumours that other, further away Resistance Groups had also 'disappeared.' He worried that his own Group must be in greatly increased danger. Might London's failure to instruct him regarding John's return be connected with all those dangerous uncertainties?

As John and Frans started moving to the stable door a sudden, thunderously loud overwhelming roar stopped them in their tracks. They gazed at one another in startled amazement for a moment then dashed outside.

They stood disbelievingly staring as a giant warplane roared over only about one hundred feet above the ground.

John shouted, 'It's a Flying Fortress! It's going to crash in that field!'

All the plane's four engines seemed to be violently roaring despite two of them trailing thick, black smoke. A huge aileron hung loose and crazily flapped beneath one wing. Ugly holes gaped in the tall rudder. Crewed by dead or dying American airmen, it shallowly angled towards a large field.

Then, as if guided by some malevolent fate, it suddenly veered to the left and headed direct for Roelant and Alies's snug farmcottage.

Frans gave an agonised shout, 'Oh God, it's going to crash on Roelant's house! Oh no!... no!...no!'

John stared with wide-eyed horror as the huge, grievously crippled plane smashed into the hapless small house.

As the terrific explosion roared out John immediately reacted. He threw himself flat on the ground.

Frans's numbed senses kept him standing frozen in shock until John shouted, 'Get down, Frans, get down!'

Only then did he dive for the ground. Then, too soon, he started rising to his feet. John restrainingly grabbed his arm. 'Wait, Frans, wait! Wait until those bullets stop flying around!'

Ignited by the explosion, hundreds of machine-gun bullets from the crashed plane were whistling about. Tracer bullets made a lethal firework display.

After what seemed a desperately long time, bullets stopped erupting. Now the only sound was the loud ugly roar of greedily engulfing flames.

'Come on, Frans, it's safe to move now.' Together they got to their feet. Together they stood and, as if mesmerized, silently motionlessly stared at the appalling mass of black smoke rising vertically into the windless air. Billowing smoke and leaping flames hid all sign of Roelant's house.

Nervous reaction now set in. Frans uncontrollably shuddered, then slowly, zombie-like, uncertainly started moving towards that tragic funeral pyre. John walked at his side for a short distance then took the lead and increased the pace towards Roelant's house – or what little might be left of Roelant's house.

The scorching heat of the roaring inferno prevented them from getting very close to the crash site. With hands sheltering smarting eyes they tried to see through the thick smoke and devouring flames. But nothing could be seen of the engulfed and pulverised cottage.

Only one thing was recognisable. Lying beyond the flames where the devastating crash had flung it was the ill-fated Flying Fortress's tail section. The huge silvery rudder jaggedly jutted from scarred grass like a macabre tombstone grimly commemorating this tragic disaster.

They saw no sign of life. They did not expect to. No one could survive that inferno.

Frans dejectedly slumped to the ground. Trembling hands cradled bowed head. Convulsive sobs choked him.

John sat beside Frans and gently placed a commiserative arm around his sagging shoulders.

The Dutchman gave free rein to his emotions. Although the young Englishman was also deeply upset by the tragic death of that entire Dutch family he resolutely controlled his feelings. He had many more experiences of violent deaths crammed into his war years than Frans had. He had seen many brave comrades violently die. He had ruthlessly killed quite a few Krauts. He did not – dared not – allow his thoughts to dwell too much on all these tragically violent deaths. He had to control his feelings if he was to continue calmly and efficiently playing his part in the grim struggle which should eventually liberate all Western Europe from the tyranny of Nazi occupation. And, of course, he had only known that Dutch family for a short time; he could not be expected to feel for them as deeply as Frans, who had known them for many years, did.

Remembering the many gentle jokes Frans had made about Roelant's grinning delight every time he finished his farmwork in time to get home and be settled at dinner with his family just as their kitchen clock chimed five, John sadly imagined Roelant, his wife, Alie and their two young boys jumping up from the table in shocked horror as they heard that huge plane thundering towards them. At least their deaths must have been quick; their terrified realisation of what was happening followed immediately after by the savage impact, the devastating explosion and the flaming inferno.

With gentle compassion be consolingly suggested this, 'Oh, Frans, at least they must all have died instantaneously. They could not have had any prolonged suffering.'

Slowly, wearily, Frans lifted his head and stared with tear dimmed eyes. 'What? ... What did you say, John?'

He more emphatically repeated his statement. 'They must have died instantly. At least we have the consolation that their deaths were mercifully quick.'

These words got through to Frans. He nodded in agreement, 'Yes John, that's true... that must be true.' He paused, he struggled to get his emotions under control. He stifled his sobs and noisily blew his nose. 'Oh, but why did they have to die?' Vaguely pointing he unsteadily swept his arm around and with anger rising and swamping his grief, he demanded, 'Why did that plane smash right into their home? Why did it not crash into one of those empty fields?'

John had already asked himself these questions, but, as usual had again found no satisfactory answers. He expressed his profound understanding by giving Frans's shoulders a quick, firm, commiserative hug.

John sat in silence for a short time then – rebuked by his S.B.S. trained militaristic senses – rose and methodically started gazing all around the surrounding countryside. Most surprisingly, every narrow farm lane, every path, every field, seemed entirely devoid of any approaching humans. But surely this strange lack of activity would not last long? Neighbouring farmers, Dutch Police and German soldiers would soon come to investigate this plane crash. This place would become dangerously crowded. He better vanish before then.

He turned to Frans who was still sitting, was mournfully staring at the leaping flames, the billowing smoke. 'I better leave you now, Frans. It would be much safer if I'm not here when the Krauts arrive.'

Slowly, as with a weary effort, Frans struggled to his feet. With an obvious further struggle he got his Resistance leadership skills back into gear. 'Oh, I am very sorry, John. I should have ordered you to get away from here before now. Yes, go, John. Hurry back to the farm. Hide in your secret room and stay there until I come and tell you it is safe to come out.'

John immediately obeyed. He started jogging away. He saw two figures approaching him on the path from the farm. Blanche and Anna were hurrying towards the crash site. As he neared them, Blanche aggitatidly gasped out a torrent of Dutch. John guessed she was anxiously asking about Roelant, Alie, and the two boys. Anna quickly confirmed this. He broke the tragic news to them.

'All dead?... All of them? Oh no, no, it can not be true! It is too terrible!... too cruelly terrible!' Anna turned to Blanche and translated. They hurled themselves into one another's arms. Weeping, gasping, they tremblingly hugged.

John emotionally looked on. A lump choked his throat. He heard the sound of a distant bell. The bell of an approaching fire-engine? Almost apologetically he said, 'I better leave you now. I'm going to hide in my secret room until Frans thinks it's safe for me to come out again.'

With a resolute effort Blanche eased herself away from Anna's trembling grasp. She recognised one word John had spoken. In a jumbled mixture of Dutch and English she distraughtly demanded, 'Frans?... Frans? Oh where is Frans?'

Pleased with this opportunity to give better news, John assured her that her husband was perfectly safe. Blanche turned to Anna for a full translation. Anna confirmed that Frans was unharmed, was waiting at the disaster site.

'I'll go to him now,' Blanche declared. 'He must be terribly upset, too. I will help him; he will help me.' As she started hurrying away Anna called after her, 'I'll follow you soon. I... I want to talk to John for just a moment.'

Without turning, Blanche raised and waved an understanding hand.

Anna threw herself into John's outstretched arms She released a flood of unrestrained tears. Her body violently trembled.

John hugged her tightly, lovingly and sympathetically.

Soon, comforted by his reassuring strength, calmed by the gentleness of his whispered sympathy, uplifted by the loving tenderness of his kisses, the wildest quiverings of Anna's fragile nerves lessened; her violent tide of tears ebbed to intermittent spasms of gasping sobs. Gradually, she got herself under control. She whispered her thankfulness that she did not have to face the terrible shock of the sudden death of that entire family by herself. John's loving sympathy helped her; prevented these tragic deaths from absolutely overwhelming her.

The loud clamour of the approaching fire-engine's bell woke John from his tender embrace. He eased himself away from Anna. He instructed, 'You better go and join Blanche and Frans now. It would seem strange – perhaps suspiciously strange to some of your untrustworthy farmer neighbours – if you were not anxiously waiting with them; were not there sharing in their terrible grief. And I better hide before Krauts come investigating this plane crash.'

Anna nodded her head in reluctant agreement. They gave a few final passionate kisses then John forced their bodies apart. He turned and started steadily walking towards the farm. Anna tearfully watched him for some moments then turned and slowly made her way to where her distraught aunt and uncle solemnly waited by that fiercely flaming funeral pyre.

Chapter Twenty Three

It was after nine that evening before Frans considered it safe for John to leave his secret hiding place and come to the farmhouse for dinner.

As was to be expected, that belated meal was a solemnly subdued occasion. Blanche and Anna hardly spoke. Their tear filled, red-rimmed eyes set in woeful faces clearly expressed their deep felt grief for that entire family – close friends and near neighbours for many years – so suddenly wiped out by what seemed such a cruelly wanton act of blind chance. They hardly touched what little food was on the plates set before them. When, speaking in English for John's sake, Frans gently urged Anna to eat some more, she rather peevishly replied in that language, 'Oh, leave me alone, Uncle. I cannot force myself to eat any more food. It would choke me.'

Then when, reverting to Dutch, Frans rather foolishly urged his wife to eat up, John needed no translation to get the gist of Blanche's violently loud, snappishly fierce reply.

After that a rather abashed Frans wisely remained silent. He concentrated his attention on his food. John, too, was largely silent, He, too, solemnly confined himself to slowly and apparently reluctantly eating. He almost guiltily felt that in this atmosphere of solemn gloom it must seem to those two distraught women something like a gluttonous unfeeling crime to selfishly indulge in hearty eating. And yet despite today's tragic deaths, his strong, healthy young body required, and demanded, this excellent food. Frans and he exchanged understanding glances as they deliberately made an effort to show no pleasure in indulging in their guilty eating.

As soon as the food was eaten and the glasses of milk drunk, Blanche started clearing the table. Anna helped her. Together they started washing up. Frans gently murmured, 'John and I will go into the sitting room for a short time.'

Blanche emphatically replied, 'Yes, but only for a little time. I am going to bed as soon as this is finished. I am exhausted.'

Anna agreed, 'I am, too. I want to rest and try to sleep.'

When the two of them were settled in the sitting room, Frans put John in the picture regarding what had happened at that crash site this evening and what was arranged for tomorrow. 'The firemen took almost two hours to put the fire out. By that time there were many people there ... our farmer neighbours; our Dutch police; Kraut soldiers and their military police. But by then it was too dark to do anything more. It was decided that the police and firemen would return tomorrow morning to sift through the debris of the house to find the bodies of the two adults and two boys.' Frans paused. He stared sadly at John for some long moments then gave a deep, sigh. 'Or to find what little remain of these four bodies. I am going to help them in that search, and... and, if necessary, help identify the bodies.' He again paused, then hurried on. 'Other Krauts, Luftwaffe officers, are coming to inspect the wreckage of the Flying Fortress. They try to get some useful information from it. They take away any bodies of American airmen they find.

'So, John, there will be much activity near here tomorrow. You will have to stay hidden all day. Although you have fake identity documents showing you are a Norwegian sailor, it will be much safer if you are not seen by any Krauts or police. All right? ...You agree?'

'Yes, yes, of course, Frans. While I'm here I am under your command. I'm only sorry I cannot help you more.' He gave a glance of sympathetic understanding. 'It's a ghastly job you face tomorrow, Frans. I am truly sorry it's impossible for me to assist you with it. I would willingly take some of the terrible burden off you if I could.'

'Thank you, John. I know you would help if it was at all possible. Yes, it is a ghastly task I face.' He gave another sad heartfelt sigh. 'But ... but it is a task that must be done.'

Hearing Anna's and Blanche's voices outside the sitting room door, Frans gasped, 'Say nothing about this horrible task to them.'

John just had time to reply, 'No, no, of course not,' before the door opened and both women entered. Blanche did not sit down. 'I'm going to bed now,' she stated, 'I'm absolutely exhausted.'

Rising from his chair, Frans said, 'I'll come with you. I'm dead tired, too.'

'Yes, I am really exhausted, too,' Anna said. 'I'll go to my bed in just a minute.'

As soon as they had the place to themselves Anna and John somehow found themselves tightly enclosed in each others arms, yet neither was conscious of having moved across the room to meet the other.

They hugged and kissed for some little time then Anna whispered, 'Oh, John, I really am very tired. I cannot go our usual walk. I must get to bed, must try to get some sleep.'

John was instantly contrite, 'Yes, Anna, get to your bed now. I'm sorry keeping you here like this. It's thoughtlessly selfish of me.'

The light of loving gratitude lit up her eyes; not just gratitude for this display of his sympathetic understanding, but profound thanks to whatever fate had so unexpectedly, so wonderfully brought John into her life, brought this great love into both their hearts in the midst of this foul war. The brilliance of love replaced the tears of weariness and sadness in her eyes. She lifted her lips to his. They kissed once more then John led her from this room and took her through to her bedroom. After whispering, 'Now try and get some sleep, Anna,' he kissed her goodnight then resolutely left.

As he entered the stable and started climbing the steep stairs to the hayloft the mare, a docile creature of habit, questioningly, whinnied as if querulously demanding to know what he meant by retiring to bed at this hour. She was well aware that this was not his usual time.

He reassured her, 'Oh, it's all right, old girl, I'm just having an early night for a change.'

After checking that the thick blackout curtain was drawn across his secret room's only window he lit one of his precious stock of candles. He quickly got settled on the large mattress lying in one corner of the room; this was his familiar, almost luxuriously comfortable bed. He started reading one of Anna's favourite books he had borrowed, but found he could not concentrate on the words. Thoughts of today's tragically cruel event insistently throbbed in his mind. He worried about how it had upset Anna and how it might further effect her. Was today's shock the worst she would suffer? Would she gradually get over it? Or might much worse delayed shock set in?

He had experience of people coping not too badly with the immediate shock of sudden, violent deaths only to later succumb to the severe nervous reaction of delayed shock. He remembered what Frans had confidentially told him about the nervous breakdown Anna had suffered as the result of tragic deaths in the past. He feared that the emotional shock of these four new deaths might trigger another breakdown.

And what if, on top of this terrible shock, he was suddenly ordered back to England? How would she cope with the additional trauma of him leaving her?... Of not knowing when she would see him again?... Of fearing – of feverishly dreading – that they might never meet again?

These worrying thoughts pounded in John's brain. They killed sleep, they denied him peaceful rest. Then with a determined effort he resolutely drew on the power and strength of all his Special Boat Section training. He forcefully ordered himself to fall asleep.

But sleep still refused to come; refused to obey these strict S.B.S. orders.

He smiled with understanding and forgiving tolerance. He knew the reason for his body refusing to obey. This disobedience was surely due to the fact that never in all his most intensive, most demanding S.B.S. training had there been any instructions on how to get his mind and body to instantly obey when they were most strangely distracted by the un-warlike state of being in love.

Yes, he thought, while being in this amazing state undoubtedly brings wondrous joy, it also brings me many heavy new burdens; vast new fears, worries and responsibilities. The decisions I make, the actions I take, will now effect not only me, but will also profoundly effect Anna.

After what seemed interminable time, he did succeed in drifting off into weary shallow sleep.

He was not allowed to enjoy this blissful state for long. It seemed he had no sooner gained sleep's relaxing ease when he was alarmingly jolted out of it.

Hardly breathing, he listened intently. The questioning neighing of the mare in her stable beneath this secret room was repeated. Obviously something – or someone – had disturbed her.

John immediately reacted. Throwing aside the blankets he silently rose from the mattress and grabbed his automatic pistol. Placed handily ready for any sudden emergency, this gun was fully loaded and had its silencer securely attached. He thumbed off the safety-catch and slid a bullet into the breech. Again he silently listened. The neighing was loudly repeated, but this time there was also another noise... the faint, indistinct murmur of a human voice.

Obeying his S.B.S. training, John's body remained calmly alert while his mind rapidly explored possible reasons for that human – or those humans – being in the stable and disturbing the mare. He glanced at his luminous watch; only ten minutes past midnight. Much too early, surely, for it to be German soldiers, their military police or the Gestapo on a stealthy search and arrest mission? Such raids were almost invariably carried out between three and four in the morning, when their victim's metabolism was at its lowest ebb, and they were least alert and less likely to offer resistance.

If not German's, who then? Someone from the farmhouse? But why would anyone come to the stable at this time?

The indistinct noises of someone climbing the steep wooden stairs, then – as if hesitantly groping in the darkness – very slowly moving along the hayloft, were followed by much louder, more definite sounds. These noises were unmistakable. That unknown person was urgently fumbling with the tangle of old reins and harnesses, the torn oilskin-coats and moth-eaten horse-blankets which hung over and concealed the door into John's secret room. As the fumblings got more frantic and the harnesses metallic clinkings and jinglings got louder, a voice suddenly increased the volume of what already sounded to John a most foolish, most alarming din. Having almost convinced himself that the person approaching this room was most likely to be Frans, John was amazed to hear that voice, for it certainly was not his – it was not a male voice!

'Is that you, Anna?' he gasped, hardly daring to believe what his senses were telling him.

'Yes. Oh yes, John, it's me! Let me in.'

'What's wrong? Are you alone?

'Oh yes, I'm alone. Oh, open the door. Let me in, John, I must see you!'

Staying alert in case of any possible deception, John unbolted and opened the door. Satisfied that Anna was alone, he held the coats, blankets and other dangling encumbrances aside to allow her to hurry into the room. As he re-bolted the door he also flicked his gun's safety-catch over to 'safe'

He turned and faced the dim shape that was all he could see of Anna in the darkness. She violently threw herself into the arms she sensed rather than saw reaching out towards her. She frantically clung to him. He fiercely hugged her and eagerly kissed her.

Feeling the violence of the nervous trembling that revealed her extreme agitation, he kissed her much more gently then, with compassionate concern, asked, 'What's the matter, Anna? Why are you here? Has something happened?'

With tears overflowing her eyes and sobs choking her voice she stammeringly whispered, 'Oh no, John, nothing more has happened, but I … I had to come to be with you. I… I could not stand being on my own endlessly remembering those four tragic deaths today. I … I felt I would go mad being by myself! I needed to be with you. Oh, I love you, John! I… I need you, I need you desperately!'

'I love you desperately, too, Anna.' Again he gently kissed her. Again he tightly hugged her. 'You know I love you deeply and passionately!'

Her tears ceased flooding quite so wildly. Her sobs did not choke quite so cruelly. He felt the violence of her trembling gradually subside. But these trembles were soon replaced by less violent, less nervous quiverings which seemed to John more like uncontrolled shivers caused by being cold. Only now did it register with him that Anna was not wearing outdoor clothes. She seemed to be clad in a lightweight dressing-gown and a thin night-gown. As far as he could make out in the vague uncertainty of the room's gloomy dimness, her ghostly pale lower legs were bare … bare and surely cold. And a pair of flimsy slippers were all that sheltered her feet. Little wonder she was shivering with cold.

Being only dressed in shirt, vest and underpants, his own bare legs were not exactly warm. He was thankful the darkness modestly hid his undignified, most un-romantic state of dress – or rather, ridiculous state of un-dress.

His compassionate thoughts swiftly returned to Anna, 'You're shivering, Anna. Are you very cold?

'Yes… Yes, I am cold. Oh, John, please let me lie and rest and get cosily warm in your bed, then I will tell you why I am here with you.'

'Yes, of course, Anna.' He smiled through the darkness. 'Come on, we'll soon get you warm in my bed.' With an arm around her, he guided her to the large mattress and gently lowered her on to it. As, kneeling on the floor, he started sweeping the blankets over her, she reached out a hand, grabbed his arm and stopped him. 'Oh, John, you must be cold as well. As far as I can see in this dimness you don't seem to be wearing all that many clothes either!'

John chuckled, 'No, I'm not. I'm thankful the room's darkness conceals my immodest state.'

'Well, come under the blankets, too. Please lie beside me and we'll get warm together. We'll just talk to one another that's all.'

John was eager to obey her suggestion, but was acutely aware that if they lay cosily intimately together it was almost inevitable that the inevitable would happen. They would eventually do much more than just innocently talk to one another. Surely their terribly frustrated flesh would be powerfully awakened, would irresistibly take over. They would passionately and urgently consummate their pent-up, long denied sexual love.

The very thought of this glorious consummation of their love involuntarily triggered excited stirrings at his genitals. There was no possibility of mistaking what his body's sensual senses wanted – most definitely, most eagerly wanted. Yet, remembering the solemn promises he had made not only to her, to Frans and Blanche, and most importantly – to himself, he certainly did not intend to allow the insistent demands of his frustrated sexual instincts to take cruelly selfish funfair advantage of Anna's very nervously upset and vulnerable present state. He wanted to, and fully intended to protect her, not harm her.

'Are you sure, Anna? Of course I want to, but would it be wise for me to get in beside you?'

'Oh yes, John, yes. I need you beside me!' In a voice trembling with tears, with violent emotion, and perhaps just a hint of annoyed frustrated impatience, she urged, 'Oh, John, don't waste any more time. Come in beside me now. I need you desperately! I need to have, to feel, to share, your reassuring strength, your warmth and comfort, your great love!'

He made no further attempt to resist her urgent commands – how could he? Gently sliding in beside her, he cosily tucked the thick blankets around them. Lying face to face they tightly hugged one another then kissed. Anna contentedly sighed, 'Now, John, we need to talk before we might be tempted to do anything more, all right?'

'Yes of course that's all right. I'm delighted, absolutely delighted, to have you share my bed. It's just that – knowing what this eager sharing is almost certainly going to lead to – I don't want to selfishly take advantage of your upset state.

'It was being on your own in your lonely room, lying hopelessly sleepless, endlessly thinking about those four tragic deaths today that drove you to my bed, my company, my love, wasn't it Anna?'

'Oh yes John, yes it was. I cannot get those cruel deaths out of my tormented mind. Oh why, why, did they have to die like that? Why didn't that plane crash harmlessly in an empty field?' Choking sobbing, weeping, Anna distraughtly gasped out those insistent questions. 'Why did it smash right into Roelant's and Alie's home?... why, oh why did they and their two innocent young boys so cruelly die?'

John replied to those unanswerable questions in the wisest way he knew. With profound sympathy, he lovingly hugged her tighter. Then, gently whispering in her ear , he tried to console her with the only consolation he had managed to find. 'Oh, Anna, at least they did not suffer long. Those four deaths must have been instantaneous. And ... and, at least Alie and Roelant had been fortunate enough to have enjoyed a good few years of real married happiness with one another and with their two loved, loving young sons, hadn't they?. Not everyone attains such happiness, do they?'

'No, they don't. Oh John, I'm scared this endless hideous war will – despite all our hopeful rosy dreams of post-war bliss together – destroy any chance of us ever attaining such happiness as they enjoyed.

'Oh, John, I hate to think of you going back to England then returning to your dangerous duties again. What if you were killed! Oh, how would I live without you?.... without even one glorious memory of us passionately consummating our great love. Oh, John, let's not be foolish any longer. Let's grasp this present opportunity... Let's make love while we can! Don't you agree? Don't you want to?'

'Yes, yes I want to! ... I passionately want to! But ... but are you sure, absolutely sure, Anna?'

'Yes, oh yes, of course I'm sure. Oh, John, please, please don't waste any more time.' Persuasively she gasped, 'Oh, John, life is so short; death is so final; we must with desperate urgency "seize the day – seize the hour!"'

She started frantically struggling out of her dressing-gown. John eagerly helped remove it, then his conscience reminded him of the solemn promises he had made and his re-awakened sense of responsibility made him say, 'Oh but, Anna, I don't have any contraceptives.'

'Oh don't worry, John, It's be all right.'

'Are you sure? I don't want to risk getting...'

With more than a hint of annoyance, with desperate impatience, she interrupted him, 'Oh yes, John, I'm sure; I'm perfectly sure! Oh why are you wasting precious time?'

He wisely wasted no more time. He threw her dressing gown-gown aside then fumblingly removed his underpants.

For a while their smoothly entwining bodies moved together with gentle loving tenderness. Then – rejoicing in at long last being freed from all its achingly frustrating strict constraints – the firm strength and furnace glowing warmth of John's body thrust with ever increasing, ever more frenzied excitement. They ceased to be two individual bodies. They became one flesh as, deliriously ecstatically, they consummated their great love.

Chapter Twenty Four

The following morning was dimmed by re-awakened memories of yesterday's violent tragic deaths. Depressed by appetite destroying thoughts of these deaths, Blanche peevishly pecked at her frugal breakfast for a short time then, impatiently pushing the plate aside, got up and resolutely forced herself to go and get on with the milking. No matter what happened, no matter how poorly one felt and how little one felt like doing it, the cows had always to be milked. The hens, too, had to be fed and their fresh laid eggs collected, but these much less skilled more mundane daily tasks were Anna's responsibility.

With as little relish as his wife, Frans picked at his food. He had no appetite for breakfast, nor for the grisly task awaiting him at that burned-out crash site this morning.

After all his tension-relieving, wondrous sexual activity last night, John this morning had a virile young man's normal healthily demanding appetite for energy replenishing food. But, chastened by observing the frugality of Blanche's and Frans's breakfasts, he nobly curtailed his doubly guilty appetite.

Anna also ate little. Body and mind were in conflict. Her glowing, fulfilled body wanted food, but her aunt and uncle's dejected state was a grim reminder of her own deep grief for yesterday's four tragic deaths. Sorrow overruled hunger and she, too, refused even the most appetizing offered food.

Following John's example, she guiltily tried to constrain her wondrous .. her wonderfully fulfilled, bright glowing new feelings. She sincerely felt deep sorrow for those four destroyed lives, and yet ... and yet, she could not ... simply could not hide from herself the rapturous tide of life-enhancing sublimely satisfied joyous love that so marvellously flooded, soared and sang through her blood and through her entire being as she gazed lovingly across that breakfast table at John.

Despite his grim thoughts of what lay before him, Frans managed an inward smile as he observantly noted the eye-sparkling, love-glowing glances Anna constantly bestowed on John. Even to him, an unromantic scientifically minded middle-aged male, it seemed glaringly obvious that what Blanche and he had anxiously discussed had at last occurred – Anna and John had become sexual lovers. Rising from the table he sighed, 'Oh, I better get ready to go and carry out my grim duties at what is left of poor Alie's and Roelant's house. You must go back to your secret room soon, John. Stay hidden there all day out of sight of any Krauts who might come over here from the crash sight.'

Turning and smiling knowingly at Anna, he ordered with mock seriousness, 'And he's to go there and demurely stay there by himself, all right, Anna?'

Shyly confusedly she blushed bright scarlet.

John's weather-beaten face glowed a shade darker as he grinned. That grin carried a hint of remorseful guilt, but also strongly hinted at a boastfully defiant touch of macho male pride.

No sooner had Frans left the kitchen than Anna and John found themselves tightly embraced in each others arms. As, for a short, voluptuously glowing time, they eagerly hugged and passionately kissed, their lovingly lingering memories of last night's rapturously fulfilling sexual bliss flamed and flared with renewed vigour and, threatened to violently overwhelm them.

With commanding strength, John summoned-up a great effort of will. Gently, but firmly, he pushed their eagerly aroused bodies reluctantly apart. Smiling, he said, 'Oh, Anna, this isn't the time or the place for passionate love-making, is it?'

With a hint of sad disappointment, and understanding agreement she returned his smile, 'No, it isn't, John. Oh, I suppose I better get these breakfast dishes washed-up and do a little – a very little- tidying-up before I feed the hens and collect the eggs. After that I better go to the dairy and try to help Blanche. She will miss the expert skill of poor Alie terribly. Perhaps, in time, I might learn to be reasonably good at milking and butter and cheese making, but never nearly as good as Blanche or poor Alie.' She paused, sobs choked her as she tearfully gasped, 'Oh, John, it's terrible to think I will never see Alie again, never hear her cheery voice and her gentle crooning which so soothed the cows as she milked them.'

John sympathetically hugged her and tenderly kissed her. 'I know, Anna, I know. I fully understand the grievous burden the tragic death of Alie, her husband, Roelant, and their two young boys is for you. I'm really sorry I can't do more to help you in your grief.'

Smiling through her tears, she murmured, 'Oh, John, John, you have helped me ... You helped me immensely in your bed last night! There's no better way you can help me!'

Making a not very successful effort to conceal the complacent vanity of his masculine ego, he grinned, 'I'm delighted my love-making efforts meet with your whole-hearted approval, Anna.'

With sad tears transmuting to happily glowing reminiscent smiles, she reassured him, 'Oh, they do, John! They most certainly do!'

He returned her smile, then sighed, 'Oh, I suppose I better obey Frans's order and go and hide myself in my secret room now.'

Giving a quick bright grin, Anna said, 'Despite Uncle Frans's hints, I might visit you, might bring you some food during the day, as long as there are no Krauts anywhere about this farm.' I certainly will visit you at night, though.' There was no mistaking the grinning roguishness with which she added, 'That's if you want me to, John ... Do you? Do you truly want me to?'

He let his amorously glowing eyes, his desperate passionate kisses, his eager hugging embraces answer for him. Then, making another resolute effort, he forced himself away from her and, urgently hurrying before that resolution failed him, made his way to his secret room above the stable.

★★★

John did not feel lonely during the day he spent hidden and alone in that room. The bright glowing memories of last night's wondrous sexual love and the eagerly anticipated promise of more, and – if that was possible – perhaps even better lovemaking tonight, filled his thoughts, beguiled his imagination and most pleasantly kept him company.

With a self-mocking grin, his unsentimental, clear-eyed insight reminded him that by increasing Anna's sexual pleasure he was self-rewardingly greatly increasing his own sexual pleasure and by honestly desiring to increase her loving pleasure I am revealing the depth and sincerity of my great love for her. And how vastly different, how infinitely better my love for Anna is compared to anything I have ever known before.

With a repulsive shudder he thought of the despicable acts of sex he had desperately and almost ashamedly performed a few times with dock-side prostitutes. Despite those tarts false smiling professional pretence and all their emphatic talk of "Love" there was never any semblance of anything remotely like this real love he was now experiencing for the first time with Anna.

But he would be as false as those deceitful smiling tarts if he did not acknowledge that there had been great sensual satisfaction, immense soul-shuddering relief to be had in those brief, furtive, frantic sweaty encounters. And while those prostitutes obviously were really only interested in making money from their tensed-up sex-starved or half drunken sailor customers, they did provide a real, a much needed war time service. For many a badly war-stressed Merchant Navy or Royal Navy sailor a desperately urgent sexual session with a dockside prostitute was the most obvious, most immediate and almost certainly the best way to gain some tension relieving forgetfulness before again facing the never-ending threat of being sent to a watery death by torpedos, bombs, mines or shells.

John smiled with understanding tolerance as he clearly remembered the first time he had made use of a prostitute's readily available services. It had been when the Battle of the Atlantic was raging at its most fierce and most deadly dangerous worst. The outcome of that vital struggle hung precariously in the balance as ever more numerous, ever more ruthlessly experienced German U-boat wolf-packs sunk ever increasing numbers of British ships.

After enduring exceptionally fierce, unrelenting U-boat attacks when almost half the convoy's merchant ships and two Royal Navy escorts had been sunk, the surviving ships, crewed by stressed, sleep-deprived exhausted men, at last gained the shelter of Nova Scotia's well protected waters and they thankfully berthed in the security of Halifax harbour.

After experiencing the wondrously reviving bliss of eight straight hours of deep sleep undisturbed by any urgent calls to Action Stations, most of those refreshed crews prepared to go ashore with keen anticipation of wholeheartedly making the most of whatever delights Halifax might offer them.

John and two other innocently inexperienced young shipmates had firmly decided that this evening they would all at last end their foolish innocent state in the beds of some Canadian prostitutes.

Once again they had been forced to endure the loud, mocking and goading insults of older sailors who accused those young conscript, still virgin sailors of being disgusting cissy milksops – perhaps even secret pansies – a disgrace to the Royal Navy uniform they were not fit to wear. After once more listening to those horny old tars with their gleeful, vividly descriptive accounts of sexual intercourse (although, of course, they used much stronger, cruder language) in countless brothels scattered over Britain's far-flung pre-war Empire, and hear them dramatically and persuasively extol the sexual act as being by far the greatest experience and pleasure in life, those three young sailors had definitely decided there must be no further delays, they must gain that experience now while they had the chance. Then if they should be killed in their next convoy at least they would have more fully lived, would have experienced the enlightening wonder of sexual intercourse before they died.

So too with Anna and I, John reflected. Should Anna or me, or both of us, ever screamingly die under sadistically torturing Gestapo hands, at least we would also have much, much, more fully lived before we died. By at last allowing our great love to gloriously soar and triumphantly realise its sublimest expression through our wondrous sexual fulfilment we have gained the highest heights of Love's summit. And surely Anna and I will survive this war. Surely our love, flourishing and strengthening, will outlive the vilest excesses of the Gestapo.

Trying to put those all too alluringly attractive thoughts of love and sex out of his mind for the present, John commanded himself to settle and concentrate on reading. He succeeded in getting engrossed in one of Anna's favourite novels and two hours of steady reading passed remarkably quickly and pleasantly.

Then, remembering and obeying his strict S.B.S. training, he lay down, drowsily rested and conserved his energy in readiness for any dramatic demands that might suddenly be made on him. He could not help grinning with self-satisfied complacency as he compared the many times he had lain conserving energy before facing the stress and dangers of fighting, killing and trying not to be killed, with the relaxed ease with which he was now resting. How much easier it was to serenely rest and relax when anticipating not going into dangerous action, but expecting soon to be with the woman you loved and be passionately making love with her.

Suddenly, with alarming violence, John's conscience troubled him.It demanded to know how much longer he intended to remain so pleasantly indulgently philandering in this cushy safe billet while the war violently raged, while some of his comrades in active S.B.S. teams and countless other Royal Navy sailors were fighting and being killed every day? He uneasily squirmed under the sharp probing severity of his self-questioning.

Then with soothing ease he answered his own question. He was only doing his duty, was correctly obeying orders by remaining – admittedly most willingly and very pleasantly – in hiding at this Dutch farm. The reply to that question of how much longer he would continue to stay being lovingly cosseted here was one to which he had no way of answering. That answer lay somewhere amongst those who made decisions in Special Operations Executive, Royal Navy Intelligence and the Netherlands Resistance Organization. When he received orders to leave here he would immediately obey them. But he was forced to admit to himself that the longer he stayed here, especially now with him so sublimely sharing his love with Anna, he felt ever increasingly more reluctant to go back to his 'normal' life of fighting, killing and risking being killed.

How terrible – yet how terribly understandable – was the thought that his great love for Anna might be beginning to make him fear death too greatly.

Chapter Twenty Five

That evening's dinner for Anna and Blanche, Frans and John, was again a subdued sombre meal. Three of them had very little appetite and John again almost guiltily made a great effort not to let his normal, healthy hunger be too obviously revealed.

As soon as John washed down the last of his food with a glass of milk, Frans rose and murmured to Blanche, 'John and I will go into the sitting- room now. Anna and you come and join us when you're finished in here, all right?'

'Sit down, John,' Frans said pointing at the large old arm chair at the side of the lounge's gleaming, blue and white tiled fireplace. Unlocking a dark oak corner cupboard he brought out a full bottle of brandy and two small crystal glasses. With slow, delicate, deliberate care he almost filled each glass. Handing one to John, he explained, 'I have been keeping this precious bottle of old, pre-war Dutch brandy to celebrate the victorious end of the war with.'

John grinned, 'Well, let's hope it won't remain slowly maturing for all that much longer before it's used for that eagerly longed for victory.'

After clinking glasses, toasting each other, and taking their first modest gulps, Frans answered John's unasked question. 'After I give Blanche and Anna a small drink of this fine old brandy I will re-lock the bottle in its cupboard. I will only bring it out again when there finally is glorious victory.' Giving something between a grin and a grimace, he added, 'Unless, of course, like now, there is a special reason for me having to use it again for ... for medicine? How do you say that in English? I cannot remember correctly.'

'Be most reluctantly forced to use that brandy for purely medicinal purposes!'

'Ah yes, "for medicinal purposes only", now I remember.'

Frans took another, a more generous gulp, then explained further, 'You see, John, I have had a…a terrible … a really terrible time today. I helped the police, the firemen and neighbouring farmers move the worst of the rubble of what was left of poor Roelant's devastated cottage then sifted through the remainder to find his, his wife's and two young sons bodies.

'Then I had the..... the appalling.... the really appalling task of trying to positively identify those four bodies.' Emotionally choked, he stared miserably at John for some long, silent moments then lifted his glass and gulped more brandy. 'Of course I did not say much to Blanche and Anna about this, but you John, who have much more experience of violent war than them, can understand that with that huge Flying Fortress crashing, exploding, then engulfing everything in raging flames, little was left to those four bodies but… but some hideously shrivelled blackened flesh and an entangled mess of charred and broken bones and skulls.' Again emotionally choked, he silently stared at John with distraught, tear filled eyes. Sighing deeply he lifted his glass and drained it in one desperate gulp.

'I am sorry to so burden you with my harrowing woes John. I hope you do not mind. I 'm not upsetting you too much, am I?'

'No, no, not at all. Frans. I fully understand. I most deeply, most sympathetically appreciate what a terrible ordeal you've been through. I know it does good to get such emotions off your chest. By sharing your ghastly experiences with me you'll, to some extent, help ease your mind, help calm your nerves.'

'Thank you John. Yes, it does me good to talk with you. I could never reveal the full hideousness of my experiences to Blanche and Anna. They are distressed enough as it is. It is much better that they do not think of.... of the terrible state of those four bodies.'

Frans lifted the bottle and poured John and himself a little more brandy. After toasting one another with sincere emotion they drained their glasses in one large, appreciative gulp.

'Ah, that's better,' Frans declared, giving a brave attempt at a carefree smile.

'Aye, I know how a good drink helps after such a grim experience.'

'You've experienced something like this yourself, John?'

'Yes, I have.' Not going into elaborate details, he told something of

151

the time his Royal Navy ship had survived after being hit by a German bomb. After the fierce fire had been extinguished and they were no longer under Luftwaffe attack, he had been one of the team faced with the grisly task of trying to find and identify what was left of the sailors who had been trapped below deck in the section of the ship engulfed by fire. 'When we finished our revolting work the captain ordered that we be issued with a generous tot of rum.' He paused, then solemnly concluded, 'Never had I been so badly in need of the reviving comfort of a large tot of extra strong navy rum!'

It was now Frans's turn to understandingly sympathize. 'Ah yes, John, I know exactly how you felt. The first thing I did when I got home this evening was to remove every stitch of my clothes. They seemed to be impregnated with death's horrors. The stench of those incinerated bodies clung to these clothes with grim tenacity. I then tried to rid myself of that terrible lingering stench in a bath as steaming hot as I could bear. I then dressed in this complete set of clothes which Blanche had most thoughtfully freshly aired and ironed and set out for me. And now the warming wonder of this noble brandy has cleared my mouth, my throat, my lungs of the lasting lingering taste of death's vile stench.'

They sat in companionable silence for a little while. Both were aware of being linked by feelings much stronger than mere friendship. They were moved by the deep, profoundly powerful trusting strength of that soldierly camaraderie that is one good thing which rises from war's blood-soaked horrors.

'Were there many Krauts investigating that crash site today?' John asked.

'Yes, quite a few, mostly Luftwaffe technicians, but fortunately they mainly worked separately from us. They collected and removed some of the scattered bits and pieces of the smashed Flying Fortress. But after that terrific explosion and raging fire I don't think they could have discovered anything really useful from that pulverized wreckage. They finished and left before us, so hopefully they will not be back again,'

'Good. So it should be safe for me to work outside here at the farm again?'

'Yes, it should. There is not so much work to do now, though. It is a good thing that, now poor Roelant is no longer here to help, almost all the potatoes and other vegetables have been harvested, carted to market and sold. And it is very good of Anna to so willingly help Blanche in the dairy now that she does not have poor Alie's expert help.'

As Frans noted the bright smiles and keen nods with which John wholeheartedly agreed with his praise of Anna, then listened to the force with which he added his own praise of her to his, it was obvious that John's feelings for Anna were much, much stronger than mere friendship's gentle kindliness. After seeing Anna's brilliant gleaming eyes dart such loving glances at John over this morning's breakfast table, and than hearing this unguarded outpouring of John's, Frans had no doubt that those two were deeply in love. He also felt certain that they were now passionately intimate sexual lovers.

Keeping his thoughts to himself for the present he listened to John now say, 'At least I can help you by mucking out the byre and stable, can't I? I'll willingly do that each day for as long as I remain here. That work will, in some small degree, ease my conscience for eating so much of Blanche's great, mouth-watering food.'

'Oh, John,' laughed Frans, 'I happily delegate the job of chief mucker-out to you! That work which poor Roelant used to do, is not labour I was ever too keen on doing myself.'

'Well, that's settled then,' John grinningly confirmed . Then, turning more serious, asked, 'Have you any idea how many more days I can expect to be employed here as "chief mucker-out"?'

Slowly shaking his head, Frans sighed, 'No, John, I'm afraid I don't know how much longer you're likely to stay here. Actually I am surprised – most surprised – that I have not received orders for you to return to England long before now.'

For some moments both men silently stared at one another. It was on the tip of John's tongue to ask more. He felt that Frans wanted to say more, but, constrained by a consciousness of the 'need to know' principle, he continued his thoughtful silence for a few more moments.

It was Frans who eventually spoke; he repeated, 'Oh no, John, I have no idea how long you will stay here. It is out of my hands. I must wait for orders from London about you.'

John grinned, 'I hope our "top brass" in London haven't completely forgotten about me.'

'Oh, I am sure they remember you John.' Frans paused, then as if uncertain whether he should say more or not, somewhat hesitantly continued, 'You see there are … are troubles, bad troubles, with some of our Dutch Resistance Groups. A number of them – I don't know how many – have "disappeared" … been betrayed to the Gestapo, we think. My own group here is still intact, but … but we have to … to "lie low" for a while. It is probably because of all these upheavals and terrible uncertainties that I have not received further orders about you, John.'

Nodding understandingly, John said 'Thank you for putting me in the picture about this, Frans. I know you can't say too much, but it's good to have some knowledge of what's happening. I will just patiently wait until you get orders about me. There's nothing else I can do, is there?' He again grinned, 'And you know, I certainly am not complaining! It's most pleasant staying at this farm with you all.'

'With us all, or with one of us in particular? With Anna, especially, is that correct? Don't you have a special – a very special, a most intimate relationship with her now?'

John felt his face foolishly flush. Not quite knowing how best to answer these rather personal questions, he silently stared for some long moments. He was baffled by the accusingly concerned? … the knowingly suggestive? tone of voice with which Frans had asked his questions.

At last, with a touch of annoyance, he defiantly stated, 'Oh, of course I especially like being with Anna. Yes, of course we have a most intimate relationship now.'

Frans gave an apologetic smile. 'Oh, I'm sorry, John, I did not mean to annoy you. I hope I didn't sound too much like an over-protective, heavy-handed father. It's just that I … Blanche and I … remembering Anna's previous nervous-breakdown cannot help being greatly concerned over how she will react when you have to part from her if the two of you have got too deeply, too passionately involved with one another.'

All hint of annoyance vanished from John's face as he contritely replied, 'Oh, Frans, it's me who should apologise to you. I'm sorry to add more burdens to the heavy weight of worries you are already carrying. It is only fair that I should explain how things are between Anna and me. Firstly I must assure you that the love between us is not any thoughtless, selfish, shallowly casual affair. We deeply, passionately and sincerely love each other. We consider ourselves morally married. We intend to marry as soon as the end of this war makes it possible.'

He paused, then as if begging for Fran's understanding tolerance, smiled, 'Oh, I must admit we have started our "honeymoon" without being legally married, but under the present extreme war-time conditions I think that's excusable, don't you?'

Frans nodded his rather uncertain agreement, 'Yes...yes, I suppose so.'

John hastened to reassure him, 'Oh, but please don't think we've been freely and casually sexually indulging ourselves for a long time – we haven't! Every evening, as we ended our stroll outside Anna's bedroom we were severely tempted to give in to our strong, natural sexual desires, but we always successfully resisted these at times almost overwhelming urges.

'Yes, we nobly resisted until last night! Then we both felt it to be the height of folly for us to continue our unnatural restrain and continually refuse to give full expression to our great love. Those terribly tragic deaths of Alie and Roelant and their two young sons decided us to consummate our love while we could. Then if one – or both – of us were killed, at least we would have, even if only for a short time, much more fully lived. Surely you can understand this, Frans? I hope you don't now think too badly of us, do you?'

'No, no, of course not. Thank you for being so frank with me. You don't mind if I tell Blanche all you've told me?'

'No, I don't mind. She's fully entitled to know as well, isn't she? I hope she'll be as understanding as you've been?'

'Oh yes, I'm sure she will. It's just that she will still be terrible worried over how Anna will react when you leave here. But, like me, she will be reassured by knowing that you truly love Anna and intend to marry her.'

'I do, Frans. I assure you I do... I solemnly promise you – as I've promised Anna – that I intend to return and marry her as soon as I can after the war's end.' John paused then thoughtfully continued, 'Only one thing – my death – will stop me returning! Before I leave here, Frans, I'll give you my home address in Keswick. If I don't return shortly after the war, you should write to my mother or sister and they will let you know what happened to me, all right?'

'Oh, John, I hope it won't come to that. But, yes, I'll keep your home address hidden away here just in case the worst should come to the worst.' He sighed, 'Oh, who knows how many of us will survive this..... this hellish, this endless seeming hellish war?' He smiled, 'It is good we have discussed these thing before the ladies arrive. We must try and be more cheerful with them.'

And they were. While Blanche got on with her eternal knitting, Frans encouraged her to tell of how well Anna had helped her in the dairy this morning. Being in Dutch, John could not follow this genuine praise of Anna, but, guessing its gist, he asked her to translate. Smiling she modestly toned down Blanche's praise. Frans laughingly joined in with his own, much more generous translation, 'Oh, you are being far too modest, Anna. You are a great help to Blanche. She could never manage all that dairy work by herself, as you well know, now that she no longer has poor Alie to assist her.'

This remark about Alie was the only reference any of them made to yesterday's sad deaths. And, with great tact they all avoided any mention of the gruesome work Frans had been employed at today. This foul war, having made them all too familiar with the ugliness of death, was now making them all the more eager to get back to everyday life's fair and homely quiet ways.

Sitting closely together, Anna and John were soon engrossed in one another's company. They were also happily engrossed in some of Anna's favourite books of poetry.

Blanche gently smiled as she got to her feet exactly at ten-fifteen, put her knitting tidily away and remarked, 'Oh, it's nice to get back to my usual pleasant routine tonight!'

As he followed his wife out of the room Frans halted at the door, cheerily grinned at Anna and John, and with eyes gleaming mischievously instructed, 'Have a good time tonight, you two ...You're only young once ... Live while you can!'

Anxious not to waste too much time before enjoying the eagerly anticipated sensual pleasures awaiting them at John's secret room, they took a shorter walk than usual. A dark screen of thick clouds hung heavily over the flat land and hid the moon and stars and muffled the roar of the stream of heavy R.A.F. bombers passing high overhead on their routine, but hazardous, "milk run" that delivered bombs to the heavily defended Ruhr.

As Anna and John entered the stable and, hand in hand, started groping their way up the steep, dark steps to the hay loft the disturbed mare stamped an annoyed hoof and gave what seemed a knowing, disapproving snort.

Anna giggled, 'Oh John, I think she knows what naughtiness we're going to get up to and she doesn't approve of it!'

John's echoing answering laughter resonated not only with honest joy but also with highly excited sexual anticipation, 'Yes I doubt our lively "hanky-panky" in my secret room will go against that strict, Victorian dictum ... I'm afraid our energetic love making *will* "frighten the horses"!'

That laughing prediction of John's was soon proved correct as the puzzled mare's questioning whinnies mingled with the noises of human lover's passionate embraces.

What John had hoped and intended came wondrously true. Tonight's sexual love was even better than last night's!

★ ★ ★

It was not until nine day later that – the tangled web of bureaucratic red-tape spun by pedantic Dutch and German officials sorted out – the funerals of Alie, Roelant, and their two young sons could finally go ahead. These multiple burials brought fresh reminders and renewed sorrows to Anna, Blanche and Frans.

John kept hidden all that day and well into evening until the last of the mourning relatives, neighbouring farmers and other dejected friends had departed.

After the grim finality of these funerals, life for all at this farm again settled to its accustomed, pleasantly familiar routine; although for Anna and John there was nothing in the least routine in the glorious glowing wonder of their love as they passionately continued their "honeymoon's" exotically erotic fulfilment.

Three days after these funerals John once more met Frans as he returned from another day of teaching. After opening the stable door for Frans to enter and park his bicycle, he stood and silently gazed his inevitable question, expecting to receive the usual negative shake of Fran's head in reply.

Today he didn't!

Instead of negatively shaking his head, Frans affirmingly nodded. 'Yes, I've received orders from London at last, John. You are flying to England tomorrow night!'

Chapter Twenty Six

John gasped; his heart violently thudded as he heard this news – this long expected, but dramatically sudden news.

He silently stared at Frans. It felt as if neither his mind nor his body knew quite how to correctly react to this startling information. Oh, of course he would obey these orders. But after his protracted cushy sojourn at this Dutch farm and his rapturously wondrous loving time with Anna it would be a violent wrench to leave here and a heart-breaking ordeal to leave her. But leave here and her he must. There was no avoiding doing his duty. And, once away, it would be exciting – perhaps at times just a bit too exciting – to be actively involved in this war's grim hazards and chances and its violent dangers once again.

'Tomorrow night? ... I fly back to England tomorrow night?'

'Yes, John, you do. It's all arranged. A Lysander aircraft is bringing in some people to a field we have used before not too far from here. That plane will then take you to England. It will land and take off under cover of night's darkness.' Frans grinned, 'We Resistance Fighters use our great "secret weapon" to help guide the R.A.F. pilot to the correct field. You will see it in use tomorrow night.'

'Good. I look forward to that. I know these highly skilled pilots need all the assistance they can get to guide them to the dark small fields they land on in German-occupied countries.'

'You have been in these Lysander planes before, John?'

'Oh yes, quite a few times.' He grinned as he told of the last time he had flown in one. 'It was in the Normandy region of France. Our S.B.S. team had successfully completed our mission. While waiting in the darkness with French Resistance Fighters we somewhat apprehensively noted how small the field seemed, how highly some trees at its far end seemed to loom. However the R.A.F. Lysander landed skilfully; two men got out, some guns and ammunition were unloaded; our team – or rather the four of us who survived – quickly got in. Less than three minutes after landing the plane turned, taxied, then with its engine roaring at full power took off into the steady wind, light rain and shrouding darkness. I remember thinking, as I was being savagely thrust back in my seat , that the plane was climbing extremely steeply. I thought of those menacingly high trees and I prayed!

'However we arrived back in England safely. After landing in heavy rain, the pilot taxied to a large hanger. Once the doors were closed, overhead lights brightly illuminated our Lysander – that single-engined, sturdily reliable, work-horse that constantly ferries secret agents and Special Forces teams into and out of German-occupied European countries, as you know, Frans.

'Well, these glaring lights also fully revealed our pilot for the first time. With his impressively large handle-bar moustache, his dark blue polka-dotted cravat and jauntily angled cap, he appeared a perfect specimen – almost a caricature – of a dare-devil "Flying Officer Kite" type of R.A.F. pilot. Ignoring the expectantly waiting Special Operations Executive Intelligence Officer, our pilot stooped to examine his aircraft's fixed undercarriage. Straightening up, he turned to face the impatient officer. Grinning widely, he thrust out both hands, revealing – like pacifying olive branches – some whippily thin shoots of trees which had been tightly wrapped around the undercarriage.

As if confirming his "Flying Officer Kite" persona, he jovially announced, 'A few feet lower and I would have pranged the jolly old kite on those tall French trees, you know! You must order those Froggies not to use that field again. It's not suitable ... it's too dangerous!'

After finishing his story John grinned at Frans, 'So I trust there are no high trees near the field I will be leaving from tomorrow night.'

'No, no, I assure you there are no high trees. There is a small wood at one side of the field, but at one end there is only a ditch, and some small bushes at the other end. Your take-off should not be .. be so alarmingly steep this time, John!'

Their grins vanished as they stared thoughtfully silently at one another. They were both thinking of the same thing ... the need to inform Anna that John was leaving tomorrow night.

'We'll need to break the upsetting news to her as gently as possible, John.'

'Yes, I agree I'll do all I can to ease the parting for her. It's a great comfort for me to know that Blanche and you will do your utmost to help her after I leave here.

'What is going to make it especially difficult for her is that, until I return after the war, she won't know how I am, where I am, what I am doing. It's most unlikely that she'll receive any information about me during the remainder of this bloody war. She won't even be certain if I am alive or not. Although perhaps her great love for me, allied to her strong feminine intuition would with vivid, dramatic certainty inform her if I was killed.' He gave a bright smile, 'But I definitely hope, by staying alive, not to put her intuitive powers to that test!'

'I know, John, I know. It won't be easy for her. Nor for you either, for that matter.'

'Yes, knowing nothing of how she is; how she's coping or even how Blanche and you are managing, will be constant nagging worries for me. Oh, let's hope to God this war does end next year!' He gave another bright smile, 'Perhaps this time for once, the war will end before Christmas – Christmas 1944, that is, and no later. Not Christmas '45, '46 or even '47!'

As he made that heartfelt wish his nerves gave a strange, tremulous, inward shudder. His tingling senses seemed to send a disturbing message surging to his brain. Flashing memory reminded him that, due to his S.B.S. team's failure to kill Professor Willem Maurik, the Germans- with that treacherous Dutch nuclear physicist's highly valued, keenly eager expert help – were now more likely to develop an atom-bomb before this war did end. And the longer the war lasted the more likely were the Germans to succeed in perfecting and using their war-winning bomb.

All the more reason for his conscience (his troubled, accusing conscience?) to remind him that the sooner he got back to playing an active important part in helping to bring the war to a successful conclusion as soon as possible, the better. He had hardly been helping to win the war by idly lingering, hiding and sexually indulging himself in this glorious love-nest, had he?

'Yes,' he assured his uneasy conscience, 'I will again resolutely and unstintingly do my utmost, use all my S.B.S. trained powers to help – "not by strength, by guile" – bring this war to an end before Christmas 1944.

'Then as soon as possible after that I will return to Holland, at last marry dear Anna, and live happily ever after!'

Sober Reason, with clear-eyed cruel logic, suddenly shattered Love's delicately fragile delicious dream It starkly reminded him that even after the defeat of Germany vicious war would most certainly continue. The Japanese were still savagely fighting in the Pacific and as that war increasingly swung in the Allies favour these Japs would ever more determinedly fight with ever more suicidal bravery in defence of their threatened homeland. And while at present that was mainly an American war, as soon as this European war was over no doubt Royal Navy Admirals would be most anxious to send their Atlantic fleet to the Pacific and gain some of the "glory" of defeating the Japs as well as the Huns.

'So I might find myself reluctantly embarked en route for Japan and nor eagerly en route for Holland and Anna.'

Frans's compassionate voice broke into John's wide ranging thoughts. 'It won't be easy, but I might manage to get some news about Anna sent to England occasionally. Despite – or perhaps in deliberate defiance of – the worst excesses of this war's disgusting foulness's, the S.O.E. in London and our Resistance leaders in The Netherlands do try whenever possible to display a touch of warm humanity by allowing some personal messages to be passed on. I suppose they realise such messages are good for morale, good for increasing our fighting resolve and spirit.'

'That's encouraging to know, Frans.' Not wanting to be discouraging he did not say so, but John was rather doubtful if any such messages about Anna would ever reach him. They certainly wouldn't while he was actively engaged in Atlantic or Russian convoys; nor when on hazardous clandestine S.B.S. operations.

★ ★ ★

Dinner that evening was once again a solemnly subdued meal. Blanche and Frans did their best not to make their deep concern for how Anna was reacting now, and how she would cope once John left her tomorrow, too glaringly obvious. However there seemed little need for them to be so discreet in keeping watch on her just now, for Anna took almost no notice of them. She only had eyes for John. Her

161

passionate, loving, agonised gaze was steadily fixed on him and him alone. She greedily drank his glorious image in while she had the chance and stored it for further use ... for bright, vivid, accurate remembrance and consoling comfort once he was no longer with her and was once again bravely facing the real danger of being cruelly killed in this terrible war's savage butchery.

In compliance with the need for maximum security she was not allowed to have photographs of John, just as he had none of her. While regretting the lack of photos, both were supremely confident that their glowing memories of each other would keep perfectly accurate visions of one another wondrously alive until they met and married after this war's end.

Enjoying their after dinner's physical ease in the sitting-room's solidly substantial comfort, they all made a convincing outward show of calmly relaxed normality. Blanche's knitting needles were blurs of determined, non-stop movement; Frans's interest seemed entirely focussed on his engrossing novel; Anna and John, sitting closer together than ever, appeared to have their minds fully engaged in the books of poetry they read, and, with Anna taking the instructive and enlightening lead, keenly discussed. But all were well aware of the unmistakable atmosphere of subdued tension enveloping the room and keeping their senses nervously taut.

Frans once or twice quietly consulted his watch then, meaningfully glancing at his wife, discreetly nodded his head towards the door. While understanding her husband's gentle hints, Blanche determinedly ignored them. Not until the inviolate, prescribed time of ten-fifteen did she rise, once again neatly put her knitting away and go out of the room by the door her husband was holding open for her. As he followed her, Frans said nothing but gave Anna and John a gentle and compassionately understanding smile.

As soon as the door firmly closed Anna's and John's bodies eagerly joined. Their lips passionately met. As they kissed and hugged Anna's brave self-control dissolved; she sobbingly wept, her embraced body uncontrollably trembled. She distraughtly gasped, 'Oh, John...John, I love you. I love you and don't want to lose you!'

Restraining his own emotions, John hugged her even more tightly, kissed her even more lovingly. 'Oh, Anna...Anna, I love you. I love you and don't want to leave you! But you know I must leave here, must

162

leave you – but only for the present – must do my duty and obey my orders. Oh, Anna, you must be brave! You will find the courage to wait with resolute self-control until I return and marry you, won't you?

'Oh, you know I will come safely through this war – as I know you will. We will be gloriously re-united, get quickly married, spend our rapturous honeymoon – our real, morally and legally sanctioned honeymoon – amongst the hills of my Lakeland homeland. Under my loving guidance you will soon get to know these hills, crags and lakes almost as well as I do.'

'Oh yes, John, I know all that. I am sure our wonderful dreams will come true.' Conjuring up a radiant smile she stifled her sobs, stared steadily into John's adoring eyes with a tear-bright, love beaming gaze and declared, 'I will keep that glorious picture of you returning, us getting married and having our wonderful honeymoon, steadily before me, Oh John, I assure you that fabulous vision will keep me steady, will greatly help me to get through the... the terrible empty vacuum of our separation until you return to me.'

A little later they curtailed their usual nightly stroll and hurried to the stable. The mare, by now quite accustomed to these nocturnal visits, merely turned her head, gave a gentle welcoming (but still suggestively knowing?) whinny as they made their way up the steep dark stairs.

Desperately urgently eagerly they made love. Through much of that night the panting gasps of fantastically wonderful passionate love mingled with the resolutely restrained, sobbing gasps of the deep sorrows of lover's parting.

At breakfast later that morning, although all agreed that they should pass the time as calmly and normally as possible on this last day that Anna and John would be together for none knew how long, they were well aware that this calm acceptance might be difficult to maintain.

Fortunately this was one of Blanche's day's for making butter and cheese. By keeping Anna energetically employed helping out with this demanding, engrossing and rewarding dairy work, Blanche hoped to make these last hours easier for her. She would have less time for giving in to the tears and lamentations of utter dejection. There was likely to be all too much time to give into these miseries in the days and weeks, the months – and years? – of anxiously waiting for John's return.

While Blanche and Anna were busy in the dairy, Frans and John were methodically making their preparations for tonight's activities which, if all went as planned, would see John safely back in England long before the night was over. In the secret room above the stable Frans unlocked a small cupboard and revealed his armoury of one Sten-gun and a neat row of spare magazines for the sub-machine gun. As he handed a tin of gun-oil and a couple of cleaning rags to John he grinned, 'It's much safer to clean and check our weapons here in this secret room where there's no danger of any Krauts smelling that gun-oil.'

John returned his grin, 'Yes, that's wise – very wise. This oil has a strong, distinctive smell, doesn't it?'

'Yes, and I don't even have the covering excuse that I'm only using it on the shot-gun I used to have for shooting rabbits. The Krauts confiscated that gun two years ago.'

Frans noted the well practised skill with which John swiftly dismantled, checked over, cleaned and reassembled his .45 calibre Colt automatic pistol, then, satisfied, firmly slapped the re-loading magazine into the gun's butt and slipped the safety-catch to 'safe'. He now tightly screwed the long, ungainly silencer on to the gun's muzzle and smiled, 'Have you seen a silencer before, Frans?'

'No, I haven't. But, more to the point, have you used that silencer, John?' Contritely grinning, he immediately apologised, 'Oh, I'm sorry, John, I should not ask such questions, should I?'

'No, you shouldn't. You know you can't expect to get detailed answers, don't you?' As he unscrewed the silencer and returned it to its webbing pouch, John smiled, 'But there's no harm – no breach of great state secrets – in letting you know that, yes, I have used that silencer; have used it stealthily silently when absolute silence and deadly stealth were imperative. That's as much as I'm going to tell you, Frans.'

'That's all you need to tell me, John. It is further reassuring proof that I can have complete confidence in you ... in your expert, experienced, skill and bravery.'

'Yes, you can, Frans, you can. Just as much as I have unlimited confidence in your absolute trustworthiness and quietly determined courage.' He remembered and smilingly repeated that remark he had made while waiting with his – now dead- S.B.S. team and those other brave Dutch Patriots, Eric and Peter, when engaged on 'Operation Waterloo', 'We are beginning to sound like members of a mutual admiration society!'

As Frans finished cleaning his Sten-gun and fitted a magazine of thirty two rounds to it, John removed four full magazines from his webbing pouches and laid them beside the other spare ammunition, 'You better keep those, Frans, they're no good to me now that I don't have a Sten-gun.'

Frans now confirmed the details of tonight's plan for getting John back to England. 'We leave here at seven; we walk cautiously through the darkness in defiance of the Krauts strictly enforced curfew. After two and a half hours we rendevous with four Patriots waiting in the small wood beside the field the Lysander plane will land in. We alertly keep guard until ten o'clock when the plane will arrive. The men in it will get out, you will get in, it will take-off.' Remembering John's story of his last trip in a Lysander, Frans laughed, 'There being no tall trees, this take-off will be easy .. won't be too steep!'

'And a few hours after that I'll revel in the luxury of drinking a steaming hot mug of great British tea, eh? That's one thing I do look forward to; it's one thing I've missed here in Holland.'

Frans again laughed, 'Oh, yes, John, I'm sorry your wondrous English tea is one thing we don't have here at present. I promise to get some after the end of the war and keep it specifically for when you return. But in the meantime you've had things that pleasantly compensated for the lack of tea, haven't you?'

'Yes, I have. Blanche's wonderfully thick, creamy milk is almost as good as our great British "char"!'

'Oh, no doubt that's true, but I was thinking more of the compensations of the wondrous times you've had with Anna.' With a suggestive stare at the neatly arranged blankets and tidily folded sheet that covered the large mattress on the floor, Frans gave what John thought was a strange, rather accusing – perhaps even a jealous? – grin as he continued, 'Especially the glorious compensations you must have had in this hidden away place, this secluded love-nest with its cosy bedroom comforts!'

John made no verbal reply, but his face betrayingly flushed. It glowed with what? With guilt? ... With remorse?... With a touch of anger? ...... annoyance that Anna and his great, deep, and supremely pure love should be hinted at as being something only consisting of selfish, self-indulgent rampant sexuality?

For a few long, silent moments the two men stared at one another.

This uneasy silence vanished as quickly as it had arisen, as John disarmingly smiled, 'Oh, Frans, surely you don't begrudge Anna and I our few hours of the greatest, the purest, happiness we have ever known?'

Frans contritely apologised, 'Oh, no, no, of course not. I did not really mean to criticize the pair of you for fulfilling your great love while you could before this war separates you and keeps you apart for God knows how long.'

As John smiled his thanks, both men felt more strongly bonded than ever by this sudden, strange suggestion of primitive masculine jealousy.

As if in further confirmation of this bond of trusting friendship, John produced two Mills hand-grenades from his webbing pouches and, grinning, handed them to Frans. 'You better keep these grenades in your small armoury; you're more likely to have occasion to use them than me. And anyway I'll get well kitted-out in England before my next S.B.S. operation.' As Frans accepted the grenades John asked. 'Do you know how to handle and use them? Have you used them before?

Smiling with modest pride, Frans replied, 'Oh yes, John, I've used these British grenades before. Only once before, admittedly, but quite effectively on that occasion!'

Frans volunteered no further information. John knew better than to ask for more, but Frans rose even higher in his estimation of how experienced and reliable he was.

'There's nothing more we can do at present in preparation for tonight's activities, John, so I think I'll revert to my peaceful role as a schoolteacher and get on with some paperwork for a few hours all right?'

'Yes, of course. I'll clean up this secret room and leave it neat and tidy for the next occupant. Then I'll muck-out the byre and stable for the last time before I leave here.'

'Yes, just you do that.' Then, laughing, Frans added, ' If I do not miss you for anything else, John, I certainly will miss you working as chief mucker-out!'

Chapter Twenty Seven

Shortly after midday, their work in the dairy finished, Blanche and Anna returned to the kitchen. Frans and John soon joined them. As Anna handed both men a glass of fresh, thick creamed, foaming milk, Frans explained, 'We will just have a light snack now; some milk and a little bread and cheese, because our dinner will be early today. We will have it about four-fifteen.' He smiled at John, 'And you and I won't have quite as large a meal as we usually have, if that's all right with you, John. You agree with me that it's best not to have too full a stomach, before setting out on this evening's activities at seven p.m., don't you?'

John nodded and grinned, 'Yes, of course I agree. That's very wise. It's as sensible as not swimming with a bloated stomach too soon after a large meal.' Both men knew they were thinking the same thing ... if they got caught up in some sudden trouble, like stumbling into an unexpected German patrol, and had to run for their lives, they would go that bit faster by not being burdened by an overloaded stomach. Likewise – as always before going on possibly dangerously violent action – they would empty their bowels before leaving this farmhouse tonight. On such occasions there was absolutely no difficulty about achieving bowel movements! Keeping these thoughts to himself, John smiled at Blanche, 'Even if today's dinner is not quite as plate-fillingly generous as usual, I'm sure it will be every bit as mouth-wateringly delicious as usual! Oh, Blanch, I don't know how I can ever thank you for all the wondrous meals I've had from you while I've been here. I will always remember them. They will remain one of the best, most treasured memories of my stay with you.'

While Frans translated this sincere praise, John beamed at Anna, 'Of course these memories of great food will certainly not be quite my greatest memory of my stay here, will they?'

Reaching across the kitchen table she tremblingly grasped his hand. While her eyes glowed with love and glittered with held back tears she summoned up a brave smile and tremulously whispered, 'No, John, I should hope not! I know you have other much, much greater memories to take with you and to treasure until we are gloriously re-united after the end of this terrible war. I know my treasured memories of you and of our great love will never die ... they will glow brightly and wondrously alive in my heart for ever!'

John lovingly smiled, tenderly squeezed her trembling hand and gulped down the emotional lump in his throat which threatened to choke him.

With compassionate understanding Frans's voice gently broke in on the self-absorbed, mutually gazing lovers, 'I'll do some more paperwork now and Blanche wants to tidy up in here then get on with preparing the early dinner, so no doubt you two will manage to pass the time pleasantly enough by yourselves for a few hours, eh?'

They did. Their remaining time together was spent in quiet happiness – that happiness subdued by thoughts of their approaching parting. These precious last hours passed all too quickly.

For a time they lingered in the sitting-room's solid comfort. With gentle care Anna neatly replaced all her borrowed books which John had brought back from his secret room. As each volume was re-united with its sacrosanct niche in the crowded bookshelves it was commented upon by one or other of them with greater or lesser enthusiasm. Once this pleasant bibliophilic task was finished they sat together on the plush old sofa and with reassuring hugs and innocently eager kisses expressed, and joyously revelled in, the glorious wonder and profound greatness of their love. Sometime later they took a final stroll along the farm's familiar paths around the harvested, bare muddy fields. It was strange to be leisurely strolling, arm in arm, in the full glow of this autumn afternoon's breezy play of slanting sunlight and high white clouds instead of in their usual, curfew defying nocturnal darkness. By unspoken mutual consent they guided their steps away from the path leading directly to the devastated ruins of Roelant's cottage. Even while being most lovingly engrossed in whispered intimate talk with Anna, John managed to keep a reasonably alert look out for any sign of menacing Germans or possibly untrustworthy neighbouring Dutch farmers. Fortunately every surrounding field seemed completely devoid of all human life except for where a distant, heavy hoofed plodding horse and a slow trundling, vegetable laden cart were labouriously moving.

As once more he lifted his gaze from Anna's upturned face and alertly scanned these flat Dutch fields, John – despite his deep sorrow at being forced to leave her – was almost guiltily conscious of a feeling almost of joy, a vague sense of anticipatory uplift at the thought that soon, if all went smoothly he should be on leave in England; would for a few precious days be gazing not at this uninspiring, drearily dull and featureless Dutch landscape, but at his inspiring, deeply loved Lakeland hills. Oh, if only Anna could be there sharing these ennobling views of hills and lakes with him. Repressing a sigh, he lovingly returned his gaze to her.

Suddenly Anna's tears overflowed in surging flood.

Gradually John's tight hugging, reassuring love eased her misery. Her weeping stopped; she dried her eyes; got her shuddering sobs under control. Again and again he passionately assured her that he would survive this war. 'Oh, Anna, our love is too powerful, too toweringly great to be destroyed. It, and we, will outlive this war's madness. I will return to you!…We will be married!'

Even as he reiterated these passionate assurances he thought of the millions who had been, were being, and would yet be killed in this war. Was he being realistic in expecting never to become one more number swelling these appalling statistics? He vividly remembered how before each dangerous S.B.S. mission, he – being so young, so superbly fit, so vitally full of life – felt (despite what reason's cold clear logic told him) it impossible that he should be killed. If anyone had to die it would be some other member of his S.B.S. team, not him. He smiled inwardly as he thought, 'The trouble is that each member of each team felt exactly the same!'

Eventually John glanced at his watch and said, 'We better start heading home now, Anna. It will soon be time for our early dinner.'

Reluctantly agreeing, she linked her arm through his and they slowly wended their way back along the familiar old paths.

That dinner was, once again, was a sombrely subdued meal. Anna ate practically nothing. Blanche slowly ate her usual modest amount. Frans and John quickly cleared their plates of the tasty but deliberately reduced portions.

As Blanche and Anna gathered up the dishes Frans hastily and – it seemed to John – rather nervously, one more time consulted his watch then said, 'Now, John, you better go to your secret room and change into your uniform.' Smiling he added, half apologetically, 'I know there's plenty time before we have to leave here, but I always like to be fully prepared well in advance, don't you?'

John returned that smile as he obediently rose from the kitchen table, 'Yes, I agree, it's always best not to have a last minute desperate rush.'

After carefully drawing the thick, blackout curtain across the secret room's small window John lit two candles and started undressing. After cleaning and loading their weapons this morning Frans had fully briefed him on tonight's planned activity and it had then been agreed that John should change back into his black S.B.S uniform. After donning all his British clothes he fastened his webbing belts and now almost empty pouches over them. It was a familiar, a strangely reassuring feel to have the heavy weight of his holstered .45 Colt automatic pistol drag at his right hip and to have the much lighter weight, but perhaps even more sinisterly menacing feel of his large, razor sharp Commando knife hang in its scabbard at his left hip. The wearing of that uniform and these weapons seemed to drag him back with unrelenting force into war's savage killing madness; they unmistakably reminded him that he was a tough, highly trained, deadly experienced killer.

Fondly looking around this room where Anna and he had experienced such glorious love he sighed. Oh, would Love ever conquer War? He again sighed as reason told him that this terrible war must be fought, must be triumphantly won and the hideous evil of Nazism destroyed if Love and loving goodness were ever to triumph and flourish.

Gathering up all his civilian Dutch clothes for return to Frans, he had a final careful look around the room checking that everything was in order, nothing had been forgotten. His keen gaze finally come to rest on the large mattress and the bedding neatly heaped upon it. Fondly remembering, he again sighed then with more than a hint of self-indulgent masculine boastfulness, smiled as he thought of how those tidily folded sheets bore witness to the passionately virile greatness of their wondrous love. He tried to remember what a mischievously grinning Anna had quoted from Hamlet: something about, "honeying and making love ... in the rank sweat of an enseamed bed"? Yes, these tell-tale sheets with their stiff starched semen stains of this lusty seaman certainly bore irrefutable proof of the glorious consummation of their great love!

He blew out the candles and left the room.

When he entered the kitchen Blanche and Anna were startled by his altered appearance. That dark uniform and these deadly weapons arranged so conveniently to hand as if ready for immediate use were most disturbing – they seemed to bring the menace of this war's ghastly deaths into this room.

Frans keenly scrutinized that transformation which had changed John from apparently being an innocent civilian to his true persona of an extremely tough and resolute S.B.S. sailor. With a gentle nod and a slight smile he gave this transformed John his wholehearted approval. He again thought how good it was to have him as an ally; how terrifying it would be to have him as an enemy.

Again sitting around the kitchen table having another glass of milk they all made a determined effort not to allow the prospect of John's imminent departure appear to weigh too heavily on them. Even Anna – though desperately distraught – succeeded in her brave effort at not allowing her distressed state to be too glaringly obvious. However they all became increasingly conscious of a gradual build up of nervous tension in this quiet room.

Having noted how frequently Frans was glancing at his watch, John was not surprised when – after yet again consulting that (unaccountably tardy?) watch – he got to his feet, saying, 'I know it's a little early, but I think we should get going now, John.'

Gently disengaging his hand from Anna's nervously trembling grip, John rose and nodded in agreement. He felt sure Frans was thinking the same as he was: There was no point in dragging out this tense waiting any longer; no sense in any further delay in the ordeal that Anna had to face. He again nodded, 'All right, Frans, I agree. We might as well get on with it.' With a forced smile and a show of eagerness he defiantly enthused, 'Let's go!...'Let's get cracking!'

As Frans slipped a small haversack on to his back then lifted his loaded Sten-gun, John held out his hand to Blanche. He was amazed when, instead of shaking his hand in farewell, she impetuously threw her arms around him, gave him a quick, tight hug, gently kissed his cheek, then with tear-filled eyes gleaming in her sad face, emotionally and haltingly gasped, 'Oh, John, soon come back.. Come back soon to Anna ... and, and to us all .'

Deeply moved by this sudden, unexpected display of such strong feelings from a normally phlegmatically un-emotional Blanche, John gulped and blurted out his appreciation, 'Thank you, Blanche, thank you very much. Yes, I will come back to Anna and to you all, just as soon as I possibly can. I promise you I will.'

After staring at his unaccountable wife with surprise that appeared almost as great as John's Frans left the kitchen and went out into the mild autumn evening's blacked-out darkness. John and Anna immediately followed him.

Standing in the concealing dimness Anna and John eagerly hugged and kissed. Even while his entire being was apparently entirely engrossed in this emotional leave-taking from Anna, another part of John – his so thoroughly and efficiently war-trained brain – noted with approval Frans's wisdom in ensuring this lingering parting took place in the open air. Not only did the darkness obscure Anna's weeping distress, but it also ensured that – with no conscious effort – his own eyes were gradually adjusting to the nocturnal darkness after being accustomed to the kitchen's tile-gleaming brightness. That keen, war-honed brain registered that Frans was silently motionlessly standing not only at a thoughtfully discreet distance from Anna and him, but also at a spot where, as his eyes adjusted to the darkness he had an unobstructed view down the farm track and across the flat fields.

Not wanting to force Frans to have to hurry him with a subtle cough, John reluctantly eased Anna's clinging body away from him. 'Oh, Anna, you better go back to the kitchen. I must go now. I must not keep Frans waiting any longer.'

With a brave effort she unwound her arms from around his body, turned, and, sobbing heart-brokenly, blindly groped her way to the farmhouse door.

John also turned and, controlling his emotions, strode over to where Frans silently waited.

For a few moments neither man spoke, then Frans said, 'Conditions look perfect tonight. Hopefully all should go smoothly to plan.'

John had already noted the excellent conditions: the high thin cloud cover; no very bright, too revealing moon; a light, steady westerly breeze and no rain. 'Yes, on a night like this the Lysander pilot should have no trouble locating the correct field.'

'That's true, and we have our special secret means of guiding that R.A.F. pilot, too.' Frans tantalisingly grinned through the darkness, 'You will see it in use when we get there, John.'

Side by side they set out along the wide path that led directly to the ruins of Roelant's farm cottage. In solemn silence they hurried past that dark heap of rubble which held the stench of death and foul decay.

Frans now took the lead on a narrower path that skirted empty fields and ran alongside deep, slightly misty ditches. Then, again side by side, they more cautiously made their way along rutted farm tracks.

The track they were following led to a narrow minor road. Frans whispered an apology, 'I'm afraid we have to risk going along this road for a while, John. At least it seems completely deserted just now.'

John grinned in reply, 'Yes, and let's hope it stays that way!'.

Unfortunately it didn't.

After uneventfully walking for twenty minutes they suddenly found the road no longer innocently deserted. One or more lorries – the darkness made it impossible to made out their exact numbers – were standing stationary a slight distance ahead of them. As they peered apprehensively through the confusing gloom the sound of a few voices were carried to them with unmistakable clearness – German voices!

Frans whispered, 'Hear that, John? ...They are Kraut soldiers. Those are Kraut army trucks.'

'Yes, I hear them. There's no mistaking these hateful voices! Why are they stopped there? ...What are we going to do about them?'

Lying on the grassy slope at the roadside, Frans remained thoughtfully staring for a while before replying, 'I don't know why they've halted there. The trouble is that just beyond these Krauts is a canal bridge we have to cross. To go by the next nearest bridge would take us too far out of our way. We would be late getting to the field where we've to rendevous with the plane.'

Both men glanced at their watches then anxiously continued staring down the road. Through the dimness they made out a small group of figures huddled around a lorry. As if barking out an order, one German voice rose commandingly louder. Frans smiled with relief, 'Ah, now I know why they have stopped there. One lorry has a puncture. That Kraut in charge ordered them to quickly change the wheel. They shouldn't take long. We will just have to wait here until they move away.' Once again he rather nervously consulted his watch, 'As long as these Krauts are quick we should still reach our field in good time.'

But, for some unaccountable reason, even after they seemed to have finished changing the wheel these German soldiers did not move off. Frans and John could clearly see their glowing pin-points of red lights as they stood around and leisurely smoked. Frans quietly cursed, 'Oh, what the hell's keeping those bloody Krauts? Why don't they go away? If they don't move soon we are going to be late for our rendevous with the Lysander.'

They both knew that the plane's R.A.F. pilot would not hang around waiting for them if they did not arrive on time. It was much too dangerous for those aircraft to spend more than two or three vulnerable minutes on the ground in German-occupied Holland.

John was just about to add his equally worried concern to Frans's when his alert ears detected the distant sound of a motor-cycle. He listened for some moments then said, 'I think that motor-bike's coming this way.' He grinned at Frans, 'Let's hope this is a Kraut Military Policeman coming to get those other Krauts moving. I hope he gives them a severe bollocking for hanging around smoking and wasting time.'

As the motor-cyclist neared them all the Krauts's cigarettes were hastily extinguished. Then both John's hopes were realised as in obedience to loudly shouted curses, barked orders and angry cries of "Schnell...Schnell!" the rebuked German soldiers smartly climbed into their trucks and quickly got them moving. The small military convoy crossed the canal bridge and continued down the narrow road.

As the Krauts dimmed headlamps and faint tail lights got ever fainter, Frans and John rose from the damp grass and cautiously made for the canal bridge. Once satisfied that no sentries had been left at it, they ran across and hurried down the dark road in the wake of the now vanished Germans.

A few miles further on they came to a crossroads where this narrow minor road joined a wider, more major road. Two farm tracks also converged on this junction where, deprived of its too revealing signs, a signpost's stout wooden trunk stood bare and forlorn. Frans unhesitatingly turned into one of these tracks and, rapidly following it, they cautiously passed a few slumbering farm cottages. Fortunately, all the more substantial farms they had to pass were situated further back from this track.

As he stopped and took a quick breather, Frans gasped, 'We are a bit later than I planned, but we should be well on time before the plane lands. The field's not far from here now.'

Younger, fitter, less in need of a reviving rest, John grinned, 'Good ...good.' Then with sincere, praise added, 'You are a great guide, Frans. I would not have found the field without your excellent help.'

Although pleased, Frans disarmingly smiled, 'Thank you, John. Oh but its little enough I do to help defeat the Krauts compared to what I'm sure you have done, and will do to defeat them.'

After carefully climbing over a barbed-wire fence, jumping over a narrow ditch and walking across a large grassy pasture Frans stood and pointed, 'The Lysander will land in that next field. Four Dutch Resistance Fighters are waiting for us in that small wood beside the field.' He grinned, 'Do you see anything strange about that field, John?'

'Yes, I do. I was just going to ask about those two lines of strange white dots palely glowing in the dark there. What are they?'

Frans gave a subdued chuckle, 'Those are our secret equipment we use to help guide the R.A.F. pilot to the correct field. Don't you remember I mentioned them before?'

'Yes, I do. But what are they?'

'They are table-tennis balls coated with luminous paint. A good idea, eh? Very light and easy to place in position to mark a safe temporary landing strip. Easily seen and gathered up after being scattered by the plane's slip-stream, too.'

'Most ingenious!... I'm impressed, Frans. Was it you who thought up this unique idea?'

After modestly admitting it was, he elaborated, 'But other Patriots helped me get enough luminous paint and assisted with painting the table tennis-balls. You haven't seen them used before?'

'No, never. Every time I've been brought in or taken out of German-occupied France or Holland by Lysanders we've always been guided by flashlights held by Resistance Fighters.'

'Yes, I know, John. We also use torches to confirm it's safe to land. Now we better go to the small wood and join up with...'

Sudden loud, desperate, warning shouts in Dutch, and frantic cries of "Krauts! ... Krauts!" came from that wood and silenced Frans. They were immediately followed by roared German commands and the vicious clamour of many machine-guns. German rifles also joined in.

Amidst the alarming confusion of this noisy din John recognised a few brief bursts of the distinctive tinny clatter of Sten-guns. But that defensive Dutch Sten-gun fire was quickly brought to an abrupt end by the overwhelming might of the surrounding German firepower.

For a few seconds of breath-held silence Frans and John indistinctly saw the dark figure of one Dutch Patriot run over the landing field. Even as they desperately hoped he would successfully elude the Krauts the silence was again broken by vicious machine-gun fire. Staring with helpless dismay they saw streams of white tracer bullets converge on that urgently running figure. Many tracers missed their moving target and streaked far beyond him. But others found their mark and extinguished their glowing brightness in that poor, brave, patriotic Dutchman's stumbling body.

Carried by its own rushing momentum and the thrusting force of German bullets, that torn bleeding body skidded along damp grass and scattered a few of the luminous table-tennis balls.

Orders were again loudly shouted in German, and while two Wehrmacht soldiers dragged the dead body to the wood's concealing darkness other soldiers neatly replaced the scattered luminous balls in their correct positions in the glowing line of balls. Then in obedience to an officer's peremptory shouts of "Schnell!... Schnell! they hurried to join their comrades hiding amongst the dark fir trees.

All this violent action had lasted less than three minutes. John and Frans had been a little too far away to effectively intervene in it despite being desperate to go to the aid of those ambushed Patriots. As they crouched in the darkness with their weapons held ready John dolefully murmured, 'Try not to take their deaths too badly, Frans. There was nothing we could do to save them. If we had intervened we would only have been killed ourselves.'

'Yes, yes, I know, John. But it's terrible seeing our brave Dutch Patriots being killed by those bloody Krauts and being unable to help them. I would feel much better if we had at least managed to kill some Krauts!'

John placed a sympathetic hand on Fran's shoulder, 'I know, Frans, I know. I feel exactly the same. But such things happen in war and there's no sense in feeling any guilt over being unable to go to their aid.'

The sound of an approaching aircraft alerted both men to their remaining imperative duty. Frans eagerly whispered, 'Oh at last we can do some real good. We can warn that Lysander not to land here now and be captured or destroyed by those waiting hidden Krauts.'

John nodded, 'Yes, we must warn them off then run like hell before those Krauts catch us.'

Frans removed the small haversack from his back and withdrew a Very pistol. Selecting a cartridge he loaded the bulky, wide barrelled pistol. 'I'll fire this red flare to warn the Lysander pilot not to land.' As he started raising his hand to fire that warning flare John stopped him, 'Wait, Frans, wait. We better put more distance between those waiting Krauts and us before you fire that flare. They don't know we're here, but once we reveal ourselves by firing it they'll come after us like pursuing devils. We better go back across this pasture, jump the ditch and get over that fence before we fire the flare. The R.A.F. pilot will see it all right and we will have a good start on the Krauts.'

Frans instantly agreed. They turned to started hurrying back the way they had come

John got across the ditch and over the fence without any trouble, but much less experienced Frans got his trousers awkwardly snagged on the fence's top strand of barbed-wire. As he helped release an annoyed, cursing Frans, John grinned, 'It's all too easy to do yourself a painful and embarrassing injury on those damned barbs! It would have been much worse if you had got caught up like that with those Krauts chasing after you, eh?'

As he pulled free from the last barb Frans also managed to grin, 'Yes, the Krauts would have caught me, wouldn't they? Oh, John, obviously I've a lot to learn from you and much to thank you for.'

They hurried away down a familiar lane for a short time then halted and, staring with upturned faces, listened to the unseen Lysander aircraft circle high above them. They now saw falsely welcoming beams of German flashlights guide the R.A.F. pilot down to the twin rows of glowing table-tennis balls and to his doom.

Even as John started saying, 'You better fire that Very pistol now,'

Frans was raising the pistol. He pulled the trigger. The small rocket went hissing high into the dark night sky. It exploded and left the flare hanging and vividly glaring its warning red.

Despite the violent pounding of their hearts, the urgent gasps of labouring lungs and noisy thuds of clumping boots as they ran, both men clearly heard the Lysander's powerful single engine roar with boosted power as the pilot instantly reacted to that sudden warning flare and steeply climbed to gain the sanctuary of the high clouds. With luck, that plane would soon be back in England.

As they hurried past the apparently still soundly slumbering farm cottages edging the lane the noise of frantically barking dogs at nearby farms drowned the distant shouts of pursuing German soldiers.

Frans and John reached the deserted crossroads and then thankfully turned into and hurried along the narrow minor road which, all going well, would lead them safely back home. Only after they had crossed that canal bridge where German trucks had delayed them earlier, did they dare stop for – at least in Frans's case – an urgently needed breather. After sitting gasping for a few minutes he recovered sufficiently to spare some breath for talk. Perhaps rather eager to show John that he was not inexperienced, he hurriedly said, 'I'm relieved we've made it safely as far as this. I was worried those Krauts might throw a cordon around this area and place sentries at the crossroads and that bridge. That's why I decided we had to keep running until we passed both places.'

With genuine appreciation John praised Frans, 'Yes, that was a wise decision you made.' He did not bother telling that he, John, had already thought of the possibility of there now being German sentries placed there long before they reached the crossroads. He grinned instead, 'With our combined experience and expertise at fighting and evading those damned bloody Krauts we make a really great team.'

Frans was about to reply when he was silenced by the sound of a distant motor-cycle. Both men listened intently as that menacing noise drew nearer. They then gave grins of relief as that sound suddenly stopped. Judging by where that motor-cycle had halted they guessed that at least one German Military Policeman was now guarding that canal bridge they had recently crossed. Exchanging quick, congratulatory glances they silently shared in the triumphant pleasure of having their foresight in quickly getting across that bridge very quickly be now so clearly vindicated.

No longer running, but keeping to a good, more sustainable steady pace they continued their return journey through the now silent and apparently Kraut-free dark Dutch landscape. As usual, this homeward journey over the now more familiar route seemed to pass much quicker than the outward one had, and without any further incidents, they arrived back at the farmhouse not too long after midnight.

Chapter Twenty Eight

Before opening the kitchen door Frans smiled, 'Oh, John, you better brace yourself. When Anna sees you've returned to her instead of being in England she'll frantically throw herself at you!'

And she did. As he entered the kitchen she stared in unbelieving amazement for a moment then jumped to her feet wildly shouting, 'John!... Oh, John!.. Oh you've come back to me!' then desperately launched herself at him.

Although expecting this loving onslaught he staggered back under the fierceness of its impact. Instantly recovering, he eagerly embraced her trembling body while she even more eagerly grabbed and joyously hugged this strong, brave lover who had so miraculously returned to her.

As they feverishly kissed she wept tears of uncontainable happiness.

While gloriously engulfed in this loving embrace, John suddenly became aware of Blanche and Frans- their much less demonstrative greetings over – standing silently staring at Anna and him. He did not detect any disapproval in their undisguised stares, but, becoming aware that this was the first time they had seen the two of them so glaringly passionately reveal their great love, he felt rather embarrassed at being so keenly scrutinized. With gentle care he eased Anna away from him and whispered. 'We better control ourselves now, Anna. Blanche and Frans are waiting to speak to us.'

After fetching one more mug, Blanch poured warmed milk into four mugs on the kitchen table and said, 'Yes, come and sit here, John, and have a warm drink with us. Frans will tell us what has happened, why you have come back here and not gone to England.'

Before doing so, however, Frans – with sudden impulsive haste – left the room. He immediately returned, firmly holding his precious bottle of pre-war brandy. He smiled at John, 'I know I'm supposed to be keeping this brandy to celebrate the victorious end of this war with, but I think we deserve a drop of it tonight.' He invitingly held the bottle out to Blanche and Anna, but they firmly refused. After pouring a little into two glasses he handed one to John then, lifting his own glass, gave a toast: 'Here's to our four brave Dutch Patriots who heroically died tonight helping to ensure that one day their, and our, dear Netherlands will be freed from the vileness of Nazi tyranny.'

John clinked his glass against Frans's then with concurring heartfelt emotion added his toast: 'To all those brave Resistance Fighters who gave their lives for Freedom.'

While both men gulped their brandy, Anna and Blanche wiped away emotional tears – tears of sincere sorrow which also brightly gleamed with deep felt patriotic pride.

Following Frans's example, John upturned his glass and drained the last few drops of brandy into his mug of warm milk. To ease the emotional tension Frans smiled, 'Ah yes, John, warm milk with a drop of brandy is much better than the only other drink we have – that really vile ersatz coffee which tastes as if it's made of sawdust. Possibly it is!'

Once they all got settled around the kitchen table Frans, speaking in Dutch for Blanche's benefit, told of what had happened this evening and explained why John had not managed to return to England. With thoughtful consideration he played down the dangers they had faced by relating each incident with undramatic understatement.

When he finished, Anna hesitantly asked, 'Oh, Uncle Frans, were those ... those four poor, brave, Patriots the Krauts ambushed members of your own Resistance Group?'

'Oh no... No, they were all in a neighbouring group. 'My'- he paused and, affectionately smiling at his wife and niece, proudly included them – 'our Resistance Group is still intact, thank God.'

With passionate sincerity Blanche reverently echoed her husband, 'Oh yes... yes we must all thank God for that.'

Anna nodded her agreement then sadly asked, 'And were all four of those Patriots definitely killed? Is there no chance that some of them might have been captured or might even have managed to evade the Krauts?'

With gentle somberness Frans replied, 'No, Anna, I'm afraid there's almost no chance that any of them escaped. It is possible that some might have been wounded and captured.' He heaved a deep sigh, 'But to be wounded, captured and then tortured by the Gestapo would be a much worse fate than to be killed outright, wouldn't it? No, I feel sure we can be thankful that at least those brave Patriots were spared extreme torture then cruel execution.'

Anna translated these last few questions and answers into English then asked, 'What do you think, John?'

Taking his time about replying he exchanged a quick, understanding glance with Frans then returned his loving, sympathetic gaze to Anna while old memories flowed and swamped his mind. He remembered when, in late Autumn 1942, his S.B.S. team had been trained in extreme winter warfare and survival in the harsh environment of Scotland's high windswept Cairngorm Mountains. They were expertly instructed by superbly tough and fit and outstandingly brave and patriotic soldiers of the Free Norwegian Army. These truly impressive modern Vikings and a larger group of other British Special Forces were preparing for a top secret mission code named 'Operation Freshman'. That very hazardous, vitally important operation, he learned later, had also been about delaying the development of a German atom-bomb by destroying their stock of heavy- water at a Norwegian Hydro-Electric plant before that vital element could be shipped to dedicated German nuclear physicists who were desperately trying to produce an atom-bomb for Hitler before the Allies produced their own war-winning bomb.

The plan of 'Operation Freshman' was for those specially trained British Commandos to be towed in three gliders across the North Sea, land deep in German-occupied Norway, link up with waiting Norwegian Resistance fighters then destroy that scarce, vital supply of heavy-water.

Fortunately for John his S.B.S. team were withdrawn from the operation almost at the last minute: for things did not go as planned.

The story which eventually emerged from a host of vague rumours and contradictory reports was a deeply tragic one. Only two gliders made it to Norway, they crash landed and most of the Commandos were killed or seriously injured. The injured survivors, instead of having their wounds treated by the German S.S. soldiers who captured them, were subjected to hideous brutality. As they lay defenceless they were viciously kicked – their broken limbs being especially selected to receive the most vicious kicks! Finally their horrible agony ended when they were all shot in the head. These executing bullets were not ordered through any humane idea of ending their suffering, but to remove the need for all the immense trouble and waste of effort that taking these wounded prisoners over many wild, snowy mountainous miles to the nearest Norwegian town would entail.

Of course John revealed none of these secret vivid memories to Anna as he gave her hand a comforting squeeze then at last answered her question. 'Oh, Anna, I agree with Frans. I feel sure those four brave Dutch Patriots were all killed outright by those Krauts who ambushed them. And, yes, I'm sure that would be the fate they preferred rather than being hideously tortured then executed by sadistic Gestapo brutes.'

With instinctive unthinking reaction John's unengaged hand rose to his head and its index finger gently touched the reassuring feel of the agony-denying cyanide suicide pill secretly taped behind his ear. Pretending only to be scratching that ear, he smiled and, deliberately striking a more positive note, warmly praised Frans. 'You did very well, Frans, bringing that Very-pistol with you.' He explained to Anna what he guessed her uncle had modestly glossed over in his account of tonight's proceedings. 'By firing that red warning flare you saved the lives of the R.A.F. pilot and possibly two or three British or Dutch agents in that Lysander aircraft. You save them from being killed, or what we've agreed is worse, being captured and tortured then executed.'

Anna added her praise to John's, then with a glowing warmth that made a secretly pleased Frans give loud voice to depreciatory protests, she translated this genuine praise into Dutch and so enabled Blanche to quietly bask with honest pride at learning this further proof of her dear husband's resourceful, bravery. After bestowing quick, warm, appreciative smiles on Anna and John she lingeringly beamed her loving and admiring gaze at a disarmingly grinning Frans.

Her bright, plump, milkmaid cheeks blushingly glowed brighter as she suddenly realized just how long she had been sitting soppily staring at her husband while in turn he, John and Anna were watching her with gentle amusement. Her face flushed with further foolish confusion as almost guiltily she sprang to her feet and vivaciously cried, 'Oh, we better not sit here all night sillily staring at one another! Drink up your milk and give me your empty mugs. It's very late. It's time we all went to our beds.' Smiling at Anna and John with understanding tolerance she mischievously added, 'To our respective beds of course, eh?'

Happily grinning, Anna nodded in agreement – an agreement she had absolutely no intention of keeping.

As Frans started following Blanche out of the kitchen he halted and said to John, 'When I'm in town teaching at my school tomorrow I'll arrange for my Resistance Group's wireless operator to get in touch with the S.O.E. in London as soon as possible. We'll explain what happened tonight that made us warn that Lysander pilot not to land. I'll also ask for fresh instructions regarding your return to England.'

John nodded, 'Yes, of course. I'm entirely in your hands – your most competent and reliable hands.'

Making a gallant effort to hide her deep concern, Anna laughingly shouted after her uncle's retreating figure, 'Tell those S.O.E. officers not to be in too great a hurry to take John away from me again!

Soon afterwards the snugly stabled mare's nocturnal rest was once again disturbed by Anna and John's hasty entrance, their hurried clamber up the dark steps to the hayloft, their impatient, noisy groping progress to and through the secret room's concealed door and their urgently eager preparing of that room's familiar bed which held so many wondrous memories and promised even more delightful erotic pleasures – these further pleasures promising to be all the more wonderful by being so utterly unexpected.

The poor, sleep-denied horse was further disturbed by Anna's loud, helpless giggles and John's subdued chuckling laughter as by the flickering light of a solitary candle they wildly impatiently threw off their clothes then dived together on to the ghostly vague white sheet so invitingly spread over that large mattress in the cool room's dim corner.

After their naked bodies had desperately eagerly moved together and then sublimely fused together Anna lay for what seemed an eternity of immensely fulfilled euphoric time by John's, drowsily relaxing side. Then, her fantastic elation suddenly overwhelmed by heart-thudding panic, she passionately gasped, 'Oh, John... John, why can't we be together like this for ever? Why do you have to leave me?'

Startled out of his blissful euphoric state he hugged her trembling body more tightly and kissed her with gentle, reassuring tenderness, then lovingly gazing into her gleaming eyes whispered, 'Oh, Anna, you know I must, sooner or later, go back to England. We cannot avoid this. But once the war is won we shall be together for ever, I promise you we will. In the meantime we must make the most of this unexpected wonderful extra time we have together for as long as it lasts, mustn't we?'

'Yes, we must!... yes, we will!'

★ ★ ★

The following afternoon John again opened the stable door and stood expectantly waiting as Frans, returning from his day of teaching, wheeled in his bicycle, stooped to unfasten his cycle-clips, straightened up and said, 'I'm afraid there's not much news today, John. We got a coded message sent to London all right, but the only order my wireless operator received from the S.O.E. was to tune in at a certain time tomorrow. Hopefully we should get instructions about your return to England then.'

John laughingly echoed Anna's sentiment, 'Oh, there's no need for them to be in too great a hurry to move me from here, you know!'

Frans was not aware of it, but that morse signal he had sent to London, arriving on top of other information recently received, sent shock waves through the Special Operations Executive officers in control of all clandestine operations in The Netherlands. That message was one more bit of evidence pointing to something badly wrong in Holland. As these deeply worried officers painstakingly studied their amassed information all these reports fitted together like pieces of a large, complex jigsaw puzzle that was gradually revealing its story. That emerging picture was a most disturbing one.

The R.A.F. pilot and three S.O.E. agents in that Lysander aircraft Frans had prevented from landing and falling into German hands did not fully realize just how fortunate they had been, for a pilot and two agents in another Lysander had landed that same night in a different part of Holland and had all been killed by waiting German soldiers. And these were only the two latest incidents of the landing sites for these aircraft having been discovered by the Germans.

It was now certain that these tragic deaths of brave British and Dutch agents (including one highly skilled and experienced female agent) had not happened by chance – by simple bad luck. The exact locations of all those landing sites must have become known to the Germans by some means or other. Perhaps some members of various Dutch Resistance Groups who had 'disappeared' might have – under extreme Gestapo torture – revealed those secret sites, or pro-German traitors might have deliberately betrayed this sensitive secret information.

What had been suspected for some time now seemed almost certain – the code used by the S.O.E. in London and by Dutch Patriots had been broken by the Germans. Some coded messages supposedly coming from reliable Dutch agents were in fact being sent by Germans or by Dutch traitors who secretly collaborated with them. The safety of many true Dutch Patriots was now gravely threatened.

These officers in charge of all Dutch operations took their definite information and their grim suspicions and dark fears to the head of S.O.E. Deeply impressed by the profound concern of these resolutely unflappable experienced officers, he, in turn, decided to take those grave problems to an even higher authority. Actually he was secretly pleased to be able to impress these subordinate officers by making immediate use of the unique special power he possessed (one of only a privileged few) of having access to the Prime Minister at any time.

As soon as he was made aware of Special Operations Executive's deep concerns, Churchill instantly became as concerned as they were. After all, the S.O.E. was his own baby; a lusty infant he had brought to life in defiance of the strongest protests of the Foreign Office, the War Office and the Admiralty. The more deeply secret, more vitally important, more deadly dangerous the operations carried out by S.O.E.'s small band of outstandingly brave and dedicated volunteer agents the more they appealed to Winston's eternally youthful romantically flamboyant irrepressible nature.

It was quickly decided that all clandestine operations in The Netherlands would be drastically curtailed until the trustworthiness of every wireless operator had been thoroughly checked out and secure new codes could be brought into use.

Through a voluptuous cloud of Havana smoke that familiar, inspiring, slightly slurred bulldog growl rumbled forth, 'We must send no more of those brave agents to their deaths.' With a touch of almost tearful emotion that amazing old man growled with renewed vigour and rising passion, 'No, we must not deliver any more of those.. those most valiant heros into the blood-drenched hands of vile Nazi Thugs!'

Not for the first time, the head of S.O.E. was truly impressed by the depth of emotional feelings that lay behind old Winston's rumbling rhetoric.

It was really amazing how deeply, sincerely, and passionately he got involved in, and concerned over, the fate of heroically brave individuals even while he was being almost overwhelmed under the weight of the vast, and ever increasing, burdens and tremendous responsibilities he was forced to carry.

One of his greatest burdens was trying to fathom out the almost unfathomable deviously contorted machinations of his implacable pre-war foe, now turned great war time ally, Stalin; while at the same time he tried, using the utmost diplomatic skill and patient forbearance, to deal with the at times almost as devious political plots and intrigues of his supposed great friend and staunch ally, President Roosevelt.

Remembering the ill-fated Dardanelles Expedition of the last war – that tragic debacle he would never forget and which still gave him nightmares – he constantly worried over the planned Allied assault on German-occupied Europe next year. He knew only too well how dangerous, how chancy and uncertain was any amphibious landing on an enemy shore; and the French coast was much more formidably defended than the Turkish coast had been.

So, with deep anxiety but keenly eager excitement, he threw himself into overseeing and often – to the great annoyance of General Eisenhower – directly interfering in the mass of meticulously detailed planning that was in progress to ensure that, as far as was humanly possible, the Allies D-Day landings in France would succeed and after establishing secure beach-heads these allied armies would break out and liberate all Western Europe.

Already worrying about post-war Europe, Churchill dreaded to think of the possible results of any failure of the D-Day landings. Not only would many thousands of British and American lives be lost, but the delay in liberating Western Europe might well result in Stalin ordering his all too victorious Soviet Army not to stop at invading and conquering all Germany, but to smash on and liberate, then subjugate, all of Western Europe as well. This all too possible scenario gave Winston even more terrible nightmares than the failure of the Dardanelles did.

Now on top of all those worries were intelligence reports that caused even greater worry. This latest top-secret intelligence suggested that the German scientists desperately trying to develop an Atomic-bomb for Hitler were greatly increasing their efforts. They had increased production of heavy-water from Norwegian Hydro-Electric plants and under tight security were transporting that vital material to new secret research laboratories being completed deep underground near the remote village of Haigerlock in Southern Germany.

Other reliable reports warned that at least two of Japan's leading physicists had arrived in Germany and by adding their expertise on nuclear fission to that of German scientists, hoped to produce an Atomic-bomb before the Americans did.

Another worry was the extent that the British, including Churchill, were being kept in the dark by Roosevelt about what progress – or lack of progress – his scientists were making in the development of what should be a truly devastating, war-winning weapon.

And only yesterday Churchill had received yet another most disturbing intelligence report. It was well known amongst those British and Americans who really were 'in the know' that the Germans were developing entirely new types of weapons. These 'Vengeance Weapons' –VI flying – bombs and V2 rockets – were, so Hitler repeatedly assured his people, even at this late stage of the war, when the tide of victory seemed to be flooding unstoppably in the Allies favour, yet going to win the war for the Germans.

This hardly seemed likely. But now there was this latest report that suggested the Germans were actively planning a much larger, longer range rocket. Only London would be within range of the German V2 rockets but with this immensely powerful new rocket – if they got sufficient time to develop it – they could hit Moscow and even New York or Washington. And there were even plans for that rocket to carry not only tons of high explosive but, if their nuclear scientists fulfilled their promises, the German Atomic-bomb.

As he once more pondered over those truly appalling possibilities, Churchill – seemingly introspectively thinking out loud – indistinctly mumbled, 'Herr Hitler must not be given time to develop these... these fiendishly monstrous new weapons. D-Day must succeed! Our vast British and American armies must sweep from France into Western Germany while Stalin's formidable Red Army smash through Poland into Eastern Germany, and between them in their vast irresistible closing vice crush to death the vile, venomous Nazi viper'

As the head of Special Operations Executive, one of those few who were fully 'in the know' attentively and admiringly stared at the Prime Minister he thought of the immense weight of awesome burdens that old man willingly carried and again reflected that although he could often be really maddening, old Winston truly was an amazing man – was a remarkably and uniquely great man!

As he finished reading through the S.O.E. file on the disturbing situation in The Netherlands, Churchill lovingly lit up another huge cigar, no less lovingly gulped from a bumper glass of malt whisky then suddenly asked, 'What about that operation, what was it's name? ... 'Operation Blenheim', wasn't it? ... dealing with those treacherous Dutch Atomic Boffins?'

'No, sir, its code name was 'Operation Waterloo'.'

Winston grinned widely, 'Operation Waterloo or Blenheim, they're much the same, aren't they? Both tremendous British victories, eh?'

'Yes, sir, they were; they certainly were!' The head of S.O.E. returned his grin, he knew how proud Winston was of his illustrious ancestor, the Duke of Marlborough, the victor of Blenheim. 'But 'Blenheim' was the correct reply to the coded challenge of 'Waterloo'.'

'Ah yes, I knew Blenheim was involved in some way! ....Well, how did 'Operation Waterloo' go?'

After hearing of the part success, part failure of that operation, Winston asked, 'So, as far as you know, only one member of that S.B.S. team has survived?'

'Yes, sir.' He explained the failure to get that survivor home by Lysander plane last night.

'Oh, I see. Well with all the uncertainties in Holland we must not risk sending another plane for him. But get that brave solitary survivor home for de-briefing as soon and as safely as you possibly can.'

'Yes, Prime Minister, I'll see to it at once.'

As he puffed out one more vast cloud of cigar smoke, Winston said, 'We need every scrap of information he can give us about why that one Dutch traitor survived. We need to know if there's any way we might still get at him to finally eliminate him before he gives yet more help to the Germans in their desperate endeavours to develop what threatens to be the ... the most fearsome ... the most terrifyingly awesome of all weapons, their Atomic-bomb.' Winston gave a profound solemn sigh then, after fortifying himself with another generous gulp of whisky, declared with passionate feeling, 'That brave S.B.S. sailor... every one of those most valiant S.B.S. sailors truly deserve our utmost endeavours to get them safely back to England from whatever hazardous missions they most nobly and heroically volunteered for!'

'Oh yes, sir, I entirely agree!... I'll do absolutely all I possibly can to get him back safely.' As he left the Prime Minister's room the head of S.O.E. was once more amazed at this latest revelation of Old Winston's real concern over the fate of one brave individual even while in the midst of making immense decisions which would affect the lives of millions and shape world history. Yes, Winston Churchill truly was an amazing man!

Chapter Twenty Nine

So the orders Frans received from London the following day were for him and his Resistance Group to quietly lie low until it was safe for them to be re-activated. He was instructed to arrange for John's return to England by whatever route he thought remained secure. Frans decided John must return by sea, via Sweden. Although longer and slower, this route should be the safest. It had been used successfully a number of times before.

These orders and warnings from London confirmed the much less reliable information Frans had gleaned from rumours being nervously passed about between various Resistance Groups. These whispers of losses and possible betrayal amongst the ranks of some of their groups were very disturbing. In many Patriots they sowed seeds of doubt about who could be trusted and who couldn't. It resolutely armed others with grim determination to ferret out all traitors and by taking merciless action against them avenge the deaths of the true Patriots who had been so vilely betrayed.

Pulling a yellow card from an inside jacket pocket, Frans smiled at John, 'What's your name?... your Norwegian name?'

Beaming a return smile, John unhesitantly replied, 'My name's Claus Idland – known to me friends, of course, as "Santa Idland!" That's my name on my Norwegian Merchant Seaman's faked identity documents, isn't it?'

'Yes, it is. You've remembered it well. Now add this card to those papers. It's already got your Norse name and signature on it. It's a pass to get you into the docks at Rotterdam. There's a small Dutch cargo ship with a completely trustworthy captain and crew berthed in one of those docks who expect to sail to Stockholm early next week. You will be on that ship. That's how you are going back home, by the long but safe route via Sweden. I don't know how you get to England from Sweden, but no doubt you will receive further instructions once you arrive there.'

As he put that yellow card with his other forged documents John asked, 'How do I get to Rotterdam docks? Do I travel furtively at night?'

'On no, John. Dressed in those civilian clothes and protected by your identity papers showing you are a Norwegian merchant sailor returning to his ship in those docks you will take my bicycle and cycle quite openly by daylight. You will meet up with a Patriot on the outskirts of Rotterdam. He will shelter you for one night, then early the following morning you will cycle with him to the docks. He works there and you will arrive when many others are turning up for work. That yellow card should get you past the police and the German sentries at the dockyard gates without any trouble. The Patriot will direct you to your ship and then, hopefully, you will have a pleasant, uneventful leisurely cruise to Sweden.'

Frans grinned, 'I almost wish I was going with you, John. I could do with a holiday. A relaxing cruise to and from Sweden would be very pleasant before winter sets in.' He gave a rueful sigh then added, 'I will show you the route to Rotterdam on your map. You must study and memorise that route. I will also show you on a detailed plan of Rotterdam docks exactly where your ship is berthed so that if anything happens to your Dutch guide you should manage to find it by yourself, all right?'

'Yes, of course. Thank you Frans. I'm impressed by your thoroughness. It gives me great confidence that things will go well.'

Frans modestly grinned, 'Thank you, John! Yes, I will make sure you are well briefed before you leave here. Oh, and another thing, John, you must remember that if you are stopped by German soldiers you are a Norwegian sailor and you only speak your native language, plus perhaps a few hesitant words of English. Should an English speaking Kraut ask you questions in that language you must pretend you don't understand him.'

John nodded, 'Yes, I'll remember that.' He smiled, 'I've been practising my "Norwegian in the last few days, too. What do you think of this: "Has ta iver deeked a spuggy on't skurl spoot? Does that sound Norwegian enough for you, Frans?'

'Yes, like real Norwegian or … or what do you English call it? … like Duble-Dutch? What does that mean, if anything?'

'It means: "Have you ever seen a sparrow on a school spout? It's in my native Cumberland's broadest local dialect, which I believe contains a lot of Norse-like words. Probably these Norse words linger on from when the Vikings ruled much of Scotland and Northern England. Anyway let's hope I don't have to put my "Norwegian" to the test. And I hope to God I don't meet a German soldier who's been based in Norway and has learned that language!'

Two days later, a Friday, John again met Frans as he returned from teaching at his school. Not waiting to be asked, Frans said, 'Yes, John, I've got news for you. Two items of news, actually. You leave here next Monday, spend the night near Rotterdam, then go into the docks and on to your ship on Tuesday. You will be hidden somewhere in the ship out of sight of any Kraut officials until it sails for Sweden on Wednesday. Everything is fully arranged for you.

'The other item is more unexpected. My brother is coming for a short visit this weekend. He is Anna's father. He comes occasionally – very occasionally – to see her.' Frans gave what to John seemed a rather cynical, disparaging grin, 'Of course this farm belongs to him. Perhaps he comes not so much to see his daughter, or even me, as to check up on how well and profitably we are running it for him. Anyway you will have to keep entirely out of his sight all the time he's here.'

John asked the question he had asked before when Frans had spoken about his older brother, 'Is he not to be trusted, then?'

Frans sighed deeply, 'Oh, John, I don't really know. I've already told you how profoundly impressed he had been by the Germans when he visited their country before the war. He greatly admired the economic prosperity, the strict discipline and patriotic fervour Hitler had given his people. I very much doubt if he still admires Hitler so much after all the misery he has inflicted on Holland and all Europe ... I fervently hope not.' He again sighed, 'Oh, it makes everything so confusingly uncertain when brother doesn't know if he can trust brother, nor a daughter know if she can trust her father.'

Remembering his experiences with various French Resistance Groups, when there was great concern over just how trustworthy certain members were, John – with deep sympathetic understanding – said, 'Yes, it will be much better for all concerned if he does not see me; does not discover you are Patriots helping me escape.'

Much more brightly Frans said, 'Well, that's settled then.' He

193

smiled, 'And you won't be kept away from Anna long, John. Only one night. My brother will sleep in the spare bedroom next to Anna's, so she better keep to her own bed that night; her father might hear her if she got up and went to join you in your secret room.

'He should arrive at lunch time on Saturday. He will travel by bicycle. Like almost all Dutchmen he gets no petrol for his car. If he still has his car, that is. It might well have been requisitioned by – his friends? – the Krauts. He will leave after lunch on Sunday. So Anna and you will still have your last romantic night together before you leave on Monday morning, all right?'

John nodded his agreement and thanks then gave a conspiratorial grin, 'I assure you that Anna and I will try to make the most of our last night together.' Of course he did not say so, but he ruefully knew that any attempt at lovemaking that last night would be severely inhibited by it now being Anna's 'awkward' time of month.

'Oh, I've just remembered, John, there is a third item of news for you. Blanche will not be here at the farm during the time my brother's staying at it. She's going to visit her mother who is getting old and frail and recently had a bad turn. Blanche is anxious to see how she is getting on, so she's going to spend that weekend with her. Blanche and my brother have never got on well together; she thinks that he – being a professor – looks down on her as being little more than a simple, poorly educated milkmaid. So it's just as well that they won't be here together. By seeing her mother and missing my brother she cleverly does two things at once, doesn't she? What is the English saying for doing that, John? I cannot quite remember it.'

'She kills two birds with one stone. Yes, that's very clever and most diplomatic of her.'

'Oh, and Blanche should be back by Sunday evening, so she will see you before you leave on Monday morning.'

'Good! I would hate to leave without seeing her and thanking her for all the excellent food she's given me.' John paused then grinned, 'Of course I've thanked her before, haven't I? How many more times will I thank her, leave here, then return, I wonder?'

'Who can tell? In the midst of this war we can be sure of nothing, no matter how well we plan.' Frans grinned, and, modestly proud of his knowledge of some British poetry, recited, ' "The best-laid schemes of mice and men gang aft a-gley", as your English poet said, John.'

194

John heartily laughed, 'Oh, Frans, you better not let any fiery Scotsmen hear you attribute that poem to an *Englishman!*'

★ ★ ★

That Friday night as Anna and John snugly intimately lay side by side in the secret room's cool autumnal darkness Anna valiantly strove to restrain her tears, tried not to let her sorrowful misery at the prospect of John leaving her on Monday morning become too overwhelmingly obvious. The thought that this was their second last night together before he left her to return to England and from there go on to face whatever dangers the hazards and chances of this most foul and savage war threw at him, filled her with trembling horror.

And, however foolishly, she could not help almost guiltily feeling her dreadful sorrow at his leaving being terribly compounded by her inability – due to that damned 'curse of Eve' – to make their last two nights together be fully fulfilled in wondrous, desperately glorious final acts of sexual love. Despite John repeatedly assuring her that it made no difference to his tremendous love for her, she still could not stop feeling this terrible guilty sense of having let him down.

Once again John reassured her. 'Oh, Anna, please don't get too distressed over this. I assure you we will gloriously make up for this when we are married after the war.'

Despite the room's dimness, she clearly saw the roguishness of the grin with which he said, 'I will patiently and chastely wait until then, I promise you I will.'

She also grinned through the darkness as she thanked him with an extra hug and, moving her lips to his, tenderly lovingly whispered, 'I, too, promise I will chastely wait for you to return to me.' She even managed an almost lighthearted giggle, 'But I don't promise that I'll wait patiently.' She again passionately hugged and kissed him, 'Oh no, John, I won't wait patiently – I'll be most terribly most anxiously impatient for you to return to me!'

Delighted by her rather nervous, but hopefully tension-easing giggling, John again gave a roughish grin, 'Anyway perhaps it's just as well I am not voluptuously indulging in too much sex just now. Probably it's best that I conserve my body's energy, keep me eyes bright and clear and hold myself wonderfully fit and perfectly attuned in readiness for my coming journey.' Then, realizing the foolishness of reminding her of the nearness of their parting, he hurriedly joked, 'So you must not upset yourself by regretting that at present you cannot use your Cleopatra-like irresistible powers to sensuously seduce me and ensnare me further in your web of erotic charms.'

His delight increased as he noted the more relaxed, more genuinely amused way in which she gigglingly asked, 'Oh, John, I'm not really such a seductive Cleopatra-like vamp, am I?'

'Oh, no, not quite! But you truly are a bewitching temptress, you know!'

With more giggles, ones that resolutely attempted to smother her threatening tears, she gaily gasped, 'Oh, John, I only wish I could really bewitch you. I would keep you snuggly here with me forever. You would never return to face the terrible horrors and dangers of your brutal war.'

'Oh, Anna... Anna, you know there's nothing I would rather do than stay here loving you forever. But... but you know I cannot. I must do my duty. I could not live with myself if I didn't! And, Anna, you know in your heart that you couldn't truly love me – you would even secretly despise me – if I was to cravenly linger here, abandon my duty and cowardly desert my brave comrades, don't you?'

With some silently escaping tears displacing the last of her tremulous giggles, she reluctantly agreed, 'Oh, I know, John. I do not really mean to play the part of an erotic Cleopatra selfishly ensnaring her Mark Antony and through an excess of hedonistic sensuous pleasures emasculate his will-power and deprive him of his sense of duty.'

John laughed, 'Emasculate your great lover?... I should damn well hope not!'

More giggles greeted this sally and he made a deliberate effort to increase her mirth by continuing, 'Oh, Anna, I hate to hear you use that word. Any talk of emasculation brings me out in a cold sweat; raises frightful fears of losing something much more precious than my will-power!'

As he hoped she would, Anna now went into worry-drowning helpless fits of giggles. His laughter eagerly joined in and their sadly constrained, but love-glowing bodies trembled together with wondrous, life-enhancing mirth.

After a while Anna managed to gasp. 'Oh, John, thank you for your love – your glorious great love. Oh, truly our wonderful love "beggars all description" doesn't it?'

'Yes, it does. It certainly does.' Recognising that quotation, John tried to answer with another appropriate quote. 'Yes, Anna, you know that "age will never wither" our supreme love nor your great beauty, don't you?'

A few days ago Anna had suddenly realised how amazingly relevant the theme of Shakespeare's 'Antony and Cleopatra' was to John and her present situation. Almost like Cleopatra's ensnaring love for Mark Antony and his obsessive love for her, Anna's passionate love of John and his great love of her could – if he stayed in ease and comfort here much longer – seriously weaken his will to return and again face the challenges and dangers of war. After re-reading that play she got John to read it. They then exhaustively and animatedly discussed its astounding relevance to themselves.

John had summed up his feelings by saying, 'Yes, Anna, it's easy to see that my loving you so much could result in my fearing death too much!'

He did not say so, but he thought it probably just as well that he was leaving this too hospitable Dutch farm on Monday morning.

Finally their sense of humour came to their aid and they had laughingly ridiculed themselves – a Royal Navy sailor of humble rank and a schoolteacher become dairymaid – for daring to foolishly compare themselves to a mighty Roman General and an immortal Egyptian Queen.

They did not know it, but soon – very soon – John would face a terrible dilemma; would have to make a tremendous decision ... a decision the consequences of which could be more historically momentous than any decision made by that proudly voluptuous Egyptian Queen or that besotted Roman General.

Chapter Thirty

Next day, the Saturday when Fran's brother was due to arrive, Blanche and Anna started the morning milking even earlier than usual. Although trying not to show it, Blanche was apprehensive at the thought of leaving Anna to do tomorrow's milking by herself. Like most skilled, dedicated milkers she thought no one could milk her cows half as well as she did. She would be most upset if she returned to discover that those unfaithful cattle had given as much milk to Anna as they gave to her.

Anna was intuitively aware of Blanche's concern; quietly amused she decided not to tell her if she got as much milk as she usually did. And, in the most unlikely event of her getting more milk than Blanche, she would not boast of this, but would, with diplomatic tact, keep this great triumph a deep secret.

Frans and John agreed it was good for Anna to be kept busy in the dairy and then with preparing food for her father's meals. The busier she was kept the less time she had to mope over the rapidly approaching time for John's departure.

Soon after breakfast, Blanche prepared to leave on her visit to her sick mother. Frans wheeled her bicycle out from the stable, then John was surprised to see her neatly load packs of her excellent home-made butter and cheese into the wickerwork basket fixed to the cycle's handlebar. Concealing a smile, he could not help thinking that surely this was a glaring case of 'taking coals to Newcastle', for he knew that Blanche's parents, with the help of their son and his wife, ran a large dairy farm. Then with sudden startling certainty he realized that Blanche, by taking these examples of her best butter and cheese, was determined to prove to her mother and – much more importantly – to her sister-in-law just how excellent her dairy products were. They were at least equal to her mother's best product and un-comparably better than what she had seen and tasted of her sister-in-law's greatest efforts.

Blanche cycled away, Anna returned to the kitchen and Frans gave John a final briefing on what was going to happen that day. 'We expect my brother, Anna's father, to arrive shortly after noon. You will have to keep out of his sight all the time he's here. If he follows his usual routine – and he is a methodical man who likes to keep to set patterns – he will go over the farm accounts with me most of the afternoon then we'll stroll around a few fields and he will cast his (as he thinks) expert eye over the dairy cattle.' Glancing at his watch he smiled, 'Now I better go and devote a few hours hard labour to sorting out these accounts ready for my brother's approval.'

Later that morning Anna hurried over to the secret room with dishes of food for John. This lovingly prepared food would sustain him during the time he remained hidden from her father.

With her face most attractively flushed from hectic unaccustomed work at the kitchen's hot stove and with eyes gleaming with modest, smiling pride at her culinary success, then alluringly flashing their love at him, an enraptured John thought she had never looked more beautiful.

For a short, delicious time they eagerly hugged and passionately kissed. Then, with a supreme effort, John loosened his hugging grip and Anna broke away from that wondrously enveloping virile embrace of his.

In a nervous flurry of desperate haste she opened the door and gasped, 'Oh. John... John, I must go back to the kitchen. My soup will be boiling over. I've still a lot to do before my father arrives.'

John grinned his apologies, 'I'm sorry I've detained you here too long, Anna, but you know it's your own fault for being so bewitchingly beautiful!... Yes, you better hurry back to your housewifely duty of sweating over Blanche's abandoned kitchen stove.'

Secretly he was somewhat surprised and very pleased at this evidence of her skill in the kitchen now it was not dominated by her aunt's commanding presence. Rather selfishly he thought this revelation of Anna's domestic skills bode well for the comfort of his future married state.

After accompanying her to the kitchen door John started to return to his secret room then he halted and stared around him. It was a lovely calm, bright autumn day. Too good a day to be completely wasted indoors, he thought. I will have to hide away all afternoon and evening, so I think I'll take a gentle stroll where I'll be able to see Anna's father arriving but remain hidden myself.

Standing amongst a small clump of concealing fir trees he was thinking it was about time to head back to his secret room when he became aware of unfamiliar movement. He intently stared. Sure enough a solitary cyclist was coming along the farm track. After moving further back into the dark trees he continued expectantly staring at that slowly approaching cyclist who must be Anna's father. This was just about the time he was expected to arrive.

It was not by mere chance that the sunshine sliding into the fir trees did so at John's back and sent bright blinding lances slanting into the eyes of the steadily nearing cyclist. Ever more clearly this crisp autumnal light revealed the glaring brightness of what seemed a mass of white hair and a wild flowing white beard.

John's heart gave a sudden violent thud! He gasped in amazement!

He recognised that white haired, white bearded cyclist. He was Professor Willem Maurik, that treacherous Dutch nuclear scientist who was helping the Germans to develop an atomic-bomb. Had 'Operation Waterloo' gone as planned, Lieutenant Smith would have killed that vile traitor at the same time as John had shot Professor Johannes de Waal, that other despicable traitor.

John had never expected to see Professor Maurick again. But there he was, amazingly turned up, apparently quite innocently cycling to that farm... To his farm?... Was that possible? Could he really be the owner of that farm? Was he Anna's father and Frans's brother? Surely such a traitor could not be brother and father of those two completely trustworthy Dutch Patriots?... No, no, surely that was impossible!

His astounded mind desperately tried to deny the evidence of his senses. Frantically searching for a possible explanation he wondered if that Professor turning up like this was a pure coincidence and that the expected cyclist – Anna's father, Frans's brother – had still to appear. He fervently hoped so. But that pious hope was quickly dashed as he heard Frans and Anna, who were waiting at the farm gate, loudly welcome that cyclist, and there was no mistaking the eager warmth with which that Professor hugged and paternally kissed Anna. Then the enthusiasm of the handshaking exchanged between him and Frans definitely suggested brotherly affection.

John's mind was a turmoil of confusion. He was torn by conflicting emotions. How could he possibly reconcile his great love for Anna, his sincere friendship with Frans, with his deep hatred of that despicable traitor who was Anna's father, Frans's brother?

How could there possibly be – as there appeared to be – harmonious compatibility between vile treachery and noble patriotism? This seemed as unlikely as an innocent rabbit harmoniously co-existing with a hungry, predatory stoat.

With an urgent effort he tried to reconcile the glaring irreconcilability of the profound motives and deep emotions that implacably divided Patriot from traitor … surely it must be impossible for these opposites to live together, even if only for a short time? This impossibility that seemingly was happening at the farm resulted in even greater confusion, even wilder tumult in John's mind.

Then his S.B.S. training – that fantastic intensive training that brought not only his body, but even more importantly, his mind to the highest possible peak of self-reliant fitness – took over and sternly issued imperative orders.

Immediately obeying these commands he sat at the foot of a fir tree, leant his back comfortably against its rough bark and, taking a few deep slow breaths, deliberately relaxed both mind and body. Then with cool, calm, logical deliberation he reviewed all the anxious uncertainties the arrival of that traitor had brought with him.

He quickly came to what he felt certain must be the correct conclusion … that Anna and Frans (and of course Blanche) were completely unaware of Professor Maurik's terrible treachery, just as he must be entirely ignorant of them being patriotic Resistance fighters.

John's certainty that this was the true explanation gave him immediate intense relief. He had never had – he never could – really believe that Frans and Anna might be – like their brother/father – secret traitors. No, he convincingly reassured himself, such treachery from such people was utterly impossible! If he could not completely trust them, he could trust absolutely no one!

Now, in further obedience to his S.B.S. training, he brought reasoning logic to calmly think over his situation and decide what course of action he must follow. Firstly he must be absolutely certain that was Professor Maurik he had just seen. He thought about 'Operation Waterloo' and conjured up a vividly accurate picture of that professor arriving by bicycle at the offices of that German controlled research establishment near Rotterdam. He compared that image with that of the man who had arrived at this farm a few minutes ago. There was no shadow of doubt. They were the one and the same person! ... The same white hair and flowing white beard; the same rotund figure still awkwardly seemingly perched high on his sturdily solid bicycle with short fat legs only reaching the pedals with straining effort. There was no mistaking that falsely benign, chubby-cheeked, jolly Father Christmas appearance that Commander Richardson had in his briefings repeatedly warned John's S.B.S. team not to be fooled by.

Yes, that undoubtedly was Professor Willem Maurik who had arrived just now.. And, yes, he must be Anna's father, be Frans's brother.

The fact of that close relationship greatly complicated things for John. If it wasn't for it, his course of action would be perfectly straightforward. With no hesitation, no qualms, no anxious questioning doubts he would shoot that obnoxious traitor dead at the first opportunity.

That clearly was his straightforward duty. Was what his logically reasoning war-trained brain urged him to do. But his reasoning brain was in violent conflict with the passionate emotions of his distraught heart.

If he did his duty, killed the traitor, how would this affect Anna? Would the bullets that killed her father just as surely kill her as well? Surely they would kill her love for him... how could she love her father's killer? The death of her father at the hands of her lover would plunge her into another, much deeper, nervous breakdown; a drastic mental collapse from which she might never recover – might never want to recover. Perhaps she would only find peace in death.

And yet if he did not kill her father, how would that compassionate act of mercy affect the war? What would be the wider implication of sparing that treacherous professor's life? If he was as great a nuclear physicist as Commander Richardson had emphatically stated he was and might be a tremendous help to the Germans in developing their atomic-bomb, then by not killing him might he, John, alter the course of world history by allowing the Germans to get an atomic weapon before the British or Americans did? Might he help the Germans win the war?

Even John's most thorough, most intensive S.B.S. training had not trained him to face such a tremendous dilemma; had not prepared him to make such a momentous decision that could effect the lives of millions for years to come. Such life or death, war-winning or war-losing decisions were normally taken by Presidents, Prime Ministers, Generals and Admirals, not by a lowly Royal Navy leading-seaman!

And yet a decision had to be made. There was no escaping that stark fact. He, and no one else, had to make that decision ... and make it soon!

'He, and no one else,' was that true? With something like a surge of immense relief he thought of a way he could legitimately share that fateful decision making with one other person, someone completely trustworthy, steady and reliable – Frans.

Then he had doubts. Would it be fair to thrust this knowledge of his brother's treachery on to him? How would Frans Maurik react to this terrible news? (John now knew this to be his correct name – previously, for greater security that surname had never been revealed to him).

After anxiously pondering these questions for a while he decided that not only would it be a great relief to share this knowledge, this momentous decision-making, but it was clearly his duty to warn Frans that his brother was a pro-German collaborator who could not be trusted. And as Frans was a science teacher, he might be able to give John some enlightening insight into his brother's obscure world of nuclear physics; could possibly give him some guidance on how important his brother's expertise might be in helping the Germans develop their atomic-bomb. Then, armed with whatever information Frans could give him, he, John, would have to make that fateful decision – would Anna's father, Professor Maurik, live or die?

Chapter Thirty One

For the remainder of that Saturday John stayed hidden in his secret room above the stable, out of sight of Professor Maurik.

He appreciatively enjoyed the food Anna had lovingly cooked for him. He gave his room a final check over and tidy up. He again cleaned and fully loaded his automatic pistol then firmly screwed the long, awkward silencer on to the end of the gun's barrel. But for most of the time, with self-imposed calmness, he sat or lay and physically rested. Again with strictly enforced calm he repeatedly reviewed the huge moral problems forced on him by his knowledge of the abysmal treachery of Anna's father, Frans's brother. His final conclusion was that there really was only one honourable course open to him. He must do his duty. He must kill Professor Maurik! (He grimly queried just how accurate was that word 'honourable'?)

But, yes, he must kill him no matter what terrible personal traumas that cruel but necessary act would cause Anna, Frans and himself. The imperative need for the greater good of humanity far outweighed the lesser personal considerations of the anguish caused to a few distraught humans.

With perhaps a touch of un-typical, but understandable weakness, John was pleased he need not make any absolutely final decision right now. Frans had promised to come and chat with him in his secret room once his brother had gone to bed. Tired after his cycle ride from Rotterdam, he was expected, as usual, to retire shortly after ten. While looking forward to having Frans's company, John also felt apprehensive over how he would react to the appalling news he must disclose to him about his brother's terrible treachery At least he had had ample time to plan the best way to break this news to him.

By ten-thirty Frans was comfortably seated opposite John in the candle-lit secret room. Smiling with tolerant amusement he told of the at times rather constrained atmosphere between his brother and himself. 'He was put in a bad mood by the farm accounts not showing anything like the profit he unreasonably expected. He seemed to think we should demand more money from the Germans for the butter and cheese we are forced to sell to them. I patiently explained we were lucky to get any money from the Krauts and not have all the food forcibly requisitioned without any payment.'

This was John's chance ... he seized it. 'Does your brother still admire the Germans then, Frans?'

All hint of amusement vanished from Frans's face. He frowned. He hesitated. Then with a sigh he said, 'Oh, I don't really know, John. We – Anna and I – did not get much out of him. Apart from his remark about getting more money from the Krauts for our food, he carefully avoided all talk of the war and of Germany and the Germans. So did we. We did not want to upset him. Despite his stoutness and ruddy faced jolly appearance, he seemed to be suffering under some nervous strain. He was rather subdued most of the time.'

'Could his nervous strain be caused by his troubled, his guilty conscience, I wonder.' John asked.

'His guilt over his great pre war admiration of the Krauts, do you mean?'

'Yes, perhaps that. But I'm sure he also has a much more definite reason for having a deeply troubled guilty conscience!'

'What do you mean?' Frans stared mystified at John then repeated, 'What do you mean? What do you know about my brother? Do you know something about him that I don't?'

John solemnly sighed, 'Yes, I'm afraid I do, Frans. I know a lot about your brother – Professor Willem Maurik, and none of it to his credit!'

Frans, amazed, silently stared for a few moments then gasped, 'How do you know his name? ... Did Anna reveal it?... Has she unwisely been talking about her father?'

John shook his head, 'No, Anna never told me. She's said nothing about her father. I was told his name in England.'

'In England? ... But.. But, who told you?.. Why were you given his name in England?'

'Before I tell you that, Frans, will you please tell me what you think your brother is doing, what he's working at? This is important. I need to know.'

More deeply mystified than ever, Frans again silently stared then openly, honestly, replied, 'My brother is working at Rotterdam University. He is a professor, a physicist. He teaches physics to his students.'

'Is that all he does? Are you sure of that?'

'Yes, as far as I know. But of course I don't know if he's doing anything else. He might also be involved in independent research. Most science professors are. But his work is another thing, like the war and the Krauts, that he does not speak about when he's here.'

John solemnly nodded, 'Yes, and there is a very good reason he does not talk about his work .. his despicable work!'

' "His despicable work ?' Frans's voice rose with his rising anger, 'Oh, for God's sake, John, stop bemusing me anymore! What do you know about him that I don't? Tell me now. Tell me how you knew his name in England.'

John apologised, 'I'm sorry, Frans, I didn't mean to upset you; although I'm afraid the news I've got for you will be very upsetting. You see, as far as I know, your brother no longer teaches at Rotterdam University. He is definitely involved in research – vitally important research for the Germans, involving physics. He is helping their scientists try to develop an entirely new, terrifying, war-winning weapon – an atomic-bomb!'

Open mouthed, wide eyed, Frans sat silently motionlessly staring at John. He seemed frozen in profound shock.

With understanding compassion John murmured, 'I'm very sorry to give you this terrible news, Frans. I had to. My seeing your brother arrive here was a terrible shock for me as well. I could hardly believe my eyes. I found it near impossible to credit what my amazed senses were telling me. But there is no mistake. That professor, your brother, is a terrible traitor! His arrival here while I am also here is an amazing coincidence. A fateful coincidence we – or I – must act on. We must decide what action to take before he leaves the farm tomorrow.'

Like a stranded fish, Frans's mouth gaped wide then snapped shut a few times before he managed to gasp, 'But... but how do you know this, John?... Surely it can't be true!... Oh, surely my brother can not be such a vile traitor!'

Setting aside the strict 'need-to-know' principle, (Surely Frans did now need to know) John gave him a full description of the part success, part failure of 'Operation Waterloo'. After pausing to let all this startling secret information sink in, he gently asked, 'You knew your brother was inclined to be pro-German, didn't you?... You also knew he was a bright, even a brilliant, physicist, didn't you?... Did you never think he might possibly help the Germans in some top-secret research involving nuclear physics?'

'Oh no... no, never! I thought he was still teaching at his university. I feared he – like, unfortunately, far too many Dutch people – might be collaborating with the Krauts to a limited extent. But, no, I never really suspected him of anything much worse; certainly nothing as terribly unforgivably vile as helping the Krauts develop an atomic bomb. To willingly do so is the worst possible treason. He is betraying not only his Dutch nation and all the Allies fighting to free Europe, but he is betraying all mankind... is betraying all the most noble principles of Science itself!'

As he gasped out these passionate condemnations of his brother's conduct Frans seemed close to tears. He paused and with an obvious effort brought himself under control. 'Oh, John, if this is true, if my brother is such a traitor, then he no longer is my brother. I renounce all kinship to him!.. He deserves to die!.. I feel I could almost kill him myself!'

'Oh, no, Frans, there's no question of you doing that. If we agree he must be killed, I will do that killing. I am well trained and all too well experienced in effective stealthy killing.'

Frans nodded his silent agreement, 'Oh, John, I hardly know what I'm saying. My mind's in turmoil. Your news is a terrible shock to me. I never thought my brother capable of such hideous treachery as to help the Krauts develop an atom bomb.'

'You don't seem very surprised that the Germans might be trying to produce such a terrible weapon, Frans.'

'No, no, not really. Ever since the publication of Einstein's 'Theories of Relativity' all nuclear physicists have – trembling with awe – realized that, theoretically at least, it should be possible to split atoms and release vast amounts of energy. If these ideas work in practise that energy could produce limitless amounts of peaceful electricity. Or it could result in almost un-imaginable death and destruction by creating then exploding atomic bombs.'

'And do you think the Germans might be ahead of the British and Americans in trying to develop such awesome weapons?'

Frans took some thoughtful time before solemnly replying, 'Yes, John, I'm afraid that's possible. Yes, that's all too possible. It was a German scientist – Otto Hahn, – if I remember correctly , who first experimentally created nuclear fission in 1938. Then the next year, Hitler set up a nuclear research programme and banned any exports of uranium from Germany. I remember reading about all this in scientific magazines at the time.'

'So it is our imperative duty to do anything we possibly can to delay the development of the Germans atomic bomb, isn't it, Frans?... Including the killing of your treacherous brother.'

Frans nodded his full agreement, 'Yes, John, it is ... we must!. But I honestly no longer regard him as being my brother. He is nothing to me but a terrible vile and dangerous enemy who must be killed at all costs!'

'Yes, and one of those most terrible costs will be the cost to poor Anna! You can renounce kinship to your brother, but he still remains Anna's father!

Suddenly, startlingly, Frans sprang to his feet. He agonisingly cried, 'Oh God ... Oh God, I've forgotten about Anna! Oh, I am sorry, John, I should have thought about how the killing of her father would effect her.' He dejectedly slumped back into his chair. He stared at John with agonised eyes, 'And how it will terribly effect you as well.'

John solemnly nodded and, with a hint of anguish in his voice, said, 'Yes, my love for Anna, her love for me and her love of her father certainly greatly complicate things, don't they? If it wasn't for these complications my duty would be quite clear and straightforward.'

For some thoughtful silent moments they stared at one another. Eventually Frans decisively stated, 'Anna must never know that her father was such a terrible traitor. She must never learn that you killed him. The knowledge of one of those things could drive her demented. The knowledge of both these things would surely be too much for her to bear ... would perhaps slowly, but surely, cruelly kill her!'

Repeatedly and seemingly endlessly they animatedly discussed and agonised over that urgent pressing problem of how best to deal with Professor Maurik while causing the least upset to Anna.

Finally they reached agreement. John would kill that despicable professor, but he would be killed in such a way as to prevent Anna from ever knowing that he had done so.

Chapter Thirty Two

After what for Frans and John had been an anxious, fretfully sleepless night they rose early in their respective rooms and methodically and as calmly as they could set about preparing for the fateful actions they had agreed to take today.

The pre-dawn dimness and Anna's self-absorbed determination to get as much milk as possible from the cows in this first milking she had attempted without Blanche being on hand with her expert help, made it easy for Frans to conceal his anxieties from her as he unobtrusively helped in byre and dairy.

With easy going resignation the younger cows accepted Anna's inexpertly coaxing, gentle stroking fingers at their teats with drowsy sighs and tolerantly gave her almost as much milk as they gave Blanche. The two older cows – mature lethargic dowagers comfortably set in their ways – turned huge doleful eyes on Anna and resentfully enquired why she was milking them? Where was their accustomed milker? Despite her best endeavours they gave Anna less than half the milk they gave Blanche.

With extra thoughtful kindness Frans carried the heavy milk pails in to the bright tiled, gleaming dairy. After Anna went to the kitchen to prepare breakfast he lingeringly loitered about in the dairy and byre until the increasingly annoyed, increasingly impatient, ever louder bellows of the milked cows could no longer be ignored. He freed them from their stalls and, led by the two annoyed dowagers, the herd made their familiar way through an opened gate into an adjacent field.

Wheeling a barrow into the byre Frans started mucking out its thick, noisome, mixture of trampled dung and straw. He did this heavy work slowly, taking many rests. The more time he spent here the less time he would spend with his brother. The less chance there would be of betraying his true feelings for that brother whom he no longer thought of as a close sibling, but regarded as a hated enemy.

Fortunately Professor Maurik seized the rare opportunity to have a luxurious long lie this Sabbath morning. He did not appear in the kitchen until almost ten-thirty. Ruefully smiling at Anna and Frans he excused his tardiness, 'I'm sorry I'm so late. The long cycle ride yesterday must have tired me more than I realised. And I've to repeat that weary journey this afternoon, too.'

While his daughter readily and cheerily forgave him and urged him to sit in and do justice to the late breakfast she had prepared, Frans excused himself for not saying much and appearing rather solemnly subdued. He apologetically explained, 'I don't know why, but I've had a most exhausting, sleepless night. And I'm not feeling very well this morning.' That lie which hopefully concealed his true feelings from his brother was, he felt, almost true, for he did feel sick – sick at heart over his brother's unforgivable treachery.

'No,' Anna sympathetically remarked, 'you're not looking well; you look quite exhausted.' She merrily grinned, 'Perhaps it is simply that you're missing Blanche so very much. Is that it, uncle, eh?' She quite often made joking remarks about how her aunt and uncle hated to be separated from one another, even – as now – for only one night.

While Professor Muarik was at his belated breakfast, John, as arranged last night, took Frans's bicycle and, unseen by anyone in the farmhouse, quickly rode away down the farm track, turned on to the minor country road and followed the route the professor would take after lunch today.

John found it strange to move over the Dutch countryside like this, quite openly and apparently innocently cycling along fully revealed in the clear brightness of this calm, fresh, autumn day. He was doing the exact opposite of his S.B.S. training, which had taught him to stay hidden during the day and to travel unseen under cover of night's darkness when operating in German-occupied countries.

As he steadily and alertly cycled along he only stopped once. Standing astride the bicycle he un-buttoned his jacket and adjusted the position of his automatic pistol, complete with long silencer. As he got the bulky gun into a slightly more comfortable position in the waist-band of his trousers, then re-fastened his concealing jacket, he ruefully grinned, thinking: I hope the bulge of that gun in my trousers wont be as glaringly obvious to any German soldiers as a certain gentleman's 'gun-bulging' trousers were to Mae West!

Even at this late hour of morning this road and the surrounding Dutch landscape seemed drowsily asleep in blissful Sabbath calm. He saw no obvious signs of human life at the two cottages he passed apart from a thin thread of grey smoke lazily rising from one chimney. Even the dark rooster proudly poised atop his dung-heap gave his belated clarion calls half-heartedly, as if he too was reluctant to disturb the drowsy somnolence of this day of rest.

He was pleased to pass these cottages without being seen. Frans had assured him that the occupiers of these two houses could be trusted, but still the fewer people who saw him the better. He was also pleased that those cottages had appeared exactly where he expected them. This reassuringly confirmed the accuracy of the map-reading instructions Frans had given him last night. He had again thoroughly studied that map earlier this morning and he knew he must be nearing the place where he would halt, would hide, would deal with Professor Maurik when he arrived en route to continue his treacherous nuclear research.

John halted, dismounted, then hid his bicycle beside a small, narrow, humpback stone bridge over a green slimed wide ditch. There were fewer shrubs beside this bridge than he had expected. After pulling out his gun and sliding a bullet into its breech, he sat down, lent against the bridge and, fairly well concealed by a bush which fortunately still retained most of its autumnal leaves, patiently waited. From this hiding place he had a clear view down that arrow-straight minor road the professor should soon be coming along.

He was pleased he was well enough hidden when, one hour later, two German lorries approached at speed along that road. Obviously those Kraut drivers were, as usual, very apprehensive of being caught in the open by eagerly searching and deadly strafing R.A.F. fighter planes. With a touch of malicious glee John grinned as he noted how reluctant those Germans were even to slow down to cross this narrow, humpback bridge. As soon they were across it they immediately increased speed. On reflection he was thankful those Krauts had crossed the bridge safely; it would have been nasty if, in their frightened haste, they had glancingly struck the stone parapet and sent heavy masonry tumbling down on him.

Some twenty minutes later he heard, then saw, three R.A.F. fighters flying in a neat V-echelon. As they passed low overhead he – reasonably confident of his aircraft recognition skills – felt sure they were Spitfires. Staring, he admired the perfection of swift, streamlined beauty which disguised their sinister menace. He wished those pilots good luck and good hunting.

There being no further distractions on the Sabbath slumbering land or in the now silent, empty sky, he had no excuse for avoiding again thinking over the unpleasantness of the task that loomed before him. The more imminent that ugly task became the uglier it seemed to become.

It was easy – all to easy – to unthinking kill when violently engaged in the savage excitements and dangers of furious battle. Then, sweating in fierce fighting's white-hot heat, you killed with something like hot-blooded, adrenalin flooded, savage lust. But to kill as he was going to do very soon was something entirely different. Such calmly calculated, cold-blooded, ruthless killing was abhorrent to his true nature. But, made resolute by the depth and intensity of his S.B.S. training, and fully convinced that the urgent necessity of this ugly act overrode all other considerations – all his humane objections; all his personal feelings – he would unflinchingly carry out this killing.

Clearly recalling Commander Richardson's repeated insistence at his briefings that they must not be deceived by Professor Maurik's benign, Santa Claus appearance; must have no compunction about killing him; that his death was vitally necessary to lessen the likelihood of the Germans developing an atomic bomb before the Allies did, John knew that this Dutch traitor's death was completely justified. By now he had resolutely steeled himself to this fact that his death was undoubtedly 'for the greater good of the greater number'.

But the additional fact of Professor Maurik being Anna's father turned what would have been an unpleasant, but straightforward necessary killing into a minefield of personal, emotional complexities involving Anna, involving Frans, and involving John himself.

The coincidence of that treacherous professor turning out to be Anna's father truly was amazing. It once more proved that fact often *was* stranger than fiction!

John fervently wished the professor would appear so that he could get this unpleasant business over and done with at last. The longer he waited the tenser he became.

His wish was granted. His alert eyes saw a solitary cyclist in the distance. As that cyclist steadily approached along the straight road John's resolutely controlled brain swiftly reacted. So too did – in a more instinctive, less well controlled manner – every tingling nerve in his tense body.

As it drew nearer the distinctive details of that approaching figure became clearer. His white hair and flowing white beard became glaringly conspicuous. There was no possible doubt. John's target, his victim, Professor Maurik was rapidly riding to his death.

One final quick check that the road was still empty on the other side of the bridge and was empty behind the cyclist; that the gun's safety-catch was off and a bullet was in the breech, and John was ready to do what was his inescapable duty.

He abruptly rose and stood blocking the narrow bridge directly in the startled cyclist's way.

Jamming on his brakes, almost falling off, the Dutch professor unsteadily stood and cursed that stupid fool who had so suddenly appeared right in front of him. Then eyes and mouth snapped wide in amazed shock and fear as he saw that huge, ugly, deadly menacing gun rise and steadily aim directly at him.

As calmly as he could John accusingly stated, 'You are a traitor helping the Krauts build an atomic bomb, Professor Maurik. You deserve to die!'

Standing in confused shock, the apparently patriarchal professor reached out unsteady hands with palms raised vertically in desperate pleading, then urgently exclaimed in excellent English, 'No, no, you do not understand! ... I...I...' His voice rose to an agonised scream as two bullets smashed through his heart.

After dragging the dead body to where he himself had hid at the side of the bridge and concealing the professor's bicycle behind other shrubs, John mounted his own bicycle and started quickly pedalling back to the farm. Hopefully the professor's body wouldn't be discovered for quite some time.

Chapter Thirty Three

Frans was waiting at the farm gate.

Dismounting, John solemnly said, 'It's done, Frans. Your brother is dead. He won't assist the Krauts any more.'

Frans nodded. He emotionally gulped, 'It had to be done. There was no escaping that... that terrible, but unescapable duty.'

Placing a hand on Fran's shoulder, John gave a sympathetic consoling squeeze. 'Yes, I know, Frans. I understand how you must feel.'

'Thank you, John, thank you.' With resolute fortitude he got himself under control. He sighed, 'Now, John, we must face Anna. We must do as we agreed last night. By telling convincing lies we must keep her from ever learning that you killed her father or that he was such a ... a despicable traitor.'

'Yes, of course. Is it arranged that I leave here this afternoon instead of tomorrow?'

'Yes, I've been on the phone. I've organised everything. You will have to leave here soon to cycle to Rotterdam and meet the Patriot who's now expecting you before this evening's curfew starts.'

'Good. I better not be here once the Krauts discover Professor Maurik is missing and then come enquiring and searching for him. Now I better break the sad news to Anna that I have to leave her now instead of having one final night with her. Where is she? In the kitchen?'

'Yes. And, John, you know that I – Blanche and I – will do everything we possibly can to help Anna and lovingly look after her once you leave her, don't you? She will be terribly upset over your departure; will endlessly worry over your safety; might sometimes despairingly think this war is never going to end and that you are never going to return and marry her. Then there will be the additional terrible anguish of her father's death. She will probably never know exactly how, or where he died. She will never learn of the part you – and I – played in his death. Fortunately with him having been involved in such top-secret work for the Germans they will almost certainly want to have very little publicity about his mysterious death.

'Now are you ready to face Anna? Have you prepared yourself not to allow the least hint of your feelings over having killed her father to escape you?'

'Yes, yes, I'll manage to hide my feelings all right. Anyway she will expect me to be upset over leaving her – as I am – and she will be so distraught herself over my sudden departure that she will hardly be in any condition to notice anything too strange about me.'

As kindly as he could Frans told Anna his prepared convincing lies that the ship taking John to Sweden was leaving a few days earlier than expected; on Tuesday morning or possibly even late on Monday, and therefore John had to leave now to be in place at Rotterdam docks tomorrow morning.

She took this news badly. She had been eagerly anticipating having one last night with John before he left tomorrow. But now this last consolation was cruelly snatched away from her.

Throwing herself despairingly into his outstretched arms she was compassionately enveloped and passionately hugged while she wept agonised tears.

Frans diplomatically left them together for almost half-an-hour, then, discreetly coughing, returned and quietly said, 'I 'm sorry, John, but you really must leave now.'

John obediently nodded and gently eased his encircling arms from around Anna's trembling body.

Making a supremely brave effort, Anna got herself almost completely under control. Arm in arm with John she went to the farm gate where Frans stood with his bicycle ready for John's use.

As they exchanged a final, expressively firm hand-shake, John said, 'Thank you, Frans, for all you've done for me. We'll meet again under happier circumstances once this war is won. Oh, and please tell Blanche I'm sorry I've missed her to say goodbye. Thank her for all her hospitable kindness to me.'

Turning to Anna, he gave her one extra strong last hug and one final passionate loving kiss. Neither of them needed any further words to express their love.

Stopping at the end of the farm track John turned, gave a quick wave to uncle and niece standing forlornly waving at the gate, then he re-mounted his bicycle and rapidly pedalled away.

Taking a different, slightly longer route than he had taken this morning, he steadily cycled along. It was wiser to keep clear of where he had killed Professor Maurik. Although unlikely, it was just possible his body had already been discovered, which would result in that place being alive with Dutch police and possibly with German Military Police.

Under Frans's tuition he had keenly studied this new route on his map, had accurately memorised it, and was now pleased to recognise and pass some of the distinctive landmarks he had noted. Going by minor and secondary roads this journey would take him fairly directly to Rotterdam and would keep him away from the greater hazards of busier main roads. While deliberately keeping his attention actively and alertly engaged in checking his route he also managed to occupy his mind with repeating his Norwegian name and details of his home address in Norway. He interspersed these repeated 'facts' with reciting the easier 'fictions' of his rehearsed speeches in his 'Norwegian' language – phrases in the broadest Cumberland dialect remembered from childhood.

All this mental activity kept him from too distressfully thinking of and agonising over how Anna was likely to cope with his sudden departure and with her father's violent death. He fervently hoped that, with the help of Blanche's and Frans's tender care, she would manage to endure these two traumas without collapsing into another nervous breakdown. However, there being nothing he could do to help her at present, he must as pragmatically as possible get on with facing the possible dangers of his own present situation.

One of the greatest of these dangers could be looming up soon. Frans had warned that German sentries sometimes guarded one large bridge he must unavoidably cross. He would soon know if any sentries were there today, for that bridge could only be about two miles away. Grinning, he reprimanded himself for thinking in miles. As a Norwegian and being in The Netherlands, he should think entirely in kilometres.

Now he clearly saw that steel bridge spanning a fairly wide, dullish brown river. But even more clearly as his sight keenly honed in on them he saw two German soldiers standing at the far end of that bridge.

He dismounted and stood holding his bicycle at the edge of the road. Hoping he was not too conspicuous he pretended to admire the view, although there was really little worthy of admiration in this dreary landscape of flat dull fields, stagnant ditches and that uninspiring river. At least these Germans were not looking this way. They appeared to be watching a group of cyclists approaching from the opposite direction.

John gazed to see how the sentries would deal with these cyclists. With real pleasure he noted that the Krauts did not stop that party. They waved them through with what to him seemed rather languid lazy gestures. He guessed those sentries were bored of standing guarding that bridge on this unimportant quiet road. With today being a Sunday probably the road was even more boringly quieter than usual.

As they passed the sentries these cyclists gave what appeared quite friendly waves. John wondered if they were known to these Germans. Might they be collaborators?

Deciding it would appear suspicious to stand here any longer, he re-mounted and slowly cycled on to the bridge. Passing these cyclists, who he now saw to be a family party of parents and three well-grown children, he, not being sure if it was normal for passing cyclists to acknowledge one another on quiet country roads, gave a rather uncertain wave (too late, he realised he should have checked this with Frans). They, the children especially, gave enthusiastic waves in return.

Once again he hurriedly rehearsed his 'Norwegian' phrases as he approached the sentries, but passionately hoped they would treat him like these other cyclists and wave him through without him needing to use that language.

They did not!

One German soldier stood in the road and held up a hand that authoritatively ordered him to halt.

John obeyed. He stood silently holding his bicycle.

The Kraut hand changed position from vertical to horizontal and reached out with beckoning fingers while its owner – a corporal – reinforced its demand by shouting in German, 'Papers!... Papers!'

There was no mistaking these words or actions. John unbuttoned his jacket, drew out his faked documents from an inside pocket and handed them over.

The German corporal painstakingly inspected these documents

and intently read the official letter typed in Dutch and German, explaining that John was a Norwegian merchant seaman returning to his ship in Rotterdam after working on a Dutch farm.

While that Kraut with typical Teutonic thoroughness and respect for official documentation and probably also with intentional, and a touch sadistic slowness and a show of authority examined and re-examined his documents and read and re-read that letter, John patiently waited. He made a supreme effort to appear calm, understandingly patient and neither too friendly nor too hostile, while all the time being conscious of a feeling of hardly daring to breathe.

And yet, while conscious of that breathless feeling and increasingly aware of the rising tide of adrenalin flooding through his veins, he quickly, but with accurate care inspected both these German soldiers. He tried to decide just how alert they were; how much of a chance he would have against them if that corporal found something suspicious in his documents or suspected something not quite right about him; thought him not really as innocent as he desperately attempted to appear, and decided to detain him. And if he did arrest him, how long would it be before they handed him over to the Gestapo for much more thorough, much more drastic interrogation?

The corporal seemed – by army standards – quite old, perhaps almost forty. His close- cropped hair was grey. Some huge, vivid, recently healed scars badly disfigured the left side of his face. The other sentry – a tall, thin, ganglingly private soldier – revealed no physical wounds but seemed to be suffering from some type of mental wound as he looked on with vague, almost blank, disinterest.

John guessed that they – like many German soldiers occupying and guarding Western Europe – were survivors of some of the terrible battles in Russia. That private soldier appeared to be still semi shell-shocked from his hideous experiences on the Eastern Front.

No doubt they hoped to remain in the comparative peace and comfort of their cushy posting in Holland until the war ended. Whether the peace of this easy posting would or wouldn't continue might be decided soon ... in the next few minutes. The boredom they had been feeling might end with more drastically dramatic excitement than they bargained for!

John had decided that if that corporal did try to arrest him, he would not docilely submit. With all his S.B.S. training and experience giving him confidence and adrenalin giving him surging dynamic strength, he thought he had a reasonable chance of killing both these not too alert Krauts before they got their rifles un-slung from their shoulders. If he acted fast he would have advantage of that vital ingredient – the element of surprise.

The corporal growled a question in German. Shaking his head, John replied in his well rehearsed 'Norwegian'.

The corporal asked more incomprehensible questions. John again replied in his incomprehensibly confusing 'Norwegian'.

With rising impatience and seemingly increasing suspicion, the corporal turned to the vacantly staring private soldier and ordered, 'Search him .. Search him.'

As the gawky soldier approached and indicated that he should hold out his arms to allow himself to be searched, John knew that all would be lost if he allowed that searching German to find and remove his hidden gun. He must prevent that. He must take immediate decisive action!

He violently thrust his bicycle at the startled soldier, took a few steps back while reaching for his automatic, drew it out and with well practised skill thumbed off the safety-catch as he raised it, and, firmly gripped in both hands, aimed at point-blank range then squeezed the trigger twice.

Shot through his heart the private was flung against the confused, startled, angrily shouting corporal. Staggering backwards that cursing German reacted too slowly. As he wildly fumbled to un-sling and aim his rifle, two .45 bullets thudded into his chest.

John gathered up his scattered documents. Fortunately none were stained with Kraut blood. He dragged both bodies off the road and rolled them out of obvious sight down the embankment at the end of the bridge. Lifting a rifle in each hand he threw them into the river. He could do nothing with the revealing pools and streaks of bright blood. He checked his bicycle. It was undamaged.

Quickly searching up and down the road he was pleased to see it was still fairly empty. Some groups of distant cyclists and a slow plodding horse and cart were its only traffic. None of them would have heard those four effectively muffled shots. He was thankful that, despite its awkwardness, he had kept that silencer screwed to his gun.

Suddenly John had a strange, strong feeling of déjà vu. He seemed to freeze and hardly seemed to breathe. He had an illusion that he had shot and killed that German corporal and private before. For what were only moments but felt like ages, he stood motionlessly engulfed in a hallucinatory trance-like state.

Then, with a violent shudder, he came out of that strange delirium and clearly and logically remembered that he had shot and killed not those Kraut soldiers before, but another German corporal and private while escaping from that research establishment at the centre of 'Operation Waterloo'.

After vigorously cycling for a few minutes he suddenly realised that in his haste to get away he was on the left side of the empty road. He immediately swung over to the right. Smiling, he wished all Europeans would follow the British example and travel on the 'correct' side of their roads!

Then more seriously he took the lesson of that error to heart. He must constantly keep his wits about him. How easy it was to make a simple mistake and how easily one such simple mistake could revealingly betray one; could result in capture and death.

With extra care he concentrated on checking that he was on the correct route.

The remainder of his journey was uneventful. As he neared the sprawling outskirts of Rotterdam the increasing numbers of houses was matched with an increase in traffic. There were many Dutch family groups on their usual Sunday outings to visit relatives, or after morning's church services out for an afternoon of fresh air and exercise. A few civilian vans and lorries passed him then two single decked trams coupled together noisily clattered and clanged by. He constantly reminded himself not to be deluded by the seemingly almost innocent normality of this pleasant passing scene.

The sudden roar of an approaching convoy of German army trucks lead by two military policeman on motor-cycles, reinforced this warning.

It took a resolute effort of will for him to continue steadily and apparently quite calmly and openly cycle along as those German soldiers neared him. His instinctive reaction was to urgently hide.

It was an indescribable feeling for him – an Englishman, a Royal Navy sailor on active duty – to so openly cycle within a few yards (shouldn't that be metres? he asked himself) of all those German soldiers he now clearly saw crammed into the backs of those passing Wehrmacht lorries.

Some ten minutes later he saw with pleasure an impressively erupting spume of grey/black smoke and violently hissing white steam as a large, dark locomotive strained to haul a long line of goods trucks along the railway track which from here on ran alongside the North side of the road. He had noted this companionship of road and rail on his map and knew the rendezvous point for meeting his waiting Dutch Patriot was not much further on.

Two windmills rising prominently behind a small wooden tea-room confirmed he had arrived at the correct place. A small boating lake, its boats neatly laid up high and dry for winter, was further confirmation. Dismounting, he wheeled his bicycle to the end of the tea-room which at this dead time of year between summer boating and winter skating, was securely locked with all its windows blankly shuttered.

Silently grinning, John once again reprimanded himself for thinking in British, not European terms. Surely here in Holland that building was a restaurant, not a tea-room. Only in Britain were there traditional tea-rooms, these noble, indispensable shrines where sedate middle-class British housewives daintily sipped refreshing tea and congratulated themselves on being so vastly superior to all coffee guzzling Huns.

A frown of serious concentration replaced that grin as he halted, un-buttoned his jacket and checked that his re-loaded automatic was ready to hand in case of sudden urgent need.

Training and experience had taught him that every rendezvous should be approached with caution. It was all too possible for those pre-arranged meeting places to be betrayed; to meet not trustworthy Patriots, but eagerly waiting hidden Germans.

Peering around the end of the silent, deserted building John saw what he hoped to see... a middle-aged Dutchman bending over his upturned bicycle, apparently completely engrossed with some repairs.

John approached him, gave the arranged code word and received the correct reply. Firmly, trustingly, appraisingly, they shook hands. Each man was favourably impressed by the other man he was meeting for the first time. Both immediately sensed a strong warm feeling of mutual trust and reliable strength. In just a few tense moments war forged stronger, more deep and sincere camaraderie than were forged in many calm, slow years of peacetime ease.

In clear, but slow and halting English the Dutchman said, 'My name is Jan.'

'And my name is John.' He smiled brightly, 'Almost the same name, and both with exactly the same aim – to defeat the Krauts!'

Jan laughed delightedly, 'Ya ... ya, we defeat the Krauts! Together we win the war! Soon we kick all the... the terrible Krauts out of poor Holland!' Descending from the blissful dream of achieving this most devoutly desired victory, he more mundanely said, 'Now we go, John. I... I guide you to my home.'

Twelve minutes later Jan introduced John to his wife. Half an hour later the three of them sat down to a dinner which, though adequate, came far short of the meals John had grown accustomed to during his stay at the farm. He knew that as this war dragged on, food shortages in Dutch cities were becoming more and more severe. So, almost ashamed of eating some of this precious food, he generously praised the meal and their self-sacrifice in insisting that he heartily ate up.

Later that night, lying revelling in the unaccustomed luxury of fresh, meticulously laundered sheets in his house-proudly prepared bed in this immaculate Dutch bedroom, John thought over today's events.

Inevitably his first, deepest, most worried thoughts were of Anna. But once again he resolutely drove his distressing worries about her out of his conscious mind and deliberately thought of other things. He was pleased at how well his escape was going. But of course it was still in its early stages; much could go wrong to prevent his safe arrival back in Britain. Summing up positive optimism, he amended that to: no... not 'prevent', but only to add unexpected delays to his safe return.

He congratulated himself on how well he had dealt with that dangerous situation with those two German sentries at that bridge.

He felt a touch of complacent pride as he thought: yes, despite all my lovemaking with Anna, all my ease and comfort at the farm, I have lost none of my deadly S.B.S. skills. There was absolutely no diminution of my fine-honed expertise as a fast, efficient killer; no delay or indecision in the speed of my reactions. Yes, all that intensive training I experienced – that unique training that took us few Special Boat Section élite not only to the very edge of what any human could be expected to endure, but often took us over that edge and made us endure the unendurable – certainly now stands me in good stead ... makes me able to confidently face whatever dangers, hardships and uncertainties fate throws at me.

He gently sighed: and no doubt I will have to use my expert skills again (again and again?) before we win this bloody war – if we do win it; if Hitler's secret weapons don't yet win it for him.

With a determined effort of will he composed himself to sleep. Drifting off, he smiled as pleasant pictures of Anna coloured his mind. He might be reasonably successful in banning too many worries about her from his conscious mind, but he knew he couldn't – didn't want to – ban her from actively invading his subconscious mind. He self-indulgently expected wondrous dreams of her to fill his sleeping hours.

He fell into deep sleep.

Chapter Thirty Four

John seemed to have no sooner dropped into sleep than he was awakened by loud banging on his bedroom door. Immediately alert, he reached for his gun lying conveniently to hand on the bedside table. He relaxed as Jan's voice announced it was time for him to get up and get ready to 'go to work' at Rotterdam docks.

'Come in, Jan, come in,' John shouted. As the door partially opened and Jan peered in, John gently laid down the gun. He had decided it would do no harm – might perhaps be positive gain – to let that Dutch Patriot see his automatic pistol with its attached silencer. Him being armed with such a deadly silent weapon should give that Dutchman extra confidence in John's experience and skill.

As Jan's wife most apologetically gave him a modest breakfast, John (with Jan acting as interpreter) assured her there was no need to apologise: 'In fact it's me who should apologise to you for eating your scarce, severely rationed food.'

Soon Jan and John were cycling side by side deeper and deeper into the centre of Rotterdam. They met ever increasing traffic. Many tramcars, crammed with yawning workers, self-importantly clamoured along and with strident bells clanged out impatient warnings. Some civilian vans and lorries and a few German army trucks trundled past them, while they in turn swiftly passed many slow plodding horses which hauled heavily laden carts. But, especially as they neared the city's vast sprawl of docks and ceaselessly busy shipyards, by far the bulk of the traffic consisted of cyclists.

John had never seen so many bicycles. From every side-street came ever more cyclists all speeding to join the throng already crowding this wide major road that lead directly to the main gates of the docks. Despite the Germans having looted many Dutch cycles, there still seemed to be not hundreds, but thousands. Staring amazed as he cycled along, part of that hurrying mass, John was forcefully reminded of a countless swarm of bees unerring homing in on their hive.

As he dismounted and drew out his forged dock pass, John gave Jan a quick confident grin, thinking there should be safety in numbers; surely the Dutch dock police or any German sentries could not thoroughly check every individual in this swarming crowd. Nor did they. His fake pass worked like a charm. A weary policeman gave that pass a cursory glance then nodded him through.

Once passed the gates that hurrying cycling mass dispersed in every direction. Jan lead John what seemed like miles – or kilometres – past dock after crowded dock until they finally reached their destination. Dismounting at a stack of large wooden crates, Jan instructed, 'Hide your bicycle here, John. It will be collect later. Collect? ... Is that correct?'

'No, it should be "collected".'

'Ah, yes, "collected" ... Now I show you your ship.'

After pointing out the ship which, hopefully, would take John safely to Sweden, Jan warmly shook his hand then cycled away to his distant workplace in that sprawling confusion of dockyards.

After a quick exchange of correct code words, John was hurried down the ship to a hiding place in an obscure store room near its bow.

All that day, all that night, and most of the following day he saw no one apart from a number of brief visits from one of the crew, a young Dutch sailor who seemed little older than a schoolboy, who brought him food and drink but could not, or would not, give him any information.

Then with immense relief he at last heard the rumble of the ship's engine starting up, felt its pulsing vibrations and recognised all the familiar sounds of a ship preparing to leave harbour. Smiling to himself he thought: 'Thank God, at last I'm en route to Sweden and home.'

After some more weary lonely hours, in which he began to fear he would spend the entire voyage hidden here like this, John was led up what seemed an endless series of vertical metal ladders and steep companion-ways until he was eventually ushered into a small, cramped dining-mess in which were crowded the ship's officers not on duty. As the captain rose and, thrusting out a huge hand, welcomed John, his impressive height and vast bulk seemed to make the room twice as crowded. Seizing John's hand in a powerful, bone-crushing grip, he said – he practically shouted – 'Welcome, John. Come, sit down. Share dinner with us.'

A generously heaped plate was set before John and the captain poured him an equally generous glass of brandy, then, raising his own brimming glass, gave emotional toasts: 'Here's to defeat of the Krauts! …Here's to victory for Allies!…Here's to Holland getting freedom back!'

After these toasts were passionately responded to, the food and yet more brandy rapidly disappeared down eager throats. Glowing faces furnaced ever fiercer; bright eyes gleamed ever brighter; voices and laughter rose ever higher. The captain's dominant voice erupted ever louder and ever deeper from his barrel chest while the thunderous laughter rumbled up from ever remoter regions of his mirth-quaking belly. Then he suddenly turned solemnly contrite and apologised for keeping John hidden for such a long time down in the remote bowels of his ship. He explained that this caution was necessary until they were at sea and well away from any risk of searching Krauts or Kraut collaborating Dutch shipping officials discovering him.

Then, reverting to jovial mirth, he half-heartedly apologised for his and his off-duty officers semi-inebriated state. His laughter again boomed out as he assured John, 'No matter how much brandy we drink, we are able to carry out all duties if sudden needed.' More laughter loudly reverberated as, accusingly staring at one broad grinning officer, the captain merrily added, 'In fact, some of crew say I do my duties better when I half-drunk!'

His booming voice dropped to what, for him, was a confidential whisper as he explained, 'But real reason we drink tonight is we are happy at being at sea. Here we free to say what we really feel. We – every member of ship's crew – is absolute trustworthy. We all hate the Krauts! We pretend to collaborate with them. But we secretly work against them.' With his drink loosened tongue disclosing more than it should, the captain jovially continued, 'We help true English friends like you, John, escape to Sweden. We help our great Dutch Patriots in other ways. Any good information we get about Kraut ships and other things go to London.'

He paused, he sighed, he gulped more brandy. 'It is big strain working with Krauts. Is bigger strain working with real Collaborators …the terrible Dutch traitors are even worse than Krauts!'

He again lifted his glass, again deeply drank, then once more his laughter thundered out, 'So we have good – as you English say, eh? – "booze-up" on first night at sea away from them all. You understand, John?... You understand big strain?'

John assured the pleased captain of his complete sympathetic understanding. His own tongue by now also foolishly drink loosened, he ramblingly continued, 'Oh yes, captain, believe me, I do know the strain of living in German-occupied Holland; know the strain of pretending to be an innocent civilian to those hateful Krauts, while all the time I am a patriotic Englishman ... a sailor serving in the Royal Navy.'

'You are British Navy sailor, John?'

'Yes, I proudly serve in the world's greatest navy – the Royal Navy!'

The captain immediately seized this excuse to passionately propose one more toast, 'To navy that is even greater than Royal Netherlands Navy – the British Royal Navy!'

Once all had, with genuine sincerity and loud eagerness drank to that toast, the captain asked, 'But why you, a British sailor, live in Holland, John? ... You are a special sailor, a Commando, yes?'

Belatedly realising he had disclosed more than he should, John gently grinned and modestly said, 'Yes, I am like a Commando; I carry out secret duties in Holland.'

The captain eagerly asked, 'You kill Krauts?'

His tongue further loosened by that last toast's generously poured and quickly drank brandy, John decided it would be foolish to allow any false modesty to constrain him – these Dutch friends put themselves at risk by taking him to freedom; surely they were entitled to know that this was a risk worth taking, that he was worth freeing – he solemnly nodded and said, 'Yes, I kill Krauts!... I have killed quite a few Krauts .. and I expect to kill more before this war's over!'

This emphatic statement caused a sudden solemn silence to fall over the staring – and admiring? – Dutch officers, then one, young and far gone in drink, eagerly asked, 'You meet, you like, Dutch Patriots?... You like Holland?... You meet, you like, nice Dutch girls, yes?'

With beaming eyes and wide grins John replied, 'The answer to each question is: Yes!... Yes!... Yes!'

The captain's booming laughter led, and almost drowned, the hearty laughter of his officers. The delighted young officer asked a more personal, more romantic question, 'Oh, John, you love nice Dutch girl, do you?'

Swept away by alcohol's gloriously un-inhibiting indiscretions, John wildly, passionately and boastfully declared, 'Yes, I do love a nice Dutch girl. But she's more than just "nice"; she's lovely! Her name is Anna! As soon as the war's over I will return to Holland and marry her!'

The captain immediately towered to his feet, raised his glass high and eagerly gave another toast, 'Here's to Anna! We all drink to John's beautiful Anna!' Once the glasses were drained his laughter again thundered out as he dramatically announced, 'After war won, we all come to your wedding, John!'

★ ★ ★

As, self-pityingly moaning, he woke late the following morning, John had only a vague memory of collapsing into this bunk in this twin berthed officer's cabin sometime late last night. He noted that the other bunk was empty; this reassuringly suggested that at least one officer had kept reasonably sober and was still alertly on duty.

The following day as dusk descended over a blacked-out harbour they were slowly approaching, he was ordered to return to his remote hiding place deep down near the ship's bows before German officials boarded the ship.

After a delay of six hours the ship started moving again, but only very, very, slowly. When he awoke next morning John noted they were still travelling at what seemed less than walking pace and the ship seemed unnaturally calm, without the slightest hint of even the most modest wave movement. He puzzled over this, but could think of no explanation.

On being freed from hiding he was ordered to report to the captain on the bridge. Then the explanation for the ship's snail-pace and un-natural calmness was obvious. They were not at sea. The ship appeared almost land-locked as it slowly travelled through a canal.

The captain's laughter boomed, 'Well, John, where do you think you are?'

John stared around as he mentally pictured a map of North West Europe. He grinned, 'I must be in Germany. This must be the Kiel Canal.'

'Yes, it is. How you like being in Germany, eh?'

'I don't! .. I don't like it at all! It feels very strange for me, an Englishman serving in the Royal Navy, to be moving through Germany, through this enemy country, this homeland of the Huns I have been fighting for the last four years.' He gazed wonderingly around the peaceful rural scene then remarked, 'So those are German children waving at us and those are German cattle grazing over there.' He thoughtfully smiled, 'These children, these cows, look no different from Dutch or British cows and children, do they?'

The captain's wide forehead furrowed into deep frowns as he gave a solemn sigh, 'No, no, they do not. These children and cows are wiser than us. Only us...us adult human animals kill one another in ... in ceaseless savage wars.'

Later, after passing under the massive iron railway bridge that rose high on its grassy embankments which were the only things like modest hills in all this flat countryside, John saw the town of Kiel in the distance. He said, 'I'm surprised the Krauts allow your ship to use this canal and go through that large German Naval base.'

'Oh no, we do not go through Kiel.' The captain explained, 'This canal comes out a few kilometres North of Kiel. We go direct into Baltic from there. No, the Krauts do not allow us in navy base.' He grinned proudly, 'But sometimes we get naval information about what is happening and send it to London. But some time we are not allowed to use canal and must go around Denmark.'

As, after leaving the Kiel Canal, they steamed down the narrow channel leading into the Baltic, John experienced stranger, even more indescribable feelings than he had felt in that German canal, for their ship was now passing close to a surfaced German U-boat heading for Kiel Naval Base. Almost instinctively his keenly trained senses itched to do something – take some violent action to destroy that enemy submarine.

It was bizarre to think that while on convoy escorting duties in the Atlantic, his Royal Navy destroyer might well have tried to locate and sink that very U-boat, while it, in turn, endeavoured to sink that hunting British warship. It felt almost like treachery to calmly sail on and do nothing. But they did. They had to.

* * *

Early the following evening the captain sent a sailor to tell John to come up to the bridge and see something interesting that, for him, would also be most unusual.

Puzzling over what this unusual sight might be, he hurried from his cabin. As he entered the bridge the captain grinned and pointed, 'You like that, John? You have not seen that for long time, eh?'

For a while John silently stared then gasped, 'No, it's many years since I've seen a sight like that.' He again fell silent and gazed at the huge, brilliant display of countless lights that magnificently lit up the harbour and sprawling city of Stockholm. Lights seemed to blaze from every window of every building. Every street, even the narrowest dockside alleyways, were ablaze with bright lamps. Every ship was unrestrainedly alight with glaring brightness.

Such a sight after four years of war – four years during which not only Britain but every war-torn European country was strictly blacked-out, was truly amazing. John stared almost disbelievingly at this fantastic blaze of light which so blatantly proclaimed Sweden's strict neutrality.

Greatly amused by John's very evident amazement, the captain laughed and asked, 'You like? ...You like bright lights of Stockholm, John?'

Rather uncertainly, John replied, 'Yes, yes, it's great to see a city brightly lit up like that.'

But was it? Were these glaring lights so assertively, so self-righteously proclaiming this country's neutrality really such a great sight? Was Sweden's peaceful prosperous brightness a glowing beacon pointing to what a better post-war Europe would become? Thoughtfully pondering such questions John could not help feeling that there was something false, even something essentially wrong, about all this proud, prosperous neutrality. And just how truly neutral was Sweden? This country was the main supplier of iron-ore to Germany. The almost indecent affluence of its people was firmly based on supplying materials to feed the German war-machine.

Yes, he thought, those Swede's are very adapt at comfortably and profitably fishing in Europe's troubled waters!

Try as he might, he could not help feeling there was something wrong, something almost unnatural about all this glaring brightness. The miseries of war's blackouts seemed much more natural! Inwardly smiling he mocked himself: I have allowed myself to be conditioned by four long years of war. The mad, topsy-turvy illogicality of war now seems almost wiser than the calm, clear logic of peace.

Having had some time to try and sort out his confused thoughts, John grinned at the captain, 'Yes, this certainly is a most attractive, brilliant peaceful scene.'

And it truly was. As their ship slowly weaved its way between Stockholm's many crowded islands, all aglow with innumerable reflected lights and while many small ferryboats self-importantly blazed their way from island to island, this really was a fair scene.

That word 'fair' triggered confused thoughts in John's mind ... triggered renewed thoughts and worries about Anna. How was she keeping?... How was she coping? But there was something more definite about that word 'fair' connected with Anna; something she had quoted from Shakespeare. He urgently groped for her quotation ...Ah, yes, now he remembered. It had been chorused by three witches in Macbeth: 'Fair is foul, and foul is fair ..' yes, that summed up his ambivalent feelings; yes, there certainly was something foul about this fair Swedish scene.

Chapter Thirty Five

The following morning, having been dropped off from the Dutch captain's taxi at the end of this wide and long street (it was wiser for him not to be seen letting anyone off directly in front of the British Legation), John, as he strode towards that Legation, guided by its jauntily waving Union Jack, was momentarily stopped in his tracks as he saw, not far beyond it, a boastfully larger flag flapping – the arrogant Nazi swastika of the German Embassy. It gave him a strange surrealistic feeling to see the flags of those deadly enemies flying almost side by side.

After having been kept waiting for a considerable time John was shown into the office of the Naval Attaché at the Legation. He immediately got the impression that that officer, a quite young First-Lieutenant, was an archetypical specimen of the worst kind of snobbishly class-conscious regular Royal Navy officer. Seated behind a large desk, he was rather slim and small, but as he almost belligerently demanded to see John's documents, he tried by his aggressive self-importance to make himself appear bigger than he actually was.

Along with his fake documents John handed over a written note and requested it be coded and radioed to London. The Naval Attaché seemed to swell even larger as he visibly bristled with annoyance at the thought of that mere leading-seaman instructing him what to do. With an effort he constrained his temper and read John's message: 'For attention Commander Richardson, Naval Intelligence, Admiralty, London. Leading-seaman J. Armstrong, S.B.S., reports that "Operation Waterloo" is now successfully completed. Both – repeat both – targets now eliminated. Await orders for return to U.K. – Message ends.'

As, standing at attention, he watched the officer read that message, John vindictively thought: That should give that snobbish twit something to think about! It did. The Lieutenant looked up at him with sudden new respect and said, 'Oh, stand at ease, Armstrong.' He knew better than to ask outright what that operation had been about; he merely thoughtfully murmured, 'Operation Waterloo, eh?'

'Yes, sir, I have successfully completed that operation.'

' Did you carry out that mission, whatever it was, entirely on your own?'

As always was acutely aware of the 'need to know' principle, and yet felt surely he was entitled to proudly and perhaps even slightly boastfully reveal a little more than he strictly should. 'No, sir, I was secretly operating in Holland as part of a five man S.B.S. team. But now I am the sole survivor of that team.'

There definitely was true respect, even reluctant admiration, in the look that officer gave John as he said, 'Oh, I see. Yes, all right then, I'll get your message coded and transmitted to London at once.'

★ ★ ★

Two nights later, lying cosily cocooned in an eiderdown filled sleeping-bag in a Norwegian Patriots mountain cabin, John musingly thought: Yes, my message and the prompt reply from Commander Richardson fairly woke up that naval attaché in Stockholm. In justice to him, he really 'got his finger out' and swiftly and efficiently organised my journey into Norway and my rendezvous with these Patriots.

As he thought of those two brave, extremely tough and fit, completely trustworthy Norwegian Freedom Fighters who had guided him from the Swedish border to this snug cabin and who lay snoringly asleep near him, he felt a wave of deep camaraderie for them and for all such great Patriots in every German-occupied country who, often under most desperate and dangerous conditions, defiantly kept the flame of hope brightly alive; retained a sure belief in Allied victory; retained the certainty of gloriously restoring Freedom to their tyrannically subjugated country.

These Norwegians seemed exceptionally dedicated to eventually achieving defeat of the Germans and returning Freedom to Norway. John diplomatically had not said so, but he felt certain they – and all such true Norwegians – were by their resolute patriotic courage doing their best to wipe out the stain on their nation inflicted by their false leader, Quisling, who had so shamefully betrayed his people. That collaborating traitor's name was now a new, a contemptible, word in the English language.

Thinking over recent events, John again compared his short time in Sweden with these last few days in Norway... and Norway again came out incomparably better.

Despite all its sufferings and dangers, all the black-out austerity under harsh German occupation, he felt Norway was a much better place to be than neutral Sweden, with all its brightly flaunted selfish prosperity based on other countries grim adversity.

Yes, life in this country with these Patriots was more real. He felt more truly alive here. Yesterday and today as, struggling slightly at first, he had determinedly kept up with those two tall, strong, effortlessly striding Norwegians, he had felt not only a sense of satisfaction at correctly doing his duty by getting himself supremely fit again, but also a flood of deep pleasure at walking through this beautiful land of snow-capped mountains, fir-clad hills and wild rushing streams and rivers. After his weeks of soft ease at that Dutch farm, all his loving sensual indulgences with Anna, all the undemanding dull flatness of Holland, he badly needed this strenuous exercise.

Before falling asleep he once again vividly thought of Anna. His familiar anxious worries about her and his dread fears over what might be happening to her constantly disturbed times like this when he had leisure to actively, longingly, lovingly, think of her.

★ ★ ★

At an isolated Norwegian village John was smuggled on to a small fishing boat. After sailing along the island dotted, fiord fretted coast all night they arrived at the correct rendezvous point and John quickly transferred to a larger fishing boat. This second boat would take him directly to Britain. It was one of a number of Norwegian fishing boats that provided a ferry service across the North Sea between the Shetland Islands and Norway, Defiantly deceiving or skilfully evading patrolling German warships and aircraft, this valiant ferrying was now so amazingly regular and reliable that it had gained the warmly affectionate accolade of being known as, 'The Shetland Bus Service'.

On each voyage these 'Shetland Buses' carried Norwegian

Resistance Fighters or British Special Forces who, operating with the utmost stealth, fought their hazardous clandestine war against the Nazi oppressors and by their gallant efforts forced the Germans to keep thousands of soldiers tied-up on defensive garrison duties in Norway.

As soon as – under cover of darkness – the 'bus' carrying John left the sheltered waters of its narrow fiord and determinedly butted its bow into smooth rolling waves of the open sea, it was obvious that the journey across the autumnal North Sea was going to be a rather stormy one. John was thankful he was a 'good sailor' and did not suffer from sea-sickness.

Despite having taken pills which – in theory – prevented sea-sickness, the two British soldiers, returning radio-operators, who were fellow passengers on this steeply rising, deeply falling and wildly rolling fishing boat were already beginning to dejectedly moan and their faces were turning a sickly shade of green.

The moonless, cloud-louring darkness seemed to make the gusting wind gust more violently; make the wild driven rain batter more dementedly; make the challenged waves fling spray more spitefully savagely over the gallant, steadfast, conquering boat.

Sitting snugly ensconced in the roomy wheel-house, John decided this rough weather, despite all its menacing 'sound and fury', posed no real threat.

He had often sailed through much worse weather on convoy escorting duties in winter's wildest North Atlantic gales. He had complete faith that the brilliant team of sturdy fishing boat and experienced Norwegian skipper would take them safely through the roughest weather. That bulky, bushily-bearded 20th century Viking standing so stoically statuesquely gripping the wheel and steering his boat with such consummate skill certainly inspired unlimited confidence in his expert seamanship.

Proving that confidence fully justified, they arrived in Lerwick harbour only one hour later than their scheduled time of arrival.

From the Shetlands John was ferried to the Orkneys. After reporting to R.N. headquarters at Scapa Flow naval base, he was again quickly ferried away; this time to the Scottish mainland.

From the North of Scotland he started a wearily long train journey to the South of England.

This journey dragged out interminably through drearily endless blacked-out night hours, sitting crammed in crowded, dimly lit carriages, everything and everyone smelling of the steam train's sooty smoke, then through almost as tediously long and dreary day time hours. As usual on long journeys on wartime's uncomfortable, overcrowded, uncertain trains there were frequent inexplicable irksome delays when the train stayed firmly halted with nothing to be seen from soot grimed carriage windows but dull, rain-swept fields and dismal drooping trees. Rain-dripping cattle in these soggy fields stood almost as motionless as the train and stared almost as resignedly at the humans in the carriages as these bored passengers forlornly stared at them.

After many changes of noisy, steam hissing, smoke belching trains, much dreary hanging around dismal, canteen-closed railway stations waiting for the late arrival of these war-delayed trains, John finally got to journey's end at the Naval Base in Poole.

After being duly processed, re-kitted and re-clad in his familiar bell-bottom R.N. uniform he reported to the medical centre at S.B.S. headquarters.

Only the Senior Naval Medical Officer at this centre had authority to remove the suicide cyanide pill held by sticking-plaster behind John's right ear.

After donning surgical gloves, that Medical Officer quickly, skilfully, and almost painlessly peeled the plaster from John's skin and hair. He then carefully placed the small, white, square-cornered lethal pill in the special container which held his entire deadly stock of extra powerful potassium of cyanide pills. After placing that container in a strong steel cupboard he securely locked it. Only he and the Commanding Officer of this S.B.S headquarters unit had a key for this cupboard.

Using an especially strong disinfectant the officer now thoroughly wiped John's skin where the pill had been hidden. Finally he removed his rubber gloves and dropped them into the metal bin which contained the other possibly contaminated items awaiting incineration.

Once this medical procedure was completed John was shown into the office of Lieutenant-Commander Payne. That officer apologetically explained, 'I'm afraid Commander Richardson is not here at present. But I am fully in the picture regarding Operation Waterloo and have been ordered to de-brief you for him. So I have been expecting you. You did really well to eliminate both targets. I am impressed. So, too, was Commander Richardson. He told me to tell you that.'

'Thank you, sir. I am pleased I eventually managed to successfully complete Operation Waterloo. But it did not go as planned. There were many difficulties before I eliminated the last, and most important target.'

Lt-Commander Payne nodded understandingly, 'Yes, I believe there were. But before we go minutely into all that there's another matter to deal with first.' Picking up a form from the Operation Waterloo file lying open on his desk, he handed it over and smiled, 'Just check that all the details are correct before I get that telegram sent.'

John quickly read the official message informing his mother that he was no longer 'missing' but was now safe in Britain and would be home on leave soon. He happily returned the form, 'Thank you, sir. I was going to ask if my mother had been informed. I was "missing-in-action . She will be overjoyed to receive that message.'

'Of course she will. It's good to be able to send a pleasant telegram for a change. I did not send it earlier. I thought it best to make sure you were safely back here before sending it. Excuse me a moment while I get it dispatched now.'

When he left to give the form to a Wren signals clerk, John reflectively thought he seemed a pleasant officer. It was decent of him to think about and personally see to that telegram before getting down to what, from the official point of view, was the much more important matter of learning every detail of what went right, what went wrong with Operation Waterloo.

Of course John had observantly noted the undulating braid strips on the Lt-Commander's jacket sleeves which proclaimed him a member of the 'Wavy Navy'. His being a Royal Navy Reserve Officer, merely serving for the duration of the war, almost certainly explained his thoughtfulness in attending to that compassionate telegram before getting down to more serious official business.

Had Commander Richardson been interviewing him, probably that regular R.N. officer would have dutifully attended to official business first, with thoughts of compassionate personal telegrams being relegated to much later.

At completion of his extensive de-briefing of John, Lt-Commander Payne said 'I'm afraid you cannot go home on leave immediately. I have to send a copy of my report on Operation Waterloo to Special Operations Executive's Headquarters. I expect they will then want to see you. As soon as they are done with you I will see that you get sent on leave....' he finished the interview with sincere praise...' on well deserved leave. You did an exceptionally good job, Armstrong.'

For two days John was kept hanging about between being interviewed by various S.O.E officers. The most senior officer made no attempt to hide his anger at John having been de-briefed by Royal Navy Intelligence before being sent to him.

John was secretly amused at this further example of the intense rivalries that existed between supposedly co-operating, but all too often jealously competing Intelligence Agencies. He knew from personal experience that R.N. Intelligence, being part of the fabulous 'Senior Service', was especially resentful of the S.O.E – that brash upstart service which so often used such unruly, un-gentlemanly methods.

Grinning, he remembered a recent newspaper cartoon that brilliantly illustrated this inter-service rivalry. A confused army motor-cycle dispatch-rider, stopped in Whitehall, surrounded by imposing Government offices on both sides of the road, asked a passing soldier, 'What side is the Admiralty on, do you know?'

The Cockney soldier paused, thought, then said, 'Cor blimey, our's I think!'

★ ★ ★

The day after his final S.O.E. interview John was allowed to go on leave.

After another not quite so long train journey, but one with the almost inevitable delay and milling confusion as he – along with many soldiers, all burdened by a heavy kit-bag on one shoulder and their rifle slung from the other shoulder – obeyed railway officials loud bellowed familiar orders to 'all change at Crewe', he arrived back in his hometown of Keswick.

Striding up the slope to his home he smiled at Skiddaw, that loved mountain which rose so familiarly beyond the town. Skiddaw seemed higher and more impressive, and he welcomed it more than ever after the dismal dull flatness of Holland.

John opened the un-locked back door and quietly entered his home's warm kitchen.

Startled by his sudden entrance, his mother turned from the hot stove and exclaimed, 'Oh, is that you, John?' Then, with her flushed face beaming, said 'I've been expecting you. I got your telegram with your great news. I'll just make you some tea.'

She started reaching up for her bright painted tea-caddy on the high mantelpiece, then stopped and turned. Being a strong, stoic, un-demonstrative Northerner who normally left all excessive open displays of emotion to soppy Southerners, but who on this special occasion- this miraculous safe return of her only son – found she could not contain her overwhelming delight.

Her eyes suddenly overflowed with tears of joy. Stretching out trembling arms she flung herself at John. She lovingly embraced him and was eagerly embraced by him. She breathlessly gasped and joyfully sobbed.

Tremulously she exclaimed, 'Oh, John! ... John! Oh, John, for a while I didn't know if you were alive or dead!... Oh, John, my own dear boy, what happened to you?... Oh, the desperate despair of getting that telegram saying you were "missing in action"... Were you wounded? Are you all right now?'

Putting convincing reassurance into his not too revealing, not entirely truthful words, John replied, 'No, Mother, I was not wounded. I'm perfectly fit and well. Things were a bit difficult for a time. My ship was operating off the coast of Norway; then I had to stay hidden from the Germans in that country for quite a while until I eventually managed to get back to Britain, that was all.'

'Oh, I see. Well thank God you did manage home safely. I had endless sleepless nights worrying over what had happened to you. I constantly prayed for your safe return. Oh, John, thank God my prayers were answered!' For some long moments deep emotions choked her voice, then she rapidly continued, 'It was terrible losing your father in that accident a few years ago. I still miss him. But I've got over the worst of my grief; one has to; life must go on. But, oh John, what if I had now lost you as well as him!... Oh John, my own dear boy, if you had been killed I don't know how I would manage to go on living without you.... Oh, I don't think I'd want to!'

Although deeply moved by this most unusual open display of profound emotion by his mother, John resolutely controlled his own emotions. Gently and sympathetically he smiled, 'Oh, mother, mother, I promise you I won't let any damned Hun kill me. Do you really think I'd allow those Jerries to prevent me returning home to you... to all your wonderful cooking and all your fabulous baking?'

After giving him a beaming smile and yet another loving hug, she chuckled, 'Oh, John, so it's only your "cupboard love that's brought you back to me, eh?' Feeling a touch ashamed of her un-typical unrestrained show of emotion, she broke away from her son, exclaiming, 'Oh John, you're still waiting for that tea I promised you. I'll make it now. You sit and rest, son. Smoke a cigarette if you want to.' She again beamed him a rapturous smile, 'I don't object to you smoking now that you're longer a mere boy, but are my grown-up handsome sailor son.' As she busied herself preparing his tea she frequently cast loving glances at John as if needing to constantly reassure herself that he truly was there; had really returned unwounded to her. Yes, she thought, he's looking really well. And, yes, he's more handsome than ever! Smilingly revealing her intense pleasure, she asked, 'Might there have been any beautiful young ladies where you were hiding from the Germans, John?'

He laughed, 'Aye, mother, there might have been.'

'Did one of them fall in love with you?'

Again merrily laughing, he replied, 'One fall in love with me, mother?... No, not one, but dozens! I had a terrible time fighting them off!'

Although taking care not to show it, he was secretly amazed at his mother's question. Was this an example of that most mysterious thing – the female maternal intuition at work? With wartime conditions being so fraught with dangers and uncertainties; with the odds against both Anna and him surviving to the end of the war being so formidable, he had decided to say nothing to his mother at present about his great love for Anna and her great love for him. But in the midst of her tremendous happiness and emotion at her son's safe return, had his mother somehow managed to pick up something of his deep, but deeply hidden, feelings for Anna? That seemed impossible. By all male rules of logic and reason this simply was just not possible.

241

Later, obeying his mother's self-denying biddings, John left her to get on with preparing dinner, and leisurely strolled down the gently sloping road in the direction his sister should appear as she returned home after her long day's work at a large market-garden on the outskirts of the town.

Brother and sister saw one another at almost the same time. Although quite a distance apart, Jean immediately recognised John in his navy blue sailor's uniform with his cap set at a jaunty angle. John also had no difficulty in recognising his sister in her distinctive Woman's Land Army uniform.

They waved to one another then John effortlessly increased his stride down the slope. Breathless from eager excitement and the efforts of determinedly hurrying up that impending slope, Jean reached out welcoming arms to John. They warmly hugged and emotionally laughed.

Then, standing back a pace, brother and sister lovingly scrutinized each other. Unconsciously echoing her mother, Jean admiringly chuckled, 'Oh, John, you're looking very well. Your uniform really suits you; it makes you look more handsome than ever!'

Although secretly pleased by her sincere flattery, he modestly laughed it off, 'Oh, Jean, you sound just like our doting mother!... you're looking very well yourself. Your face is fair blooming with health and beauty.' He laughed, 'and your uniform really suits you as well!'

Both these admiring statements were true. His sister had never looked so well. Attractively tanned with constantly working outdoors and now animated with loving, welcoming pleasure, her face beamingly glowed. And her Woman's Land Army uniform of bosom hugging green jumper, corduroy breeches and long, thick, woollen stockings really did – even with all its practical, 'down-to-earth' utilitarian aspect – quite amazingly emphasize and flatter the pure femininity of her fine figure.

The initial welcoming excitement over, they happily leisurely walked side by side up the gentle incline towards their home. Suddenly Jean exclaimed, 'Oh, John, before we go in to mother please tell me what really happened to you during that time when you were "missing-in-action". It was a hideously distressing time for mother and me, not knowing if you were alive or dead; uncertain if we would

242

ever see you again or not. Oh, what happened to you? Why couldn't the Navy give us any more definite information about you?'

John had been expecting this. He had his part true, part false answer ready. He certainly was not going to increase his mother's and sister's deep worries about him by letting them know that he was a member of the S.B.S., was frequently engaged in hazardous operations in German-occupied Western Europe. He told his sister he had been engaged in 'normal' naval sea-going duties and that his ship had been sunk near Norway. After being rescued by Norwegian fisherman he was hidden in their country until his escape and return to Britain could be arranged. 'As some of the crew of my ship died when she sank and some, like me, survived and were hidden from the Germans in Norway for a considerable time, the Admiralty could only report us "missing-in-action" until they received definite confirmation of which sailors had actually survived.'

He paused and gazed sympathetically at his sister. 'Oh, Jean, believe me I fully understand what a terribly distressing time that must have been for mother and you. I hope it never happens again.'

'No, I hope not. It would be terrible for mother to go through such an ordeal again.' She smiled brightly at him, 'You're now back safe and sound, that's all that matters. Come on, let's hurry home. I'm hungry, aren't you?'

★ ★ ★

The following day was calm, bright and unusually mild for late autumn. John joyfully took advantage of this glorious weather to make the pilgrimage he made every time he was home on leave – to the summit of Skiddaw.

Glowing in eager early morning sunshine, that mountain was looking its glorious best as it heaved up that steep bulk which sheltered Keswick from the North and provided that attractive small town with its dominating backdrop.

John found it wondrously exhilarating to freely and openly step out towards Skiddaw – that familiar mountain hr fondly thought of as almost being his own special, personal hill; his own, intimate, 'Shangri La.'

After the flatness of Holland, it was delightful to be climbing his favourite homeland hill again. His superbly fit young body soon adjusted to the path's steepness. His eager feet quickly regained their regular, rhythmic, tireless, mountaineer's stride.

But his mind took longer to adjust than his body did. When he spotted a couple of people on the path a good way below him his almost instinctive immediate reaction was to look for concealing cover from which to alertly observe these distant figures and quickly decide if they might pose a dangerous threat to him. Smiling, he self-mockingly castigated himself for being so foolish. These were no feared and loathed Germans. There were none of that despicable Kraut race here, thank God!

Standing at the summit cairn he gazed around with passionate eagerness at that familiar never changing – yet ever changing – scene of Derwentwater sparklingly revealed amidst its enclosing jumble of tumbling hills and its smoother, mistily obscured fells.

After getting himself comfortably seated he expectantly opened his rucksack to see what food his mother had surreptitiously slipped into it. He gently shook his head. He smiled with warm emotional fondness as he saw the abundant – the generously over-abundant – amount of sandwiches she had secreted there.

After the huge breakfast his mother had prepared for him and had dotingly insisted he devour every morsel of, he was not yet really hungry. But he would force himself to eat all those sandwiches. His mother would be most disappointed if he arrived home with some un-eaten sandwiches. She would worry about his poor appetite; would anxiously enquire if he was feeling all right.

He again warmly and fondly smiled as he thought that at least she was hardly likely to enquire – as she often did when he was a boy – about his bowel movements, or lack of them, and whether he was in need of a restorative laxative!

From loving thoughts of his mother's cosseting love of him; her tremendous delight at having him safely home; her determination to abundantly look after her son's 'inner man', it was an easy transition for his mind to longingly turn to thoughts of that other woman who loved him with a different kind of love – a love in its own way every bit as deep and sincere as his mother's maternal love, but also greatly heightened by the demanding urges of sexual passion – Anna.

Remembering how vividly Anna had described her unbounded delight at being at this summit, the first mountain she had ever climbed, and how greedily she had devoured the views revealed to her, and how eagerly she had planned to return here the next year, it was easy for John to imagine her sitting at this very spot surrounded by her tired but volubly excited party of young Dutch students.

The start of this horrendous war had forced the cancellation of Anna's plans to return. Would the eventual end of this devastating war allow her to return? Would she – now his wife – tiredly but happily contentedly sit here beside him, with his arm lovingly encircling her waist?

Giving a deep sad sigh he despairingly feared he was painting far too rosy a picture of their post-war life together.

This war was so terribly full of so many terrible uncertainties. Perhaps the greatest uncertainty was just how much longer it would continue for. Surely it would be madly rash to think it might end this present year, 1943. But mightn't it be reasonable to hope it would finish before the end of next year? Perhaps – for once – the war really would be over by that Christmas!

John's mind now anxiously turned to much more immediate concerns over Anna. Had she got over the worst of her distress at the suddenness of his departure from her? Were the Gestapo investigating Professor Maurik's violent death? Might they be cruelly interrogating Anna – and also Frans and Blanche – over the mysterious killing? He shuddered at that awful thought. Then, obeying his S.B.S training, he determinedly tried to force it out of his conscious mind. Yes, he resolutely decided, he must think positively, must be hopefully optimistic. All this war's terrible dangers and difficulties would be overcome. Anna and he *would* survive this war; *would* get married once it ended; *would* spend their honeymoon in his Lake District and happily and lovingly sit together here on top of Skiddaw.

But, try as he might, he could not entirely ban all pessimism. Doubts again arose and with insistent insidious logic questioned the likelihood of this dream ever becoming reality. Was it really likely that Anna and he would both survive this war then meet up and marry?

★ ★ ★

The un-seasonally mild, bright weather lured John outdoors at every opportunity. He keenly welcomed the demanding efforts of all the hard physical exercise with which he cycled uphill on the narrow, twisting, almost traffic-free roads that undulated over his beloved Lakeland countryside. And then, after sweatily straining uphill for miles, how delightful it was to hunch low on the handlebars and, rejoicing in the wildly overflowing exuberance of his health, strength and freedom, rapidly gain downhill speed and have the road spin past beneath him in a blur of swift pleasure and ease.

And always it was wonderful to cycle along on the 'correct' side of the road without having to worry about the danger of being stopped by any Krauts.

During all this time – being wholly engrossed in his exhilarating physical efforts and pleasures – he happily forgot all his pessimistic doubts, all his deep worries about what was happening to Anna.

Then, leaving his bicycle by the roadside, how eagerly his legs got into the familiar, steady pacing regular rhythm of a natural Fellsman. He could – and did – keep up that steady pace hour after hour, mile after effortless tireless mile.

As, once more, he strode along Helvellyn's narrow, steep and stony Striding Edge he rejoiced in the awareness of just how superbly fit his body was; there was real sensual pleasure in the easy with which it traversed this long – this sublimely long, wild, and starkly beautiful ridge.

While his feet tirelessly strode his soul exultantly soared. With semi-articulate thoughts delightfully soaring he felt something of what Wordsworth had so wondrously poetically experienced on this hill, on this very ridge, and through that sublime experience had – 'recollecting in tranquillity' – discovered that truly we humans 'are greater than we know.'

Chapter Thirty Six

The seven days of John's leave passed all too quickly.

On his last evening at home his mother, despite the strict food rationing, managed to surpass all her previous efforts with the amount and excellent quality of the food she provided for his final dinner.

John and his sister did full justice to the glorious meal. They hungrily cleared their first heaped plates and did the same to the only slightly smaller second helpings. Despite her son and daughter's repeated urgings, their mother took very little, As she slowly and sparingly ate she got immense pure maternal pleasure from seeing them – especially her brave, handsome sailor son – eat with such keen appetites.

Unlike these two glowingly healthy young people, she had little need for a lot of food to keep her going. As, happily contentedly, she observed her son and daughter so openly and honestly revel in their enjoyment of all her eagerly prepared food she flushed with a blissful surge of maternal pride. Aglow with maternity's pure, deep, unselfish love she actually felt herself again more sustenance from each generous forkful they hungrily crammed into their appreciative mouths than they did!

Only one thing prevented her loving happiness from being complete... the ugly shadow cast by the imminence of her son's departure.

★ ★ ★

Early the following morning, replete from last night's feast and the large breakfast his mother insisted he ate, John once more left the peaceful love and comforts of his home and the blissful peace of his Lakeland Hills for the grim uncertainties and dangers of war.

★ ★ ★

There being no immediate need for his keen-honed S.B.S. skills, John was once again sent on 'normal' sea-going, convoy-escorting duties. So, five days later, he was aboard a large, modern Royal Navy destroyer; was the highly trained, well experienced expert seaman/gunner in charge of a set of high-precision, high-velocity twin barrelled oerlikon anti-aircraft guns on that ship which was moored in the Clyde Estuary.

Looking around the familiar water of this huge estuary – the gateway through which most of Britain's vital wartime convoys departure from and eagerly returned to – John had never seen these well sheltered, well guarded waters so crowded. Amongst the many convoy-protecting warships moored here were three of that new class of R.N. warships – escort aircraft-carriers. The squat, ungainly ugliness of these ex-merchant ships converted into escorting aircraft-carriers was made all the more conspicuous, all the more ugly, in comparison to the sleek, slim, rakish lines of the destroyers anchored near them.

Merchant ships of every type and size crowded this huge and attractively hill-enclosed Scottish estuary. But amongst all this vast, varied fleet one ship was outstandingly prominent. The huge size of the Cunard liner *Queen Mary* effortlessly dominated the scene. The drabness of her battleship grey paint did little to diminish the majesty of this truly impressive ship; it could not lessen the graceful lines of her hull or the nobility of her three large, symmetrically raked funnels.

In the immense build-up in preparation for the coming invasion and liberation of Western Europe that liner, and her sister ship the *Queen Elizabeth*, were playing a notable part. Making voyage after voyage – each time carrying more than seven thousand soldiers – they ferried an entire American Army across the North Atlantic. They did this without the loss of a single soldier. This was achieved despite the desperate longings of every German U-boat captain to sink one of these troop-crammed liners and gain glory and, as Hitler had promised, be rewarded with the highest order of the Iron Cross.

★ ★ ★

After passing through the thick wired, large meshed boom that stretched from shore to shore and denied the Clyde Estuary to U-boats, and after fussily shepherding thirty seven scattered merchant ships and persuading them to become a neat convoy, John's destroyer took up the lead position and guided these ships and the other escorting warships into the Atlantic.

Six hours out from the Clyde they ran into a fierce South Westerly gale and for the next three days the convoy slowly and tenaciously battered its way Westwards.

Having nothing to sustain him but thick bacon sandwiches and mugs of hot, sweet cocoa during these three storm-tossed days, John longingly dreamt of the large delightful dinners his mother had so lovingly made for him on his recent leave. But he – like every other sailor on this convoy – happily consoled himself with the reassuring thought that at least the violence of this food and sleep depriving storm made it virtually impossible for any U-boats to effectively attack them.

However they did not enjoy complete freedom from U-boat attack in the calmer seas of their return voyage. This Eastward heading convoy was the largest one John had ever seen. Consisting of more than eighty large, heavily laden British and American merchant ships it stretched for miles.

Looking around as he stood on starboard watch on his destroyer's open bridge, John felt pleasantly reassured as he saw how many escorting warships were protecting these precious merchant ships. All the American merchant ships he could see were exactly uniform in shape and size. They were 'Liberty Ships'; those standard, 10,000 ton welded ships which American shipyards were mass-producing at a truly remarkable rate.

All suitable deck space on these ships was crammed with extra cargo. Through powerful binoculars John could clearly make out the unmistakable bulky shape of Sherman tanks and huge, multi-wheeled army trucks overshadowing the much smaller and neater shapes of the wingless fuselages of fighter aircraft. Looking like thoughtfully gift-wrapped American presents to Britain, each item of deck cargo was neatly cocooned in some form of transparent coating which protected it from the insidiously corroding damage of salt spray.

In the centre of the convoy was a newly commissioned Royal Navy escort-aircraft carrier. Planes from this carrier and most of the long-range, four-engined Liberator aircraft operating over the North Atlantic were now equipped with extra sensitive radar which could locate the tiny target of a surfaced U-boat's conning-tower from considerable distances. Although many R.N. officers were most reluctant to acknowledge this, it did seem that aircraft were now sinking more U-boats than their warships were.

The sudden startling booming noise of a torpedo exploding against a large merchant ship at the tail of the convoy proved that at least one U-boat had successfully evaded both aircraft and warships. Being at the head of the convoy, John's destroyer had to leave it to other escorting warships to hunt for – and eventually destroy – that U-boat.

This was the only enemy action they experienced on the entire voyage. Like many another veteran in this almost five year long battle against U-boats, John thankfully reflected that the loss of only one ship out of more than eighty was a tremendous, a wonderful, improvement over the grim times in 1941 and 1942, and even in the early months of this year, 1943, when the losses of merchant ships (and all too many of their brave crews) had been truly horrendous. He believed that many convoys were now suffering absolutely no losses and many more U-boats were now being sunk than allied ships were. He again thoughtfully reflected that of course this struggle for control of the North Atlantic was one battle that had to be decisively won before the battle to invade and liberate Europe could be undertaken.

Not for the first time he wondered what part he would play in the liberation of Western Europe. Although he could not entirely prevent some slight apprehension, he was confident he would resolutely carry out whatever duties he was given. And, after all, the sooner Europe was freed the sooner he would – hopefully – be re-united with Anna.

As soon as his destroyer moored in the welcome shelter of the Clyde Estuary, John received orders to report immediately to S.B.S. headquarters in Poole. If he felt any sudden slight touch of fear at these orders, knowing that every S.B.S. mission was always dangerous, that suggestion of fear was forcibly subjugated under a surge of excitement, almost exaltation, at the thought of his keen-honed, highly trained S.B.S. skills being once again put to the test of decisive action.

Chapter Thirty Seven

Ten men of two experienced S.B.S. teams attentively listened as Commander Richardson briefed them. 'Both teams will practise for "Operation Starlight . But only one team will be chosen to go on that mission.'

He knew, as they did, that there would be keen competition to be the chosen team even though none of these men at present had any idea of what this operation would entail or just how dangerous it was likely to be. As he stared at these ten strong, tough, fit young sailors sitting before him, the Commander once again thought: 'Yes, all these S.B.S. men certainly are exceptionally brave and resourceful... yes, truly they are the bravest of the brave... the elité of the elité!'

He grinned at them, 'I must admit that it's not only to make you keenly competitive that I've both your teams training for this mission which only one team will carry out. No, I'm afraid your training might well result in some injuries, so I must ensure I have at least five entirely fit men to make up one team.' Again grinning, he explained, 'Before you go on "Operation Starlight our friends in the R.A.F. are going to fly you on a little jaunt. They will take you to Ringway Airfield, near Manchester, which is their main parachute training centre. There you will practise a few H.A.L.O. jumps.'

This news was greeted with a chorus of loud, melodramatic groans of feigned horror and dismay followed by wide grins and somewhat uncertain laughter. All these men had done H.A.L.O. parachute jumps as part of their training. They had no desire to do any more of those nerve-wracking 'High Altitude Low Opening' jumps again. Now they were going to do more of them. Then after these practise jumps they would probably be doing one more jump – into some part of some German-occupied country. It was a daunting prospect.

Commander Richardson's next remarks instantly made the prospect facing these brave men even more daunting. 'I know you have all done those jumps before – have jumped from your aircraft at a high altitude; have fallen many thousands of feet; have opened your parachute at, or less than, one thousand feet above the ground; have landed safely and – most importantly – have all landed close together.

'You are going to make a few more of these practise jumps in daylight.' The Commander paused, stared steadily at these now rather apprehensive S.B.S. sailors, then confirmed their worst apprehensions: 'Then you will make some practise H.A.L.O. jumps in the darkness of night.' There was little or no feigning of the loud gasps of dismay that greeted this news!

★ ★ ★

Three days later, having successfully completed their day and night H.A.L.O. jumps with only two men being disabled by severely sprained ankles, these ten S.B.S. sailors were flown direct from Ringway parachute training centre to an R.A.F. airfield in Suffolk. They were then driven to a nearby manor-house. This imposing mansion was now a S.O.E base; was only one of many such grand old English houses taken over by this rapidly expanding Intelligence Organisation. It was the proliferation of such commandeered bases that caused one of their officers to facetiously declare that S.O.E stood not so much for 'Special Operations Executive,' but rather for 'Stately 'Omes of England'! Commander Richardson welcomed these ten men to this 'Stately 'ome'; quickly selected the five man team who would carry out 'Operation Starlight,' then intensively briefed them.

This team would do a night time H.A.L.O parachute drop into Holland near Utrecht. Would link up with waiting Dutch Resistance Fighters who would guide them to a German detention camp at Amersfoort where captured Dutch Patriots were held and were brutally interrogated before either being executed or sent to concentration camps in Germany for further interrogations then disposal in gas chambers.

'Given suitable weather, you fly out on 'Operation Starlight' tomorrow night.' The Commander explained the need for speed. 'You must free these Dutch Patriots in Amersfoort camp before any more are executed or sent to Germany. But there is one prisoner who is more important than all the others. He is Professor Paul Van Karson. You must find him, free him, and bring him back to England. We believe the Germans plan to send him to Germany soon for intensive interrogation by some of their scientists. You must prevent that happening. You must bring him safely back to England. That is your urgent imperative duty. Is that clearly understood, gentlemen?'

Once the collective briefing was finished Commander Richardson took John aside to give him, and him alone, more information about Professor Van Karson. But first he sincerely praised him. 'This is the first opportunity I've had to congratulate you, Armstrong, on successfully completing "Operation Waterloo. "You really did marvellously well to eliminate both targets, especially after the other four members of your team were killed. I noted your remarks in your detail report on Lieutenant Smith deserving the posthumous award of a medal for his outstanding bravery.

'I have added my strong recommendation to yours. It is now up to "the powers that be" to decide if he gets a "gong" or not. I rather doubt if he will though... not when he was on S.B.S duties. As you know, everything involving S.B.S operations is kept very strictly hush-hush.'

'Yes, I appreciate that, sir. Thank you for adding your recommendations anyway.'

'Now, regarding Professor Van Karson, I'm sure you will be pleased that this time you will be freeing, not killing, this important Dutch scientist.'

John nodded and smiled, 'Yes, sir, that will be a pleasant change .'

'Actually "Operation Starlight" is really a follow-up to "Operation Waterloo. Professor Van Karson is also a nuclear physicist, seemingly quite a brilliant one, but unlike those two treacherous scientists you eliminated, he refused to do any work on helping to develop the Germans atomic bomb. In fact he does the opposite. He feeds us with any information he can get regarding progress of this potentially war-winning German secret weapon. He has been doing this extremely dangerous, vitally important undercover work for quite some time. But now the Huns have caught him. They are going to take him to Germany, torture all information out of him then kill him. That brave Dutchman deserves better than that, doesn't he?'

'Yes sir, he does; he certainly does.'

'I am confident that your S.B.S team will save him and bring him to England. But should it turn out that he has already been tortured and is in too poor physical condition to escape and travel with you to the Dutch coast and keep the arranged rendezvous with a British submarine, you must give him a cyanide suicide pill and save him from any further torture. But according to our latest most reliable gen he has not yet been tortured. It seems the Huns are saving that refinement for when they get him into Germany.'

Commander Richardson concluded by saying, 'As you, Armstrong, are one of the few who know about the terrible possibility of the Germans getting an atomic bomb before the Allies do, I have put you – and only you in your team – fully in the picture regarding the importance of saving Professor Van Karson .Disclose none of this secret knowledge you have to any of your comrades. They all know he is a most important scientist, but only you know exactly just how important he is.'

Chapter Thirty Eight

The flight from Suffolk to near Amersfoort took little more than half an hour.

To the five S.B.S. sailors sitting tensely waiting to do their parachute jump into night shrouded Holland it seemed much longer. It took strong nerves and resolute courage to do any H.A.L.O. jump, but to do one at night into enemy-held country took exceptional nerve and courage. Even these exceptional men were feeling the strain.

The team leader, Lieutenant Anderson, tried to ease the tension by means of some avuncular jocularity. Appreciating his tension relieving efforts and honestly amused by the best of his jokes, all the others interspersed their chuckles and laughter with jokes of their own. More than ever, every member of that united team felt most strongly and securely enveloped within the great warmth and depth of their noble camaraderie.

After some ten minutes the easeful laughter and lively banter gradually subsided then faded away and, slightly more relaxed, every man continued the journey in thoughtful, self-absorbed silence.

Most of John's thoughts were of Anna. It was strange to think he would soon be back in her country. But of course it would be a case of him being 'so near and yet so far' from her. He still had no knowledge of what had happened to her since he had so precipitately left her.

Suddenly a foolish, but vividly bright thought flared to life in his brain. He pictured Anna imprisoned in that German detention camp at Amersfoort. He saw himself gallantly rescue her. He imagined her staring unbelievingly then wildly flinging herself into her miraculously returned hero's outstretched arms.

Then when Lt. Anderson learned that Anna and he were engaged to be married, surely that officer would compassionately allow Anna to return to England with them. Then there would be no need for them to impatiently wait until the war's end; they would be married in Keswick on John's next leave. They would ....

Speeding high through the dark night sky the R.A.F. plane hit turbulence and gave a sudden violent sideways lurch.

John was jolted out of his pleasant, foolish, rosy dream. He self-mockingly smiled at himself. For Anna to be a prisoner in that camp, and for him to rescue her was surely much too unlikely; would be a fairy tale come true. He would be a knight in shining armour riding to save his beloved damsel from a fierce dragon – the fierce, vile, Nazi dragon.

For Anna to be imprisoned in that camp would be too great a coincidence. And yet, amazing coincidences did happen ... like that traitor, Professor Maurik, turning out to be Anna's father. Truth often was stranger than fiction. Might not another amazing coincidence happen?

Lt. Anderson's voice loudly announcing, 'Five minutes to go! Do your final checks now,' brought John back to the present unpleasant reality. At least his rosy pipe-dream about rescuing Anna had kept him from too vividly imagining the horrors of the H.A.L.O. jump that was now imminent.

The icy blast of night air as the aircraft's door was opened told them their tense wait was almost over. All felt apprehension replaced by something like relief that their inactive waiting was over at last.

A shout of 'Go!...Go!...Go!...' and within seconds all five men were falling at a tremendous rate through cold dark space towards unseen Blacked out Holland.

In free fall in that awful darkness John's eyes were glued to the altimeter strapped to his left wrist. Counting off the feet in hundreds the fluorescent numbers frantically revolved like a mad, demented fruit machine. John gambled his life on that altimeter's accuracy.

At one thousand feet he violently hit the button that opened his parachute.

He heard the sharp crack of the 'chute opening. Gasping, he felt the harness sadistically snatch at his crotch.

As after the terrifying speed of his free fall this gentle swaying parachute descent seemed amazingly sedate and leisurely.

Gazing down into the darkness he saw a darker darkness coming rushing up to meet him and immediately all sedateness vanished.

A few more tense moments then he was safely down on damp Dutch soil.

The distinctive musical whistling call of a plover was instantly echoed by three answering calls from nearby. John added his plover call to this strange, well rehearsed nocturnal chorus and confirmed that the entire S.B.S team were safely down and had landed close together.

Guns were pointed and breaths held as shadowy figures slowly approached. Shouts of, 'Starlight!... Starlight!' immediately eased the tension as Dutch Patriots identified themselves. There were warm greetings and firm handshakes.

These brave, patriotic Dutchmen lead the S.B.S. team through the silent darkness to Amersfoort camp. Slowly, stealthily, they crawled to the camp's high fence. A large gap was quickly cut through the barded wire.

While the Dutch Patriots stayed and kept guard at this gap the five S.B.S men passed swiftly but silently through. Merging into the dim shade of a hut they became darker shades... deadly dangerous shadows highly skilled in the black arts of stealthy killing.

A solitary patrolling German sentry was quickly, easily, silently dealt with.

The German soldier standing at the search-light on the camp's only tower posed a much greater danger. The silent killing of him required different skills. Every member of that S.B.S team was an accurate marksman in a wide variety of weapons, but was also a specialist in some chose weapon. John's choice was a crossbow. At any reasonable range his modern crossbow, fitted with a telescopic sight, was a deadly accurate silent weapon.

Standing in the concealing darkness of the hut nearest the searchlight tower he studied his target. With the cross wires of his night-sight covering the sentry's neck, John gently squeezed the trigger. The crossbow's bolt sped silently and accurately into that German soldier's throat and immediately ended all threat from him.

The way was now clear to rescue Professor Van Karson and free as many captured Dutch Patriots as possible.

Lieutenant Anderson threw open the door of hut number three, switched on the light and loudly announced, 'We are Englander's!' He then called out for Professor Paul Van Karson.

Startled and bemused the Professor, a darkly bearded man in his late forties, came hesitantly stumbling forward. His identity was checked. He was calmed and reassured; was informed he was being taken to freedom in England.

Once the Professor was safely guided through the gap in the fence more than fifty other Dutch Patriots thankfully – some almost disbelievingly, some fearful of being lead into a cruel Nazi trap – hurried from the squalid foulness of their overcrowded huts and then, trembling with eagerness, urgently scrambled through that inviting gap.

Welcomed by their waiting countrymen, they were quickly sorted into smaller groups then each dispersing group was guided to some safe place of concealment from which in due course they could resume their noble struggle against the hated German oppressors.

Once the Professor and the other freed Dutchmen were well clear of the camp the S.B.S presented their 'visiting card' to the Krauts. The sound of male voices rising loudly in vigorous renderings of patriotic Teutonic songs suggested that a party was going on in the camp's officer's mess. Swiftly following these sounds to their source, Leading-seaman Johnstone – the S.B.S team's specialist in hand-grenades – removed the pin from a Mills bomb, eased open the door of the officer's mess, rolled the ugly grey bomb towards the crowded tables then slammed the door shut.

As he ran to join his waiting comrades the grenade exploded with its familiar, impressively loud deadly roar.

Travelling with steady pace and alert caution through their blacked-out, curfewed, German patrolled native countryside, two Dutch Patriots expertly guided the S.B.S team, with Professor Van Karson well protected in their midst, further and further away from the drastically stirred-up hive of that German camp.

Securely shepherded, warmly encouraged and occasionally gently chivied by his calm, experienced British rescuers the professor gallantly did his utmost not to slow the progress of the entire party too much. But, being older and – especially after his time in the squalid misery and semi-starvation of German custody – much less fit than all the others, he found it an exhausting effort to keep up with them.

Anxiously observing the Professor's increasing exhaustion Lieutenant Anderson had a discreet word with their two Dutch guides.

Quietly elated at having been chosen to take part in this obviously very important rescue mission, both these keen young Dutchmen were increasingly inclined to move rather more quickly than was quite wise. Contritely abashed, they promised to slow their pace to accommodate the struggling Professor.

Grinning, the Royal Navy officer explained, 'The speed of every convoy is determined by the speed of the slowest ship in the convoy.'

After another hour of slow progress the entire party sat and, still alert, rested for half-hour. then Professor Van Karson giving a determined display of renewed vigour, they set out on the final part of their fraught journey to the Dutch 'safe-house' where they would be securely hidden.

All the following day they thankfully ate, rested, and slept in a secret extension to that safe-house's large cellar.

At night they emerged again cautiously travelled many dark kilometres then reached a certain point on the Dutch coast. There they rendezvoused with a waiting Royal Navy submarine.

★ ★ ★

During the next month Professor Van Karson was frequently interviewed by a number of eminent British scientists. These boffins – especially the extremely worried physicists – were desperately anxious to receive every scrap of information or astute well-informed speculation that Dutchman could give them on how far advanced were the German's with the development of their atomic bomb.

The British scientific establishment was keen to keep this important Dutch physicist in Britain; however after a heated bout of 'horse-trading' between Churchill and Roosevelt their intelligence agencies sealed a deal and Professor Van Karson was 'given' to the Americans.

As soon as he received security clearance the Professor started helping some of world's greatest scientists with their top-secret 'Manhattan Project'... that urgent race to develop an atomic bomb in America before the German's (perhaps even the Japanese?) perfected their own nuclear weapons.

Chapter Thirty Nine

Once the rescued Dutch professor was handed over to an eagerly waiting high-ranking S.O.E. officer, Lieutenant Anderson's S.B.S team disembarked from their discreetly berthed submarine.

They were quickly driven to yet another S.O.E 'Stately 'Ome' somewhere in Southern England.

When the Colonel in charge of this secret Intelligence Establishment had fully de-briefed them on 'Operation Starlight' he sincerely praised their effort and concluded by saying, 'Yes, gentlemen, a truly perfect operation carried out perfectly'.

Modestly basking in this unexpected praise the five young sailors self-deprecatingly grinned at one another. John also secretly grinned at himself as he thought 'Only one thing makes this perfect operation not quite perfect for me … the fact that Anna was not held captive in that German camp and that I was not able to gallantly rescue her, bring her to England and marry her.'

Early the following morning Lt. Anderson was given a map and ordered to lead his team from this 'Stately 'Ome' and, travelling inconspicuously on foot, report to S.B.S headquarters in Poole within twelve hours.

They made it to Poole in ten hours, and this was achieved despite having to make many time-consuming detours around army camps and bases. Almost every second field in this corner of England seemed to have been taken over by the British or American army.

Moving with swift skilled stealth they passed unseen and unchallenged around countless numbers of tanks, trucks, all sizes of artillery and huge heaps of ammunition. Arranged in neat rows and concealed from the air under cosy cocoons of camouflage netting, this mighty mass of military equipment held a suggestion of barely contained impatience..... of eagerly wanting to be put to violent use.

They sensed no similar feeling of impatience, of wanting to be put to the test of battle, by the completely untested young American sentries un-alertly guarding their tented camps.

As these battle-hardened S.B.S. sailors watched a long column of British soldiers pass them on a sweatily strenuous route march they sensed a palpable aura of resolute determination from these mostly young and un-tested soldiers. They seemed imbued with quiet confidence... a strong feeling that they would grimly do their duty when, the long waiting and intensive training over, they waded ashore on some well fortified, tenaciously defended French beach.

Their strongly fostered regimental pride, that great 'Esprit De Corps', immensely strengthened these soldiers confidence that when they were put to this supreme test – and it was looming ever nearer – none of them would let their loyal comrades down.

The S.B.S sailors silently wished these inexperienced young soldiers the best of luck when they faced the traumatic trial of going into battle for the first time.

★ ★ ★

Throughout that autumn, then all winter, and then ever more frequently and urgently as winter's gales gave way to the gentler breezes of spring and then to the smiling warmth of the momentous early summer of 1944 every S.B.S team was engaged time after time on most important and usually most dangerous operations in German-occupied Western Europe. With unflinching bravery these unsung heroes secretly prepared the way and helped ensure that when the imminent, the vastly complex, extremely hazardous British and American amphibious military landings took place on carefully selected French beaches which these S.B.S teams had painstaking reconnoitred, they would be successful.

Whenever the weather permitted – and often even when the uncertain winter weather barely permitted it – John's team stealthily operated as frogmen in various parts of the strongly fortified French shore between Calais and Boulogne.

Not quite all of these dangerous missions were carried out in complete stealth and silence. Sometimes, using techniques that deliberately caused noisily spectacular explosions, they demolished a number of German underwater obstacles at beaches near Calais.

Not having been put fully in the picture, none of these S.B.S sailors knew it but they were a part – a small, but important part – of 'Operation Fortitude'. This top-secret operation was the largest and most successful British and American deception campaign of the entire war. It succeeded in fooling Hitler into believing that when the Allies amphibious assault against his formidable 'Atlantic Wall' took place it would be launched against beaches in the Pas de Calais area. He therefore ordered that the already strong coastal defences in this area be even further strengthened. He also ordered that most of his Western Army's reserves – including the vitally important Panzer Divisions – be kept in this Northern part of France.

This was what the Allied deception planners had hoped for; the further Hitler's Panzers were from the Normandy beaches the better the chance of the Allies invasion being successful.

* * *

By the middle of May, 1944 it was obvious that D-Day – the day when vast British and American Armies would storm ashore on French beaches – was rapidly approaching. It was impossible to keep all the immense preparations for this tremendous undertaking completely secret.

Everyone involved in this historic event, code named 'Operation Overlord', from Churchill and Roosevelt; Generals Eisenhower and Montgomery and all other 'top-brass' fully in the know, down to the youngest, least experienced private soldier tremulously waiting in anticipation of going into battle for the first time was irresistibly caught up in the excitement, the hidden fears and deep worries about what would happen on D-Day. Despite all its years of meticulous planning 'Operation Overlord' was still a desperate gamble. From the highest to the lowest the feeling of deep, but strongly controlled apprehension was palpable .... would D-Day succeed or fail?... would you personally survive or die?

* * *

Two weeks before the planned date for D-Day John's S.B.S team were in Normandy. After being landed by a Lysander aircraft in a night-shrouded field behind the coastal town of Arromanches they were warmly greeted by the French Resistance Leader for this district who, for greater security, was know to them only as 'Léon'.

At a carefully selected 'safe-house' near Arromanches the extra Sten-guns and ammunition the S.B.S men had brought were distributed to Léon's team of Resistance Fighters. The British sailors were impressed by the eagerness with which these patriotic Frenchmen wanted to put those sub-machines guns to good use by killing some of the hated Boche with them.

Likewise, the French Patriots were greatly impressed by the amount of plastic explosives these British had brought with them and by the supremely confident way they handled it. The Frenchmen eagerly learned how to handle this dangerously un-stable putty-like explosive almost as well as these experienced experts did.

Every night Léon's team of patriots used their intimate knowledge of their Normandy homeland to guide the British experts to the important targets they had been instructed to find, thoroughly inspect, and – at some – set hidden explosive charges.

As the shore in front of Arromanches – code-named 'Gold Beach' – was to be one of the main landing places for the British Army on D-Day, the neutralization of these various targets by the brave Frenchmen and experienced British S.B.S. sailors was vital. Their dangerous clandestine actions should save the lives of many British soldiers as, desperately vulnerable, they waded ashore on that momentous day.

As May gave way to the first week of June the long, bright evenings got even longer and ever brighter. These British and French teams, now well integrated and working smoothly together, had to wait even later before it was dark enough to leave their safe-house and successfully continue their stealthy work.

During the night of the third of June they completed the last of their allotted pre-invasion tasks. Stealthily and ruthlessly they 'neutralized' certain key German military personnel and a number of obnoxious French traitors who worked with these Germans.

Now they had nothing to do but wait.....alertly, keenly and impatiently wait for D-day.

The following evening five S.B.S. sailors and six French Patriots were crowded into a gloomy attic room in their safe-house near Arromanches. After a good meal, all were leisurely smoking strong French cigarettes and appreciatively drinking a final glass of red wine. The talk and laughter died as Léon, the middle-aged schoolteacher leader of this district's Resistance Fighters, unlocked a cupboard, shifted aside a jumble of clothes, hinged up three floorboards then lifted out a clandestine wireless set. After he plugged-in and switched-on the cumbersome pre-war wireless everyone silently waited for the wireless's valves to warm up. To the impatient waiting Frenchmen they seemed to take much longer than usual to heat up.

At last there was a crackle of static then the familiar dot-dot-dot-dash morse for the letter 'V' ... the 'V for Victory' call sign of the Free French Radio. Every Frenchman tensely listening to the stream of French flowing to them from London eagerly hoped to hear, inserted amongst news items, a special coded message telling them that the long awaited British and American assault on German-occupied France was underway.

At last that uplifting, heart-pounding message came through loud and clear. It was emphatically repeated three times.... 'The dice are on the carpet!'

This was the message the S.B.S. team were also expecting. D-Day would be at dawn tomorrow, the fifth of June, 1944

Crowded together, the eleven men stood and raised their glasses as Léon gave emotional toasts: 'Here's to success for D-Day tomorrow!... Here's Victory to the Allies; defeat to the Boche.... Here's to the return of Freedom to France!'

As soon as their glasses were drained the oldest French Patriot started quietly and tremulously singing the Marseillaise. With quavering voices and eyes streaming tears the other Frenchmen emotionally joined in. As the British sailors whole-heartedly added their voices to this patriotic singing even the most phlegmatic of these tough, battle-hardened, resolute men felt a hint of emotional moisture blurring his eyesight.

All eleven men fell silent as a sudden strong gust of wind hammered heavy rain against the attic windows. All listened apprehensively as increasingly frequent gusts savagely battered against the shuddering windows. The British sailors felt even more apprehensive than the Frenchmen; they had personal experience of an unexpected un-seasonal storm seriously disrupting a well-planned naval operation. They feared that if these fierce gusts developed into a full summer gale tomorrow's planned invasion might be gravely jeopardized. Again from personal experience of amphibious landing exercises they knew how easily small, flat-bottomed landing-craft could be swamped or capsized in even a moderate surf.

Lieutenant Anderson, the S.B.S. leader, voiced his team's unspoken thoughts: 'I hope that wind dies down as quickly as it sprung up.'

'Yes,' Leading-seaman John Armstrong fervently replied, 'Yes, let's hope to God it does!'

The Lieutenant turned to Léon, 'Anyway, after receiving that code message we must all obey our orders. No matter what the weather's like we must be ready and waiting at our pre-arranged targets in the expectation – the hope – that the invasion will go ahead at dawn tomorrow as planned. You agree?

'Yes, yes, of course I agree'. Léon stood silently staring as another fierce gust shook the attic's windows, then he passionately gasped, 'Oh I hope there's no delay. I hope the weather calms. Surely the invasion will start tomorrow!'

★ ★ ★

Three hours later, under cover darkness, the French Patriots and British sailors left the safe-house. All the French and Lt Anderson with two of his S.B.S team headed inland to their various targets. The other two members of his team – Leading-seaman John Armstrong and Bill Kemp – went in the opposite direction. They headed towards the Normandy coast. As they neared the unseen shore they became increasingly aware of – and increasingly anxious about – the strength of the wind gusting in from the sea. They distinctly tasted the agitated sea's salty breath on their lips.

Stealthily following the familiar, previously reconnoitred route through the dark lanes and narrow, cobbled streets of the sleepy, blacked-out town of Arromanches and skilfully evading patrolling German sentries they safely reached their target – a seaside villa named, 'Bon Sejour'.

Like most houses on, or overlooking, this part of the Normandy coast the villa had been taken over by the German Army. Many of these commandeered buildings were now fortified strong-points, part of Hitler's formidable 'Atlantic Wall' which he hoped was now strong enough to deter or defeat any planned Allied amphibious landings in Western Europe. The Germans were using the ground floor of villa 'Bon Sejour' as their main telephonic communications centre for their defences in this part of Normandy. This military telephone exchange was John's and Bill's target. As soon as they were certain that D-Day was underway they would, by 'neutralizing' this centre, severely disrupt communications between the Germans coastal observations posts and gun-emplacements and their local headquarters, and, in turn, the local commanders would be unable to send reliable information to their commanding officer in his inland headquarters, nor would they be able to receive orders from him.

Using the key provided by Léon, John noiselessly opened a small door set in the gloomily dark obscurity of the landward side of the villa. After following Bill through the dim doorway he pulled the door shut and locked it from the inside. Portioned off from the rest of the building, narrow, and steep wooden stairs led directly from this doorway to what had been the servants spartan sleeping quarters in the attic. The bedrooms beneath the attic were now dormitories where off-duty German Army telephonists lived and slept.

After silently standing close together for some time while their eyes tried to adapt to the almost complete blackness, John whispered, 'We better take our boots off now'.

'Yes, sure,' Bill agreed. He whispered, 'Let's hope we don't get too many splinters in our feet.'

Sitting on the bottom stairs they quickly removed their boots, then, carrying them, slowly groped and tip-toed their way up the old, alarmingly creaky wooden stairs. Holding their breaths they sneaked past the bolted door that led into the Germans dormitory. Continuing noiselessly upwards they reached the attic.

The bare, dusty and slightly uneven floorboards of the attic did not seem as noisily creaky as the stairs – not quite! Nor was the darkness in this large, almost empty attic room quite so utterly dark as the stairs. The room's two small windows allowed the night sky to reveal its less sombre dimness.

Acutely conscious of the German soldiers in the bedrooms beneath them, John and Bill moved on their stockened feet with infinitely slow and delicate care. Placing their Sten-guns and other weapons beside them, ready for instant use should that be necessary, they got themselves settled as comfortably as possible on the hard floorboards and sleeplessly and stoically waited for dawn – a dawn that would bring the long awaited Allied assault on German-occupied France.

Or would it?

Anxiously listening to the wind gusting and whistling around this seaside villa's high attic these experienced S.B.S. sailors fervently prayed that the weather would calm down before dawn. But even if it did, they knew that the angry surf – its roaring sound now magnified by the night's darkness – would continue to intimidatingly growl for a considerable time after the wind dropped.

Might D-Day have to be delayed?

Or worse, much worse, might it go ahead as planned at dawn today and might that fiercely restless surf turn D-Day into disaster?.... A disaster infinitely worse than the blood-soaked tragic failure of the amphibious landing at Dieppe in 1942?

Chapter Forty

At the first faintest hint of dawn John and Bill silently made their way to the attic's windows. Watching night's gloom being steadily conquered by the sun's most welcome warming glow they anxiously and expectantly waited to see what full daylight would reveal.

Would today, the 5th June, 1944, be an historic day?

Would they see a vast armada heading for that barded-wire and obstacle strewn Arromanches beach which spread out right in front of them?

At last dawn's pure fresh light revealed a brightly glittering sea... a sea alive with sparkling waves, but a sea bereft of any sign of an approaching British armada. John whispered his disappointment, 'D-Day must be postponed.'

'Yes, it must,' Bill sombrely replied. 'Postponed for how long do you think?'

'If the wind continues to drop and that surf gets calmer perhaps it will only be delayed for 24 hours. Perhaps D-Day will go ahead at dawn tomorrow. Anyway, obeying our orders, we will wait here in the hope that it does go ahead tomorrow.'

★ ★ ★

That inactive silent day spent in their attic room, always acutely aware that any careless noisy movement might betray them to the German soldiers in the rooms beneath them, was one of the longest, most wearisome days these two men had ever spent. They found this tense waiting, silently cooped up in their dreary, dusty attic more deeply, subtly, nerve-rackingly testing than active fighting was. Only their fantastically tough and thorough S.B.S training saw them through it;

enabled them to keep the unavoidable tension securely under control.

Eventually the endless daylight hours gave way to the even longer, more dreary nighttime hours.

As he silently and wearily lay through these interminable hours John often thought of Anna. He let the lively activities of his mind and imagination compensate for the unavoidable inactivity of his body.

Eagerly longing to be re-united with Anna he desperately hoped that this war would end soon. His love of her was as deep, sincere, and strong as ever. At times he self-indulgently revelled in gloriously pleasant memories of their wondrous amorous nights together in their secret secluded love-rest at her Dutch farm.

Then after a while, these warm glowing vividly bright pictures of their fantastically fulfilling love-making were superseded by forcefully insistent worries ... deep worries over how any longer delay to D-Day than just 24 hours might affect Anna. What if D-Day did – like Dieppe – turn into a horrible disaster? Such an outcome tomorrow – if the Allies invasion did go ahead tomorrow – might result in the war dragging on for another one, or more years. How could Anna cope with any such further delay in him returning to marry her?

John tried to imagine how any long delay in bringing this war to a victorious conclusion was likely to effect not only Anna, but all the brave Resistance Fighters in every German-occupied country. The terrible news of the failure of the British and American invasion and liberation of France would send shock-waves of despair through every one of those Freedom Fighters; they would despondently fear there never would be an Allied victory; freedom might never be returned to them. And in those extra years of Nazi tyranny how many more of them would be caught by the Gestapo, be tortured then shot?... or be sent to slave-labour in Germany, then, reduced to starving skeletal zombies, be disposed of in some concentration camp's gas-chamber and furnace?

With urgent resolute determination John forced thoughts of any such terrible fate befalling Anna out of his mind. Then with a flare of inwardly directed anger he ordered his conscious brain not to harbour, nor dare articulate, the fearful treacherous thought that Anna might already be dead.

She was alive, she would survive, she would cope with any delay in him returning to marry her!

Forcing his thoughts to less personal worries and remembering the briefings given by Commander Richardson before 'Operation Waterloo' when he disclosed the desperate efforts German scientists were making to develop an atomic bomb, John was fearful that an Allied disaster on D-Day might result in these dedicated Nazi physicists gaining sufficient time to perfect their awesome bomb. The consequences of that outcome did not bear thinking about!

D-Day must succeed tomorrow...... Bill and he would do everything in their power to help ensure its success.

★ ★ ★

John Armstrong and Bill Kemp were not the only ones sleeplessly worrying about what would happen tomorrow.

Secreted behind blacked-out windows, electric lights glared all night in almost every room of Southwick House. This Georgian-style mansion was yet another 'stately 'Ome of England' commandeered by the military. It was not another secret S.O.E base, but was General Eisenhower's forwards headquarters near Portsmouth from which he and his 'top-brass' were poised to direct 'Operation Overlord' once it at long last got under way.

Bad weather on the 4th and worse weather forecast for the planned day for the D-Day landings, the 5th June, 1944, had forced General Eisenhower – the Supreme Allied Commander for 'Operation Overlord' – to order that this vast, incredibly complex amphibious undertaking be postponed for 24 hours.

Now, early in the morning of the 5th., Eisenhower and all his most senior British and American officers were gathered around a large, document strewn table in the library of Southwick House. Every officer anxiously listened as the top R.A.F. meteorologist gave his latest report. There was no guarantee, but he hoped for a favourable 'window' in the weather tomorrow. The wind should not exceed Force Three, and the cloud ceiling might be high enough to permit all air operations as planned. The forecast for a few days after the 6th was less favourable.

The vital decision had to be made ... should D-Day go ahead tomorrow or be again delayed?

Small and cocky British General, Sir Bernard Montgomery, was the first to speak up. He was most emphatically all for going ahead tomorrow.

American Generals Bradley and Patton were also, but more hesitantly, for going ahead tomorrow.

Air Marshall Leigh-Mallory was rather more doubtful. He was not happy with the uncertainty of the weather forecast.

Admiral Sir Bertram Ramsey, the officer in command of the entire naval side of 'Operation Overlord' authoritatively spoke up, 'A final, irrevocable decision has to be made now. Many of the tens of thousands soldiers crammed overlong in overcrowded troopships are already violently seasick. They cannot be kept cooped up much longer. They must be landed at dawn on the Normandy beaches tomorrow, or be disembarked in England instead.'

A tense silence fell over the room. All eyes focussed on the Supreme Commander. He – and he alone – had to make the tremendous decision.

General Eisenhower who, grim-faced and mostly silently, had sat intently listening to the varying opinions of these sombre officers, frowned as another shower of heavy rain was driven against the room's tall, narrow windows. He inwardly cursed this God-damn awful English weather. These Brits had assured him that June was usually one of the calmest, brightest English summer months. If this rain and gale tormented weather was typical of their best summer month, he dreaded to think what their worst summer month must be like!

Should he order D-Day to go ahead or not?... almost Hamlet like, he found it difficult to come to a definite decision... to go, or not to go, that is the question!

He thought of some of the consequences of any long delay. President Roosevelt, who was strongly pressing him for a major (and popular) American victory in Europe before the presidential elections later this year, would be extremely disappointed and displeased.

Winston Churchill, too, would be most disappointed, but his main concern would be how to break the news of any lengthy delay to his great wartime 'friend' – Josef Stalin. For more than a year Stalin had been demanding that the British and Americans opened a Second Front in Western Europe to take some pressure off the Russian Army who were taking much more than their fair share of the bloody battle against the Nazis. Winston could all too vividly imagine how furious Stalin would be at any further delay in the Western Allies opening that Second Front.

271

But, General Eisenhower grimly thought as he agonised over the fatal decision he had to make, the fury of Stalin would be nothing to the fury of tens of thousands of bereaved Americans, British and Canadian next-of-kin if they thought the lives of their soldier sons, husbands or brothers had been recklessly thrown away in a D-Day landing that the unsuitable weather had made far too risky an operation.

Another nagging worry for him was the knowledge that ninety percent of his American soldiers had no battle experience. How well would those un-tested young soldiers react when they waded ashore on a Normandy beach tenaciously, defended by resolute German soldiers?... and many of these enemy soldiers were tough, battle-hardened veterans of years of brutal fighting on the Russia Front.

Every man in that crowded, but apprehensively silent room felt increasingly conscious of the mounting tension. There must be no more delay. The Supreme Commander must give a definite decision now.

Two more agonizingly long, slow minutes passed as Eisenhower lit up one more of his almost chain-smoked cigarettes, then, sitting with shoulders hunched in what seemed near to utter exhaustion, silently smoked it.

He made up his mind. He also decided how he would announce his momentous decision. These anxious, stressed officers wanted no long speech. He would give his clear order in a few blunt words. He would leave the high-flown rhetoric to old Winston... he, with his many years of wartime experience, was much better at it!

The Supreme Allied Commander savagely stubbed out his cigarette in the large, half-full glass ashtray in front of him then rose to his feet. He straightened his shoulders. He gave each of his most senior officers a quick, resolute stare. These officers steadily returned his stare and stood tensely waiting.

Loudly and decisively General Eisenhower uttered the historic words, 'Okay, gentlemen, let's go!'

'Operation Overlord' – the greatest, most important amphibious assault of all time was underway!

★ ★ ★

At the first hint of dawn John Armstrong and Bill Kemp silently rose from the hard attic floorboards and stealthily made their way through the uncertain dimness to the two small windows.

The same thought was in both their minds: would today – the 6th June, 1944 – be D-Day?

Would daylight reveal a vast armada sailing in towards the beaches in front of and on both sides of this small Normandy town of Arromanches?..... Would they, from their attic windows in the villa 'Bon Sojour' have a grandstand view of a tremendous historic event?... Would they witness the first – and the most risky and dangerous – stage of the British and American attempt to liberate all Western Europe from Nazi tyranny?

Or – as yesterday – would dawn again disappoint: reveal nothing but an empty sea?

These experienced sailors noted with rising hope that the worst of yesterday's summer gale had blown itself out, but the noise of the as yet unseen surf suggested that an angry swell was still running.

John whispered, 'Conditions are much better today. Surely the invasion will now go ahead.?'

Bill nodded, 'Yes it better! I don't fancy being cooped up in this damn attic much longer!'

Eventually dawn's brightness overpowered night's darkness, but even yet the empty, or ship crowded sea was not revealed to them. Thick white mist concealed everything.

Both sailors silently, but viciously, cursed. Was that sea never going to be revealed to them?

The long minutes silently passed. John and Bill got increasingly despondent: they feared they would have to endure another weary day, another even more dreary night in this attic.

Then with dramatic suddenness the sun's eager strength burned away the concealing mist and at last disclosed the glittering sea – but not an empty sea!

These two Royal Navy sailors stared in wide-eyed amazement. They choked with profound emotion; they gasped with immense inarticulate pride. They had a unique view of this historic D-Day invasion. No other Englishmen were seeing it as they were seeing it!

The entire sea was crammed with ships. There were ships of all shapes and sizes. This vast armada were not distant dots on the far horizon . Having taken advantage of the concealing mist many ships were already quite close to the Normandy landing sites. Flotillas of infantry landing-craft and larger tank landing-craft were steadily making for these French beaches. Royal Navy destroyers assiduously guarded crowded troopships as they urgently disembarked many more British soldiers into other landing-craft. Behind these troopships sleek cruisers keenly patrolled. Some miles beyond the cruisers two battleships loomed and with their majestic display of impressive might gave extra protection to the vulnerable troopships and brought apprehensive soldiers heartening assurance that the Royal Naval was doing all that was humanly possible to get them safely ashore.

As if mesmerized, John and Bill continued staring for what seemed an immense time, but was less than half a minute. The most amazing thing about this fantastic sight was the incredible silence. There was no gunfire either from the ships or shore. The whole world seemed to be waiting with bated breath.

The German sentries viewing that immense armada were as mesmerized as John and Bill. But while these British sailors were held motionless with awe and pride, the Boche were paralysed with shock and fear.

Bright muzzle-flashes from the heavy guns of the battleships H.M.S. Nelson and H.M.S Rodney as they simultaneously fired broadsides signalled the end of the uncanny silence.

It took a few seconds for the thunderous roar of these guns to reach the shore and set off a bedlam of terrifying noise, smoke and confusion.

Shaken German sentries belatedly activated shrieking klaxons.

Every warship eagerly followed the lead of the battleships. Accurately aimed at carefully pre-selected targets, volley after volley of massive naval firepower rained down on the German coastal defences. Huge shells from the battleships smashed with devastating effect into the largest, most menacing concrete gun-emplacements guarding the Arromanches beaches.

John grinned at Bill, 'I hope to God no warship has been mistakenly given this villa as its target.'

'No, lets' hope not.'

John again grinned, 'I think we can safety put our boots on now .

274

No Jerry in the rooms below us will hear us moving about now, not with all this din.'

'Yeah, we could do a clog-dance and they wouldn't hear us. Anyway none of them'll be in the bedrooms now, will they?..... they'll all be on duty in their communications rooms, won't they?'

'Yes, they will.' John imagined those German soldiers' reaction when they heard the warning klaxons and the gunfire: how precipitously they would leap out of bed, how quickly throw on their uniforms and urgently dash downstairs to their allotted place at telephone exchange or wireless console. 'And that's where we better head for too and 'neutralise' them before they send information to, and pass on orders from their headquarters.'

Two minutes later, their boots and webbing gear on and weapons checked, they were ready. Both men felt the familiar, nerve tingling excitement of a surge of adrenalin. After being silently inactively cooped up in this attic for so long they experienced a definite touch of eagerness to be actively – even though dangerously – moving again and doing their best to help ensure the success of D-Day.

Unknowingly echoing the words of General Eisenhower, John said, 'Okay, Bill, let's go!'

Chapter Forty One

Tense with ruthless determination, John and Bill once again put their fine-honed killing skills into use.

They stormed into the villa's communications room. At point-blank range they fired four quick bursts from their Sten-guns. Four dead or dying German soldiers collapsed onto the floor.

John smashed up all the wireless equipment while Bill, using his specialist knowledge, swapped over some lines at the telephone console and then disconnected or cut others. Hopefully when senior German officers at their inland headquarters tried to phone collaborating French civilians at Arromanches to get information on what was happening at the coast these re-routed lines would add further confusion to these officers already confused picture.

Their task successfully completed, John and Bill stood in the shelter of the front door of the villa and gazed around at the vast, violent, noisy drama unfolding all around them.

British warships were still furiously pounding some of the German coastal defences. The many high, white spouts of tormented water rising amongst the steadily approaching landing-craft proved that, despite the fierce naval bombardment, some German guns were still all too actively and accurately firing.

At one place large and small landing-craft had already beached and were urgently unloading their cargoes of tanks and infantry. German machine-guns were viciously chattering their message of hate at the desperately exposed and vulnerable British soldiers wading ashore.

'Poor buggers!... Poor brave buggers!' John compassionately gasped. 'I hope most of them manage off that beach safely.'

Bill nodded his heart-felt silent agreement.

Those two brave men were deeply moved by witnessing the

tremendous courage of all those other brave men facing enemy shells, mortar-bombs and machine-guns on that terribly exposed open beach.

Some British soldiers made it to the comparative safety of the sand dunes. Many did not.

After fiercely cursing the unseen Krauts who were bringing savage death to those brave British soldiers, Bill said, 'I feel we should go and try to silence those bloody machine-gunners, don't you, John?'

'Yes, I feel the same, Bill, but...' A deluge of naval shells exploding near the villa and between them and the beach where the British soldiers were, threw them to the floor. When the deadly din died they scrambled to their feet and John said, 'If we tried to get to those Kraut machine-gunners we would be hit by our own naval guns. We better follow orders, head inland and meet up with Lieutenant Anderson, Léon and the others.'

Keeping to the rutted lanes and narrow cobbled streets they had approached by, they hurried through the uncannily deserted town of Arromanches. Most French civilians were sheltering in cellars. Most German soldiers were already at their posts, manning their costal defences or were being held in reserve many miles inland, nervously uncertainly waiting until their senior officers had a much clearer picture of what was happening at their sector of the Normandy coast.

Only their week of moving about this 'hedgerow country' with the French Patriots, and their expert map-reading skills guided John and Bill accurately through this confusing Norman Countryside. Its intricate patchwork of small cornfields, densely packed orchards and hazel copses; its many identical sleepy hamlets and modest grey stone farms really were confusing. Adding extra confusion were the many similar looking narrow sunken lanes they had to cautiously navigate. All those constricting lanes were bounded by ancient, densely thick and in-penetrable hedges growing on high, enclosing banks.

As they again halted to consult their map, John said, 'I hope our Generals know what this countryside's like and have planned accordingly. It looks a place much easier to defend than to attack through.'

'Yeah,' Bill said, 'and after occupying it for four years the Krauts will be familiar with every inch of it. I doubt our P.B.I. (Poor Bloody Infantry) lads will have a tough time fighting their way through here.'

Almost exactly on time they reached the rendezvous point where Lt. Anderson and Léon were waiting with their now well integrated team of S.B.S sailors and French Resistance Fighters

After the warm greetings were over, John confirmed that the German communications centre at the coastal villa and its four occupants had been successfully 'neutralised.'

'Good,' Lt Anderson said, 'We've successfully completed our first tasks, too. After 'neutralising' the sentries at our first bridge we removed the demolition charges the Boche had set, then guarded the bridge until our paratroopers, who had dropped quite a way from their planned landing zone, eventually arrived. They will guard that bridge until soldiers from the beach-head arrive and advance over it. Other Paratroops had already captured two more bridges nearer the beach-head.'

The young lieutenant smiled, 'No doubt when the history of D-Day is written the Paratroops will get all the credit and glory for capturing these three bridges intact.'

John grinned, 'Ah well, being the S.BS., the most secret section of the "Silent Service", we're used to receiving no public recognition of all our... our most gallant efforts, aren't we?'

'Anyway,' Lt. Anderson continued, 'after handing over to the Paras, we hurried to our next targets: two smaller bridges further inland. We quickly demolished them. Now no counter-attacking Germans will be able to use them. And now we better all press-on to our next targets.' Guided by Léon, the entire group moved silently and as rapidly as experienced caution dictated through this familiar but now desperately dangerous Normandy countryside where every hedgerow could conceal Boche sentries and every bend in a lane could suddenly reveal alertly advancing Boche soldiers.

And the hated Germans were not the only danger.

Guns of Royal Navy warships were now firing at targets well behind the beaches where British soldiers had established rather precarious bridge-heads. Shells from the two battleships were reaching targets deeper and deeper inland. Some of those huge shells landed at a distance which every one of the anxiously hurrying group thought much to close for comfort. The noise of those exploding shells was tremendous.

R.A.F heavy bombers passing high overhead and low-flying, savage strafing fighters added their reverberating thunder to the din of British gunfire; so too did German artillery and flack guns.

There was a terrific explosion – a noise that for some awesome moments drowned all other sounds – as a German ammunition dump, hit by Naval shells or Air Force bombs, volcanically exploded.

Hurrying on, these patriotic Frenchmen and experienced British S.B.S sailors were all too well aware of their vulnerability in this strange, uncertain 'no-man's-land' between the British and Germans fighting at the beaches and the German reserves further inland. Surely some of those reserve Boche soldiers must also be moving through this neatly chequered, thickly hedgerowed countryside, but be moving in the opposite direction from them.

Managing not to bump into any Boche, the group reached their next target … a 'giant wuerzburg' German radar station.

Stealthily using their deadly skills the S.B.S team quickly and silently 'neutralised' the two sentries. They expertly positioned their plastic explosives and set short fuses.

Lying at a safe distance the entire group watched as explosions demolished the control building and sent the large circular radar dish crazily spiralling to the ground. The French and British exchanged congratulatory smiles. Lt. Anderson said, 'A good job well done!'

They hurried on to their next target.

A few hours later two more Boche sentries were stealthily dealt with; plastic explosives were positioned and fuses set. Three simultaneous explosions demolished two buildings at this important German radio communications centre and brought its tall wireless mast crashing down.

Jubilant at this latest success against the hated Boche the French Patriots were in danger of becoming over-confident. Beaming brightly, Léon complacently said, 'This is becoming quite routine now, is it not?'

Lt. Anderson nodded and grinned, then warned, ' Yes, it almost seems routine, Léon, but don't get too complacent. From grim experience I know how quickly and easily triumph can turn to disaster.'

His equally experienced S.B.S comrades nodded their full agreement.

'Come on, we better get moving again,' Lt. Anderson said. 'We must be well away from this place before it's swamped with vengefully searching Boche soldiers.'

Once again they hurried on to their next target.

As afternoon gave way to evening they lay hidden at the edge of a small orchard and gazed at their latest target – another radar station.

This was one of Germans best and most important radar installations in this district. The large, rectangular metallic mesh of this 'FREYA' radar unit conspicuously reared and revolved at the top of a grassy mound. Rising almost two hundred feet above sea-level in this flat Normandy countryside, this mound was graced by being called 'a hill'

While Lt. Anderson and Léon carefully inspected that target through their binoculars, John Armstrong smiled to himself as he remembered how when they had reconnoitred here last week their French guides had almost reverently talked of this 'hill'. Now, seeing it once more, John again disparagingly compared it to the real hills of his Lakeland Homeland; especially to Skidaw, his 'own' hill; that hill Anna and he were going to climb together once all this fighting and killing was over.

But this French 'hill' and its surroundings were different, alarmingly dangerously different, from what they had been last week. There were many more flak guns. The 'hill' bristled with small, multi-barrelled guns which – as many R.A.F. fighter pilots had discovered to their cost when trying to strafe that radar unit – threw up a terrifying barrage of small, but lethal shells. Five German Army trucks and three armoured-cars were halted near the foot of the 'hill'. More trucks and a column of marching Boche soldiers were approaching along a narrow road.

Lt. Anderson frowned and slowly shook his head, 'Well, Léon, there will be nothing "routine" about trying to destroy that target now, eh?'

'No, no, it will be far from "routine"! Do you really think we might still manage to destroy it?'

Every man in the tense silent group apprehensively waited for the Lieutenant's reply. Whether they lived or died might well depend on what he decided!

Lt. Anderson took his time about replying. He hastily glanced at each man in turn. He lifted his binoculars and again studied their target, the 'hill' and its approaches. The tension increased. He lowered his binoculars. 'We'll just wait here for a while and see what happens.'

More Boche armoured cars, trucks and marching soldiers arrived and halted beside the other Boche. Officers shouted orders and soon all the Germans and all their vehicles vanished into the protective obscurity of an oak wood at the foot of the radar 'hill.'

'It looks as if they're massing there ready for to counter-attack the beach-head tomorrow, doesn't it?... anyway we've no change of getting near our target now. We'll move away from here,' Lt. Anderson decided. We'll head for our next target – the bridge at Caen Canal. Let's hope no Boche are there.'

Léon eagerly agreed with the Lieutenant's wise decision. All the others exchanged relieved smiles.

After cautiously moving a safe distance away from the Boche they followed their example and hid in a small wood. There they lay and rested, ate and drank. It would safer to move through this Boche infested countryside once they were protected by night's concealing cloak.

They did not speak much as they lay relaxing. Eating and drinking were more urgently important than talk.

Almost replete, Bill Kemp eventually glanced at his watch then remarked, 'It'll soon be the end D-Day. It's been a long, long day, hasn't it?'

'Yes, a really long, eventful day right enough,' John Armstrong replied. He grinned, 'It's a day I'm sure all of us here would hate to have missed, eh?'

All agreed. Léon smiled, 'Yes, in years to come we will boast to our children and grandchildren of our part in helping to librate France on this long ... this historic, heroic long, long day!'

★ ★ ★

They, and all those who had fought ashore were not the only ones for whom D-Day had been a long, weary day.

For all the officers at Southwick House- the Supreme Allied Headquarters from which D-Day was commanded – it had also been a long day... A long, extremely anxious, but not as dangerous a day!

Almost an hour after midnight on this momentous day General Eisenhower, the Supreme Allied Commander, was still at his desk. His Senior Intelligence Officer entered his office and handed the General the document he was waiting for.

Eisenhower stubbed out his cigarette and put on his reading glasses. He anxiously read the latest, the most complete summary of how things had gone on D-Day.

Gains far exceeded losses. Out of the five thousand Allied ships taking part the only serious losses had been suffered by the landing-craft. These losses had been unavoidable. Almost eleven thousand Allied aircraft had been involved in one way or another. Amazingly few had been lost. Almost one hundred and sixty thousand Allied soldiers had been successfully landed, and had established beach-heads, at five parts of the Normandy coast.

General Eisenhower quickly read through the detailed reports on how securely each beach-head was now established. Worryingly, none was as firmly secure as had been planned.

Apprehensively he turned to the final item in this document..... the casualty figures for all Allied soldiers. A total of about ten thousand soldiers, American, British and Canadian, had been killed or seriously wounded on D-Day.

The General sighed deeply as, sadly and pityingly, he imagined all those thousands of dreaded telegrams that would soon be arriving at so many homes in America, Britain and Canada.

He looked up at his waiting Intelligence Officer, 'Ten thousands casualties in one day... a high, sad price to pay!'

'Yes, Sir, it is; it certainly is. But at least it's nothing like as bad as we had feared and had allowed for in our planning.'

'Yeah, that's true. How many casualties had we expected?'

'At least twenty thousand. Double the actual number today.'

Eisenhower remembered his last meeting with Churchill. Although always displaying utmost confidence in public, Old Winston had at that private, well lubricated lunch revealed one of his despairing 'black dog' moods. All too vividly he recalled the disastrous failure of amphibious Dardanelles landings in the last World War. Fearfully he envisaged another tragic failure. Trembling with emotion, Winston pictured those five Normandy beaches "Choked with the dead and dying flower of young British and American manhood. Briefly, wearily, Eisenhower smiled, 'Well thank God we don't have to send twenty thousand telegrams!'

'No, thankfully we don't, sir. D-Day has been a great success!..... a wonderful historic success with far fewer casualties than we dared expect'.

General Eisenhower nodded, 'Yeah, well let's hope D-Day plus one, and all the following days and weeks are equally successful. Let's hope we successfully beat off the Krauts when they assault our beach-heads. Their counter-attack could be launched any time now, couldn't it?'

'Yes, sir, it could. Almost certainly they will attack soon, before we get more and more men and supplies ashore' .

Chapter Forty-Two

Under cover of the early morning darkness of D–Day+1, Lt. Anderson's British and French team reached their next target – a major bridge over the Caen Canal. Surprised and pleased to find no German sentries here, they quickly set about their task.

They had previously de-fused the demolition charges set under the bridge by the Germans; they now removed these explosives and dropped them into the murky waters of the canal.

It was planned that later today British troops would smash out of their Arromanches beach-head and, crossing the canal by this intact bridge, capture and free the town of Caen.

Lt. Anderson smiled, 'That task didn't take long. We'll move on to the next bridge now. O.K., let's get cracking!'

★ ★ ★

Nearing the bridge as dawn brightened the scene they hurried along a narrow sunken lane until their way was blocked by four halted British Sherman tanks. Large, white, five-pointed identification stars glared brightly on the surprisingly high sides of each tank.

Hurrying forward, the Lieutenant introduced himself to the army officer in command, 'Lt. Anderson, Royal Navy.'

'Royal Navy, eh? What's the navy doing here? You've strayed far from your ship, surely.'

'We're S.B.S – the Special Boat Section of the Royal Navy. We're carrying out special duties.'

'S.B.S? – never heard of them!'

Lt. Anderson smiled, 'No. Few people have. And this is Léon. He and his comrades are local French Resistance Fighters. They have expertly guided and helped us.'

'Oh, I see. I'm Major Dawson.' He stabbed a finger at the map spread on the back of his tank. 'We're hoping to cross that small bridge over the canal, but we've outrun the troops who should be with us. You haven't seen any British infantry, have you?'

'No, we haven't; you're the first British army unit we've met up with.'

Léon and two other Frenchmen were standing in front of the tank. With outstretched arms and wild gesticulations they were having an animated discussion.

Major Dawson whispered to Lt. Anderson, 'What are those Froggies going on about?' Almost as if he had heard that question, Léon came to the rear of the tank and said, 'We don't think your tanks will manage across that small bridge. We think it might be too narrow for them.'

After some further lively discussion the Major decided 'We won't wait any longer for our infantry. We'll press on and try to cross the bridge. "Old Monty" (General Montgomery) is very keen to get some tanks across that canal and into Caen before the Jerries counter-attack.'

'We'll come with you,' Lt. Anderson said. 'We'll check the Boche haven't set explosives at the bridge. They hadn't when we checked it a few day's ago.'

★ ★ ★

Moving at a snail's pace and scraping the stone parapet, Major Dawson's leading tank made it across the small bridge with only a few inches to spare on each side.

As the second tank started creeping across, a sound was heard that drowned out the ugly noise of metal agonising against stone – the loud, unmistakable, frightening sound of rapidly approaching German Panzers.

The rumble, clatter and grumble of these tanks grew louder as the first two of a column of Panzers appeared on the far side of the canal. Monstrously large, toad squat, evil black, they halted. Their turrets swivelled. Their guns intimidatingly pointed and eagerly searched for targets.

Major Dawson's tank fired. The two British tanks not yet over the bridge joined in.. Two shells went wide. One supposedly armour-piercing shell glancingly struck the side of a Panzer, blazed a shower of sparks, then went harmlessly ricocheting away. Both Panzers fired. Major Dawson's tank and the one still labouriously negotiating the bridge exploded into flames.

The two remaining British tanks fired again. Again their shells went wide.

Watching from the shelter of a deep ditch, Lt. Anderson's team helplessly looked on as the two British tanks turned and urgently made for the concealing protection of the sunken lane and its high earth bank and thick hedge. The Panzers fired again and only one tank made it to safety. The other exploded in a volcanic eruption of leaping flames.

Half a mile along the lane the one surviving British tank halted. Lt. Anderson's team caught up with it.

The tank commander – a Second Lieutenant who seemed little more than a youth – stood up in the open turret. His face was deathly white. His voice trembled with shock as he apologetically blurted out to Lt. Anderson, 'I... I'm sorry I reacted like that I... I should have stayed and fought, shouldn't I?'

'And be savagely and uselessly killed like all the others? You were right to retreat and to live to fight another day. Your Sherman tanks are no match for those Panzers, are they? Those German tanks are huge. Do you think they are the new, formidable "Tigers"?'

Some colour came back into the young army officers face. His voice grew steadier as he eagerly seized the thoughtfully offered excuse for his precipitous retreat which he feared must have seemed like cowardice in the face of the enemy. 'Yes I'm sure these Panzers are the latest German "Tiger Tanks". In fact I think they might even be "King Tigers". Armed with an 88 mm. gun and protected with exceptionally good, thick armour, these "King Tigers" are truly fearsome monsters. No British or American tank has much chance against them. We were warned there might be some about here.'

'Yes,' Lt. Anderson said, 'Léon's Resistance Group got word to London that a S.S. Panzer Division was now stationed East of Caen and were equipped with some huge new type of tanks.'

Léon nodded, 'Yes, and we warned that with those giant tanks being manned by Hitler's own S.S. (SCHUTZE-STAFFEL) Panzer soldiers – every one a former "Hitler Youth, and now a ruthless, fanatical Nazi – they would be a ..... a tremendously powerful and formidable enemy facing the British soldiers when they landed here.'

For some moments all the British and French stood silently solemnly staring at the three columns of thick black oily smoke steadily rising from the funeral pyres of Major Dawson and the crews of his three engulfed Sherman tanks. The same thought was in every mind:'I hope to God they all died instantly when their tanks exploded into flames.' The possibility of them being trapped alive for a time in those roaring infernos did not bear thinking about!

They learned later that those Panzers crews contemptuously nick-named those terribly vulnerable Sherman tanks, 'The British Tommies tin-cans.' Then after seeing the deadly ease with which one Panzer shell would turn a Sherman tank into a blazing wreck, they re-named them, 'the Tommy-roasters.'

Lt. Anderson snapped out of this sad, solemn, reflective mood. Decisions had to be made. He had to make them. He ordered the young tank officer, 'You drive back towards the shore. Meet up with our troops. Find some senior officers and warn them to expect a German counter-attack soon. Alert them to the severe threat from these Panzers.' He turned to his expectant waiting French and S.B.S teams. 'We'll go back to the bridge we removed the Boche explosions from this morning. I think these Panzers will try to cross the canal by that bridge. The small bridge here must be too narrow for their huge, wide, "Tiger tanks. Right everyone, let's get cracking. We must make it to that bridge before the Panzers do!'

★ ★ ★

They did make it – but only just!

After fixing the last of their plastic explosives under the bridge, but not setting the fuses, they had a final quick exchange of views about the best, the most effective action to take. Having removed the Germans demolition changes earlier in the expectation that British troops would soon be crossing this bridge, would it be wise of them to now demolish it? Would those Panzers actually head for this canal crossing? Were British forces already pushing forward from the beaches toward this bridge?

There was no certainty. There was great confusion. There was much noise of artillery, mortars and machine-guns; much billowing, obscuring smoke; many clouds of dust sent up by speeding vehicles – tanks?.... trucks?....British?.... German? The most intensive fighting seemed to be towards the small town of Douvres.

Suddenly they heard another sound; a noise that got ever louder, grew ever more menacing as a column of Panzers appeared on the far side of the canal and, throwing up clouds of dust, made rapid progress towards this bridge. As those awesomely impressive German tanks thundered ever nearer they arrogantly smothered all lesser sounds.

No time now for uncertainty or hesitation. Lt. Anderson shouted, 'Come on, set the fuses!'

John Armstrong threw himself down beside the Lieutenant at the edge of the bridge, and, reaching down to the demolition charges, they set half-minute fuses.

Leading-seaman 'Johnnie' Johnstone, the S.B.S teams's explosives expert, and Bill Kemp did the same at the opposite side.

Leaping to his feet, Lt. Anderson shouted, 'Run!.... Run like Hell!'

The entire British and French group ran then threw themselves into a deep ditch as the leading Panzer fired a vicious burst of machine-gun fire.

The demolition charges exploded.

One end of the heavy iron bridge seemed to reluctantly rise, hang lazily suspended, then shudderingly collapse into the canal.

The frustrated Panzers halted. There would be a delay – a perhaps vital delay – in their planned counter-attack on the British beachheads.

★ ★ ★

After stealthily by-passing a large group of German infantry soldiers silently waiting around a deserted, badly damaged French farm, Lt. Anderson's team alertly continued on toward where they hoped to see not more field-grey German Army uniforms, but dull khaki British Army uniforms.

Forty minutes later after passing through the vaguely defined, ever changing, 'no-mans-land' between the opposing armies where they were in danger of being fired at by both sides, they were at last surrounded by khaki uniforms.

They were guided to a Divisional Headquarters where Lt. Anderson gave the commanding Brigadier information and warnings about the German Panzers and infantry he had seen.

While the officers conferred, the other S.B.S sailors and the Frenchmen were given large mugs of steaming hot tea and British cigarettes. Lèon and his countrymen thoroughly enjoyed the British 'fags', but seemed much less keen on the British army tea, so thickly sweetened with condensed milk. John Armstrong laughed, What's the matter, Léon don't you like our great British 'char'?'

The Frenchmen laughed in reply, 'A love of that 'char' must be an acquired taste. It is a taste I have not yet acquired! I do not want to..... to, how do you say it?..... to look at the gift-horse in the mouth?..... but I think I will stick to our great French wines and leave the 'char' to you.' He mollifyingly grinned, 'But your British 'fags' are great!'

As the war in this part of Normandy was now being fought on a large scale by increasingly large numbers of British soldiers the Brigadier had no further need of the stealthy skills of these S.B.S sailors. Nor were the services of these brave, Patriotic Frenchmen required at present.

The French Patriots were anxious to return to their homes and families; were desperately hoping to find their houses intact, their families safe.

Before parting, the British and French warmly shook hands. These Frenchmen had been greatly impressed by the calm self-control and competent authority of these brave, exceptionally well trained and greatly experienced S.B.S sailors. These British, in turn, had been most impressed by the depth of patriotic fervour and the great emotional commitment of these Frenchmen as they nobly helped free their beloved country from Boche tyranny.

As he gripped Lt. Anderson's hand Léon said, 'You will come back and visit us here in Normandy after the war is won, won't you?'

'Yes,' the smiling officer promised, 'we'll certainly visit you once we've finally defeated the bloody Boche. Let's hope that happens soon: before Christmas this year, perhaps?'

While John Armstrong apparently joined in with as much enthusiasm as his S.B.S comrades in this promise to make an early post-war visit to Normandy, he had absolutely no intention of doing so. He had other, more important, plans. Certainly he would return to the European mainland as soon as possible after the war, but definitely not to France. He would be in Holland, would be re-united with his Anna!

The following morning the five S.B.S sailors arrived at Arromanches. They were amazed at the transformation that had taken place here since D-Day. Where there had been wide open beaches there was now a large, sheltered harbour. This 'Mulberry Harbour' had been kept top-secret. Consisting of massive concrete boxes, it had been towed from as far away as the Clyde Estuary to this beach. They were set in lines then flooded to form enclosing breakwaters and landing jetties. A really impressive achievement!

A seemingly ceaseless flow of reinforcing soldiers were streaming ashore at this amazing harbour. Thousands of tons of the huge variety of ammunitions and other supplies required to keep this British army fighting were also pouring ashore.

Surely this vast army would – with the American, the Canadian, and other Allies armies – soon break out of their bridgeheads and drive the Germans out of France, Belgium and Holland...or would they?

The S.B.S team got a 'lift' on a Royal Navy minesweeper and late that afternoon they disembarked at their headquarters in Poole Harbour.

After a few days in Poole they, with two other S.B.S teams were sent to another S.O.E 'Stately 'Ome' near Elham , not far inland from Dover.

For some days they had an easy, restful time. These greatly experienced, now unusually idle S.B.S veterans increasingly wondered if this pleasant idleness was the calm before some extremely violent storm. Were their S.O.E officers busily planning something really special for them?

The fifteen S.B.S sailors wisely made the most of their enforced leisure. On the evening of the 12th June, 1944 they were again light-heartedly enjoying a friendly game of cricket. As John Armstrong sat with other members of his team waiting their turn with ball or bat he, and they, leisurely drank beer and smoked cigarettes. John sighed contentedly. This was a pleasant change from what they were used to. It was a perfect calm, cloudless, warm June evening. The lawns sweeping from the stately manor house to the large and picturesque pond made a perfect setting for this most English of sports..

Beyond the glittering pond many venerable apple trees unstintingly displayed their fluffy white haze of candy-floss. This mellow Kentish countryside was joyously proving itself to truly be 'the Garden of England'.

John had another gulp of beer then smiled at Bill Kemp who sat near him. 'This is a far cry from war, isn't it?'

Bill grinned, 'Yes, it's blissfully remote from all the fighting, all the killing.'

Lt. Anderson also grinned, 'Wouldn't it be great if this peaceful tranquillity was to last and spread over all Europe?'

Unfortunately it didn't.

All their exhilarating dreams of spreading peace; all their comradely banter and laughter abruptly ceased and the cricketers reluctantly stopped playing.

The strange noise – a noise such as none had heard before – which halted their innocent play grew louder, grew more menacing.

All eyes stared up and searched the Eastern sky.

All keenly gazed at the strange, small, jet-propelled aircraft streaking across and menacingly violating the pleasant evening sky. In synchronized movement every one swivelled and kept their eyes linked to that peculiar object until, steadily heading towards London, it disappeared.

Loud exclamations, animated discussions and wild speculations broke out once that strange thing was out of sight and its unfamiliar noise died away. 'What was that?'... 'Is it one of ours?'... 'Have we developed some new kind of plane?'... 'Is it a sinister new German secret weapon?' Many questions, no definite answers!

John Armstrong said nothing to his companions, but clearly remembered the briefing Commander Richardson had given before 'Operation Waterloo'. That Intelligence Officer had warned of the dangers posed by secret new weapons the Germans were developing. He had mentioned a jet-propelled pilotless plane, or 'flying-bomb'. That small jet-aircraft must be one of these new 'flying bombs'.

This was confirmed the following morning by Colonel Dobbs, the senior S.O.E. officer at this establishment. He smiled around at the three teams of S.B.S. sailors sitting before him, 'I'm sorry your game of cricket was interrupted yesterday evening. It was not, as usual, a case of "rain stopped play", but "strange plane stopped play", eh!... And I hope your innocent sleep was not disturbed too much by those other strange planes – "flying-bombs actually – that roared overhead in the wee small hours this morning'.

The Colonel now turned serious, 'It's all right for us to joke, but it's no joke for the poor Londoners at the receiving end of those flying-bombs. Once the jet engine falls silent those pilotless planes drop steeply down. It must be nerve-wracking waiting to see exactly where they're going to land and explode.'

Col Dobbs fully briefed them on those flying-bombs; on the sloping concrete ramps they were fired from and the location of these ramps in the Calais region of France. He concluded, 'We are waiting for more detailed photos of the exact positions of these ramps from R.A.F. reconnaissance planes and for more information from local French Patriots in that region. Once we get that "gen you will go in and destroy as many flying-bombs as possible before they are launched against us.'

A few days later the Germans VI (Vengeance One) retaliation campaign with their flying-bombs (Which Cockneys quickly nick-named 'Doodle-bugs') got under way in earnest with the launch of two hundred against London.

And so too did the S.B.S. campaign against these deadly 'Doodle-bugs'. These fifteen S.B.S. sailors, organised in three teams and stealthily operating at night, resolutely carried out this dangerous work.

They hid in the darkness until the sudden flare of a flying-bomb's jet engine thundering into life revealed the exact location of its launching ramp. As the 'Doodle-bug' soared into its fixed course towards London Lt. Anderson's team cautiously advanced through the returned darkness. Waiting until German Army technicians had the next flying-bomb on the ramp and were engrossed in preparing it for launch, they stealthily moved the last few yards forward and then quickly killed these Germans. They had already silently dealt with the sentries.

Plastic explosives were fixed on the flying-bomb, the concrete ramp and in the buildings housing more flying-bombs and jet fuel.

The five S.B.S. sailors rushed away, threw themselves down at a safe distance and eagerly counted off the minutes until the fuses blew.

The almost simultaneous explosion of all the flying-bombs, warheads and their volatile fuel created a hugely satisfyingly finale to the teams efforts.

Once the noise died down Lt. Anderson enthusiastically exclaimed, 'A good job brilliantly carried out, lads!'

All the others grinned their agreement. John Armstrong voiced their thoughts, 'Yes, it's great that our efforts here will save dozens or even hundreds of lives in London.'

As the summer days, weeks and months passed more than eight thousand flying-bombs were fired against London. Many were shot down by R.A.F. fighters and Army anti-aircraft guns before they reached their target. These Army gunners and R.A.F. pilots received much well deserved public praise.

Of course the S.B.S. teams received absolutely no public acknowledgement of their heroic efforts that destroyed many flying-bombs before they were launched at England.

Chapter Forty Three

By the end of August, 1944 Allied Armies had rapidly advanced through France; had driven the Germans out of that country; had returned freedom to the French.

The liberation of the Calais region by Canadian soldiers finally halted the assault on London by German flying-bombs.

The S.B.S. teams who had so bravely, so resolutely, so successfully destroyed flying-bombs in France were again resting in the S.O.E. 'Stately 'Ome' near Elham. As they relaxed, drank beer and smoked fags their stained nerves eased; tension was relieved; used up adrenaline was renewed.

Perhaps the greatest restorative, the noblest bringer of tranquil rest, were the light-heartedly played games of cricket. And this time neither rain nor strange planes disrupted their joyful play.

★ ★ ★

On the morning of 8th September British newspapers headlined a speech of Government minister, Duncan Sandys, in which he boastfully announced that the 'Battle of London' was over. He assured Londoners they could go about their daytime business in complete security; could sleep sound at night free from the threat of those damn 'doodle-bugs' The Germans awesome secret Vengeance Weapons on which Hitler set such great store, had turned out to be something of a damp squib and now they could no longer reach London.

Rarely was a politicians promise of complete security so quickly, so decisively proved false as that promise of Duncan Sandys.

Shortly before seven that same evening Londoners heard a sound they had never heard before in all the years of the Blitz – the sonic boom of the Germans V2 (Vengeance Weapon Two) long range ballistic rocket. The loud explosion that immediately followed that sonic boom sounded all too familiar to war-weary, but still- despite everything Hitler had flung against them- remarkably cheery Londoners.

Soon afterwards a second V2 rocket was launched from near The Hague in Holland. That thirteen ton missile with its two ton warhead and almost eight tons of fuel soared vertically in impressive flaming ascent, went higher than any man-made object had gone before, hurled itself two hundred miles through the stratosphere at unparalleled speed then descended almost vertically on central London.

With the descent of those two ballistic rockets something like panic descended over the Whitehall centres of power. Many Government Ministers joined Duncan Sandys in a deep 'Slough of Despond' as, all too vividly, they saw London being helplessly pounded into a Bunyanish 'City of Destruction.' But Winston Churchill exploded in wrath – like these Hun rockets he, too, went 'ballistic'!

At a hastily convened emergency meeting of senior Intelligence Officers, Scientists, Generals and Air Marshals, Winston demanded to know why their recent Intelligence Reports had now proved to be so wrong. These reports had assured him that the Air Force's devastating raids on the factories producing those German V2 rockets and the acute shortage of various commodities in Germany made it impossible for these rockets to go into service for at least another six months, and then only in very limited numbers. They had also reported that there was a strong possibility that the war would be won well before then. These reports now seemed wildly over-optimistic!

Winston's anger flared through an eruption of cigar smoke and as he snatched the huge soggy-ended Havana from his emotional lips some spittle dribbled. Some of the keenly watching officers wryly thought: at least dear old Winston's not – as his arch-enemy, Hitler, is reputed to do – foaming at the mouth ... not quite!

Winston deep-throatedly growled, 'All your great experts got it wrong about the V1 flying-bombs and about this V2 ballistic rocket. Will they get it wrong about the Hun's V3 weapon?' He paused, he drew deeply on his cigar, he glared gloomily around at all the officers. 'And what might the Hun's V3, or V4 or V5 weapons be? I... I have despairing black-dog bouts of worrying that one of them will be an atomic-bomb. I have nightmares of that Hun nuclear weapon exploding and devastating the whole of London!'

He again paused then quietly said, 'I know our best boffins assure us that Herr Hitler is at least two years away from getting an atomic-bomb.'

Emotionally, almost weepingly, almost pleadingly, Winston begged, 'Oh let's hope to God our experts do not get it wrong once again!'

All those gathered with Winston in the War Room deep under The Admiralty felt a slight tremor, saw the lights momentarily flicker as one more V2 rocket landed and exploded somewhere close by. This latest German rocket seemed to defiantly and mockingly emphasize just how wrong our best British experts had got their confident predictions.

★ ★ ★

Ripples from that touch of near panic in Whitehall surged guiltily outwards from the centre of power and, aggressively touching many Government Departments, spread the blame for this grave failure of Intelligence gathering and analysis over as wide a range of culprits as possible.

The Special Operations Executive came in for a share of this blame. In an effort to redeem themselves, orders came from S.O.E. Headquarters to the commanding officer at their establishment near Elham for S.B.S. teams to go into Holland and destroy as many V2 rockets as possible before they were launched against London.

And so, a few days later, Colonel Dobbs was again briefing three S.B.S. teams on a new German vengeance weapon – their V2 ballistic rocket. 'As with their flying-bombs, the Germans have brought these new weapons into use much sooner than we had expected. And, unlike the flying-bombs, we have absolutely no defence against them. They soar so high and travel so fast that fighter planes and anti-aircraft guns are useless against them.

'Being fired from large mobile transporters they are much harder to locate than the flying-bombs were with their fixed launch ramps. These transporters and rockets are kept hidden in woods and are only brought out to open clearings shortly before they are launched. So you gentlemen – you well experienced veterans – can fully appreciate just how difficult a task it will be to locate and destroy those fearsome weapons.'

The Colonel paused, gazed steadily at all those silent, attentive, resolute faces starring up at him, then declared with feeling, 'I know that if it is at all possible to find and destroy some of those rockets you are the men who will carry out this most important, most worthwhile task bravely, resolutely and successfully!'

Colonel Dobbs again paused while his sincere flattery ripped over his audience, then continued, 'The R.A.F. Bomber Boys are doing all they can to disrupted and delay production of these rockets . So with their effort combined with yours, hopefully we should prevent too many rockets falling on London. After more than five years of war; the terrible Blitz of 1940/41; the lesser "Baby Blitz" of 1943/44; then the attacks by flying-bombs, the poor, long suffering Londoners don't deserve another Blitz inflicted on them by these rockets against which there is no defence, no warning, no way of knowing where the next rocket will land.'

After showing on a map of Holland the region around The Hague where these V2 rockets were mainly being fired from, the Colonel encouragingly said, 'Fortunately the Dutch Resistance Group in that area are now well organised and are most keen to help. As some of you know, there was considerable disruption in many Dutch groups last year. There were many betrayals. Now, however, we are confident that all the betrayers have been "eliminated . Secure new codes are now in use. All the Dutch Patriots you will work with are completely trustworthy. Putting not only their own lives, but also the lives of their families at risk, they will hide you during the day and guide you at night to the woods where they think Kraut rockets are being launched from.'

Although of course he did not know it, as John Armstrong attentively listened to the Colonel's revealing briefing he felt the same worries as Churchill had felt. Like Winston, he feared that if the Germans V1, and then their V2 weapons had come into use much sooner than expected, was it possible that the Hun's next Vengeance Weapon might give us yet another nasty surprise?..... be deployed much quicker than expected?.... And might that weapon be an atomic bomb?

He fervently hoped that his actions in killing the treacherous, pro-German Dutch nuclear Physicists Professor Johannes de Waal and Anna's father, Professor Willem Maurik, had helped in some degree to delay the development of the Germans atomic bomb.

From thoughts of Anna's treacherous father John's mind swiftly shifted to much pleasanter thoughts of Anna herself. It would be strange to be in her country again, be so near, yet so far from her. He knew he could not ask the Dutch Patriots he would be working with about her, or about her Uncle Frans. For greater security each Resistance Group kept details of its members strictly secret from all other Groups.

The day before they left for Holland the S.BS men were given an excellent dinner in the large dining-room of that truly imposing S.O.E. 'Stately 'Ome', a dinner perhaps not quite as elaborately sumptuous as pre-war dinners had been here, but certainly the best meal these men had enjoyed since the start of the war.

John Armstrong laughed, 'They're feeding us up like fighting-cocks before we go into battle tomorrow!'

'Yes,' Bill Kemp agreed. 'Or perhaps more like condemned murders getting an excellent meal on the eve of being hanged, eh?'

.

★ ★ ★

Lying hidden in the night-shrouded gloom of the wood they had been guided to by Dutch Patriots, Lt. Anderson's S.B.S team saw their first V2 rocket being launched about half a mile from them.

The noise rose to a shrieking crescendo. The flames savagely glared and wickedly spread. The volcanic smoke obscured everything as the giant rocket lifted off. All combined to make a Dante-ish Inferno.

Rising high and fast in vertical flight that rocket was an awesomely impressive sight as its flaming power screamed it ever higher up through the dark sky.

All these keenly watching S.B.S sailors agreed: that rocket was much more terrible, much more awesome than any of the flying-bombs they had seen launched. So, too, they later agreed, after the German Army sentries and technicians had been dealt with and plastic explosives set, was the tremendous explosion of these rocket's two ton war-heads and eight tons of fuel!

As autumnal weeks then months passed more and more V2 rockets fell on London. The efforts of the S.B.S and brave Dutch Patriots to destroy rockets before they were launched became increasingly dangerous. The Germans guarded the rockets with more sentries. The combined S.B.S. and Dutch attacked with larger teams. The Dutch and

British suffered casualties. Five Dutchmen were killed. Lt. Anderson and two others in his team were killed. John Armstrong and Bill Kemp were the only survivors of the original team. They were transferred to another S.B.S. unit. They helped destroy two more rockets. Then because of the increasing casualties and the ever more hazardous nature of these attacks, they were called off – at least for a time.

★ ★ ★

After a few voyages on 'Normal', now largely uneventful, almost stress-free, sea-going convoy escorting duties, John again became a member of another S.B.S. team. Bill Kemp was also in this team. So too were others they had worked with before. All were pleased to meet up again. They were pleased at the prospect of working together again as a tough, resolute, well experienced reliable team.

They did not know it, but all those qualities of toughness, of resolution, of outright bravery would be greatly needed, would be put to extreme test on their next missions.

British soldiers had recently freed the Belgian city of Antwerp; had wrested it from the Germans with its huge harbour almost intact.

All Allied commanders, especially General Montgomery, were extremely anxious to have the huge amounts of supplies needed for their armies in Belgium and Northern France brought in through that port instead of having them trucked all the way from Normandy. However Antwerp harbour could not be used until the waterway leading to it had been cleared of German artillery batteries firmly established on both banks of the Scheldt River and estuary.

The Germans entrenched in their strong positions on the sides of the Scheldt were frantically determined to deny the Allies the use of Antwerp Harbour. They knew that once that harbour was opened to Allied ships vast quantities of war supplies would be shipped through there in preparation for the final British and American assault across the Rhine into their beloved German Homeland. Many of the young S.S. Nazi defenders were determined to fight to the death to prevent this happening.

So the clearing of the Scheldt waterways turned into some of the most savage and most bloody fighting of the entire military campaign in Western Europe.

Paddling silently at night in canoes or inflatable dinghies and stealthily crawling through the darkness, S.B.S. teams managed to destroy some of the dug-in German guns that dominated this vital waterway. The destruction of these guns helped reduce the still grievous number of casualties amongst Royal Marine Commandos and British and Canadian soldiers grimly struggling to dislodge the fanatic Nazis from their well prepared defences.

This ruthless fighting in which no quarter was given, no – or next to no – prisoners were taken, lasted almost until the end of November. Only after heavy bombardment from the battleship H.M.S. Warspite, and further landings by amphibious forces were the Germans tenaciously defending the Scheldt Estuary on both sides of the commanding narrows at Flushing finally, and bloodily, defeated.

Operating in their usual stealthy, unpublicized way S.B.S. teams played an important part in what was in effect another – a mini – D–Day invasion.

As soon as all the Scheldt waterways were swept clear of German mines the first Allied ships, after having been delayed for three months, sailed into Antwerp harbour and started unloading vast amounts of vital military supplies.

Many of the exhausted British and Canadian soldiers – the fortunate survivors – who had bourne the brunt of all this desperate and costly fighting were given much needed and well deserved leave and rest in now German-free Belgium. The luckiest ones were sent to Brussels where they lost no time in desperately eagerly savouring many of the sensual delights of that city's amazingly war-free carnival atmosphere.

Others – thankful to be alive and to be in one piece – uncomplainingly made do with the perhaps less hectic, but to them truly delightful sensual pleasures to be found in Antwerp. After being all too familiar with sudden violent death for all too long, they determined to live; to avidly enjoy all the pleasures of drink and sex and as many of the care-free gaieties of life as were available here.

Even the S.B.S. teams were allowed some leave for rest and recreation in Antwerp. Even these bravest, toughest men were in need of some reviving relaxation.

★ ★ ★

On the last evening of their leave all these S.B.S. sailors met up again. Tomorrow they would be going different ways. Some were ordered back to their headquarters in Poole. Some were being attached to British or Canadian army units to help prepare for the many river and canal crossings that faced these soldiers. All these obstacles would have to be overcome when they advanced towards the German border.

After a good dinner, with the red, vinegary house-wine thrown in free (some said it should instead have been thrown away!) in one of the many Antwerp restaurants offering cut-price meals to the heroic Allied soldiers who had freed Belgium from the Krauts, the group of S.B.S. sailors leisurely made their way towards a favourite bar handily situated between the vibrant gaiety of the city centre and the dockside red light district.

They stopped in front of the alluring glittery attractions of the Rex Cinema. Many Allied soldiers were eagerly crowding into this cinema to see its English language films. Some of the sailors, the ones with weaker stomachs and all too strong memories of their recent miserable hung-over alcoholic state, decided to go into the cinema rather than inflict more drunken misery on themselves. After good-humouredly mocking these comrades as renegade milk-sops, the remainder of the group continued on their way.

The bar was happily noisily crowded. Many allied soldiers were vivaciously enjoying the last of their leave before returning to the chances, hardships and dangers of war. Some heavily made -up women, prostitutes or amateur good-time girls were brazenly prominent with their loud, forced laughter. Their eagerly offered services were much in demand.

The S.B.S. sailors struggled to a table in front of a large plate glass window and immediately got down to pleasurable business of seriously drinking. John Armstrong and Bill Kemp had thought about going into that cinema with the other 'milk-sop' renegades, but had been persuaded to do the 'correct' manly thing and drink with the 'real' men.

Petty Officer Tom Wright's large body shook with laughter as, holding up his third pint of gassy Belgian beer, he said, 'This is a damn sight better than sitting in the dark watching shadows buggering about on a cinema screen, isn't it?'

'Yes,' John laughingly agreed, 'it's great now, but it won't be so good tomorrow morning when we suffer another terrible hang-over!'

Leading-seaman 'Jock' Brown jovially joined in; he put on an exaggeratedly mournful 'Heiland' accent, 'Aye, man, all us poor sinners will hae tae Calvinisticly suffer for a'oor sinful pleasures!'

As the evening raced on and ever more pints were downed the talk grew louder and happier. The jokes got wilder. Different songs were sung at the same time by friendly rival groups of soldiers. The sailors joined in the bawdy singing with one or other group.

The British Military Police had been instructed to leave those battle stressed soldiers alone no matter how drunk they got, unless they got up to anything too extreme. And there were no officers in this bar to put a damper on proceedings. Officers and humble 'other ranks' could work together and die together, but they most definitely could not socialize together!

The noisy song and laughter was suddenly dramatically drowned and stilled by a much louder noise – a sound they had not heard before – the sonic boom of a German V 2 rocket. Arms were protectively thrown over eyes as the plate glass windows violently quivered. Fortunately they did not smash, nor did they a few seconds later when the more violent, more terrifying explosion of the rocket's two ton warhead shook the building. That frightful noise's shock waves of fear miraculously sobered up the not too far gone soldiers and sailors.

'What the hell was that?' demanded Jock Brown.

'God knows what it was!' Bill Kemp exclaimed. 'There was no noise of Jerry planes; no air-raid warning.'

'I think it must have been a Kraut rocket exploding,' John Armstrong said.

'I thought they were only being fired at London,' said Tom Wright.

'Perhaps they were. But now that Antwerp harbour's open to our ships they might be starting to aim them here as well.'

'Aye, John,' Jock Brown agreed, 'I bet that's what's happening.'

Two army sergeants and some other soldiers were moving towards the door. Petty Officer Wright said, 'Come on, lads, we better go with them. We must find where that rocket landed. See if we can help.'

As they hurried down the wide street towards the city centre a

British army jeep roared up, violently braked, and the young, white faced Military Policeman gasped, 'I... I was coming for you lot. Coming to get you to help.'

'What's happened? Is it a Kraut rocket? Where has it landed?' demanded P.O. Wright.

'Yes,' the M.P. said, 'it's a Kraut rocket. It.. It landed right on that picture house down the road there. The...the Rex Cinema.'

'Oh God, no! That's where some of our lads went! Come on, let's do what we can to help.' The Petty Officer started running. The others followed him.

As they reached that cinema – or rather the ugly heap of smouldering rubble where the Rex Cinema had been – a hideous sight was revealed. A scene of utter carnage. Mutilated human bodies and parts of bodies were scattered all around.

They recognised what was left of one body's blood soaked uniform as being that of one of their S.B.S. comrades. There was little left of his head to identify him by..

These tough, war hardened veterans had seen dead bodies before, but what they were seeing now was something different. The large number of bodies lying here, the ghastly ugliness of their mutilated condition and, perhaps worst of all, the careless indifferent disorder with which all the bits and pieces of bodies were scattered about was worse, far worse, than anything they had seen before. Faces paled, then greened. Stomachs queasily churned. The food and wine and beer they had so enjoyed this evening was violently spewed up. Their vile mess's of steaming vomit added further disgusting ugliness to the already disgustingly ugly scene.

Petty Officer Tom Wright was the first to recover. He decided, 'We'll leave the dead alone for now. We'll try to find and help any injured survivors.'

As they searchingly scrambled and stumbled over the smoking rubble John Armstrong shouted, 'There's someone buried here. I hear them moaning.

After frantically heaving bricks and smashed concrete aside, they found a young, blonde haired Belgian woman. Her despairing moans increased as they eased her free. She gave a convulsive shudder, then died.

Belgian civilian ambulances and fire engines had now arrived. British and Canadian army ambulances also soon arrived. The search for survivors quickly became well organised. But not many of the cinema's audience survived the devastating carnage caused by that German V2 rocket smashing through the roof and exploding amidst them.

★ ★ ★

John Armstrong was allocated to Petty Officer Wright's S.B.S. team, which, in turn was attached to a Canadian Army Regiment stationed some miles outside Antwerp.

Many soldiers from this regiment had been amongst the seven hundred Allied servicemen killed or seriously wounded in the Rex Cinema on that evening of 17th December, 1944. Almost four hundred Belgian civilians had also been killed or severely injured. These were by far the worst casualties inflicted by a single V2 rocket.

When that S.B.S team learned the full extent of these military and civilian casualties they all greed they would, despite the high risk, willingly go back into Holland and by destroying more V2 rockets help prevent such disasters happening again in Antwerp or in London.★ They would have absolutely no compunction about ruthlessly killing the German technicians servicing these rockets!

John Armstrong summed up their feelings, 'It would be good to avenge the deaths of our S.B.S comrades. Their deaths while on leave, while sitting relaxing in that cinema seem more than usually cruel, especially after they had survived all that savage fighting and bloody killing at the Scheldt.'

★ (After the war, John was surprised to learn that more V2 rockets had actually been fired against Antwerp than against London. 1,190 were launched at London: 1,610 at Antwerp)

Chapter Forty Four

Christmas neared and the miserable December weather got ever more miserable. Day after day thick layers of dark clouds hung low overhead and brought freezing mists, unrelenting rain, slithery soaking sleet or blinding cloaking snow. The British and American Tactical Air Forces were grounded. Soldiers of the Allied Armies – 'the poor bloody infantry' – shivered and cursed as they soaked and froze in their flooded fox-holes. In places the churned, all engulfing mud was of First World War volume and tenacity. The fighting ground – or squelched – to a halt.

Weary Allied Commanders were lulled into a false sense of security. Surely after being ignominiously driven out of France and Belgium the German Army must be in a much worse state, must be more miserable and exhausted than the victorious British and American Armies were? Those Commanders confidently decided they could safely go on early Christmas holiday while the exhausted Allied soldiers and the even more exhausted German soldiers rested in a state of wary, weary, comatose stalemate.

Puritanical General Montgomery went home to England. General Eisenhower and some other American Generals went to enjoy the fleshpots of Paris.

Then once again when least expected the Germans sprang a sudden, amazing, nasty surprise.

A large, powerful, German Army that the Allies did not know was there came thundering out of the concealing mist and snow. As in 1940, Panzers again led the way and smashed through the weakly defended Ardennes Forest. They intended to re-capture Brussels and Antwerp.

As rumours of this fantastic, almost unbelievable German attack spread they caused real panic. Would the British or American Army manage to stop those formidable and fast Tiger Panzers before they reached Brussels? Would those fearsome, those amazing Krauts smash aside all resistance by the shocked and surprised Allied Armies?

Not only Belgian and French civilians were caught up in this panic. At the Canadian Army depot near Antwerp where they were now based, Petty Officer Wright's S.B.S team were overhauling inflatable dinghies they would use when they advanced into Holland and then – hopefully – into Germany. This work came to a sudden halt as a Canadian sergeant came running and urgently shouted at them, 'Leave those boats. Get your guns and gear. Get ready for action. We've to defend this depot from the Krauts!'

'The Krauts?' P.O. Wright exclaimed. 'What are you talking about? The Krauts are nowhere near here!'

'They might be here soon, though!' The sergeant breathlessly explained, 'They've attacked through Luxemburg. Their Panzers have almost reached Brussels! They're heading for Antwerp. We've to stop them re-capturing that vital harbour.'

As the Canadians and British anxiously waited for German soldiers to appear, more, and even wilder, rumours flew around ....thousands of German Paratroops had landed in Belgium. They were everywhere! Evoking memories of 1940 when Britain expected to be invaded, there were 'authentic' stories of some of those Kraut paratroops being disguised as nuns! Germans in American uniforms and in captured jeeps were racing around everywhere causing mayhem and spreading immense confusion.

An hour past with no sight or sound of Krauts. The waiting soldiers relaxed. They became convinced that this great scare was based on nothing but false rumours. Some thought it might even be a training exercise to test their state of readiness.

Then a strange sound startled them . With alarming suddenness three medium sized, twin engine warplanes the like of which none had seen before, came screaming low overhead. And these strange Kraut aircraft, their evil black crosses clearly visible, really did scream, for they were jet-propelled.

Flying level beneath the pressing clouds they skilfully skimmed over a nearby airfield and accurately strafing and bombing, destroyed many neatly lined-up R.A.F aircraft. The Air Force received a bigger shock and were caught even more defencelessly off guard than the Army. After boasting they had practically wiped out the Luftwaffe it was a tremendously demoralising blow to be so suddenly, so unexpectedly, so devastatingly attacked by that 'non-existent' Luftwaffe. And what was even more humiliating to R.A.F. pride was that they had been attacked by those amazing new Messerschmitt 262 jet planes – the first jets to come into service in any Air Force!

Allied Intelligence Agencies knew the Germans were building a jet-propelled warplane, but our best experts confidently declared it could not come into service for at least eight months, and by that time they expected the war would be victoriously won. Once again these great, over-confident 'experts' had got their predictions badly wrong!

As the noise of those screaming jets faded away the staring, startled Canadian soldiers voiced their amazement: 'What the hell were those?'...'Where did those bastards come from?' ..... 'Trust the bloody Krauts to surprise us!'.... 'Yeah, and what other nasty surprises have they got hidden up their sleeves?'

Petty Officer Wright solemnly said,'After seeing that amazing display of Kraut skill and power we better take those reports of them trying to re-capture Brussels and Antwerp extremely seriously!'

Jock Brown grinned, 'Aye, and after that damned startling surprise perhaps those stories of Jerry paratroopers being disguised as nuns might no be so farfetched after all!'

John Armstrong joined in the laughter. He kept his anxious thoughts to himself. After learning how badly wrong our best experts had got their predictions about the Germans V1 flying-bomb, their V2 rocket, and now their jet plane, he was increasingly worried that those same 'experts' would also be proved hopelessly wrong in predicting that the Germans were reassuringly far away from successfully developing an atomic-bomb. Might their atom bomb turn out to be their next, their most terrifying, Vengeance Weapon? Might that new V weapon, like its predecessors, devastatingly appear long before the Allies expected? Might the Allies planned, war-winning, Spring Offensive come too late?

Were our Generals planning to free Holland before they launched that final Offensive against Germany? Would his S.B.S. team help in the fight to bring freedom to The Netherlands? Almost certainly they would. Was it impossible that he might find himself near Anna's farm?.... impossible that he might meet her, free her – also Blanche and Frans – and once more, even if only for a brief time again make sublime passionate love with her before the devastating explosions of German atomic-bombs decisively altered everything?

John's rosy romantic dream of being wonderfully re-united with Anna was violently blown away by the decidedly un-romantic voice of a Canadian Sergeant-major loudly shouting orders.

★ ★ ★

After a week of great confusion, of wildly flying rumours, of fierce fighting and savage dying, the German assault towards Brussels and Antwerp was halted. It took another five weeks of bloody fighting before the battle that became known as 'The Battle of the Bulge' was finally won by the Allies. What was left of what had been a formidable, greatly feared German Army dejectedly retreated back to the homeland lair from which it had so amazingly, so unexpectedly attacked with such fanatical determination.

As Winter drearily dragged on towards Spring the Canadian soldiers based outside Antwerp grew accustomed to the noise of the sonic booms and loud explosions as many German V2 rockets fell on that city and its important harbour. P.O. Wright's S.B.S. team had the warm glowing consolation that at least they could do something to reduce the numbers of rockets falling on Antwerp and London. They, and other S.B.S. teams, went into Holland as often as possible and with the indispensable help of local Dutch Patriots destroyed many rockets before they could be launched.

On their last two missions into Holland they had been pleasantly surprised at how few German sentries were defending these particular rockets. They did not know that many German soldiers had been secretly withdrawn from The Netherlands and most other occupied countries to reinforce their armies in Germany as they prepared for the desperate last ditch defence of their Homeland.

Near the end of March that S.B.S. team were again in Holland. As they and their guiding Dutch Patriots stealthily made their way through the dismal, misty, midnight darkness of a forest of fir trees the sudden noisy roar and fierce glaring flames of an igniting V2 rocket unmistakenly confirmed that they had once again been correctly guided to a mobile launch site by their outstandingly keen, brave, and absolutely trustworthy Dutch comrades.

After patiently waiting until the sinisterly impressive bright glowing rocket accelerated out of sight high in the mist shrouded night sky and their eyes had re-adjusted to the returned darkness, the British and Dutch group again stealthily moved towards that now accurately pin-pointed launch site.

Caught by complete surprise, the German sentries and rocket technicians were swiftly and ruthlessly dealt with. Plastic explosives were quickly set at the rocket's warhead and large, full, fuel tank.

Lying at a safe distance the Dutch and British counted down the minutes, then the seconds until the eagerly awaited explosives should destroy that rocket and its large launcher truck. Their tense wait was well rewarded as, exactly on time, an enormous explosion brilliantly flared the startled night sky then sensationally reverberated across the blacked-out Dutch countryside. The alert watchers felt the earth momentarily tremble under their flattened bodies. They heard small pieces of hot debris hissingly pitter-patter through nearby fir trees like a shower of demented hailstones.

All were elated by the thought that they had prevented that rocket from being launched; might well have saved many lives in some crowded building in London or Antwerp.

P.O. Wright gave voice to these thoughts, 'A noble mission nobly carried out. Well done, lads!' His grinning glance swept over the S.B.S. sailors then over the proud Dutch Patriots as he included them in his sincere praise, 'We're a great team, aren't we?... Okay, now we better get moving before hordes of rudely awakened Krauts come searching for us.'

The first of the team were emerging from the forest's solemn silent darkness when a savage burst of sub-machine-gun fire caught them. Violently caught them: viciously killed them.

The three others in the S.B.S. team immediately reacted. They spread out then cautiously moved towards the dark ditch where the gunfire had come from. As they crouchingly advanced every sense was on knife-edged alert, every gun was keenly pointing, every trigger-finger was nerved to instantly squeeze.

A dark figure suddenly rose and frantically ran from the ditch.

Bullets from three Sten-guns thudded into the running body.

The British sailors gathered around the dead German soldier. In the dim uncertain light his white face looked youthful; seemed almost boyishly innocent.

John Armstrong compassionately murmured,'Oh, the poor bugger's hardly more than a boy.'

'Aye,' said Jock Brown, 'but no doubt he was a Hitler Youth. Was a fanatic young Nazi. He certainly was old enough to shoot and kill, wasn't he?'

'Yes, yes, I know he was.' John inspected the German's sub-machine gun. It was unloaded. 'Yes, we did well to kill him before he had time to re-load.'

They turned their attention to their shot comrades. Agonised groans revealed that at least one was not dead – not yet.

Two Dutch Patriots were unmistakably dead. So was Petty Officer Wright. The anguished groans were coming from Bill Kemp.

John and Jock knelt on opposite sides of Bill. Peering through the dimness they hurriedly examined him. Judging from the almost continuous low, guttural moaning sounds that seemed to erupt from deep within his tortured body, Bill's wounds were agonisingly serious. Just how serious was quickly confirmed by his compassionate comrades' gently searching hands as they felt a mess of blood soggily soaking through Bill's uniform at his chest and upper stomach. Further proof of the seriousness of his injuries was provided by every breath he took. Each desperate breath pulsed more blood up to further saturate his already saturated uniform.

John and Jock looked at one another across Bill's savaged body. Slowly they shook their heads. They thought that two or more bullets had smashed into Bill's chest and stomach. They guessed he was beyond all medical help. Certainly he was beyond anything they could do to really help him. And yet they felt they must try to do something to bring him some relief from the grievous pain he was so obviously suffering.

It was Bill himself who suggested the only real – the extremely drastic – relief they could bring him. He weakly raised his right hand from where it had been grasping his bloodied stomach and tried to reach up towards his ear. A searing agonising spasm of pain forced a louder groan from his tortured nerves and dropped his trembling hand back down to again desperately clutch at his stomach.

The worst of the spasm passed and Bill lifted an imploring gaze to John's compassionate eyes. Making a tremendous effort he gasped, 'The pill, John. The... the cyanide pill!'

John's instinctive reaction was to emphatically say, 'Oh no. I can't give you that pill.' But he didn't. Instead he said, 'Hold on, Bill. We'll do something to help you.

Another violent spasm brought another despairing groan. Summoning up deep reserves of strength, Bill somehow managed to clearly articulate, 'Oh, John, for God's sake give me that pill. You...you know I'm done for, don't you?'

John could not refuse that desperate plea. It would be stupid to think Bill would believe any reassuring lies. It would be cruel to needlessly prolong his agony.

Before acting on the decision he had already taken, John lifted his pitying gaze from Bill and stared for a few moments at Jock.

Sensing John's unspoken request for his moral support, Jock nodded his agreement and sympathetic understanding.

Both men knew that they dared not linger here much longer. German soldiers must surely be on their way to investigate that noisy destruction of their V2 rocket and to search for those responsible for destroying it. If Bill was alive when searching Krauts found him they would hardly treat him tenderly. If they did give him medical attention it would only be so that he could be handed over to the Gestapo for savage investigation then execution. Much better to use that suicide cyanide pill each S.B.S. sailor had taped behind his ear when on dangerous missions in German-occupied countries.

After nodding his thanks in acknowledgement of Jock's sympathetic agreement, John reached behind Bill's ear and searched for his suicide pill. Taking a firm grip of the plaster that held the pill secure, he gave it a sharp pull. Despite being terribly engrossed with the real pain of his bullet wounds, Bill still flinched away from the lesser pain of some hairs being pulled out with that plaster.

John immediately apologised with genuine but foolish contrition, 'Oh, I'm sorry giving you that extra pain, Bill.'

Another violent spasm of anguish seared up from his stomach and grabbed all Bill's attention; it instantly drowned the minor pain of a few pulled hairs.

As he waited for that spasm to pass and for Bill's grinding groans to ease, John inspected the small, uniquely shaped white suicide pill he gingerly held in his hand. To ensure that pill with its deadly concentrate of cyanide would never be mistaken for any innocent pill it was square shaped with each corner being sharp to the touch. Its deliberately difficult shape prevented it from being swallowed whole.

Once Bill's anguish seemed to slightly ease John lifted his head a bit higher and moved the suicide pill towards his trembling lips.

Sensing John's reluctance to actually place the cyanide pill in his mouth, Bill made a gallant effort to spare John the anguish of having to carry out this humane but repulsive act of mercy killing. Lifting his hand from his stomach he held it up to take the pill and gasped, 'I'll do it myself, John.'

Deeply moved by Bill's thoughtfulness in the midst of his torturing pain, John put the pill in his trembling hand. As Bill tried to move his weak, heavy hand towards his mouth the pill fell from his slippery, blood-soaked fingers. He gave a despairing sigh that turned into a tortured groan and dropped his hand to again clutch at his stomach.

John found the pill and found resolution to do what he must to do spare Bill further needless pain. He put the cyanide pill in Bill's gaping mouth then firmly forced his mouth shut. With authority blended with compassion he instructed, 'Now crush it up, then swallow it down, Bill.'

With a great, brave, struggling effort Bill eventually got the crushed poison down his throat while John forcefully held his mouth shut.

As both men waited for the cyanide to do its deadly work Bill held John's deeply compassionate gaze with his own flickering troubled gaze that seemed to hold a whole range of emotions; There was a suggestion of courageous resolution; of trembling fear; but perhaps most of all an immense thankfulness that he was not facing his last moments alone. His slide towards death was eased by having that brave comrade hold him and envelop him in deep, sincere, compassion.

Bill's body gave a violent convulsive shudder. He gave a final groaning sigh. He died.

Even in the midst of genuine grief at this death of a good S.B.S comrade John's throughtly war-trained mind registered the comforting fact that what that Royal Navy medical officer had told them was true: those cyanide pills did bring painless death in half a minute.

The voice of a Dutch patriot shouting a loud waring alerted all the others to the dangers facing them. The dim lights of two German Army trucks were rapidly moving towards them. John rose and picked up Bill's Sten-gun. The guns of their other three dead comrades were already in the hands of anxiously waiting Dutch Patriots. It was now time to leave these dead British and Dutch comrades to companionably mourn one another while their living comrades got on with the desperately serious business of trying to stay alive themselves.

They succeeded in that endeavour – for the present at least! After hiding while the German Army trucks passed them, they reached a Dutch safe-house without encountering any more Krauts. Securely hidden in the spacious cellar of this large Dutch house the three S.B.S sailors now had an easy time of resting, eating and sleeping; of conserving their energy and building up their strength until night time when, if all went, they would, returning by the way they had come, leave German – occupied Holland and get back into allied controlled Belgium.

They deeply felt for their Dutch comrades and sincerely commiserated with them as they set out on the distressing task of informing the families of the two lost Dutchmen that these brave Patriots had been killed by the Krauts.

They also thought of their own dead British comrades. They sadly imagined the shattering grief of the families as the dreaded Admiralty telegrams arrived and announced the death of Bill Kemp and Tom Wright.

These S.B.S sailors did not know it then, but that mission to destroy that V2 rocket was memorable not only because of the sad loss of their brave comrades but was also memorable in a larger historic sense. That V2 rocket they saw being launched last night (the 27th March, 1945) was the last German rocket to be fired against London. The rocket they destroyed before it too could be launched had been the only remaining rocket that was fully serviceable. So no more of these dangerous combined Dutch and British missions to destroy those formidable rockets were needed.

If these S.B.S men had had this information then, they would have been under no illusion that their great experience and expertise in so many ways of killing would not soon be put to use again on other – perhaps even more dangerous- missions.

Chapter Forty Five

Sure enough their S.B.S. skills were all too soon again put to stealthy and efficient use!

After a massive build up of supplies and months of detailed planning the Allies great Spring Offensive across the Rhine and deep into Germany was almost ready to start. What hopefully should be the final assault against Hitler's battered and beleaguered Third Reich would be on a truly gigantic scale. Vast American armies were poised facing Southern and central Germany. The British army was also waiting in the more Northerly part of Central Germany while the Canadians were even further North waiting to free the parts of Holland still occupied by the Germans then to push on into the extreme North of Germany.

And these were only the Western Allies armies. Massive Soviet armies were already well into Eastern Germany. Halted little more that thirty miles from Berlin more than two million Soviet soldiers were poised to surround then capture the fanatically defended German Capital.

The synchronized attacks from East and West started in early April. Before dawn of the day of the great offensive thousands of Allied paratroops landed East of the Rhine.

Stealthily paddling their black, inflatable dinghy John's S.B.S team also crossed the Rhine under cover of darkness. Their task was to locate and 'eliminate' any German machine-guns positioned on the far bank of this part of the river and so greatly reduce the number of casualties the Canadians would suffer when their soldiers crossed here at dawn.

After some extremely hazardous hours of moving, fighting, killing and avoiding being killed in the confusing darkness, they had successfully destroyed three German machine-guns and had killed all the machine-gunners. The elation they felt at the success of their mission was dampened by having had two of their comrades killed.

At dawn John and the other two surviving S.B.S sailors lay hidden and watched the Canadian soldiers cross the Rhine. Their crossing here was now almost unopposed. When the first group of the Canadians were re-united with the three S.B.S men their commanding officer, Colonel Macdonald, eagerly greeted them. 'You did a great job! It was marvellous not to be greeted by a hail of Kraut machine-gun bullets when we were stuck like sitting ducks in those God-damn slow boats.

The other Canadians expressed their whole-hearted agreement with the officer's praise by giving them cheery grins, thumbs up signs and friendly slaps on the back.

At other places the Rhine crossings were much more fiercely opposed, but once the bulk of the American, British and Canadian armies were firmly established across that river – the last major natural barrier protecting the German homeland– organised resistance largely collapsed .

Most of the German army units which should have been attempting to halt the Canadian advance through Holland had already retreated into Germany. The disorganised, spasmodic resistance some German soldiers did put up was usually quite quickly overcome by the accurate firepower of Canadians tanks and artillery.

John, with the two other surviving members of their S.B.S team, travelled with the Canadians as they rapidly pushed ever further North through Holland. All the soldiers of the this liberating Allied Army received a deliriously rapturous welcome in every hamlet, village and town they passed through as they continued their relentless effort to drive the last Kraut out of The Netherlands and to ruthlessly kill any who put up resistance. For many of those cheering, waving Dutch it seemed almost unbelievable that the day of Liberation had, after such a long, long, weary wait at last arrived.

John was as wholeheartedly overjoyed as any of his comrades at the rapturous welcome they received as they brought Freedom to yet another Dutch community. The one deep regret he felt in the midst of all this overwhelming joy he kept to himself: the fact that they had by-passed and were now well away from the part of Holland he would much prefer to be.... The part where Anna lived.

As they moved on from Holland into Northern Germany they received nothing but dourly unsmiling hostile stares from the few German civilians they saw in the strangely, almost eerily, silent and deserted neat, flat, German countryside.

Then, just as they were in danger of being lulled into a foolish lack of alertness by the unopposed ease with which they were moving through the German homeland, they would be suddenly, violently reminded that those tough, deadly dangerous Krauts were not finished yet, not quite.

As the first Canadian armoured cars or jeeps drove into some village seemingly deserted by the German Army, a lethal shower of hand-grenades would cascade down on them from the village's highest buildings: a church tower or a hotel balcony. Then machine-guns would open up from these vantage points to add to the carnage. Usually this desperate, last-ditch resistance was put up by young, fanatic Hitler Youths or by older, tougher, perhaps even more fanatical Nazi S.S. veterans who, even at this late stage of a lost war, were willing to die for Hitler, their idolized Führer.

The incensed comrades of the killed Canadian soldiers reacted with fury. This being Germany, they were under none of the constraints that had applied in Holland where they had tried to inflict as little damage as possible on Dutch property.

They brought their tanks up to the edge of the German village and, firing at point-blank range, blasted shell after shell into the church and hotel and any other suspect building where those fanatic Nazis might be hiding out. They continued firing until satisfied that no hostile Krauts were left alive in the devastated village.

After a few incidents like this, with the death of a number of their furthest advanced soldiers, the Canadians moved at a slower, more cautious pace. Even when opposed by no more than a few well concealed Kraut snipers the weary Canadian soldiers did not take on those greatly outnumbered snipers in the always slow and dangerous house-to-house, room-to-room classical infantry clearing-out operations they had been trained in, but waited until their tanks came up and drastically dealt with those deadly lurking Kraut snipers.

Now, nearing the end of April and what must surely be also near the end of this long, bloody, devastating war, none of the Allied soldiers wanted to take any foolish useless risk of being killed in its final days. Their Commanding Officers felt the same; did not want to order any of their men to a cruel, needless death when the war was now almost won.

The Canadian officers reluctance to send their soldiers to an unnecessary death was reinforced by the great news – or unconfirmed rumour? – that reached them on the 1st May, 1945. The story was that, when surrounded by the victorious Soviet Army, Hitler had committed suicide in his huge concrete headquarters bunker in Berlin. This story quickly and jubilantly swept through all ranks of the Allied Armies as they continued their cautious advance from the West ever deeper into Germany.

Then the news that Grand Admiral Doenitz had been announced as Hitler's successor and Commander of all German Armed Forces seemed to confirm that Hitler really was dead. Surely the war would now end? Surely that Admiral had been appointed to negotiate the best possible terms for a German surrender?

John's three man S.B.S. team was with the first Canadian soldiers to reach the River Ems. Finding a major road bridge across that German river intact and un-guarded they crossed it then quickly checked the bridge for demolition charges. There were none. This advance party guarded the bridge until the main body of the Canadians arrived an rapidly crossed over. The S.B.S. men were profoundly thankful that, as at the Rhine, they had not to stealthily paddle across that river and neutralize German machine-guns defending it.

While the bulk of the Canadian Army pushed on towards Bremerhaven a smaller unit, including the S.B.S. team, headed for the other important German Naval Base at Emden. About ten kilometres from Emden the main road was blocked by many fallen trees. Driving slowly and anxiously alert for the danger of being caught in an ambush, the Canadians took a minor road through a thick fir forest.

While two of their jeeps scouted ahead of them the remainder of the Canadian vehicles halted. Fifteen minutes later the small advance party returned and the captain in charge halted beside Colonel MacDonald's jeep. 'What's the matter, Captain Colbert?' asked the Colonel. 'You look as if you've seen a ghost. Did you bump into some Krauts?'

'No, sir. We didn't see any Krauts. But we did see – and smell – something, some Hellhole, the Krauts have abandoned.'

'What do you mean, Captain, "some Hellhole"?'

'It's a type of prison camp. It must be one of those hideous German concentration camps we've heard vague reports about.'

'Are there still prisoners in the camp?'

'Yes, sir. There seem to be hundreds, if not thousands of them. But...but they're not like normal prisoners. They're more like ghastly zombies; starved living skeletons who can hardly walk, can barely manage to crawl. And... and the stench from that camp is vile, is really revolting.'

Col. MacDonald had already noted that the other seven soldiers who had been with Captain Colbert seemed even more distraught than that officer was. Four of the youngest ones had violently vomited at the camp and were miserably white faced. Even Sgt. Martin, one of his toughest, most experienced, most reliable soldiers was looking decidedly queasy. 'Okay, Captain,' the Colonel said, 'we better all go and see this "Hellhole" for ourselves.'

The condition of the starved, barely living humans at this German Concentration Camp well hidden in the thick forest and the vileness of the stench permeating the entire camp and its surroundings were worse – far worse – than any of the Canadians or British could have imagined in their worst nightmares.

Colonel MacDonald ordered his soldiers to split into small groups, thoroughly explore this sprawling camp, then bring detailed reports of the full extent of its horrors back to him.

With his two S.B.S. comrades beside him, John Armstrong threw open the door of one of the squat wooden barracks that stretched in dismal rows all over the camp. Assaulted by the awful stench that belched from the open doorway the three men staggered back.

Holding a handkerchief over his mouth and nostrils, John forced himself to enter the gloomily dim room. Originally built to house three hundred prisoners, this barrack was now hideously crammed with almost three thousand bodies. Just how many of those tragic bodies were alive and how many were dead it was impossible to say.

Row upon row of barely living or already dead grotesquely thin bodies were jammed closely together in wooden bunks that rose like a warehouse's stacked shelves from the straw and excretement littered floor almost to the ceiling. Most of the dying had defecated where they lay. The stench was appalling. All were covered with a crawling blanket of lice.

With his elbow resting on a corpse an emaciated old Jewish man feebly attempted to wave at John. Only that faint movement of his skeletal hand and the suggestion of a welcoming smile courageously moving his lips proved that he, too , was not a corpse.

A little girl, doubled up with gnawing hunger pains, cried pitifully for help and weakly begged 'Wasser, wasser.' She, like all the others, had received no food or water for some days.

A patriarchal, bushily-bearded Rabbi tripped over a dead body as he attempted to hurry towards John with a strength he must have tenaciously stored for this day of liberation. Gripping John's right hand with both of his, the Rabbi raised it to his cold, trembling lips and kissed it. With tears coursing down his hollow cheeks he lifted his head and mumbled a heartfelt prayer.

With eyes blurred by sympathetic tears John saw a 'thing' slowly move from one of the building's darkest corners and, after labouriously clambering over two corpses, slowly crawl towards him. Too weak to rise from the floor, the 'thing' – a haggard, grey haired old woman – patted the toe of one of his boots in a simple, loving, child-like manner.

With gentle care John disengaged himself from the Rabbi and the old woman. Pointing at his watch he said, 'We'll be back soon with help for you all.'

He joined his two S.B.S. comrades who, despite all their war-honed toughness, had not been able to advance beyond the open doorway, but stood – silent and queasily pale – peering in with deep, compassion, but even deeper, nerve-freezing revulsion at the nauseating sights nightmarishly half revealed in the building's filthy stinking gloom.

A touch shame-facedly they met John's understanding glance as he said, 'Perhaps we better have a quick look around behind these huts before we report back to Colonel MacDonald.'

They did not think it possible that they could find worse horrors than the hideous horrors they'd discovered in that crammed hut. But they did!

A strange persistent buzzing sound guided them to a large clearing in the fir trees beyond the camp's huts. As they neared the source of this mysterious noise their nostrils were attacked by a stench even more disgusting than any of the vile smells they had encountered before.

With handkerchiefs again pressed to nose and mouth, John slowly but resolutely advanced towards the forest clearing. His two companions even more slowly and much more reluctantly followed him.

What all three already suspected was all too definitely confirmed. That ceaseless ugly buzzing noise was made by a mass of flies. There were thousands of these large, black, frantically active flies. They formed a keenly crawling, excitedly rising and falling ghoulish pall over the huge pit that took up much of this forest clearing.

And in this deep pit there seemed to be almost as many naked, emaciated, decomposing human bodies as there were loudly gloating, greedily feeding flies.

Making a determined effort, John and his two comrades forced themselves to scrutinize that revolting sight.

Pathetically indecent in their nudity, tumbled layers of corpses of men, women and of children were promiscuously tangled together. In the places where a thin scattering of soil had been hastily thrown over the top layer of bodies it seemed as if some of these 'corpses' had been buried when they were not quite dead.

Despite their terribly weak state some of them had – obeying Nature's insistent Life Force – managed to scrape through the suffocating soil in a last desperate effort to tenaciously stay alive if only for a few extra minutes of a cruel, pointless life. Their gaunt, anguished heads now lay motionless on the displaced soil while stick-thin arms stuck up and claw-like hands imploringly reached up to Heaven in unavailing prayer.

'Oh God,' John exclaimed, 'some of those poor souls must have been buried alive.' He paused, he sighed deeply, 'Atrocities like this make you hate all Krauts and all things German, don't they? How could those Germans who boast of being such a cultured civilized people inflict such awful atrocities on their fellow Europeans? Perhaps it's just as well we haven't captured any of this camp's Kraut guards. I would shoot or hang all of them at once without bothering to wait for any proper legal trial.'

'Aye, I know. I feel exactly the same,' said Jock Brown. 'But wouldn't shooting or hanging be too quick, too humane a death for the Kraut bastards who ran this concentration camp and inflicted such .... such almost unbelievable terrible misery, suffering and torture on their victims... some of them small, innocent children?'

The third S.B.S. sailor, Tom Priestly, solemnly nodded in agreement then passionately asked, 'Yes, don't the inhuman bastards who inflicted such hideous torture deserve to suffer some avenging torture themselves?'

'Yes, perhaps they do,' John rather reluctantly agreed. Again he deeply and despairingly sighed, 'And so all those terrible hateful things that happened here might well go on to endlessly engender other terrible hateful things.'

For some long, solemn, silent moments the three men stood beside that large pit so disgustingly crammed with its hideously obscene human debris. Then John thought he saw some faint movement amongst some of the heaped corpses at the far side of the pit – a movement definitely different from the incessant noisily active movements of the mass of black flies. He pointed and gasped, 'I think some of those bodies are still alive. I'm sure there's something moving over there.'

The three of them walked around the pit and forced themselves to look closely at what John had thought was the faint movements of some still living 'corpses.'

There were definite movements, but not movements made by any living 'corpse', but made by things vivaciously living on these corpses.

An upheaval of large, plump, white maggots were a writhing loathsome mess in a number of the decomposing corpses burst bellies.

This gruesome sight coming on top of all the other disgusting horrors they had witnessed at this camp proved too much for Jock and Tom. They turned, took a few shaky steps away then were violently sick. John's strong stomach held out for a couple of queasy minutes as he fought to control his nausea then he too gushed a torrent of vomit.

Once his heaving stomach had nothing more to bring up, John resolutely forced his mind to re-gain control of his body. Sympathetically he wanly smiled at his white-faced comrades. 'You two poor buggers look as bad as I feel. There's nothing we can do here; come on, lets get away from this Hellish place.'

They followed a path leading towards a brick building with two high chimneys. A hazy column of greyish/black smoke waveringly rose from each chimney and drifted a thin fog of what seemed like black soot into the calm air.

As they neared the building a group of Canadian soldiers come out of it. They recognised Sergeant Josef Komorowski. He and his five companions were of Polish descent. The S.B.S. sailors noted that these Canadians were rather white-faced as if they too had seen some ghastly horror.

They had!

After the parties greeted one another John asked Sgt. Komorowski, 'What's in that building?'

'Oh gee, John, you don't want to see what's in there. It's full of yet more horrors; furnaces where the Krauts must have disposed of many starved corpses. Each furnace is stuffed overfull with corpses. They are slowly smouldering away.'

'Oh, in that case I don't think we'll bother going in there.'

As they stood talking some spots of black soot fell on them. Giving a savage curse Sgt. Komorowski drew out his handkerchief and urgently wiped away the smear of greasy soot that disfigured his forehead

After having wiped away a large greasy spot from his left cheek John shuddered with revulsion as he inspected the filthy smudge that fouled his khaki handkerchief. Scowling, he said, 'This horrible soot is coming from the smouldering bodies in those furnaces, isn't it?'

'Yeah, it is. It sure as Hell is.' Josef Komorowski emotionally thought of his relations in Poland. Some of them were thought to have died in a German concentration camp like this one. He, too scowled. He, too, shuddered as he gasped in a tear-choked voice, 'And to think that Hitler wanted to rule the world!'

Breaking the tense, compassionate silence that had fallen over the Canadian soldiers and British sailors, Jock Brown said, 'Aye, and he thought that his Nazi Third Reich would last for a thousand years!'

Getting his feelings under control, Sgt. Komorowski said, 'Okay, lads, we've seen enough. We better go and report to Colonel Mac.'

★ ★ ★

Colonel MacDonald stood in his jeep and addressed his troops who, having delivered their shocking reports, were silently crowded around him.' I've already been in touch with Headquarters. They're sending a team of specialists medical personnel and supplies to sort out things at this camp. They should arrive tomorrow. In the meantime we will do what we can for the poor, starving souls here.' Glancing at Major Turow, his medical officer, the Colonel continued, 'Doc Turow has warned you not to give the starving prisoners any too rich food too quickly. Even one candy bar could be too much for their impoverished stomachs to cope with properly. You could quite literally kill them with kindness!

'We have all heard them pathetically pleading for water; that is what they need more than anything else. Our cooks are organizing gallons of tea for them; tea thick with condensed milk and sweet with sugar, but not too hot. In their urgency to drink they would scald themselves if the tea was boiling hot.

'Now Major Turow will say a bit more on the medical problems we face.'

The Major stood up in the jeep when the Colonel sat down. He glanced at some notes he had made. 'By far the biggest threat we face is an outbreak of typhus. There already is a widespread plague of dysentery in the camp. The medical orderlies and myself will wear surgical masks when we go into the filthily overcrowded huts and all of you who volunteer to help us will wear handkerchiefs soaked in strong disinfectant.

'The first thing we will do is to give the living that urgently needed life-saving tea. Then we must separate the barely living from the already dead. That's about all we can do until the special medical team arrives tomorrow.'

Colonel Macdonald resumed his stand on the jeep. 'Thank you, Major. Now let's not waste any more of your time, doc. Get cracking with....' The Colonel stopped and frowned disapprovingly at the beaming grin on the face of Sgt. Wilson, his chief wireless operator, as, holding aloft a fluttering message form, he forced his way through the crowd of surprised soldiers. In this camp of hideous horrors that sergeant's glowing grin seemed obscenely out of place.

Thrusting the message form up to the Colonel and still grinning, Sgt. Wilson said, 'These very important messages have just arrived, sir.'

Continuing his disapproving stare, Col. Macdonald snatched the flimsy sheet of paper. After quickly reading the message he again stared at Sgt. Wilson, but his disapproving frown had been replaced by a smile.

As their commanding officer more slowly re-read these messages all the soldiers silently and greedily stared and speculatively wondered what was this important news that the Colonel and Sgt. Wilson found so cheerful?

Colonel Macdonald smiled around at all those staring, battle-weary faces then said, 'Okay, boys, I won't keep you in suspense any longer. After all the horrors you've seen here today you deserve to hear some brighter and better news. And this message I've just received from Headquarters is really great... Actually there are two messages. The first one informs us that the German Army defending Berlin has surrendered to the encircling Soviet Army.' Smiling, the Colonel patiently waited until his 'boys' cheers, laughter and excitement died down then faded to an expectant silence as they eagerly waited in hope of perhaps hearing even greater news in the second message.

'The other message from Headquarters is of more direct, immediate concern to us all. It informs us that senior German officers have agreed to meet Field Marshal Montgomery at Lüneburg Heath tomorrow, the 4th May, 1945, and sign the unconditional surrender of all German Forces in North West Germany, The Netherlands and Denmark. So in effect the war is over for us!'

This time the cheers were unrestrained; they continued longer, were much louder and more triumphantly jubilant. So too was the wild excitement of all the laughter, the handshaking and back-slapping that expressed their thankfulness that this war was over and that they had survived it.

Waiting until the storm of noisy excitement was not quite so loud, Colonel MacDonald again stood up in the jeep and addressed his exultant 'boys.' 'No doubt we will manage to conjure up some liquor to help us really celebrate the end of almost six long and bloody years of war. But we must not start celebrating until tonight. Before that we must do everything we can to help those poor starving souls in this camp.' He smiled at Major Turow, 'Okay, doc you are now in charge of our humane relief work. Let's all get on with it.'

★ ★ ★

Early that evening some reconnoitring Canadian soldiers discovered three waggons left locked and abandoned by the Germans on a siding outside the concentration camp. After making sure they were not booby-trapped, they smashed the locks then searched through the waggons. They were delighted to find the first two of them crammed with all types of food. They were even more delighted at what they found in the third waggon. Alongside a high heap of tinned food was a stack of crates; each crate held twelve bottles of schnapps.

As they keenly inspected this fabulous hoard it seemed obvious to the rejoicing soldiers that all this food and drink must have been intended for the camp's privileged Nazi guards and must have arrived shortly before the unexpectedly rapid advance of the Canadian Army had forced these despicable sadistic inhuman guards to flee for their lives.

It would now be real poetic justice that most of this freed food would, once their stomachs could cope with it, feed the Kraut's poor starved prisoners.

It would also be real ironic justice that those Canadian soldiers who had liberated this concentration camp would, by 'liberating' all these bottles of schnapps, receive their well deserved reward directly from those fled Kraut guards. They would celebrate the surrender of the German Army and the victorious end of the war with some of that defeated Army's own, extra strong and fiery schnapps.

As – taking two bottles with them as proof, and having tasted some of this fierce, high proof schnapps – these Canadian soldiers hurried to share their great news with their comrades at the camp they laughingly congratulated one another that they now really had something worthy to celebrate with

★ ★ ★

By midnight most of the 'liberated' bottles of schnapps had been emptied. With foolishly eagre liberality this raw harsh spirit had been almost masochistically poured down gasping, burning, Canadian and British throats.

For a time this fierce alcoholic spirit uproariously enlivened the spirits of these celebrating men, then, all too soon and all too drastically, the fierceness of this raw alcohol took its toll; turned inebriated good cheer to depressed cursing, to despairing moaning, to violent and revolting vomiting and miserable self-loathing.

For a time John Armstrong wisely restricted the amount of that 'liberated firewater' he allowed down his assaulted throat and into his protesting stomach, but then, mockingly chivvied by his most definitely, most determinedly non-abstentious uproarious comrades, he eventually succumbed to the powerful alluring temptation of allowing drunken forgetfulness to blot out the all too vivid memories of the horrors he had seen here today.

As the noise of victorious rejoicing increasingly gave way to the moans of drunken misery John – still much too sober to really forget all today's hideous horrors – felt an urgent need to be by himself for a while. He felt that in the peace of secluded solitude he might manage to sort out his troubled disordered thoughts; might manage to calm his confused conflicting emotions; would try to ease his deeply scarred nerves and feelings with optimistic hopes that tomorrow's end of this long and terrible war might allow him to be soon re-united with his Anna and, revelling in post-war peace, and together forever, they would make love, kindness and compassion triumphantly take over from war's horrors.

As he reasonably steadily walked towards the dark fir trees surrounding the camp John saw a tall, bulky figure stumble towards him out of the nocturnal gloom. He instantly recognised Sgt. Josef Komorowski. The Canadian/ Polish sergeant did not recognise John until he almost bumped into him, but then loudly and warmly greeted him like a long lost brother. As he flung an arm around John's shoulders he raised the bottle of schnapps firmly gripped in his other hand and with joyous enthusiasm clattered it against John's bottle in soldierly brotherly greeting. John was amazed that both bottles did not shatter under the over-enthusiastic impact.

'Are you okay, John?... Where are you going?'

'Yeah, I'm okay. I'm just going into this forest for a while.'

'Oh, I see.' The merrily un-sober Canadian soldier laughed uproariously, 'Yeah, that's where I've just come from. You do crap in woods too, John?' As he staggered off towards the camp Sgt. Komorowski shouted over his shoulder, 'Don't be long, John. Come back before I finish all the schnapps!'

Despite what that sergeant thought, John was not going to seek relief for his troubled bowels, but, hopefully, was going to get some relief for his troubled soul. That soul was seriously confused and uneasy not only at all the horrors he had seen here today, but by vivid memories of some of the hideous, ruthless killings this terrible war had forced him to carry out.

After getting comfortably settled on the deep dry litter of pine needles at the foot of a tall fir tree and resting his back on its rough grey bark John lifted his bottle to the profoundly silent, calmly aloof starry night sky and inspected its contents. His first thought was that it was half empty. But then, quietly chuckling he remembered Jock Brown's invariable reaction when confronted with a part full whisky bottle: 'Only dour pessimists think that bottle's half empty; all true optimists rejoice that it's half full.'Yes, his bottle of schnapps was happily half full!

In an effort to control his erratic wandering thoughts he decided to have another brain-clearing drink. Unscrewing the bottle's metal cap – but, unlike Jock with his whisky corks – retaining that cap, John guided the raw spirits to his mouth and gulped down one more savagely fiery, throat strangling, stomach-burning, eye-watering dram. As his abused body gave a protesting shudder he once again ruefully thought, 'Yes, undoubtedly there is something decidedly masochistic about inflicting such 'pleasure' on oneself!'

A gentle breeze playfully stirred the fir's high top and sent a few pine needles dancing down. One needle fell on John's left cheek: landed on the exact spot where that repulsive greasy smudge from the concentration camp's body-consuming furnaces had landed.

In his uneasy, not exactly sober state that innocent needle felt like another loathsome smudge. As he violently wiped away that non-existent sooty stain he suddenly remembered how upsetting Anna had found Dickens' macabre scene in *Bleak House* when the body of a character – Mr. Krook, an eccentric rag and bone dealer – had been consumed by a fantastic act of spontaneous combustion . Little had been left of his greasy, un-washed, gin-sodden body but a dense smoky obscurity thicker than the worst London fog, an all pervading disgusting stench and a repulsive rain of oily black soot.

But humans can always be trusted to come up with a reality far, far worse that the ugliest of fiction's fantasy. The horror and one-off uniqueness of that 19th century fictitious act of spontaneous combustion was now completely overshadowed by the 20th century not spontaneous, but, deliberate, meticulously planned acts of victim – destroying combustion in the Nazis satanic mass-production furnaces.

John tortured himself with the horrendous thought that Anna might – as he knew some Dutch Resistance Patriots had – have ended her life in a German concentration camp's furnace.

This unbearable thought made him suddenly sure – absolutely sure – that all his stealthy ruthless killings and all the large scale deaths of German civilians and wholesale destruction of their cities by Allied aircraft were fully justified. These savage actions had played an important part in ensuring a quicker end of the war and a quicker liberation of the incredibly tenacious survivors in the German concentration camps.

In a desperate effort to anaesthetize that too cruel, but – as an almost sober, logically reasoning part of his brain insisted – all too possible scenario of Anna's end, he lifted his bottle and forced himself to gulp down more of that fierce 'firewater'.

As his gasping throat eased and his smarting eyes ceased watering he seemed to distinctly hear Anna's voice emphatically exclaim, 'Oh, John! John! I'm safe, I'm perfectly safe!.... I'm waiting, endlessly waiting for you to return to me.'

Was that voice of Anna's a drunken illusion? Was he merely hearing his alcohol stimulated imagination tell him things he desperately wanted to hear?

With sudden sharp clearness a vivid scene in another of Anna's favourite novels – *Jane Eyre* – flared in John's mind. Although many miles apart, Jane heard her passionately loved Edward Fairfax Rochester send his unmistakable voice crying out to her in what seemed tortured anguish, 'Jane! Jane! Jane!'

Without hesitation, without doubt, she responded to that impassioned call.

Should John do the same? Should he immediately set out to be re-united with Anna? In his un-sober, excited state he was tempted. He missed her terribly. And now that 'psychic' message told him that she desperately wanting him to return to her. This war was now more or less over; surely all his deadly, stealthy, killing skills were no longer required? Wouldn't he be justified in setting off this very minute?

Giving a deep, dismissive sigh he thrust away thoughts of carrying out such a tempting course of action. Such an unauthorised action would be an act of desertion – he would be A.W.O.L. (Absent without leave), be a despicable deserter from the Royal Navy. And worse –

much worse – he would let down all his trusting, trustworthy S.B.S. comrades. No, he would never become a deserter!

After resolutely dismissing the temptation of immediately returning to Anna from his mind, he remembered how animatedly Anna and he had discussed both these powerful fictitious events that were now so vividly present in this thoughts. They soon agreed that Krook's spontaneous combustion seemed most unlikely. But when it came to the 'psychic' voice that Jane Eyre had distinctly heard they were sharply divided. John's logically reasoning male brain made him extremely sceptical. Guided by instinctive feelings, by intuitive 'knowledge' deeper and truer than mere logic, Anna powerfully, passionately and persuasively argued that the wonderful magical mystical non-scientific power of love could sometimes transcend all the 'normal' rules of soul-less Science.

So, John bemusedly wondered, had he really heard Anna's voice with its reassuring message?

Engrossed in these thoughts he almost dropped his bottle.

Grinning, he gripped it tighter and mused, 'There the answer. The spiritual message I received came not from some para-normal power, but from the powerful spirits in that bottle!'

No longer grinning but again feeling confused and uncertain he started to raise the part-full bottle to his mouth. Then, thinking better of it, he resolutely screwed the nobly retained metal cap back on. Too much drinking here by himself would only lead to too much un-wise, un-healthy stultifying introversion. Much better to go back and share what little schnapps was left with Sgt. Komorowski and the others.

★ ★ ★

Once again Josef Komorowski greeted John like a long lost brother. Laughing loudly, he bellowed, 'Welcome back, John. You've had a very long crap in the woods!'

Laughing almost as loudly, John declared, 'I've discovered that the whole of life is nothing but a lot of craps: the only real relief comes from a bottle of schnapps!'

'Oh gee, John, you're a poet and you don't know it! That's very funny.'

Pointing and grinning John said, 'Those dismal comrades of yours don't seen to find it, or anything else, very funny.' Earlier in this evening's bout of drinking he had noted with some surprise and much quiet amusement just how these Canadian/ Polish soldiers had – true to their Slav origins – so determinedly set about what seemed the grim necessity rather than the pleasure of getting hopelessly leg-lessly drunk as quickly as possible. Like true Poles they had knocked back each brimming glass of fiery schnapps in one desperate, masochistic gulp. Despite their good-hearted jeering at his non-Slavonic ways John had, after attempting to gulp down his first glass, resolutely drank it and his succeeding glasses in a much wiser, more frugal way.

As the evening wore on these drunken soldiers were – again in a truly Slavonic way – either on a glorious, uproarious, carefree 'high' or, sometimes only a few minutes later, were sunk in a gloomy trough of almost suicidal despair . They were now in a deep, dismal, comatose low.

Only Josef Komorowski was on a happy, uplifting high. He grinned at John, 'I give them sage advice....I shake them out of their Polish depression.' Grabbing the shoulders of the two nearest slumped soldiers he shook them violently and loudly exclaimed, 'Come on, lads, schnapp out of it !'

He bellowed unrestrainedly at his own great joke. John's laughter loudly and appreciatively joined in. In his not quite sober state that did seem a great joke.

Chapter Forty Six

Despite the self-inflicted misery of throbbing hangovers, the Canadians soldiers and the three S.B.S. sailors were up early the following morning and were soon again conscientiously attending to the concentration camp's freed prisoners. The uncomplaining stoic courage of these emaciated victims whose sufferings and miseries were uncomparably worse than anything their helpers were suffering, made these compassionate British and Canadians ashamed of their earlier rueful complaints to one another about the terrible agony of their hung-over state.

Gallons of well-sweetened warm tea were again brewed-up and quickly given to the grateful, thirsty still semi-starving victims. Under the direction of the medical officer, Major Turow, small amounts of easily digested food were carefully rationed out to those he thought were strong enough to cope with it.

The wasted skeletal corpses of those who had died during the night were gently removed from amongst those who were still holding on to life with fierce tenacity.

Late in the afternoon the expected team of medical and hygiene experts arrived at the camp. They brought truck loads of urgently needed special supplies. They immediately set about their humane work.

Then Col. Macdonald received a message confirming that the Germans had signed their unconditional surrender to Field Marshall Montgomery at Lüneburg Heath. So the war in this part of Europe was now officially over.

The Colonel received a second message; it informed him that a small party of Royal Navy officers would arrive tomorrow morning. He was ordered to prepare the S.B.S sailors and an escorting group of his soldiers to accompany these officers deeper into Northern

Germany to receive the surrender of an important German naval base.

So the following afternoon John Armstrong, Jock Brown and Tom Priestley, those three veteran members of that greatest, most skilled, most secretive of all British Special Forces – the Royal Navy's Special Boat Section – were standing at attention on the stern of a large, modern, German destroyer moored in Cuxhaven's extensive and apparently not too badly bomb-damaged naval base

Captain Medhurst, the R.N. officer in command of this operation, tried not to make his exultation too glaringly obvious to the dourly watching German sailors as he quickly hauled down the German ensign with its vile swastika then slowly and steadily raised the White Ensign of the Royal Navy in its place.

He made no attempt to hide the elated pride with which he saluted that noble flag.

As the three S.B.S sailors saluted that bravely fluttering White Ensign they, too, were deeply moved by profound feelings. This simple symbolic act of replacing one naval ensign with another one confirmed to them more than Col Macdonald's announcement had done that the war really was over; that the Royal Navy had finally defeated the German Navy. Each one of them was justifiably, though modestly and secretly, proud of the part he had played in bringing this eagerly longed for historic act about.

At the completion of this unique, moving, short ceremony all four British sailors tried to diplomatically control the excited emotions that glowed their faces. They did not want the exhilaration they felt to appear to be too triumphantly gloating to the line of defeated and despondent German sailors who stood on the deck of this ex-German, now British warship and stared in sullen sulky silence or more openly allowed their dark scowls to reveal the true depth of their continuing smouldering hatred.

After having been trying to kill one another for almost six long and bloody years and having seen many good brave comrades die, it was hardly to be expected that those German and British sailors would very quickly or easily become really friendly.

As, making for the gangway, they smartly passed that line of scowling Krauts those Royal Navy sailors were greatly reassured by the alertness of the well-armed Canadian soldiers who stood protectively waiting on the dockside.

The party of British and Canadians went to find the three other R.N. officers who had been left at another part of this large naval base.

John Armstrong thought it most strange that those officers had not been present at the ceremonious surrender of that German warship. Surely such an unforgettable, once in a lifetime, historic experience was one that no Royal Navy officer would willingly have wanted to miss. But, being merely a humble leading-seaman, his was not to reason why these officers had been absent. Not having been put fully in the picture by Captain Medhurst, there was a lot John and his two S.B.S. comrades did not know.

They did not know that units of Montgomery's triumphant army had, by racing to the Baltic at Lubeck, prevented Stalin's victorious Red Army from advancing any further West into defeated Northern Germany or even into Denmark. Nor did they know that British soldiers had already captured the German Navy's largest naval base at Kiel and also the large, important city of Hamburg.

Only after Captain Medhurst received new orders direct from London did he announce that their entire party of soldiers and sailors were immediately heading as quickly as possible to the shipyards of Hamburg. But only he and his fellow R.N. officers knew why they were in such a hurry to get to Hamburg when it was already firmly under British Army control.

Those naval officers knew that their speedy dash to Hamburg was only one of the many frantic races that British and American army units had made, and were still making in the final stages of this war. There were many important German research establishments the Western Allies desperately wanted their experts to examine and get as much information as possible from before these facilities were taken over by the Russian Army.

The Russians had already taken over the extensive establishment at Peenemünde where the Germans had developed their V1 flying-bombs and V2 long range rockets, although the most important German scientists had fled Westward and were now in American hands.

Racing in front of a token force of the Free French Army who were slowly advancing into Germany, a large American Army unit succeeded in getting to the German town of Hechingen before these annoyed Frenchmen did, or – much more importantly – before the

Russians did.. At a research establishment in this town many of the best German physicists were working feverishly trying to produce an atomic bomb before the Allies did. The Americans captured most of thee scientists. They were quickly taken out of reach of the Russians. Some two tons of uranium, two tons of heavy water and ten tons of carbon were also rapidly removed by the Americans.

One of the reasons Stalin ordered the Red Army to urgently (and with complete disregard of the very heavy losses they would suffer) surround then capture Berlin before the Western Allies reached the German Capital was so that the secrets of the German nuclear programme kept at the Kaiser Wilhelm Institute for Physics be captured by the Russians and not by the Americans. The stores of uranium oxide discovered at this Institute were taken to Moscow and ultimately helped the Russians with their atomic programme.

The rush to get to the shipyards at Hamburg was also connected with that frantic effort by the Germans to develop a nuclear weapon. Royal Navy Intelligence had received information that if the Germans succeeded in making an atomic bomb they would try to get it to New York harbour in one of the large new submarines they were building and then it would be exploded with devastating, war-winning effect.

The surrender of decisively defeated Germany had removed that terrifying threat. But for Royal Navy Intelligence the end of the war in no way lessened the urgency with which they wanted to obtain full details of those large new German U-boats which had been reported to be going to be powered by some entirely new kind of engine. British Admirals wanted to get their hands on those fantastic new engines before any one else did.

So Captain Medhust, a senior R.N. Intelligence officer, his team of three expert naval technocrats and their escorting S.B.S sailors and Canadian soldiers urgently raced towards Hamburg.

Passing through that devastated city as quickly as its bomb-cratered and rubble heaped streets permitted they made for the shipbuilding yards that lined the River Elbe. Eventually they found what they were searching for: the three giant, almost completed U-boats that sat on bomb-damaged slipways. One submarine lay on its side like a mortally stricken beast. One was trapped under the contorted skeleton of a collapsed steel gantry. The third huge U-boat appeared to be more or less intact. It gave an impression of terrible longing: of desperate impatience to slide into the dark river water that so tantalizingly lapped at its stern.

The four expert R.N. officers and the three S.B.S sailors were awed by the size of these submarines. They were almost three times longer than any U-boat they had ever seen.

After a quick inspection of the intact submarine then a hurried scrutiny of the mass of technical documents and blueprints systematically filed in the bomb-proof vaults of this shipyards head office those British naval experts were absolutely amazed at how entirely new and novel the design of the engines for these large U-boats were. They had never seen anything like them. They knew the Royal Navy had nothing comparable. Unlike all existing submarines, these huge new 'WALTHER' class of U-boats would not, when surfaced, be propelled by a diesel engine, and, when submerged, by electric batteries, but their fantastic, truly revolutionary new engine, using hydrogen- peroxide, would propel them both on the surface and underwater. It would give them speeds far in excess of the Royal Navy's convoy-escorting corvettes.

Captain Medhurst voiced all these awed R.N. officers' thoughts. 'Thank God the Germans never managed to bring these terrifying monsters into service. Had they got enough of them into action they might well have won the Battle of the Atlantic for the Huns.'

The most junior officer, a mere war-time member of the Volunteer Reserve, thinking of the extensive bomb-damage at this shipyard, said, 'Yes, sir, we must hand it to the R.A.F. bomber boys; they seem to have done a great job of delaying the production of these U-boats.'

John Armstrong and his two S.B.S. comrades exchanged discreet, secretly amused glances; they thought that junior officer was being more than a little naive in expressing such praise of the R.A.F. to a senior, regular, R.N. officer.

And, sure enough, Captain Medhurst's reply, when it eventually came, was little more than a brief grunted, decidedly reluctant agreement.

★ ★ ★

After a few days all the Canadian soldiers returned to their regiments and left the three S.B.S sailors to continue to act as bodyguards to the four expert R.N. officers as they thoroughly examined the huge U-boat and systematically sifted through the mass of technical documentation relating to it and to its fantastic new type of engine.

For more than a week these sailors carried out their rather boring, but necessary, bodyguard duties, then a detachment of Royal Marines arrived and relieved them. They were now ordered to accompany and again more or less act as bodyguards to two other R.N. officers who were to make a quick survey of most major naval bases in Germany.

After having inspected and reported on conditions, Emden, Cuxhaven and Kiel they sailed on a R.N. destroyer to inspect the naval base with its massive, impressive, concrete U-boat pens on the small island of Heligoland.

These officers now proceeded to Norway to inspect the U-boat pens at Bergen and other ex-German naval bases in that country. The three S.B.S. sailors went with them although of course they should no longer be required as bodyguards. The situation and atmosphere in recently freed Norway was entirely different from the barely concealed resentful hostility they had encountered in ignominiously defeated Germany. After having suffered five long miserable years of brutal German tyranny the Norwegian people were rejoicing in the wonder of their restored freedom.

In some of the small coastal towns and fishing villages the five man Royal Navy party passed through they were the first British servicemen the Norwegians had seen. They were invariably greeted and treated as liberating heroes. Sometimes the welcoming generosity of the Norwegians was so unstintingly great that it forced that British naval party to – un-reluctantly – stay overnight in their hospitable host's village instead of merely driving through.

John Armstrong, Jock Brown and Tom Priestly laughingly, an perhaps not quite soberly, agreed amongst themselves that, 'We certainly don't need to act as bodyguards to these officers; not in this wonderful country amongst those great people.' Instead they called themselves the officers chaperons. They should try to ensure that these two young officers did carry out their duties and were not completely overwhelmed by the great hospitality of the genuinely appreciative Norwegians.

But who was to chaperone the chaperoner? Almost every Norwegian home was open to them. Food and drink was forced on them. They gloried in meals of unlimited helpings of succulent salmon and other only slightly less delightful fresh caught fish.

When the Norwegians learned that John had been in Norway before and had travelled on a 'Shetland Bus' he received an especially warm welcome and extra praise. He, in turn, warmly and sincerely praised all the patriotic Norwegian Resistance Fighters as being some of the greatest and bravest of all Europe's Freedom Fighters.

John had another secret link to those Norwegian Patriots, but he discretely continued to keep this link secret. Just as a small, exceptionally brave and determined group of these Patriots had seriously delayed the development of the Germans atomic bomb by destroying some of the heavy water the Kraut scientists needed to get from Norway for their nuclear programme, so, too, John had helped delay development of that terrifying weapon by killing those two treacherous Dutch nuclear physicists who had been helping the Germans in their desperate effort to get an atomic bomb before the Americans did.

The fact that the most important of those two Dutch collaborators had turned out to be Anna's father had been a truly amazing coincidence; a terrible complication that John could well have done without; a complication that often disturbed the dark, silent, midnight minutes when he lay restlessly worrying as he tried to fall asleep. How had Anna reacted to her father's inexplicable death? Had Frans succeeded in keeping secret from her the terrible fact that her father had been a despicable traitor and that John had, patriotically doing his duty, killed him?

Often in these fretful sleepless minutes John fervently wished he had been ordered to go to Holland instead of revelling in all this most enjoyable Norwegian hospitality. If he had been stationed in the Netherlands surely he would have managed to get to Anna; would know that she was alive and well. Or would have discovered that she was.... was what?... was not well?.. Was not alive? Summing up all the strength of his S.B.S trained mind he resolutely forced such negatively pessimistic self-torturing thoughts away. Anna *was* alive ! She *was* well!

Now that the war was over it shouldn't be too long before he was demobilised from the navy, and, once a civilian, there would be nothing to stop him from hurrying to Holland to be re-united with Anna.

But of course, as his logically reasoning brain cruelly reminded him, it was only the war in Europe that was over. The war in the Far East was still being fiercely fought and there seemed no prospect of it ending soon. Might he be sent with expert, experienced S.B.S. teams to pave the way for the huge Allied Army that would have to land on the Japanese mainland to bring this war to a successful end? Such a savagely resisted invasion would have to be on a much, much vaster scale – and would result in far, far heavier casualties- than the Normandy D-Day landings . Might he be one of the fatal casualties? He shuddered at the thought.

As he again thought of how he and those Norwegian Patriots had helped delay the development of the Germans atomic bomb (although he had no way of knowing just how much they had delayed it, or how close the Krauts had come to getting their bomb) John felt something that seemed a flash of inspired insight. He had a strong positive feeling that the Americans must be close to getting their own atomic bomb. Or quite possibly they already had one. Might he have helped to bring this about? Might Professor van Karson, that Dutch nuclear physicist whom John's S.B.S. team had freed from the Krauts and taken to England in 'Operation Starlight', have gone on to the United States to help develop their bomb?

If the Americans did have their own bomb surely the use of that frightful weapon against Japan would make any huge – and costly – invasion of that country unnecessary.

But, still in shock after the unexpected sudden death of President Roosevelt, would new, un-tested President Truman find the courage and determination to order the use of the American atomic bomb? The decision to use such a terrible weapon was a truly awesome decision for anyone to make, but that new President, and he alone had to make it. John felt sure that if Truman was convinced that its use would save many American lives he would order it to be immediately used. And the lives of many British and Commonwealth soldiers would also be saved.

★ ★ ★

After some pleasant weeks of having food and drink hospitably forced on them and some enjoyably strenuous climbing on impressively high and beautiful Norwegians mountains the three S.B.S. sailors began to think that their leisurely, relaxing, post-war sojourn in Norway was too good to last.

It was!

Near the end of July they received orders to immediately return to S.B.S. Headquarters at Poole Harbour.

The day after their arrival at Poole, Lieutenant Johnstone, who had led them on a number of hazardous missions, cheerily greeted them.'Welcome home, lads. It's good to see the lost sheep return to the fold.You're all looking very well. I believe you've had a most pleasant leisurely time in time Norway.'The young officer brightly smiled, 'It's a good thing you enjoyed your time there, for that's the last pleasant leisure you're likely to enjoy for quite a while.You've to report to the medical officer this morning to get some extra inoculations.'

This news was greeted with loud, melodramatic groans. 'What new inoculations are we to get, sir?' John Armstrong warily asked.

John and his two comrades sensed a hint of sadistic amusement in Lt. Johnstone's grinning reply. 'You've to get jabs for malaria and various other tropical diseases.'

There was no melodramatic amusement in the noise that greeted this information; these were genuine groans of dismay.

'So we're heading for the Far East to finish off the Japs for the Yankees, are we?' asked Tom Priestly.

'Aye, where else would we be going that needed protection from all those tropical diseases?' Jock Brown asked in turn. 'Trust us S.B.S. to be sent for when there's stealthy and dangerous fighting to be done.'

'Yes,' Lt. Johnstone confirmed, 'we're heading East to prepare the way for the invasion and defeated of Japan.' He scrutinized their sternly set faces. Obviously they were not happy at this news. Nor was he. Hadn't they done more than enough in this long and bloody war? Weren't there plenty of younger, keener, less war-weary men to do the work in the Far East that these brave veterans had been uncomplainingly doing for the last four years in Europe? The S.B.S. officer sighed, 'I'm sorry. I know how you feel. I feel the same. But we must obey orders. We can only hope that the Japs will be quickly defeated.' He smiled, 'Now you must report to the M.O. and take your jabs like true heroes. I had mine a week ago. I don't mind telling you that the after-effects were not very pleasant.'

Jock Brown managed a mischievous grin, 'Thank you for those cheery, consoling words, sir.'

★ ★ ★

After a few days of real pain then almost a week of nagging unease the ill-effects of their inoculations wore off and the three S.B.S. sailors were declared fit enough to be sent to fight in the Far East. Lt. Johnstone briefed them, 'We're getting V.I.P. (Very Important Persons) treatment, lads. We're not going on a slow troopship. We are being flown to Egypt and then on to India. Where we go from there I don't know.' He grinned, ' 'But no doubt we'll find out soon enough, eh?' He thought the grins he received in reply were rather forced. The Lieutenant continued 'Anyway we're due to fly out on the 8th August. That's just three days to wait. I'm sorry you haven't had embarkation leave before you go out East. I tried to get it for you but I'm afraid the "powers that be" seem to want us out fighting the Japs in rather a hurry. Perhaps they regard the pleasant time you had in Norway as the leave you were due.'

They decided to have a farewell booze-up before they left 'Dear Old Blighty'. They did not know it then, but they chose an historic day for this celebration – the sixth of August, 1945.

As they slowly, blearily and tormentedly returned to consciousness the following morning they heard the astounding news that yesterday some entirely new and terrifying powerful weapon had been exploded over, and had destroyed the Japanese city of Hiroshima. As yet there were no reports of the number of human casualties.

It seemed certain that the explosion of this American atomic bomb over Japan must make the Japanese surrender.

But it did not. They insanely continue to fight on. They fanatically continue to 'gloriously' die.

Lieutenant Johnstone – suffering from a hang-over himself – informed the rather woebegone S.B.S sailors that he had some good news for them, news that should help them recover their spirits. 'Our planned flight to the East to tomorrow has been cancelled. Been cancelled, or perhaps only postponed. We've to wait here at Poole until we receive further orders.'

They whole-heartedly welcomed this news. They loudly, and

scientifically ignorantly, speculated about just exactly what an atomic bomb was. Only John had heard of such a weapon before. In his 'Operation Waterloo' briefings he had been given some indication of what terrible destruction such a bomb could cause. He continued to keep his secret knowledge to himself. He was profoundly thankful that the world's first atomic bomb had exploded over Japan and not over Britain or the United States. He again wondered just how much his and the Norwegian Patriots actions had helped bring this desired outcome about.

Like his comrades, John was awed at the thought of what devastation one single bomb could cause. With them he shudderingly wondered what other terrifying Frankensteinish monstrosities the scientific boffins might create in the future .

Two day later another atomic bomb was dropped on Japan. It destroyed the city of Nagasaki.

But still the Japanese did not surrender.

They continued to fanatically fight. They continued to senselessly die. And, of greater concern to Allied commanders, they continued to kill all too many American, British and Commonwealth soldiers, sailors, and marines. If only the use of more atomic bombs would bring about the end of all this needless killing so be it. By their mad, misguided, stubborn refusal to surrender the Japs were bringing this nuclear horror on themselves.

After five tense days of nuclear sabre-rattling, with President Truman darkly hinting of having a whole arsenal of atomic bombs, his great bluff (for he had only one more nuclear weapon ready for use) achieved its desired end of bringing the war to an end. The Japanese unconditionally surrendered on the 14 August 1945.

Truman's great atomic bluff also stopped Stalin's formidable Red Army from grabbling any more territory in the Far East.

Millions hysterically celebrated the fantastic news that – at long, long last – the Second World War was over.

As John rejoiced with his rejoicing comrades he optimistically thought, 'Surely I will soon be demobbed from the navy. Surely I will soon be re-united with Anna.'

Chapter Forty Seven

The Royal Navy, however, was in no great hurry to return John to civilian life.

Of course he was only one of many thousands of R.N. sailors who, having willingly 'done their bit' during the long and bloody war, now keenly desired to become civilians again. Yet here he was almost three months after the end of the war against Japan still serving on a Royal Navy warship.

This warship was not a fast, sleek destroyer, nor was it a huge, impressive battleship; it was a small, humble, ex-trawler now minesweeper. It was one of the fleet of minesweepers carrying out the hardly glamorous or exciting but very necessary duty of sweeping the North Sea free of the many British and German minefield that for six years had closed off large parts of these waters.

After all his adrenalin flooding, stomach churning wartime S.B.S. duties John found this minesweeping a dull business as sweep after sweep was monotonously and endlessly repeated. His boring, undemanding duties gave him too much time to think of, and worry about Anna. When – oh when – would he be free to return to her?

At first there was some excitement each time a mine was cut free of its mooring cable and bobbed to the surface. There was keen competition amongst the crew to be the one to explode the large, darkly menacing drifting mine by your accurate rifle-fire from a safe distance.

Using his fine-honed S.B.S. marksman's skills John quickly proved himself the greatest expert at hitting and exploding these mines. Again at first it was exciting to see the mine explode, fountain a giant column of white water impressively high, hold it for gravity defying seconds then Niagra the violated water back down. But after a time even this regularly repeated excitement began to pall. It palled almost as much as the taste of the large haddocks and other fish that were served to them at almost every meal palled. Fish – all kinds of fish – were the ship's cook's favourite food. He, formerly a cook on peacetime trawlers, revelled in the abundance of fish that – dead or merely stunned – littered the sea's surface after the explosion of every mine. He longingly looked forward to the time when, demobbed from the Royal Navy, he would again sail on trawlers; would eagerly join in the bonanza of fish that the North Sea would yield once all its minefields were cleared. Meanwhile he made the most of the tormented sea's culinary bounty.

The crew did not rejoice with him. The skipper agreed with his moaning, fish-satiated crew. He ordered the cook, 'Let's have something different from fish now and again.' He grinned, 'Even your thick slices of fried Spam would make a welcome change from your endless fish dishes.'

At the end of two weeks of this monotonous minesweeping John felt increasingly restless and unsettled. This foretaste of the mundaneness of 'normal' peacetime life was difficult to cope with after his years of wartime excitements, dangers and violent activity. He largely succeeded in hiding his restlessness from his shipmates but he could not hide it from himself. The transition from war to peace was not easy. How would he adjust to peacetime after he left the Navy and was no longer buoyed up by the deep camaraderie of many good comrades?

He would urgently need the great love and profound understanding of his wife, Anna, to help him successfully adjust to his new peacetime civilian life. And how much would Anna need his deep love and sympathetic understanding to help her after all her grim years under German tyranny; under the constant threat of betrayal, of Gestapo torture then execution? At times during her almost two year state of being held in dreadful limbo; of not knowing if he was alive or dead; of constantly worrying about when – if ever – he would return to her, surely Anna must have been desolate .... must have felt completely neglected and forgotten.

Yes, they would desperately need each others love to get over all their wartime horrors.

★ ★ ★

When the minesweeper berthed in the naval base at Hull to be re-fuelled and re-provisioned before again setting out on yet more minesweeping duties, John was delighted to receive orders to report to S.B.S. headquarters at Poole. Hopefully he would not serve on any more long, weary, mine clearing voyages but would be heading for demob from the navy at long last.

He was!

Four days later he had gone through the elaborate procedure that transformed him from being a leading-seaman in the Royal Navy to being a civilian. He had been issued with many documents that confirmed his status as a civilian. Although the war was over, food, clothes, petrol and most other things were still strictly rationed. Armed with his new ration book and his railway travel pass and rewarded with a little – a very little – money as a gratuity for his war service from his grateful, but un-generous government, John was en route for his home town of Keswick.

Despite it now being peacetime the trains were still overcrowded with kitbag laden soldiers, sailors and airmen; were still subject to long, inexplicable delays that could no longer be blamed on German air raids. At least night-time journeys were much cheerier now that there was no dreary wartime black-out. All lights could – and did brightly blaze as if in celebration.

Eventually John reached Keswick. Unhampered by the haversack slung over his right shoulder and the cardboard case containing his demob suit and other civilian clothes which jauntily swung from his left hand he joyfully strode up the slope to his home. The dismal drizzle he had encountered outside Keswick railway station had died away. A weak afternoon sun smiled down and transmuted the sloping row of gray old cottages to things of bright glittery splendour.

Halting at a familiar, well loved spot, John got the first sight of 'his mountain' – Skiddaw. Although its peak was hidden by clinging mists its lower slopes rejoiced in the autumnal sun's brave smiling glow. John, too, rejoiced. His mountain, his town, were giving him a bright welcome; were adding their welcome to the ones he would receive from his mother and sister. He was sure his mother would be slaving over her kitchen stove cooking and baking in eager anticipation of her prodigal son's return.

She was!

The face his mother turned to him as he entered the cosy homely warmth of her kitchen was glowing, was bright flushed with the heat of the stove, with a rush of joy and a hot flood of maternal love.

After their brief, firm hugging embrace John was held at arm's length by his beaming mother; was keenly inspected by her steady gaze despite her eyes being blurred by emotion. 'You're looking very well, John. You've put on a little weight. You look more handsome than ever in your sailor's uniform.'

He laughed, 'Aye, perhaps so, mother, but I think you are a wee bit biassed. Anyway this will be almost the last time I'll be wearing this uniform.'

'So you are demobbed from the navy at last, are you? I was not sure if you were just on leave and would be going back or not.' She lovingly hugged him again. 'Oh thank God you're home for good, son. Thank God you came through the war safely. I worried about you constantly during all those long, terrible six years of war.'

'Oh, mother, you didn't think I was going to let any damn Huns get the better of me, did you?'

She hugged him even more tightly. She seemed reluctant to let him go.

Although deeply moved by his mother's display of emotion, John resolutely kept his own emotions under strict control. 'Oh mother, believe me I do understand what a hideous time those six long years must have been for you. I'm terribly sorry to have brought such almost unbearable misery on you.' He smiled encouragingly, 'But such terrible wartime horrors belong to the past. We are now in peacetime. We must all make the most of Peace.'

His mother instantly agreed, 'And the first peacetime thing I must do for you, son, is to give you some tea and fresh made scones.'

As she happily sat beside her returned son at the kitchen table and eagerly encouraged him to eat more scones Mrs Armstrong suddenly remembered something. 'Oh John, I have a letter for you. It arrived about a week ago. I've been keeping it safe in my bedroom.' She hurried away to get it.

John's heart thudded. Could this be a letter from Anna? Or be a letter from Frans telling him about Anna?...Telling him what about Anna?

345

As soon he saw the bulky official envelope with its O.H.M.S (On His Majesties Service) markings he knew it was not from Anna or from Frans. He tore it open and extracted the civilian passport he had applied for over a month ago. Now, covered by this passport, he was properly equipped to go to Holland.

Alert with instinctive apprehension Mrs Armstrong asked, 'What's that, son?'

'It's my passport, mother. My civilian passport.'

With dismay she asked, 'Oh John, what do you want a passport for? You've only just come home; surely you've not going away abroad again soon?'

'Yes, mother, I'm afraid I am. I'm going to Holland. I must go there. You see, I must be re-united with Anna, the Dutch woman I love and intend to marry.' Taking pity on his mother's shocked state John fondly smiled, 'I'm sorry to have sprung this news so suddenly and unexpectedly on you. I know it must be a terrible shock for you. Come on, sit down and pour out more tea for both of us and I'll tell you all about it; all about Anna's great love of me and my great love of her.'

For many happy minutes John eagerly enlightened his mother on how he had met Anna Maurik when hidden at her farm in Holland; on how quickly, how deeply and sincerely they had fallen in love. He said nothing of how wonderfully Anna and he had sexually consummated their great love. However, as she keenly noted the glowing eagerness with which her son described Anna and their overwhelming love, his mother's intuition strongly hinted to her something of this passionately active side of John's powerful love. Her first protective motherly fear was that some sly, scheming, worldly foreign female had seduced her innocent son. Then on reflection she thought: 'Oh John is not a fool. After six years in the navy surely he is not innocent; was not inexperienced.'

As she listened to the passionate intensity with which John continued to express his love for Anna, his mother became convinced – convinced beyond almost any doubt – that this love was no mere casual wartime affair but was the genuine thing.

John concluded by saying, 'So you see, mother, I must go to Holland. I must return to Anna. After the long, terribly stressful wait Anna has suffered there must be no further delays; we must be married as soon as possible in Holland. Now that you know how deeply, how truly we love one another I go with your wholehearted blessing, don't I?'

'Oh yes, son, as long as you truly love each other that's all that matters. Yes, I give you my sincerest blessing and deepest wishes for Anna's and your happiness. I look forward to welcoming Anna as your bride to my home.'

After thoughtfully pouring yet more tea she said, 'Oh John, I had no idea you carried out such secret mission in German-occupied countries. They must have been very dangerous, weren't they?'

He self-depreciatingly grinned, 'Oh, I admit now that some of them were quite dangerous, but most were hardly more hazardous than my normal sea-going naval duties. Anyway you had enough to worry about with me being away at sea without also knowing and worrying about my clandestine S.B.S duties. None of our next-of-kin were allowed to know anything about us taking part in these most secret missions.' He again grinned, 'In fact practically no one knows about these important secret missions..... they would hardly be secret if many knew about them, would they?'

Violent spluttering and hissings from a large pot of stew as its neglected gravy spilled over hurtled Mrs. Armstrong from the kitchen table to her hot stove. While his mother was happily occupied at the stove John drank up the last of his many cups of tea and thought of the secrets he would never divulge to her, nor to anyone else.

He would never burden her with the fact that the war had forced him to ruthlessly carry out many – all too many – stealthy, cold-blooded killings. There was one dark secret that, more than any other, he would keep from her, and from Anna: the fact that one victim of his ruthless but fully justified killings had been Anna's treacherous father. That was a burden he would continue to carry alone. Or almost alone. Frans shared that knowledge with him, but he, too, could be trusted to conscientiously keep it as deep a secret as John did. But quite possibly he was finding the keeping of that secret from Anna a more difficult burden to cope with than S.B.S. trained John was.

John's real test would come after he was married to Anna. He rather apprehensively wondered just how much strain it might be to constantly be on guard against ever allowing the slightest hint of his secret knowledge of her father's death escape him during all the years that (hopefully) Anna and he would be together.

What if he talked in his sleep? His peacetime sleep might well be disturbed as body and soul tried to adjust from war's dangers, its high excitements, its deadly killings and terrible traumas.

As long as Frans and he did not inadvertently reveal the truth about Professor Maurik's death there should be no way that that sensitive information could escape. Certainly it should not be revealed from any official sources. Everything to do with the S.B.S was still kept strictly secret. All details of 'Operations Waterloo' would now be hidden away in the deepest, most secure, most secret vaults of Special Operations Executive and Royal Navy Intelligence archives.

John thoughts were interrupted as his mother, turning from the stove and her now controlled stew pot, smiled and asked, 'Do you want some more tea, son?'

'Oh no, mother, no more tea please. I've had enough to float a ship. In fact I'll need to go and empty out my bilges!'

'Well, when you've done that why don't you walk down to meet Jean? She should be on her way home now.'

John's sister, Jean, was still working in the same market-garden on the outskirts of Keswick. She was still wearing her distinctive Woman's Land Army uniform. Brother and sister warmly greeted one another. After the usual jocular, but sincere, remarks on how well the other looked; how beautiful, how handsome they were in their respective uniforms they got down to exchanging news. John – unusually – did most of the talking. He had much to tell his sister and much to discretely keep secret from her. He told her what she already knew: how eagerly their mother was looking forward to having him home for good now the war was over and he was no longer in the navy. He then revealed how disappointed she had been when she learned he was leaving her very soon to go to Holland. Then with happy eagerness he explained how quickly, how completely she was reconciled to his leaving once she knew the imperative urgency of his need to be re-united with Anna Maurik, the Dutch woman he loved and intended to marry.

Jean was womanly and sisterly excited by John's thrilling romantic news. She eagerly asked question after question about Anna, about the greatness of their love, about the profound excitements, the supreme joys and the great dangers they must have shared while he was hidden at her farm in German-occupied Holland.

Her emotional feminine feelings, her imaginative intuitive empathy were wonderfully heightened by the fact that she herself was in love; was also hoping to be married soon... quite soon, but not quite as soon as John hoped to marry.

Like John and Anna, the war had separated her from her fiancée. He, Tom Kershaw, was still in the army, was now stationed in defeated, devastated, sullen Germany. Being three years younger that John, having only served as a soldier for the last eighteen months of the war, it would be at least another year before he was demobbed and could return home to Keswick as a civilian and marry Jean.

Giving a wistful smile Jean said, 'Oh, John, its a great pity Tom's in Germany and your Anna's in Holland; we could have had a wonderful double wedding here in Keswick.'

John sighed, 'I'm afraid that's not to be. I cannot wait for Tom to be demobbed. I must return to Holland almost immediately..... in about three days time.'

'Oh, as soon as that, John? I didn't realize you were leaving quite so quickly.'

' I must! I must get back to Anna. I must find out how she is and learn how she's coped with the long stressful wait for me to return to her.' It was a relief to share with his sympathetic sister some of his worries about what might have happened to Anna since he'd left her. Might she have been captured and tortured by the Gestapo? Was she now free but still mentally and physically suffering from the effects of torture? As with his mother, he did not burden Jean with his deepest fear; that vital question that tortured with almost ceaseless nagging persistence ..... was Anna still alive?

Now that she was aware of the urgent necessity of John's immediate return to Holland, Jean — just as their mother had done — gave him her blessings and sincerest wishes for a happy outcome to his exciting romantic quest. She, too, looked forward to meeting and welcoming his Dutch bride. Anna would become the sister she did not have.

★ ★ ★

Mrs. Armstrong, ruddy-faced and beaming, presided happily over her fiercely hot cooking range.

Her daughter put the final touches to the three settings on the kitchen table where they were about to have their first generous post-war dinner together. They were profoundly thankful they had all survived the war and could celebrated as a complete re-united family when so many, so terribly many, could not. Giving the well arrange table a last quietly pleased scrutiny, Jean turned to John, smiled and asked, 'What's in that large cardboard box that looks something like a suitcase in the corner there? Is it yours, John? Did you bring it home with you?'

He laughed, 'Yes Jean, its mine. It's a farewell present from the navy, or rather, from a grateful Government for my noble war service. It contains my civilian demob suit.'

His mother turned from her demanding stove, she fondly smiled, 'Why don't you try that suit on, son, and let us see how well you look as a civilian.'

His sister said, 'Yes, go on, John. It'll be funny to see you dressed as a civilian again.'

'Aye, after six years of wearing this Royal Navy uniform it'll be very strange to be in civies again.' He thought of, but said nothing of the number of hazardous times he had worn civilian Dutch and French clothes while operating in these German-occupied countries.

Fifteen minutes later he threw the kitchen door wide open and entered with an extravagant theatrical flourish and a grin, 'Well, mother, Jean, how do I look?'

Mother and daughter gaped then laughed. 'Oh, son, I hardly recognise you in these bonny new civilian clothes!' … 'No, it doesn't seem the real you dressed in that civie suit, John. You're not nearly as handsome as in your Royal Navy uniform!'

John's laughter joined their, 'No, I hardly recognised myself in the bedroom mirror.' He glanced down at his fawnish two-piece demob suit which was a surprisingly good fit, then sweeping off his dark brown trilby demob hat, grinned, 'I feel like a cockney spiv in this civie outfit. However I suppose I'll just have to get used to it, won't I?'

★ ★ ★

John woke early the following morning. He hurried to his bedroom window and scrutinized as much of the view as the dim dawn revealed. Thick white mist, dewy moist and tenacious clinging, further obscured the scene. But, well experienced in Lakeland weather, he was not discouraged. He was sure the mist would clear soon and the day would turn into one blessed by brilliant autumnal splendour. It would be perfect for his planned climb of 'his mountain'- Skiddaw .

When he entered the breakfast kitchen his sister was busy at the stove while his mother was engrossed in preparing a large heap of sandwiches to fortify him on his climbing expedition.

Resignedly shaking his head, he laughed, 'Oh, mother, you're making enough food to feed an army!' He turned to his sister, 'Can you come with me, Jean, to help me get through all those sandwiches?'

'I'd love to, John, but no, I can't. I must go to work. We're very busy at the market garden and farm just now.'

Mrs. Armstrong beamed at her son, 'Never mind, John, I'm sure it won't be too long before your wife Anna, climbs Skiddaw with you and shares your food on the summit.'

John had told his mother and sister about Anna having climbed Skiddaw with a party of Dutch students shortly before the war and her and his resolute intention to climb it together as husband and wife as soon as possible after the war was won. He suddenly felt a powerful surge of great emotion.... a feeling of deep love for those three women in his life: his mother, his sister, and most powerfully, most passionately, for Anna. Instinctively concealing those strong emotions he gave a broad grin, 'Yes, I agree, mother, it shouldn't be long until Anna sits on top of "my" mountain with me'

Three hours later he was sitting by himself on the summit of Skiddaw and once again the thoroughness of his knowledge of this district's weather was confirmed. His confidence that the thick mist would rapidly disperse was now fully vindicated. Leisurely stretching out on smooth, sheep-cropped turf he contentedly rested and revelled in "his" mountain's calm, mist free, sun bright glory while some of dawn's dense white mist still draped its smothering duvet over Derwentwater's drowsy surface. Other tattered remnants of sun-vanquished mist hazed narrow valleys and precariously clung to the steepest hills deepest gullies.

For some precious timeless time he was, as always, held enthralled by the wondrous Lakeland panorama set out before him. How vastly different was this visit to Skiddaw from all the wartime visits he had snatched before retuning to the stealthily ruthless, vitally necessary killings his demanding S.B.S. duties forced on him. This time, thank God, from here, from this ennobling, uplifting pilgrimage, there would be no descent back down to that terrible war, to those savage killings.

But his tremendous relief at being freed from war was again overshadowed by dark fears of what might have happened to Anna since he'd last seen her. Had she survived the war as un-harmed as he? Would she really sit beside him here quite soon.... in a few months, or even a few weeks? Was that being much too optimistic? Then that vital question again forced its torture on him: Was Anna still alive?

Chapter Forty Eight

Two mornings later Mrs Armstrong was again busily preparing a heap of sandwiches for her son to take with him, not to fortify him on Skiddaw, but to sustain him on his long journey to Holland.

★ ★ ★

Despite its small size and the almost Victorian age of the corridor-less passenger carriages augmenting its goods trucks, many laden with metallic clanking milk churns, the early morning train that approached Carlisle on the minor branch line from Keswick did so with a series of fussy, self-important toots of its whistle as if to assert it was in no way awed by the size and mighty power of the L.M.S. (London, Midlands & Scottish) locomotive that was effortlessly hauling the Glasgow to London express towards Carlisle Central Station on a much busier, much more important neighbouring line.

With sandwich laden rucksack on back and wheeling his sturdy old bicycle John alighted from the slow local train. He was immediately engulfed in a bedlam of billowing acrid smoke, noisy hissing stream and frantic movements of rushing, luggage laden crowds. The bustling railway station reverberated with wartime memoirs.

How often he'd thankfully alighted here on his way home on leave from the navy. How many times he'd obediently boarded a train here at the expiry of his short leave and was hurried back to face war's tremendous challenges and dangers. How often he'd wondered if he would survive his dangerous duties and return to this station again. Today it was crowded with boyish-faced army conscripts. Too young to have fought in the war, these rookies khaki tunics were conspicuously blank in comparison to the multi-coloured campaign ribbons that proudly rainbowed the tunics of older, battle-tested soldiers.

After hurrying to another platform John stowed his bicycle in the guard's van of the waiting train that would take him to Hull.

At last the strong, briny, distinctly fishy smell of the wind gusting from the North Sea, familiar to him from when he'd sailed from here on minesweepers, announced as definitely as the porter's shouted announcement that his train had arrived at Hull.

Soon afterwards he was comfortably ensconced in his berth on the Dutch ferry. Tomorrow morning he would be in Holland. Tomorrow evening he should be with Anna. His heart thudded excitedly at that thought. For a time the prospect of Anna and him being re-united kept him restlessly from sleep. Then the well remembered soothing motions of a ship getting underway on a calm sea lulled him to sleep.

At the first touch of dawn's light John was on deck eagerly searching Eastwards for a sight of The Netherlands. Just as the dim line of that flat coast came into view there was a warning shout from a crewman on lookout duty. That loud shout and the violent turn the ship made were obvious signs of there being some danger. Peering in the direction the crew were pointing, John made out the darkly sinister shape of a drifting mine. No need to ask why the ship had suddenly changed course. Thank God it had! It would have been a terribly ironic ending for him if, after surviving all the many dangers of six years of war, he had died on what should have been a peaceful voyage on a peacetime ferry.

Only slightly behind schedule the ferry docked at its usual berth in the Hook of Holland. A minimum of formalities were quickly gone through. John's virgin passport was stamped and handed back to him by a smiling Dutch official who said, 'Welcome to The Netherlands. I hope you have an enjoyable time in our country. Have you been here before?'

It was John's turn to smile, 'Oh yes...yes, I've been in Holland before; quite a few times in fact. But I never had a proper passport before.'

The puzzled official waited for an explanation. John enlightened him. 'It was during the war. My Sten-gun and other weapons were the only passport I needed.'

'Oh, I see. I understand.' The customs officer stood, reached across his desk and shook John's hand. 'Oh well, you are more than ever welcome to our grateful country.'

Reminding himself to ride on the 'wrong' side of the Dutch roads, John mounted his bicycle and quickly cycled out of the harbour and through the small, tidy town and then eagerly set out on the narrow, quiet road that would lead him to Anna. The route he must take had been well studied on, and well memorised from the large scale British military map of this part of The Netherlands he had 'borrowed'.

It felt strange to be quite freely and openly cycling through this Dutch countryside and not be constantly alert for German soldiers.

At first his instinctive reaction when he did see a vehicle approaching on the amazingly traffic-free country roads was to jump off his bicycle and hide. However he quickly conquered this wartime instinct and soon viewed all approaching traffic quite calmly. The younger drivers of passing trucks cheerfully returned his friendly wave, but many of the elderly Dutch peasants sitting with solid solemnity on vegetable laden carts allowed as little trace of a friendly smile to distort their dour, heavy jowled features as their stoic plodding horses did.

Despite the urgency of his desire to meet up with Anna again, he forced himself to take occasional rests from his arduous pedalling. He sat, checked his position and the remainder of his route on the large-scale map, then finished off the last of the more than abundant load of sandwiches his mother had forced on him.

As, at last, he drew near to Anna's farm he recognised the small stone bridge he was rapidly approaching. He stopped, dismounted and propped his bicycle against the narrow, humpback bridge's low parapet. There was no mistaking this place. This was where he had confronted then shot dead that treacherous Dutchman, Professor Maurik. There grown larger, and brighter with extra autumnal leaves was the bush he had hidden behind. With every detail vividly clear John re-lived that tense scene. He remembered his exact accusation: 'You are a traitor helping the Krauts build an atomic bomb, Professor Maurik. You deserve to die!' Then that traitor's desperate pleading: 'No, no, you do not understand. I....I....' Then his voice rising in an agonised scream as two bullets smashed through his heart.

It was an ordeal, was almost a physical agony for John to so clearly

355

re-live this ruthless cold–blooded killing of that Dutchman. His white haired, flowing bearded appearance had seemed so innocent, so benign. And there was the terrible extra burden of knowing that that despicable traitor was Anna's father.

Re-mounting his bicycle John continued his journey.

★ ★ ★

Now he cycled up the muddy lane leading to Anna's farm, and there was Frans carrying a bundle of hay into the stable.

John called out 'Hello, Frans. How are you? It's good to see you again.'

'John?...John? Is that really you , John?'

They warmly shook hands. They robustly clapped one another on the back. 'Oh, Frans, it's great to see you once more; to see you looking so fit and well.' John was about to say more; was going to ask about Anna, but saw Blanche appear at the kitchen door. He smiled and waved to her.

'See who's here, Blanche,' Frans shouted in Dutch, 'John's come back to us at last.'

Bursting with tearful joy, Blanche embraced and hugged and emotionally kissed John. In a mixture of Dutch and English she welcomed him 'home'. When the wildest exuberance of her welcome had subsided the three of them stood together all giving beaming smiles. Then, after quickly looking around in hope of catching sight of Anna but seeing no sign of her, John with increasing apprehension asked the vital questions he now almost feared to hear answered. 'Is Anna all right? Is she here? Is she in the kitchen?'

'No, she is not here,' Frans replied; then, seeing John's dismay, hastened to reassure him.

'But, yes she is all right. She is well; is quite well.' Frans started to explain further but Blanche interrupted him, 'Oh, Frans, don't keep John standing outside here.' Smiling, she hospitably ushered him into the house and, proudly using her best English (a language she had been studying under her husband's tuition) said, 'Please, come in kitchen, John.'

As John obediently entered the well remembered room urgent questions throbbed and flared and scorched his brain. Why, if Anna was "all right, was quite well , was she not here at this farm with her aunt and uncle waiting for him to return to her as she had faithfully promised she would? Where was she? What had happened to her? Then came a heart-chilling thought: weary of the long, endless seeming wait for his return, fearing he had been killed, had she married someone else? But no, no, surely not! He refused to believe that Anna would commit such a treacherous act, There must be some other, some more innocent reason for her not being here lovingly waiting for him.

Containing his impatience to get answers to these tormenting questions, John again obeyed Blanche's hospitable instructions as, smiling and pointing, she urged, 'Sit down, please, John' Then, hurrying to the hot stove, cheerfully added, 'I get you coffee.'

'Yes', Frans confirmed as he settled opposite John at the kitchen table, 'thankfully we now have some real coffee to offer you and not the awful wartime sawdust that was sold as Erstaz coffee.'

John's observant gaze surveyed the familiar, large, bright, spotless kitchen. It seemed even brighter than he remembered it. It was. This extra brightness was easily explained. The heavy dark curtains that in compliance with the Kraut's strict wartime blackout restrictions had obscured the room's windows were gone; were replaced by light, bright, semi transparent lacy curtains. Kitchen shelves that had been bare were now lined with an attractive array of large blue and white Delft plates. The gleaming lustre of these antique plates added their gay brightness to the room. He correctly surmised that during the war these precious plates, possibly family heirlooms, had been hidden in some secure cellar safe from the greedy hands of looting Huns and from the bombs of German – or British or American – warplanes. Peace had restored them to their rightful proud place.

For some few more seconds he scrutinized the kitchen then his eyes honed in on Frans.

Attempting to equal the soul-searching intenseness of that piercing gaze Frans met it and held it. He saw asked in those staring eyes the urgent questions about Anna that were tormenting John.

'I....I am sorry, John, for the delay in telling you everything that's happened to Anna' He paused, gathered his thoughts then continued. 'Anna is staying in a hospital... a sort of convalescent hospital in the small town of Lopik, some ten kilometres from here. Physically she is quite well.... in fact she is almost perfectly well. However her mind is troubled. But not too badly I assure you, John. She had a ..an .another nervous breakdown shortly after you left her.'

John nodded, 'Oh, I see. I remember you were afraid my suddenly leaving her then her father's sudden, violent death at almost the same time would be too much for her to bear; might trigger another breakdown.'

'Yes, John, that's exactly what happened.'

John cast a quick almost furtive glance at Blanche. Engrossed in pouring steaming coffee into three mugs she did not appear to be listening to them. He lowered his voice. 'Did Anna ever find out what actually happened to her father?'

Frans in turn cast his wife a quick sideways glance before warily replying. 'No. Neither she nor anyone else knows what happened to him. The Krauts and our Dutch police investigated his unexplained death. They repeatedly interrogated the three of us at this farm. Despite poor Anna's terrible distraught state the Krauts kept cruelly questioning her. When Blanche and I protested we were threatened with being sent to a concentration camp or to slave labour.' Frans paused, again quickly glanced at his absorbed wife then stated, 'If the Krauts or the Dutch police did discover something about Professor Maurik's death they kept it secret; they certainly never told us anything about it.'

John gave a slight nod. That almost imperceptible movement informed Frans that he understood the message, clear to him but concealed from Blanche, in that reply. It was an immense relief to know that the secret knowledge of how Anna's father, Frans's brother, had died was still a profound secret shared by no one but Frans and himself.

Blanche brought over the mugs of coffee and joined them at the table. She reached over and gently touched John's hand. She struggled to translate her thoughts into reassuring English words. 'Oh, John, please, do not worry too much about Anna. I know she will be made well once she sees you.

Frans fondly smiled. That smile was in appreciation of his wife's greatly improved English and of her desire to reassure John about Anna. He hastened to confirm her confident statement. 'Yes, John, I am sure what Blanche says is true. Once Anna sees you and knows that you have, as promised returned, to marry her she will fully recover from her depression.'

'Yes, I certainly hope so too. But just how bad is her depression?'

'Oh I am sorry, John, depression is not the right word, not now.' Frans frantically searched for the correct English word. 'No, Anna is no longer deeply or seriously depressed I assure you, though for a time she was badly depressed. After you left her she collapsed into a miserable, weeping, deeply despairing state. For a while – some months – she continued living at the farm with us and we, (here once again Frans fondly smiled at his wife) especially Blanche, tenderly nursed her and did everything we could to help her. However as it became clear that poor Anna was making no progress with us it was decided, with her agreement, that she should go into hospital to receive better, more professional nursing and psychiatric care.' Frans paused then lifted his mug and sipped at the hot coffee.

After sipping his own coffee John asked, 'And the hospital, the doctors and nurses, have managed to really help Anna, have they?'

'Yes, they have. She is much better than she was. She used to sit in the hospital lounge in a dull listless way; seemed to be completely ap...apathetic? Yes apathetic. But now she takes more interest in things. She willingly takes an active part in helping to keep the hospital's colourful flower garden neat and tidy. About two months ago she asked me to bring her a few of her favourite books. Now she spends many hours quite contentedly reading these books. In her best, most animated moods she will cheerfully and intelligently discuss with me the novel she is currently reading.

'So you see, John, she is making very good progress. The doctors are so pleased with her recovery that they say she will be fit to return home to this farm in about a week's time.'

Blanche had been keenly following Frans's English. She got the gist of his meaning. She smiled and again reached across the kitchen table to companionably touch John's hand. Once more she reassured him, 'Oh, John, what Frans says is true. Anna is much, much better and I am sure your return to her will complete her recovery.'

John nodded and smiled his thanks. 'You know that, under your, and the doctor's, guidance, I will do absolutely everything I can to help Anna fully recover. How soon can I see her?'

'Either Blanche or I, or both of us, visit Anna almost every day,' Frans said. 'So tomorrow afternoon at the usual visiting time you will come with us to see her.' He smiled with compassionate understanding, 'I hope you manage to contain your impatience to see her until then, John.'

John returned his smile, 'Yes, I will. I'll have to, won't I? Thank you Frans. Thank you both for all you've done to help Anna. I am deeply in your debt.'

★ ★ ★

'Doctor De Hooft, this is John Armstrong, the brave Englishman I have told you about. He has come back to The Netherlands to marry my niece, Anna Maurik.' Frans turned to John, 'Dr De Hooft is the senior physician at this hospital. His compassionate psychiatric treatment has greatly helped Anna's recovery.'

The neat, smallish, white haired doctor rose and hurried round his paper-littered desk. He firmly grasped and enthusiastically shook John's hand. Speaking excellent English he said, 'I am very pleased to meet you, John, Frans has told me much about you. It is great that you've survived the war and have returned to keep your promise to marry Anna. Her most terrible incessant fear – the cause of her deepest distress – was that you might have been killed by the Krauts after you left her to return to your dangerous duties. I feel sure that Anna's great delight when she sees you again, safe and well, then learns that you still love her and intend to marry her will be the best – the only- medicine she needs to bring about her complete recovery.'

In a quick, cheerful, lively way Dr. De Hooft shook hands with Blanche and Frans. He then apologised, 'Oh, I'm sorry keeping you standing.' He bustled about and pushed forward a chair. 'Here, sit down, Blanche. Sit down Frans, John.' He resumed his seat behind his desk. In a more thoughtful professional manner he said, 'Yes, John, I am sure your safe return will bring about Anna's full recovery. But we must ensure her wondrous joy and tremendous excitement when she sees you again is not too much for her, does not overwhelm her and make her hysterical.' He paused then said, 'Excuse me one moment.' Lifting up the internal phone he spoke in rapid Dutch. He explained to John, 'I have asked the hospital's matron to come to my office.'

A few minutes later, after Matron Bolivier had been introduced to

John and his presence here explained, she and the doctor led him, and Blanche and Frans, to the lounge where, as the matron had confirmed, Anna was sitting engrossed in reading.

As instructed John, Blanche and Frans stood back near the lounge's door while the doctor and matron approached Anna. Doctor De Hooft smiled, 'Good afternoon, Anna. I am sorry to disturb your reading but there is a visitor come to see you.'

For a moment Anna's expression as she looked up at the doctor was one of slight annoyance; some displeasure at being disturbed in her reading. Then she relented. She smiled.

Watching with experienced professional eyes that alertly, but not too obviously, observed their patient, doctor and matron noted with silent approval the calm care of a true book-lover with which Anna placed her bookmark between the correct pages before gently placing the novel on the low table beside her armchair. She then calmly smiled again and asked the doctor, 'Who is my visitor? Is it Uncle Frans; or is it Aunt Blanche?'

'They are both here, but there is also a special... a very special visitor; someone who has come all the way from England to see you, Anna.' Doctor De Hooft beamed, 'You will be delighted to see him, I assure you.' Then he gently cautioned, 'But please try not to get too over excited when you see him.'

The doctor stepped aside and gestured John forward.

Anna gave an audible gasp. Her heart thudded wildly. She sat silent, motionless, transfixed. She stared with astounded eyes. For some tremulous uncertain cosmic moments she hardly dared believe the evidence of her senses.

'John!...John!... Is that really you, John?'

'Yes, Anna, it's me! I've returned to marry you as I promised I would.'

Anna was not conscious of springing to her feet. John was barely aware of rushing towards her. But somehow their agitated bodies unerringly met. Gloriously met, fiercely embraced and greedily kissed. Kissed with a hungry urgency that ignited the frustrated passion of their re-united love.

For a time John happily lost himself in the intensity of their reaffirmed love. Then he became rather embarrassingly aware of the doctor's, the matron's and Blanche's and Frans's alertly watching presence. With gentle insistence he tried to ease Anna's tenacious embracing arms from around his love besieged body. He gaily laughed, 'Oh, Anna, Anna, you'll hug me to death. Please let me breathe!'

Anna reluctantly eased her trembling grip and raised joyous brimming eyes to meet John's tender, loving, unwavering gaze. She smiled ecstatically, 'Oh, John, its wonderful, its almost unbelievable, that you've come back safely and that we are going to be married soon.' Her glowing rapture was suddenly overshadowed by hideous memories. 'Oh, John, after you left me to try to make your way back to England I constantly dreaded that you might have been killed by the Krauts. That dread tortured me every day and denied me sleep each night.' These relived memories set her body violently shuddering. She sobbed, 'Oh, and when I did fall into exhausted sleep the nightmares I suffered were worse – far worse – than my daytime fears for you. In these awful night-time horrors I saw you being hideously tortured by sadistic Gestapo monsters. I all too vividly heard their gloating laughter as you desperately pleaded then wildly screamed. When – shivering, sweating and panicking – I burst out of these dreadful nightmares I still heard your dying screams exploding through my demented brain.'

With overflowing imploring eyes repeating the message of her tremulous voice she pleaded, 'Oh, John don't ever leave me again. Please, please, promise you will never leave me again.'

John compassionately hugged her. He kissed her gently. 'Anna, I promise I will never leave you again. Now the war's over there's nothing can part us again. We will be married soon and then we'll be together for the rest of our lives, I promise you.' Smiling lovingly he gave her yet more reassurance, 'All war's deadly dangers, its sad partings and terrible worries belong to the past; they are over and done with; we must put them behind us. Together we must – we will – make ourselves a wonderful peacetime life. We will make it not only for ourselves but for our yet unborn children, won't we, Anna?'

Blissfully uplifted by John's reassuring promise and exhilarated by his prediction of their future conjugal happiness Anna's nervous shudders eased; her distraught sobs ceased – became inarticulate emotion choked gasps of pleasure as she eagerly nodded her agreement, smiled her thanks and rosily pictured a wondrous vision of their life together.

Although John's love and happiness equalled – or almost equalled – Anna's, his senses were not quite so completely overwhelmed as hers. He was not entirely unaware of the other people in this hospital lounge. The longer their passionate embrace continued the more embarrassingly conscious he became of just how many pairs of human eyes were watching them. He felt that the analytical professional gaze with which the doctor and matron were observing Anna and him contained not only deep psychological understanding but also genuine human warmth and compassion.

Perhaps the mature, formidable looking matron allowed some hint of the more tender aspects of her strongly controlled femininity to be revealed in the barely heard sympathetic sighs that escaped her as she observed this romantic tableau.

Being unconstrained by any professional considerations, Blanche made no attempt to hide the emotional effect of this romantic scene on her; she joyfully sobbed and made gentle dabbing motions at her overflowing eyes with a dainty cambric handkerchief.

Even Frans was forced to defensively bring his handkerchief into use a few times to blow his nose and smother his emotions.

Doctor De Hooft come forward and placed a gentle hand on Anna's shoulder. 'Why don't John and you sit at that small table?' He turned to Blanche and Frans, 'Join them there. I am sure the four of you will have plenty to discuss and much to arrange.' He then addressed Matron Bolivier, 'Perhaps you could kindly organise some coffee for them, matron?'

Then, smiling at John, the doctor asked, 'Or would you prefer some tea? Now that the war's over, at long, long last we have real coffee and even some great, genuine English tea to offer you, John.'

'Thank you, doctor. Yes, a cup of tea – the cup that cheers, but does not inebriate – would be most welcome.'

Matron Bolivier allowed one of her bright and sincere smiles to enliven her stern professional expression as she cheerily enquired, 'Tea for you all?'

Beaming her an answering smile, Anna replied for the entire party, 'Yes, please, matron. We will all celebrate this wonderful reunion with that great British drink – tea.' Giving John a loving, remembering grin she hastily amended that to, 'Or with "char" … a good hot cup of really strong British "char", eh, John?'

Doctor and Matron exchanged a quick, professional glance. They noted with genuine pleasure Anna's re-born vivacious brightness. They thought it bode well for her future happiness.

★ ★ ★

About two hours later Dr De Hooft and Matron Bolivier returned to the emptying hospital lounge. Visiting time was almost over. Anna, John, Blanche and Frans still sat around that table. Their emptied teacups had been cleared away. The doctor smiled down at them. 'Well, Anna how do you feel? Not too tired after the great excitement of John's return are you?'

'Oh no, doctor. I'm not in the least tired!'

Doctor and Matron again exchanged a quick understanding glance. The matron's stern features were again enlivened by a sincere smile as she said, 'No, Anna, you don't look at all tired. In fact you look the brightest, the most alert and happy I have ever seen you.' She grinned at John, 'I think your returning to be re-united with Anna and the confirmation of your great love of her has provided a complete cure – the only cure she needed – for all her nervous troubles.'

The doctor beamed his agreement, 'Yes, exactly, Matron. As you know, Anna, we were going to let you home to Blanche's and Frans's care in about a week's time, but after having discussed it, Matron and I agree that there's really no reason why you should not go home today. Would you like that?'

Anna sprang to her feet. Her glowing face glowed ever brighter. 'Oh, yes, yes, doctor, I would love to go home today.' Grasping his hand with both of hers she gasped, 'Thank you, doctor. Oh, thank you!'

She turned to Matron Bolivier and reached out eager hands towards her, 'And thank you , too, Matron. Thank you for your kind, understanding care of me.' She disarmingly smiled, 'I hope I was not too difficult, too upsetting, too unreasonable a patient.'

The matron reacted warmly to this sincere appreciation of her professional efforts. 'Oh, no, Anna, you were never too difficult a patient, not really. And, you know, it is truly wonderful for me – for all the doctors and nurses and me – to now see your complete recovery.'

Instead of seizing hold of matron's hands, Anna impulsively threw both arms around her buxom body in an emotional embrace.

For a few moments matron warmly returned that tight embrace, then, reverting to her best professional manner, declared, 'Now then, as you are going home today we better see about getting your clothes and other things packed ready for you to take with you, hadn't we?'

Chapter Forty Nine

In the evening of that memorable day, after having, thanks to Blanche's special effort, enjoyed a delightful festive dinner in the farmhouse's spotless kitchen, the pleasantly replete four of them – Anna, Blanche, Frans and John – sat companionably together in the adjoining lounge.

Like the kitchen, this room was brightened by having its dark, wartime blackout curtains replaced by lighter, more colourful ones. This cheerful brightness was augmented by a pair of large blue and white vases and some smaller, most attractive Delft ornaments.

With arms lovingly embracing one another, Anna and John sat close together on the small leather settee on one side of the bright tiled fireplace while Blanche and Frans were comfortably settled in armchairs across from them.

Sublimely self-engrossed in their profound love and overwhelming happiness Anna and John had no need for any books or any other distractions. But Frans held a large slim book conspicuously wide open with both hands and discreetly attempted to hide behind it so as not to make his sympathetic but gently amused observation of those two young lovers too obvious.

Blanche attempted to disguise her emotional observation of Anna and John by apparently being completely engrossed with her knitting. But the expert skill and amazing dexterity of her motion-blurred fingers left her eyes quite free to gaze her full at these so wonderfully re-united young lovers.

After a while, as at the hospital, John became embarassingly aware of just what a foolish, soppy pair of besotted lovers Anna and he must appear to the sympathetic but also gently amused middle-aged eyes of Blanche and Frans. He lessened the pressure of his embracing arm and with gentle care eased his body a little away from the alluring warmth of Anna's lovely body.

With instinctive feminine empathy Anna knew that the reduced pressure of John's arm and the slight withdrawal of his strong body was in no way due to any lessening of his love for her, but was entirely due to his – oh so English – embarrassment at appearing too soppy, too foolishly love-sick to her watching aunt and uncle. She herself felt so gloriously overwhelmed by the greatness of her love that she would have happily entirely ignored Blanche and Frans; would have adoringly embraced John all evening. However, taking pity on his foolish Anglo-Saxon embarrassed unease (and loving him all the more for it) she gently eased her reluctant body away from his. She removed her possessive arm from around him. Smiling into his appreciative eyes she grasped his free hand and with an impish act of pretence maidenly, modestly placed their innocent hands, with their perhaps not quite so innocent intertwined fingers, sedately on the leather of the settee now exposed between their bodies.

She mockingly smiled across at her relations. 'Oh, Uncle Frans, you needn't pretend to be reading that book. We know you are not interested in it. And we know you don't need to use your eyes much for your knitting, Aunt Blanche. Both of you need your eyes for nothing but observing John and I.'

Frans laughed and gently laid his un-needed book down. He smiled apologetically, 'I'm sorry, Anna, and you too John. I didn't intend my spying on you to be quite so obvious. Please forgive me.'

Blanche's fingers momentarily ceased their industrious motion as she gave a disarming smile, 'I must apologise as well. But, you know, it is so wonderful to see you so utterly happy again, Anna; to see you gloriously re-united with your faithful John, that I can not deny myself the pleasure of watching the pair of you.' She paused, set her nimble fingers to work again, smiled around at the three others in this comfortable room then gave a contented sigh, 'Yes, its truly wonderful to have the four of us, all safe and well, back together again after the war's terrible dangers and its almost unbearable separations, isn't it? We must all make the most of this delightful domestic bliss while it lasts, mustn't we?'

Frans fondly smiled at his wife and eagerly agreed, 'Yes, we must, we certainly must.' With what almost seemed like equal fondness he smiled at Anna and John, 'Yes, we must make the most of each others company while we can. After all it will only be about two weeks until you get married and then leave here for England.'

'Oh, Uncle Frans,' gasped Anna, 'do you honestly think John and I will really be able to get married in just two weeks time? Such a short wait for our wedding seems almost too good to be true.'

'I don't think there's any reason why it shouldn't take place then. As I've already told you, I've asked the hospital padre, Pastor Van Karson, about this and he assures me that it will only take him about ten or twelve days to get a special marriage licence for you.'

'And he's willing to perform our wedding in the hospital's small chapel, isn't he?'

'Yes, Anna, he is. As I've already told you (like all frantic wedding preparations the hasty planning of all the details were gone over time after time) he assured me that it would be a treat for him to hold a wedding in that hospital chapel instead of conducting the all to frequent funerals of deceased patients there.'

'Yes,' Blanche confirmed, 'I spoke to him as well, and not only to him but to Matron Bolivier. She and all the nurses are delighted at the prospect of having one of their former patients married in the hospital's attractive small chapel. But of course it really is a very small chapel which can't seat many. You are sure you do want a quiet wedding with just a few guests, aren't you, Anna?'

'O yes, I'm certain. I – we – don't want a large elaborate wedding.' Glowing with love she beamed at her miraculously returned fiancée, 'Do we, John?'

He squeezed her fingers and grinned, 'I'm entirely in your hands. I agree to whatever you want, Anna.'

Frans nodded, 'Yes, I think you are wise to have a quiet wedding with only some close relations and a few special guests. As you can well imagine, John, although it is over six months since the end of the war – the war in Europe that is – we Dutch people are still violently divided by that war. Are divided by foul festering feelings; by vivid memories of fearful atrocities; by deadly hatreds between our brave, noble Patriots and our – unfortunately all too many – loathsome collaborators.' He paused for a moment. His steady gaze met and held John's steady gaze. Both men knew they were thinking of the same thing. Were again remembering one particular Dutch collaborator…

that terrible, despicable traitor, Professor Willem Maurik, who had been Frans's brother, had been Anna's father.

'Yes,' reiterated Frans, 'It will be wise to have only a few friends, good, true, patriotic friends at your wedding, Anna.'

'Yes, exactly, uncle. It's a great pity my brother Jan won't be able to be at my wedding.'

'He's still in the Royal Netherlands Navy, is he?' John asked.

'Yes he is. He was serving in the Pacific war and now his ship is based in the Dutch East Indies. He does not get home to Holland on leave and he does not expect to be demobbed from our navy for a least four months.' She grinned at John, 'I certainly don't want to put off our wedding until he comes home, do you?'

'No, definitely not!' He returned her grin, 'I might just about manage to contain my impatience for two weeks but definitely not for four months.'

For some blissful wistful moments they silently gazed at one another then John sighed, 'It's also a great pity that my mother and sister won't manage to the wedding either. They don't have passports and it would take at least a month for them to get one. Perhaps instead of them I could have a few of the Dutch Patriots who sheltered me and helped me evade the Krauts as honoured guests at our wedding.'

'Yes, certainly,' Anna immediately agreed. 'Some of our best friends who were members of Uncle Frans's local Resistance Group will also be special guests at the wedding. Oh, John, it's a shame you don't have your Royal Navy uniform with you. If you had, and my brother Jan was here in his Dutch naval uniform too, you would have been a pair of really brave and handsome looking sailors, wouldn't you?'

John laughed, 'Aye, perhaps. But I'm not keen to wear my uniform again. It belongs to my wartime past. Our wedding will take me into our brighter peacetime future.' He smiled at Frans, 'Perhaps I could borrow a good Dutch civilian suit from you. It wouldn't be the first time you've kitted me out in Dutch civies, would it?'

Naturally this talk of clothes for the wedding lead Blanche and Anna into a delightful discussion – in rapid, excited Dutch – of the immense problem of what frock Anna would wear on that special occasion.

As all the pros and cons of Anna's various frocks were being debated with unfailing interest Frans grinned, 'Oh, John, you don't know how lucky you are. Not understanding Dutch you've no option but to stay silent until the ladies eventually agree on the correct frock.'

For those four people reunited in that comfortable room the hours flew un-noticed by as details of this imminent wedding were endlessly discussed.

Only when the large, quietly ticking marble clock on the mantlepiece pointed to ten-fifteen did Blanche, with a sudden start, realise the time – that sacrosanct time when she invariably put down her knitting and retired to bed. She gasped, 'Oh, look, it's bedtime already!' She smiled at Anna and John, 'All this wonderful romantic excitement is all very well, but I still have to get up early tomorrow morning. The cows always have to be milked, no matter what is going on. I'm certainly ready for my bed. I feel exhausted after this long, eventful day.' She gave a fond, concerned smile, 'What about you, Anna? You're looking rather tired after all today's great excitement. Aren't you needing to get to your bed?'

'Yes, I must admit I do feel quite tired. Just Frans and you go to bed now. John and I will only stay here for a little while longer.' She smiled reassuringly at Blanche then ruefully grinned at John. 'And I promise you we will then go to our respective beds – our most respectable respective beds.'

'Good, good! Frans and I don't want to be sour old spoilsports, but we honestly believe that that sleeping arrangement is for the best until you are married. Your bed is prepared for you in your own bedroom, Anna, and John has his in the guest bedroom.'

Almost as soon as they had the room to themselves, only delaying until the first of the eager embraces and passionate kisses had been indulged in, did Anna ask, 'Oh, John, are you sure you don't really too much mind us not sleeping together tonight.'

Earlier this evening, in the little time they had been by themselves, she had almost tearfully explained her inability to have sexual intercourse this week. She feared this unavoidable delay before they consummated their re-united love might be a big disappointment for John. She was delighted by his assurance that, after waiting two years, he would manage to wait another week, or even two weeks, if she wanted to delay that consummation until their wedding night. That was exactly what she had hoped to hear. She was convinced that their wondrous illicit lovemaking when John had been hidden at this farm had been entirely justified by the dangerous, uncertain, unnatural conditions of wartime. She now felt that the return of peacetime conditions required their future lovemaking to be done under the sanctity of the married state.

John reaffirmed the assurances he had given earlier, 'Oh, please don't worry about that, Anna. The decision about when we sleep together is entirely up to you and I agree with whatever you decide.'

★ ★ ★

These two weeks seemed all too short to attend to all the details of their wedding. As the days passed ever more swiftly Blanch and Anna got ever more – not unpleasantly – flustered while John laughed, 'Thank God we're having a small and simple wedding; we would never have managed to organise a large, elaborate one in time, would we?'

Despite all the pressures on her time, Anna resolutely ensured that she spent an hour or two each day out strolling or cycling with John. On a couple of occasions they were away on their bicycles for most of the day. Not only did they both enjoy the healthy, invigorating freshness of the autumnal air, but the gentle exercise helped build up Anna's physical strength after her time in hospital.

On the first of those enjoyable days they cycled to the farm where John had been hidden for one night. As he led the way into the muddy farmyard he saw a familiar old horse standing stoically by itself in the shafts of a high-sided cart. The cart was heaped with a familiar load. Anna joined him as he halted beside the horse and cart.

Two Dutch farmers came out of the stable. One was middle-aged and lame. Assisted by his stout walking stick he limped towards them. His taller, white-bearded father followed him. Both Dutchmen peered inquisitively at the two unknown cyclists.

John laughed and pointed at the cart's load, 'No need to hide me under that heap of turnips this time, is there?'

As Anna translated the English words into Dutch both farmers exclaimed, 'Oh, its John!.... It's John!' Beaming they eagerly shook his hand and warmly welcomed him back to their farm. With Anna translating for him the old father excitedly and proudly enthused, 'No, John, no need now to hide you under smelly turnips to evade the stinking Krauts! We certainly fooled those Kraut sentries at that bridge, didn't we?' He laughed uproariously at the memory of how ingeniously he had taken John past those duped German soldiers. The triumphant bellowing joy of his laughter was contagious; the three others joined in with laughter almost as unrestrained as his.

Once all had regained something approaching calm sobriety Anna and John were ushered into the farmhouse kitchen and received a warm welcome from the two women in that snug room. The old Dutch farmer seized this opportunity to repeat to his wife and daughter-in-law the story of John and the cart load of turnips.

Soon all were sitting around the hospitable kitchen table and food and drink were being urged on John and Anna. When Anna explained the most important reason for their visit – to invite them all to be guests at John and her wedding – the invitation was joyfully accepted. The three children at this farm were included in the invitation. The two girls were still at school and the boy, Theo, was at college. The only sadness to temporarily subdue this pleasant gathering was when John enquired about Wims, the youth who, with Theo, had courageously helped him evade the Krauts. Anna solemnly translated the sad news, 'Poor Wims is dead. It seems he was guiding two British airmen towards safety when they suddenly encountered a patrol of German soldiers. Wims and one of the British airmen were shot and died. The other airman escaped. After the war young Wims's bravery was recognised by him being posthumously awarded a special medal.'

John sighed, 'Poor brave Wims. He certainly deserved that medal.'

★ ★ ★

A Few days later they again went cycling to meet up with and invite to their wedding two other Dutch people who had helped John evade the Germans – the pastor and his wife known only to him by their Christian names, Johannes and Hilda.

After a little difficulty retracing the route they arrived at the correct grey church with its distinctive squat tower. John laughed, 'Thank God I don't have to sleep in this church's damp, dark and ghostly crypt again.'

Wheeling their bicycles they crunched up the wide gravel path towards the parsonage. Remembering what had happened to brave,

372

patriotic young Wims, John felt a sudden shiver of apprehension. 'Oh, I hope to God dear Hilda and good old Johannes have survived the war all right.'

He felt a wondrous surge of emotion as he saw two familiar elderly figures appear from round the side of the parsonage. They had been feeding their hens. Hilda carried an egg laden basket with cautious care. With what seemed jaunty pleasure Johannes swung an empty pail.

They stopped and stared at the two strangers.

John called out, 'Hello Hilda. Hello Johannes.'

'Oh, it's John...it's John!' Hilda put down her basket and hurried towards him with outstretched arms. They emotionally embraced and tenderly kissed. Johannes patiently waited until the most violent of his wife's rapturous greetings were over then seized John's hand and firmly shook it. John introduced Anna to them.

Hilda found it difficult to control her excitement at John having survived the war; having returned to visit Johannes and her; having invited them to his wedding to that lovely Dutch girl. Once more she joyously enthused, 'Oh, John, it's wonderful to see you here again. Johannes and I often used to talk about you and wonder if you were alive; wonder if we would ever see you again.'

Thinking she was perhaps getting just a touch too tearfully emotional, John asked, 'How did you manage with those German Army officers who were billeted on you? Did they stay long?

She smiled, 'Oh, we managed things so that we saw very little of those horrible Krauts.'

'Yes,' Johannes confirmed, 'we were fortunate. Those officers were kept so busy re-organising and re-equipping their decimated panzer division that they used our parsonage for practically nothing but sleeping in. And they only stayed here for six weeks.'

John laughed, 'So, Hilda, you had no opportunity to put rat-poison in the food of those Kraut officers as you threatened to do!'

★ ★ ★

It was their wedding day. The hospital's small chapel was crowded with friends and relations. Almost all those guests had been patriotic Resistance fighters or had indirectly helped those brave Dutch Patriots. Doctor De Hooft, Matron Bolivier and some nurses were honoured guests. Other nurses, snatching a short respite from their duties, stood crammed together with a few less seriously ill patients at the back of the chapel. The unique joy and excitement of this special occasion seemed to permeate the entire hospital.

After the hospital's padre, Pastor Van Karson, had pronounced John and Anna man and wife he invited Pastor Johannes Sterrenburg to bestow his additional blessing on this holy union. He did so with pleasure, sincerity and experienced skill, then with continuing sincere emotion said, 'I see this ceremony we have been privileged to witness here today as not just the joining together of this handsome young Englishman and this lovely young Dutch woman, but also the symbolic joining together of our Dutch people with the British people. We Dutch will always remember that in our time of dreadful defeat and darkest despondency in 1940 the British nation alone – under Winston Churchill's inspired, inspiring leadership – kept the flame of freedom alight. We owe an immense debt of gratitude to the thousands of British soldiers who lost their lives in the struggle to restore freedom to us.'

The pastor paused and glanced around his attentive audience where many were murmuring and nodding their wholehearted agreement. He then directly addressed John, 'And we owe special gratitude to quietly resolute British heroes like you, John, who dauntlessly carried out many dangerous missions in our Kraut controlled country and by your example helped keep our own Freedom Fighters courage and resolve and belief in eventual victory alive.'

★ ★ ★

In ever recently liberated, war ravished European country – and even in proud, victorious Britain – these post-war months were a time of continuing shortages and strict food rationing. Despite all the scarcities and drab austerity in The Netherlands a former member of Frans's Resistance Group who owned a small hotel in Lopik managed to provide a tasty and fairly substantial dinner for the wedding party. A generous supply of alcohol played no small part in ensuring that this festive occasion was enjoyed by all.

An hour after the last of the meal had been eaten, all the laudatory speeches made and all the congratulatory toasts drunk, Anna and John managed to slip away from the hotel without having to endure too boisterous or bawdy a send off.

Their honeymoon journey to England would start tomorrow. Tonight, at long last, John would elatedly share with an equally elated Anna the hitherto sacrosanct sanctuary of that double bed in her farmhouse bedroom.

★ ★ ★

All four humans in that farmhouse slept late the following morning. John and Anna were blissfully exhausted after their glorious wedding night. Frans's anguished body this 'morning after the night before' was suffering for his alcoholic excesses at the wedding feast. Blanche was also exhausted, not from any excessive alcoholic or sexual indulgence, but from the strains of the last two weeks of ceaseless preparations for Anna's marriage and then the culminating joyous excitement of the wedding itself.

The loud and increasingly querulous bellowings of the cows waiting to be milked forced themselves on Blanche's drowsy consciousness. She realised it was long past their normal milking time. With guilty haste she heaved herself out of bed and into her working clothes. Her repeated demands that Frans follow her example were met with self-pitying moans, indistinct mutterings and the sulky turning away of his pain-wracked body.

Rather later than intended, John and Anna cycled away from the farm on the first stage of their honeymoon journey.

At the Hook of Holland ferry terminal the Dutch customs officer who had checked John into The Netherlands was again on duty. Recognising John he gave him a friendly greeting. 'Well, did you have a good time in our country?'

'Yes, an excellent time. It couldn't have been better.' He proudly introduced Anna, 'I've got myself a wonderful Dutch wife.'

After giving congratulatory handshakes and his best wishes the officer smiled at John, 'I won't charge you any customs duty on this precious Dutch item you are taking out of the country.'

John laughed, 'No, I should hope not.'

Anna joined in his laughter, 'No, the only duty John and I are interested in are our conjugal duties.' She gave her husband an impish grin, 'And we fully intend to continue carrying out those glorious duties I assure you!'

Chapter Fifty

For the next two weeks they leisurely travelled around Yorkshire. They had no fixed itinerary. Day after joyous day they went wherever flighty fancy took them. They cycled along many miles of winding, climbing quiet roads. They carefree rambled over vast expanses of windswept heather moors. Sometimes they took old, almost Victorian trains that wheezed their sedate steamy way along half forgotten, half overgrown meandering country lines. They alighted at tiny, out of the way moorland stations where often a languid, bushy-bearded station-master would seem surprised, perhaps even slightly annoyed, that two strangers should alight here and disturb the Rip Van Winkle sleep of his station. (Little did those innocent rustic wraiths guess what a horrid Beeching fate lay in wait for them and their torpid railway line).

The sublimely happy couple spent many memorable passionate nights in remote, stout walled, snugly hospitable moorland inns. Often the sturdy innkeeper's buxom wife would insist they eat up their substantial breakfasts so they could be given generous second helpings. What her feminine intuition told her yesterday had been confirmed by last night's squeaky protests of the inn's belaboured best double bed... they were a pair of newly-weds. And if any further proof was needed it was provided by these shyly proud glances the young bride could not refrain from bestowing on her gold wedding-ring.

Laughing, their hostess would ignore their protests, would declare, 'Na, lad, ye must eat up. Ye must finish off every morsel.' Turning twinkling eyes on confused, blushing Anna would knowingly grin, 'Eh, lass, yer husband must eat up; must eat up tae keep his strength up mustn't he?'

Leaving the breakfast-room she would give John a wicked impish wink.

The time they spent in the attractive ancient town of York was rather more spiritual, was something of an uplifting pilgrimage. Hand in hand they halted and stared and gasped at the overwhelming multi-pinnacled magnificence of York Minster. They were even more awed by the interior beauty of this cathedral's heaven-soaring splendour. Almost instinctively they sat and offered up silent prayers.

Anna emotionally prayed for her dead mother, father and brother who had all, directly or indirectly, been killed by the war. Her soldier brother had died fighting the invading Germans in 1940. Her mother's grief at her youngest son's death and the stress of not knowing if her other son, thought to be serving in the Royal Netherlands Navy, was alive or was also dead, had hastened her own death. Anna only knew what the Dutch police had told her about her father's death: he had been shot dead by a person – or persons – unknown. Once again she wondered who had killed her father..... and why? She tried, and more or less succeeded, in sincerely praying for forgiveness of those responsible for his death... whoever they were.

John rendered up silent prayers of profound thanksgiving, unbounded thanks that Anna and he had survived the war; had both kept faith by their mutual promises; had at last been reunited, been gloriously joined together in holy matrimony. He could not be entirely sure that these – or any other prayers to any other Gods – did any good, but surely they did no harm? He did not (he was sure there was no need to) pray for any Divine or human forgiveness for any of the foul deeds he had carried out during his wartime S.B.S. activities. The use of some unpleasant, 'not quite cricket' methods was fair when – as they had – they helped speed the defeat of Hitler's vile Nazi tyranny.

A few days later, cycling Westwards, they arrived at a crossroads where two workmen were erecting a signpost. Only now, six months after the end of the war were some County Councils getting round to replacing signposts that had been removed in 1940 when Britain faced the threat of German invasion. The removal of the nations signposts was intended to further confuse any disorientated invading Huns.

One re-erected, re-painted sign pointed towards the North Pennines. They headed there and then pushed on into the Southern Lake District. Day after delightful day they leisurely cycled up the length of Windermere then wandered, rambled and explored around Ambleside and Grasmere. This wonderful landscape was proudly glowing the bright glory of its autumnal splendour.

As they stared over glittery water to rugged slopes of bronzed birch and bracken John beamed at Anna, 'Oh it's great to be back home in The Lakes. Yorkshire's moors and dales are all very fine, but they simply cannot compare with this glory, can they?'

Anna delighted in her husband's delight, 'Oh John, it's wonderful – it's almost unbelievably wonderful – that this glorious landscape in now going to be my homeland as well as yours.'

With this golden aesthetic glory by day plus the exultant passionate delights of their honeymoon nights Anna and John were happier than they had ever been. They experienced sublime happiness far, far greater than they had thought possible.

On one of their rambles John halted and pointed, 'I'm sure that's Dove Cottage over there.'

'Dove Cottage? What's that, John?'

'It was William Wordsworth's home for many years.'

'Oh, I would love to visit it. Is it open to the public?'

'Yes, it is. It's a Wordsworth museum, or was before the war. My father, who loved Wordsworth's poetry, took me as a boy to visit it. But I was too young to appreciate those dreary papers in those musty rooms. I remember I wanted to go fishing instead.'

The curator at Dove Cottage warmly welcomed them then apologised, 'The museum's rather disorganised at present.' She pointed at stacks of cardboard boxes, 'We've only now received that lot of Wordsworth manuscripts back after them being hidden away during the war in deep bank vaults safe from any stray German bombs.'

'Yes, it's the same in my country,' Anna said. 'Our Dutch art galleries are only now re-hanging their Rembrandt's and other masterpieces after them being stored away safe from bombs or from the foul hands of plundering Krauts.'

With sympathetic understanding, and some secret amusement, John – not for the first time – noted how keen Anna was to make it quite clear that her European accent was Dutch…was most definitely not German.

The curator nodded and smiled, 'Would you like you like to see some of Wordsworth's manuscripts?'

Anna eagerly answered for them both, 'Oh, yes we would love to. Are the public allowed to actually handle these manuscripts?'

'No, not really. But I'll make an exception for you. Handle them very carefully.'

They were thrilled to hold these faded and stained precious papers even though the scrawled writing was almost completely un-decipherable.

Anna found, lifted and read a page that was more legible. She gave a sudden, startled gasp. John looked up from his straining effort to decipher Wordsworth's wild, inspirational scrawl. 'What is it, Anna? What's the matter?'

She, beamed a glowing smile at him, 'Oh no doubt I'm being very foolish, but I was profoundly moved by a few lines from Wordsworth's magnificent Immortality Ode.'

'Well read them to me. I want to know what moved you so much.'

Hesitantly and rather shyly she read aloud:

Behold the Child among his new-born blisses,
A six years' Darling of a pigmy size!
See, where 'mid work of his own hand he lies.
Fretted by sallies of his mother's kisses,
With light upon him from his father's eyes!

'Oh, John, I saw that lovely picture of perfect domestic bliss so clearly. I felt it was exactly describing us – you, me, and our own little son – as we'll all be in a few years time.'

John too was moved as he also clearly pictured that blissful scene. He murmured, 'Yes, Anna, that's just exactly how it will be.'

★ ★ ★

The nearer they came to John's homeland at Derwentwater the higher his spirits soared. With something like eager, innocent, proprietary pride he pointed out to his wife special features in this wonderful landscape known to him, and loved by him since childhood.

Anna once again delighted in her husband's delight. Even though now a veteran wife almost three weeks married her sensitive nerves still thrilled and tingled every time she thought of or referred to John as "her husband. (Was there perhaps also a touch of some innocent proprietary pride here?)

Beaming with pleasure John pointed, 'Look, Anna, there's Skiddaw, my own mountain nobly rising above my hometown of Keswick.'

'Oh, John, that's wonderful! Oh how I've longed to see "your mountain again. How often, I've dreamt of sitting on its summit with you as you promised we would. I often feared we would never fulfill that promise; would never achieve that sublime summit of love-fulfilled happiness.'

John hugged her and gently kissed her, 'Well, we have. Or we soon will. As long as you're sure you are fit enough, we will reach Skiddaw's summit next week.'

Only one thing slighted clouded Anna's pleasure at this time. Despite John's repeated assurances, she could not entirely free herself from some apprehension at the prospect of meeting his mother for the first time.

Most seriously courting young women had gone through the ordeal of first meeting their prospective mother-in-law long before their actual wedding, but Anna still had that trial to face. The unique circumstances of John's and her 'courtship' under the hazardous conditions prevailing in German-occupied Holland and then their hasty marriage in post-war Holland had prevented her from meeting her mother-in-law before now.

As they wheeled their bicycles up the slope towards John's home he again tried to calm his nervous wife, 'I assure you, Anna, there's no need to be too apprehensive at meeting my mother and sister. Both of them will warmly welcome you; will quickly make you feel at home.'

John threw open the kitchen door of his home and ushered his flushed and tremulous wife into the warm room. His mother and sister were sitting enjoying a late afternoon cup of tea. Two teacups slopped and clattered into saucers. Startled and flustered, the excited mother and daughter leapt to their feet. John smiled at his mother, 'Mrs Armstrong, I want you to meet Mrs Armstrong!'

He gently urged his shyly hanging back wife forward, 'Anna, this is my mother.'

The two Mrs Armstrong's met, shock hands, then, as one, embraced, hugged and kissed one another's cheeks. John looked on with smiling delight as his mother warmly welcomed his wife.

'Welcome to our home, Anna. From now on this house is your home as much as it is John's. I hope the pair of you will be as happy here as John's father and I were.'

'Oh, thank you, Mrs Armstrong, thank you. I am sure we will be.'

John turned to his sister and smiled an apology, 'I'm sorry to keep you waiting there, Jean.... Anna, this is my sister – your sister-in-law Jean Armstrong.'

More embraces, more hugs, more kisses; another warm welcome to what was now their shared home.

'Would you like a cup of tea, Anna?' Mrs Armstrong asked. 'Or do you prefer coffee?'

'Oh, tea please, thank you. I used to drink coffee, but John has educated me in the superior qualities of tea.' She smiled at her mother-in-law, 'Now I drink practically nothing but your great British char!'

'Good, good! A most wise decision. Yes, John has always been very fond of his char.'

Jean said, 'Just all of you sit at the table and I'll make a fresh pot of tea.'

Later, they all again sat around that kitchen table and enjoyed the substantial and tasty dinner Mrs Armstrong had cooked for them. As with great appreciative pleasure John spooned the last of the rich, thick, rice pudding into his replete mouth he smiled across the table. 'That was a wonderful meal, mother. Thank you very much. Your cooking skills are as great as ever.' Anna's and Jean's equally sincere praise augmented his.

Flushed, smiling, and modestly beaming Mrs Armstrong dismissed their praise. 'Oh, it was a real pleasure for me to cook the first meal for your lovely wife, Anna and you in this house. I'm sure it will only be the first of many meals we will all share here. Had I known the exact day you were arriving I would have prepared a much more special dinner for you.'

'Oh, mother, we need nothing any more special than this excellent meal I assure you. Anna and I were not sure when we would arrive home. We sent postcards to give you some idea when to expect us.'

'Yes, it was good of you to send them, to think of us when you were so happily engrossed in your honeymoon.'

'I thought about sending you a telegram, then decided against it. Even though the war's over I thought the arrival of a telegram might still alarm you.'

'Yes, it would have. After the many dreaded wartime telegrams announcing tragic news to next-of-kin, I will always associate telegrams with sudden deaths or other grim news. I still all to clearly remember that dreadful telegram from the Admiralty informing me you were "missing in action, feared dead." Yes, John, it was most thoughtful of you to send me postcards instead of a telegram.'

Anna was listening with intense interest. She knew there were many parts of John's long, varied and dangerous war service that even she – his deeply loving and deeply loved wife – as yet knew nothing of. She would like to learn more about what must be his truly impressive war record. She hoped, and expected, that during their future years together he would – in his own good time – reveal most, if not all, his secret exploits to her, even if he disclosed them to no one else. She had come to the wise decision to respect her husband's reluctance to tell her much about his war experiences, but still she could not resist saying, 'Oh, John, I didn't know you had been reported as being "missing in action". When was that? What happened to you to make the Admiralty send your poor mother such an appalling telegram?'

Anna's questions confronted John with a quite a dilemma. He did not want to directly lie to his wife, yet he was forced to! He must not – would never – tell he anything about that most secret mission 'Operation Waterloo' which had resulted not only in that dramatic telegram being sent to his mother, but had also resulted in the death of Anna's father. At all costs Anna must never learn the truth about his part in her father's violent death. If the keeping of that truth from her required him to tell her lies so be it. Surely this was an occasion when well-meaning lies were much better than the all too terrible truth.

Not only, Anna, but John's mother and sister were waiting for his answer. Clearly remembering the false tale he had told his mother explaining that very upsetting telegram, he now repeated it correct in every detail.

He explained that his Royal Navy warship had been sunk near the Norwegian coast; that many of the crew had been killed, but he and a few others had been rescued and then hidden by Norwegian Patriots. For quite a while they had been out of touch with London, but eventually arrangements were made for the survivors to return via a

'Shetland Bus' to Britain. He told this false story so convincingly (embellishing it with clearly remembered details from the time when he had actually sailed from Norway on one of those incredibly reliable 'buses') that he almost became convinced of its truth himself.

These lies occasioned by his mother's mention of that upsetting telegram reminded John how constantly he would have to guard against allowing the least hint of the truth about treacherous Professor Maurik's death escape him. He was confident that his tough, intensive S.B.S. training – his mental toughness even more than his physical toughness – which had let hm cope with the worst that war had thrown at him would just as reliably see him through the different challenges of peace.

His sister now spoke up, 'Oh, John, out of what must be your many interesting war experiences that experience in Norway is almost the only one you've ever told us about. Surely now the war's over you can tell us more about your secret activities. How, for instance, when serving in the Royal Navy did you manage to meet (here she smiled at her sister-in-law) and woo Anna in the heart of German-occupied Holland?'

John thought it supremely ironic that the only wartime experience he had told them about was the only one that was not true. He patiently explained, 'You see, Jean, although the war's over, my activities in Holland when I met Anna (here he lovingly smiled at his wife) are still being kept profound secrets. In fact all our S.B.S. activities, and there were many of them, were – and are – extremely secret. Perhaps in thirty – or, more likely, fifty – years time our secret exploits will be made known to the public. In the meantime all involved in these stealthy S.B.S. operations are, even in peacetime, still covered not only by the Official Secrets Act, but also by other more stringent oaths of secrecy we signed.'

He gave a self-mocking modest grin, 'Yes, all our S.B.S. operations were real hush, hush, cloak and dagger stuff!'

Not wanting to worry his wife, mother and sister, he said nothing of it to them, but he was well aware that though demobbed from the Royal Navy he was still in the naval reserves and, should some national emergency require it, could be called back to serve in the S.B.S. again. In fact officially he was supposed to keep his naval uniform in good order in case he had to once more wear it.

Eager to change the subject, he again praised his mother's cooking then asked, 'Are things a bit easier now, mother? Do you get more food in your rations now that the war's over?'

This, he knew, was a subject close to his mother's heart. In his admiring eyes she was symbolic of all the older British housewives who for six weary years had uncomplainingly stood for seemingly endless hours, often in the worst of winter's freezing misery, in patient queues outside grocers and other shops. By their humbly heroic selfless efforts these stoic women ensured that their menfolk had sufficient good, filling meals to sustain them in their vital war work.

As if these cares were not enough most of these noble mothers suffered under the extra worry of what might be happening to their endangered soldier sons.

John's mother rose to his bait. With indignant vigour she corrected him. 'Oh, no, son, in many ways things are even worse than they were during the worst depth of the war. Everywhere in Britain everything is grim austerity. Clothes and some items of food are even more severely rationed than they were during the war.' Somewhat wearily she sighed, 'Oh, yes, things are really grim.'

Suddenly she smiled, 'Oh, dear, I'm a real moaning minnie, aren't I? I hope I don't sound too much like "Itma's" dear old, ever complaining Mrs Mop, do I?'

Her daughter laughed, 'Yes, mother, you do rather remind us of the B.B.C.'s wonderfully funny Mrs Mop!'

Even as his wife and he joined in the laughter John's thoughts flew to another occasion when the great morale boosting wartime humour of "Itma" and Mrs Mop had been mentioned. That had also been connected with 'Operation Waterloo'. Strange how things seemed destined to lead back to that ruthless, blood-soaked secret operation. It had been Eric and Peter, the two brave Dutch Patriots who had, after guiding the S.B.S. team to their target, light-heartedly remarked that they had now to wait for the arrival of the two Dutch Mrs Mops before the operation could go ahead. And these Dutch charwomen had turned out to be real Mrs Mops, complete with clanging pails and sodden mops. John fervently hoped that Peter and Erik had survived the war.

Mrs Armstrong beamed a blissful maternal smile on her son, 'But our present shortages are nothing now that all the fighting and killing are over and that our sons have returned to us.'

Instinctively she and the three others fell silent for a few solemn moments as they thought of all the too, too many mother's sons who had not returned.

Turning to her daughter-in-law, Mrs Armstrong asked, 'What are things like in your country, Anna? Are....'

Smiling, John interrupted her, 'Oh, mother, England is now Anna's country!'

'Oh, yes, of course. I'm sorry , Anna, I'm sorry.' Perhaps a touch irritably she continued, 'Well, Anna, are there bad shortages in Holland, too?'

'Oh yes. Many shortages. Food is scarce and strictly rationed. But, largely thanks to the millions of dollars of "Marshal Aid the Americans are pouring into Western Europe, things are steadily getting better. Fortunately, living deep in the country at our farm, food was never too scarce with us. Things were much, much worse in the Dutch cities, especially Rotterdam. During the last months before your British and Canadian soldiers finally managed to liberate all of The Netherlands food got so scarce that some people were forced to eat not only horsemeat, which was not really too bad, but even to eat dogs and cats.'

Once again they all fell solemnly silent.

Wanting to raise their saddened spirits, John asked Anna (although he knew the answer) 'What was it the starving people in Rotterdam used to call the poor stray cats they had to climb after, capture, kill and eat?'

'Oh no doubt it was sad black humour, but such humour helped the Dutch people to endure the dreadful years under German occupation. Wanting to salve their consciences over being forced to eat these poor cats they pretended they were rabbits. And so these unfortunate cats became known as "roof rabbits !'

Once their slightly uneasy laughter died down Jean said, 'I can confirm that. At one of the farms where I work in the Land Army they took in two young Dutch boys suffering from malnutrition to feed up for a few months just after the end of the war. The farmer shot a brace of large, plump rabbits and his wife made a mouth-watering rabbit stew. However the Dutch boys refused to eat it. Although hungry, they pushed their full plates away when they saw the rabbits. After considerable confusion the farmer's wife realised the boys thought that what they were being offered was cat stew. It took some hasty drawings of rabbits to convince them it was rabbits in the stew – not cats. Once convinced, and delighted with the taste, they wolfed the stew down with desperate urgency.'

When Anna went to the toilet John's mother reached across the table and grasped his hand with both of hers. 'Oh, son, I think you've made a wise decision marrying Anna. I'm sure she'll be a great wife for you. I'm sure the two of you will be very happy.'

John laughed, 'Thank you, mother. We are very happy I assure you. From the first moment I saw her I knew she was the one for me.'

Despite the sincerity of her praise of her son's wife – she had intuitively taken to her from the first – Mrs Armstrong could not quite prevent feeling a slight, but definite, pang of jealousy of that younger Mrs Armstrong who had supplanted her place in John's heart. She consoled herself with the thought that this was an understandable feeling that every loving mother must experience. No doubt it was worse when, as in her case, she had only the one son.

Anna returned and, cheerfully but firmly defying her mother-in-law's protests, insisted on helping with the washing up.

John sat at complacent masculine ease and enjoyed the luxury of his post-dinner cigarette. As he gazed around this cosy kitchen – the warm heart of this happy house – he was filled with quiet contentment. Everything in this room was familiar. Almost nothing was changed from his childhood days; that same large brown kettle still steamed on the always hot, assiduously black-leaded pot-bellied iron stove where his mother had seemingly endlessly cooked and baked; those same frequently used thick, heavy blue and white plates and other dishes (minus the cup he had dropped and smashed) still decorated the old oak sideboard and enhanced the room with their modest gleam.

How many times in quiet moments during dangerous S.B.S. missions he'd wondered if he would survive to see this familiar kitchen, with his mother and sister busy in it, again.

While engrossed in his musing thoughts he half listened to those three most important women in his life as with effortless skill they got on with washing up and putting away all the dishes, pots and pans while at the same time ceaselessly carrying on an engrossing and cheerily animated three way conversation.

Much of this intriguing feminine talk seemed to centre on questions to Anna about their wedding... Where exactly had the ceremony been held?...... How many of her relations and other guests had been at it? (Reiterated genuine regret from her in-laws that they had not been able to attend it) .... Despite the food shortages did they have a good after-wedding meal?..... Had many photographs been taken? Mother and daughter sympathised with, and joined in Anna's impatience to see the wedding photos that must have been developed by now and should arrive from Holland soon.

Not wanting to shift the limelight from her brother's and new sister's wedding glory, Jean – although eager to – nobly refrained from going on too much about her own wedding plans. Surely in the coming weeks and months there would be plenty of more suitable opportunities to indulge in cosy intimate womanly/sisterly chats about her intended, Tom Kershaw, and their pending marriage. The obvious power and wonder of Anna's and John's conjugal happiness made Jean more impatient than ever for her own wedding and married bliss. Once more she silently cursed the hard-hearted British Army for keeping Tom in Germany and being in no hurry to demob him.

Chapter Fifty One

For much of the next two days John and Anna were kept busy seeing about getting Anna's new nationality as the wife of an English husband officially recognised then getting this British citizen issued with all the ration books and coupons she was entitled to. Without these documents she was unable to buy any of the many foods still strictly rationed. Even new clothes would be banned to her until she got her clothing coupons.

The petty bureaucrats they dealt with told them Anna could not be issued with ration books until they saw the correct documents confirming her new status as a British subject. Then another Government department's bureaucrats demanded to see her ration books as proof that she really was a British citizen before they could issue documents confirming this.

On the second day of being shunted about from department to department; from office to office; from official to official and at times kept waiting, seemingly forgotten, for long spells, John finally lost his rag. 'My God,' he raged, 'we've defeated the Nazis, it's about time we got round to defeating all you thousands of petty, puffed-up self-important bureaucratic twits who want to hold on to your wartime powers as long as you possibly can. Armed with a little more power some of you would be as tyrannical as dear departed Herr Hitler!'

He insisted on seeing one of the department's 'top brass'. Once they did gain access to the highest official things moved more smoothly. They were promised ration books would be ready for Anna when she returned next morning.

As, arm in arm, they strolled home they saw a large ginger cat voluptuously making the most of the October sunshine on the flat roof of a garden shed. John laughed, 'Oh, Anna, if that Civil Servant keeps his word and you get your ration books tomorrow, you won't need to go, almost starving, hunting after that plump "roof-rabbit !'

★ ★ ★

A few days later Anna and John sat together on the summit of Skiddaw. For some delightful self-engrossed minutes they ignored the magnificent views stretching out around them. With gentle congratulatory kisses they celebrated having achieved their wartime ambition of the two of them climbing John's "own mountain in the calm wonder of post-war peace.

Eventually they forced their gazes away from one another and commanded their eyes to drink in those neglected Lakeland views.

After staring, awed to silence, for some blissful moments John sighed, 'Oh, Anna, isn't it wonderful up here on "my mountain ? Wouldn't it be great if our life together could continue like this forever?..... one endless honeymoon of making love and climbing, hiking and cycling.'

With twinkling eyes Anna joined in his wishful daydreaming, 'And eating? We would have to eat to keep up our strength to revel in all those active delights, wouldn't we? And we would also need some time for the more leisurely delights of reading, wouldn't we?.... I know I would.'

John laughed then ruefully sighed, 'Aye, there's the rub. I suppose I'll have to work to get money for food and for books to feed our minds. I have about ten days of my fully – but certainly not generous – paid demob leave from the Royal Navy left. After that I will have to work, but I'm not quite sure what work I'm fit for. Almost the only skills I've got are my highly trained skills in different ways of killing Germans.' He grinned, 'But now the war's over I don't suppose there's a great demand for these skills.'

Anna laughed, 'No, there won't be. Your desperately needed valuable skills were at a premium for six long war years, weren't they? Surely a grateful country will do something about re-training you for some type of peace-related work?'

'Aye, perhaps. I will call at the Labour Exchange tomorrow and see what work or training they can offer. Meanwhile we're wise to make the most of this bright weather, this glorious "Indian Summer , while we can.'

★ ★ ★

'Yes,' the helpful, elderly civil servant at Keswick's employment exchange said, 'I can well appreciate that after your long, active and hazardous war service you don't want to, or you wouldn't really be able to settle down to any too dull and boring a routine job; certainly not to any dreary, inactive sedentary work.'

John was pleasantly surprised at how helpful this official was .... a great improvement on the pompous unhelpful bureaucrats Anna and he had encountered a few days ago.

With fingers that were a blur of rippling movement and seemed as sure and nimble as any flashy card-sharp's, the civil servant flicked through a bundle of jobs vacant index cards. As he gave each card a negative shake of his head he dismissively mumbled, 'Oh, no, I don't think so' ..... 'Oh, no, that's hardly suitable'...... 'No, no, not suitable at all!'

Just as John began to fear he would not find anything to suit him, the conscientious official beamed, 'Ah, here's something more like. How about forestry work? That's physically active and it's out in the open air.'

'Yes, yes, that's more interesting. My late father was a forester. I would be following in his footsteps.' John paused for a few thoughtful moments then his face clouded, 'I have only one serious qualm about doing forestry work. You see, my father was killed by a tree he was felling. My mother would constantly worry that the same fate might befall me. After her terrible worries about me all during the war I would hate to impose that new burden of worry on her during my years of peacetime forestry work.'

'No, no, that would be too cruel a weight of worry for your mother to bear.' After flicking through a few more cards the official smiled, 'Ah, this job's just come in. It might well be exactly what you're looking for.'

So the following morning, armed with a form (in duplicate) from the Labour Exchange, John, with Anna accompanying him, set out on

391

a cycle ride to Bassenthwaite Lake. As they cycled along by the lake the impressive bulk of Skiddaw loomed invitingly above them. It felt strange to be merely travelling past John's "own" mountain instead of climbing it. But the imperative need for John to find employment kept them on the straight and narrow path of duty. Their goal today was not the top of that mountain but the far end of this lake.

They saw the stately grey bulk of Ravenscrag House tower above neighbouring trees. John knew that before the war this large mansion had been a posh, expensive public school. It had been requisitioned by the army for secret wartime uses. Now it seemed it was a posh school again. And here, perhaps, was where he would find work.

Before quite reaching the imposing, many-towered old mansion they dismounted and stood staring around them. Their admiring gazes swept across the shimmering lake to wooded slopes and shaggy hills. Anna gasped, 'Oh, John, wouldn't it be wonderful to live here? Oh, I hope and pray you'll get a job at this place.'

John was directed to an office at the top of a wide, curving sweep of marble stairs. With quiet amusement he read the varnish gleaming wooden name-plate on the door which proudly announced: 'Brigadier Rutherford, Commanding Officer.' Confirmation that this was the correct office was supplied by the name inked on a sheet of paper tacked above the name-plate: 'Edmund Turner, assistant principal, Ravenscrag School.'

As he shook hands with John, Mr. Turner smiled, 'Despite that plate on the door this is no longer the Brigadier's office. For the present it's mine, although I'm afraid I never rose to higher rank than First Lieutenant in the Royal Navy.'

John returned his smiled, 'Well, sir, you did better than me. I was only a leading-seaman in the Senior Service. Some details of my war service are in that document from the Labour Exchange.'

After reading this information Mr. Turner said, 'I see you carried out some special duties while in the Navy; were you in the Royal Marines Commandos?'

'No, sir, not the Commandos. The S.B.S.'

'Oh, I see.' He seemed impressed. 'We heard very little about the exploits of the S.B.S, but according to what we did hear – always just vague rumours, perhaps exaggerated rumours, rather than reliable facts – you were tougher and even more daring than the Commandos.'

John gave a broad grin, 'Yes, sir, we were! Without being too boastful, I can unequivocally state that to successfully complete our secret S.B.S. missions we had to be – we were – much tougher and more stealthily daring than not only the Commandos but any other special forces, British or of any other nationality.' He paused and gave another wide grin, 'I'm sorry, that does sound very boastful, doesn't it?.... It just happens to be the truth!'

'Well, you've certainly convinced me. What special S.B.S. skills do you have that could be used to instruct pupils at this school in various, often strenuous and demanding, outdoor activities?'

'I've done many testing long-distance hikes and climbs over wild country carrying a heavily laden rucksack; I've camped and skied and done snow and ice climbing in some quite atrocious winter conditions; I'm skilled at rock-climbing and abseiling on spray lashed sea cliffs and on high remote mountain faces. I'm an expert frogman and canoeist. I'm quite an experienced parachutist too.'

Edmund Turner laughed, 'A really impressive list. I don't think the school could use your parachuting expertise, but all those other skills are exactly what we're looking for. I think you will be perfect for this work of instructing the boys in these challenging, character forming activities.'

'I hope so, sir, we – my wife and I – would love to live and work here in the midst of this glorious Lakeland countryside.'

'Is your wife with you? Is she waiting outside?'

'Yes, she is.'

'Oh well, we better not keeping her waiting any longer. Come with me and I'll show both of you around this place.' As he made for the door he halted and pointed at a table covered by layers of official documents; there were pages after pages of Government rules and regulations about getting priority for any type of building work; there were heaps of different coloured forms (mostly in triplicate) to apply for scare building materials; there were forms for builders to counter-sign once – and if – precious resources were allocated to them. 'I like any excuse to get away from all that Government red tape for a while. That official bumph takes up so much of my time I'm hard pushed to get on with my academic duties.' He gave an optimistic smile, 'However, once we do finally get all the post-war renovations completed and can accommodate the full complement of staff and pupils this will once again be a great school ... one of the very best!'

He led John and Anna across the mansion's cobbled back courtyard to a row of grey stone buildings which had once been stables and coach-houses with living quarters for grooms and coachmen above. He opened two large doors and revealed an ex-army ambulance and fire engine. 'Part of your work, Mr Armstrong, would be to help organise and keep in perfect order the school's own fire service and mountain rescue service based on those two vehicles. You do drive, don't you?'

'Oh, yes, I've got a driving licence. I'm afraid I'm not an experienced mechanic though.' John smiled, 'Thanks to my S.B.S. training I'm much more skilful at stealthily putting vehicles out of use, rather than maintaining them.'

Mr Turner laughed, 'Oh, I'm sure you'll soon adjust to the more constructive peacetime work all right.' As he opened another two large doors he apologised, 'I'm sorry all this gear is in such a disorganised jumble. That would be your first task, Mr Armstrong, to get all those things sorted out and checked over. Some of those canoes might need patching up.'

All the things here were also ex-army stuff. There was an untidily stranded flotilla of about twenty canoes, complete with paddles and life jackets; there was a stricken forest of long wooden skies and ski-poles; there were heaped hillocks of rucksacks and khaki or camouflage clothing. Tents of various sizes and colours were draped over rafters and cascaded to the floor in kaleidoscopic confusion.

Finally, and perhaps most importantly, they were shown through the small stone cottage which had once been a gardener's (one of the four who had kept the mansion's extensive gardens in immaculate order in its Victorian heyday), had been army officers billets during the war, and was now to be to be their home if John got this job.

★ ★ ★

He did get the job

Two weeks later they moved into that cottage.

Late in the evening of that first, busy and exciting day in their new home Anna and John sat together on the small sofa facing the open fire where remnants of small birch logs were glowing their final brave brightness before smouldering into pale, powdery grey ash.

As Anna snuggled even more comfortably into the warmth of

John's strong body he hugged her even more tightly. She sighed contentedly, 'Oh, John, isn't it wonderful to be here together, just the two of us in our own home? Oh, how many times I've dreampt of this.' She gave a sudden involuntary shudder, 'Oh, but how many other deeply depressed times I despaired of ever gaining such happiness.'

'Well you – we – have gained it. Yes, we are amazingly lucky to have found such great happiness.' He smiled into her gleaming eyes, 'But, in all humbleness, I think we deserved to find it.' After glancing around the plain, sparsely furnished small room with appreciative pleasure he laughed, 'Yes, it's true, it's very true what the old song says: "Be it ever so humble, there's no place like home. '

They fully realised just how fortunate they were to have a home of their own (although of course, they did not actually own this tied-cottage) for in this dreary time of post-war austerity and, it seemed, ever more scarcities, by far the most severe scarcity was the desperate shortage of housing.

Tens of thousands of British houses had been destroyed and many others had been badly damaged by German bombs, flying-bombs and V2 rockets. Now Government Ministers gave repeated assurances that they were initiating an urgent programme of repairing all the country's bomb-damaged houses and were going to build thousands of small, quickly erected prefabricated houses. But so far those assurances remained nothing but politicians doubtful promises and had made no impact on the nation's housing shortages.

The steady flood of servicemen being demobbed back into 'civvy street' who – having 'done their bit' to win the war – were now keenly (many revelling in the novelty of their newly married state) doing their much more pleasant duty of bringing the post-war' baby-boom' into being.

They and their eager wives managed to conscientiously carry out this duty despite the often frustrating and embarrassing lack of much real conjugal privacy in the overcrowded homes they shared with spying and giggling or noisy squalling siblings and with parents or with large, sometimes not particularly friendly families of in-laws.

With silent contentment John again glanced around the small room then again smiled into Anna's gleaming eyes. 'Yes, we are truly fortunate to have this wonderful, humble, wee cottage to ourselves. As the fire's now out let's head for our first night in our new bedroom where my mother's large double bed must be getting impatient waiting for us to initiate it into its new home.'

Anna nodded and giggled, 'I'm as eager as you to get to that bed. It was very good of your mother to insist on giving us it as an extra wedding present.'

It was John's turn to nod in agreement, 'Yes, it was. We would have found it rather difficult to manage without it.' He smiled with warm affection as he remembered how his mother had reacted to the discovery that the only beds in this cottage were a pair of narrow, ex-army iron bunk-beds. Blushing with charming old-fashioned modesty she immediately offered them her large double-bed. With eyes glittering oblique hints of what her innocent rural upbringing forbade her to openly talk of, she said, 'No doubt these bunk-beds were fine for solitary soldiers, but they are hardly suitable for a recently married young couple like you, are they?'

In this time of post-war austerity only 'Utility' type furniture was being produced and even these basic units were scarce. John's mother had given them various other items of furniture in addition to the bed and Anna and he were quite content with what they had. They would buy extra furniture once they had saved enough to be able to pay for it in cash. For the present, after six years of receiving nothing but his miserly poor Royal Navy pay and after the un-grudged expenses of their honeymoon, money was scare with them. They certainly would not get themselves into debt by purchasing things through hire-purchase. There was thought to be something rather disreputable about buying anything on the 'never-never;' it was something only reverted to by the poorest and most feckless.

Anna and John rose together from the snug intimacy of the small sofa and hurried into their unfamiliar new bedroom. To mark this special occasion a coal and log fire brightly flamed in the small grate. It danced its flickering light over the surprised ceiling and brought a brighter blush to the brilliant pink of the eiderdown quilt covering the gifted double-bed.

★ ★ ★

John attended training courses with R.A.F. Mountain Rescue Teams; he was instructed in firefighting by officers of Carlisle's Fire Brigade; he attended Red Cross courses on giving emergency medical treatment.

As the months passed he built up all those positive skills and gained ever increasing peacetime experience to augment his savage wartime experiences. After years of using all his many dark and deadly skills to kill people it was wonderfully uplifting to learn all these fine new skills which would save people. Perhaps each life he saved in the future would compensate for the regrettably necessary killings he had carried out during the war. Yes, surely by helping with the life-saving bright grace of Peace he would help redeem his War's darkest past.

Then − all too bright in memory's vivid glare − he suddenly remembered the horrors of the German Concentration Camp he had helped liberate and he was certain that even the most ruthless of his wartime killings needed no peacetime redeeming, for by these killings he had helped end the vile Nazi tyranny that had brought these horrendous camps into being and with cold-blooded Teutonic efficiency kept them going right to the end of the war.

John also found it wonderfully uplifting to lead the school's eager pupils on strenuous hiking, climbing and camping expeditions knowing that they did so to benefit their physical and mental health and to increase their aesthetic appreciation of this district's wild mountainous beauty and not to have any stealthy killings, and evading being killed, as the main object of these adventurous excursions.

He was thrilled when one of the keenest of the pupils he was training became the first from this school to win a Gold Award from the recently formed Duke of Edinburgh Outward Bound Scheme.

When Mr Edmund Turner's Irish Setter bitch gave birth to five pups one sturdy male pup was, as promised, given in due course to a delighted John and Anna. Once strong enough, this setter − named 'Rebel' − became a firm favourite with the boys as it keenly accompanied them on long hikes.

On many other even more perfect days there would be just the three of them − Anna, John and tireless Rebel − striding over delightful miles of high Lakeland hills and rugged fells. Eventually for Anna the more strenuous of these excursions were reluctantly abandoned as her first pregnancy developed. Then, four years into their marriage, their son was born. 'Oh, John, are you sure you don't mind us calling our son by the Dutch name, Willem, after my father?'

'No, no, Anna, Willem is fine. When he gets older perhaps he might want to use the more English name of William. However Willem is fine with me if that's the name you want for him.' Despite his assurances to Anna, in the deepest depths of his being John was not at all happy at the name of Anna's treacherous father being bestowed – even in all innocence – on their son. However, keeping his secret knowledge of her father's death forever hidden from Anna over-rode all other considerations. In their four happy years together he had not allowed the least hint of this secret to inadvertently escape him. Even in the worst of his – fortunately now much less frequent – post-war nightmares nothing relating to her father's death that would have alerted and alarmed Anna had escaped from him. The only words she ever recognised in the midst of his wildest ravings were loud warning cries of 'Look out! Those are bloody Krauts over there!'

So he certainly was not going to risk jeopardising this deep secret by raising any objections to his son being named after Anna's father.

Another three and a half quiet, useful and happy years past until Anna gave birth to their daughter. John suffered no secrets qualms over the name bestowed on her. She was christened Elizabeth, after his mother.

Anna and John's family was now complete.

Their happiness was now complete.

One evening in the January following their daughter's Spring birth the cosy small sitting room of their cottage presented a picture of perfect domestic bliss.

Their four year old son, Willem, lay on the rug in front of the glowing open fire; the tip of his tongue protruded as with engrossed concentration he selected the best crayons to colour in the outlined pictures in his drawing book. Their dog, Rebel, lay comfortably stretched out beside Willem. The Irish Setter's ruddy colours gleamed a brighter glossy red in the flickering glare of the log fire. When Rebel's tail thumped in sleepy pleasure little Willem smiled up at his father and whispered, 'Oh, dad, Rebel's dreaming of running over the hills with us, isn't he?'

Held lovingly secure on her mother's lap, Willem's small sister, Elizabeth, chortled with inarticulate infant pleasure as her wide, bright, wonder-filled eyes drank in every detail of the glorious scene of snug, homely human and domestic warmth that enveloped her with comfort and inviolate security.

As John gazed around this tranquil scene of domestic bliss he too drank in every detail with thankful pleasure. The passing years had added some extra modest comforts to this room, had most importantly, crowded its shelves with a glorious host of Anna's and his books; but his thoughts did not linger too long over the room's pleasant inanimate objects, his eyes instead smiled on his wife and daughter, moved down to the blissful sleeping dog then beamed in on his son. Those lines of poetry Anna had prophetically quoted at Wordsworth's cottage during their honeymoon came echoing back to him. With his loving gaze fixed on his son he gently murmured the two lines he clearly remember:

See, where 'mid work of his own hand he lies,
With light upon him from his father's eyes!

After giving John a gentle appreciative chuckle, Anna lent over her daughter, smothered her with kisses then deliberately mis-quoted three lines:

Behold the child among her new-born blisses,
A six months Darling of a pigmy size,
Fretted by sallies of her mother's kisses.

She laughed, 'Oh, John, we ought to apologise to Wordsworth for muddling up his great poetry.'

As winter's first blizzard battered snow with ever increasing ferocity against the cottage's small-paned old windows it set them rattling in their weathered frames. Extra strong gusts howled mournful sighs down the chimney and sent the pleasant primitive scent of birch smoke to enhance the room's snug comfort. Not only the perfuming wood smoke but all those howls, rattles and sighs seemed to greatly increase the warmth and cosy snugness of this homely room.

Once again John's eager gaze drank in this picture of wondrous bliss; once again he smiled at Anna, 'With that blizzard raging outside while all of us are revelling in the great comfort of this blazing log fire within, this is – to switch authors – a real Dickensian scene of perfect family bliss, isn't it?'

Every creature in this modest room, the four humans and the one dog, were happy – were quietly contentedly happy.

Epilogue

Flowing by with time's usual swift, un-noticed stealth a full fifteen years had passed since the birth of Elizabeth Armstrong. It was now the year 1968.

With a generous glass of Glenlivet malt whisky (diluted with a miserly splash of water) grasped in his right hand John Armstrong sat at relaxed ease in a large, chintz-covered armchair in the comfortable lounge of Mr. & Mrs Edmund Turner's flat attached to Ravenscrag School. Edmund Turner was now Principal of this splendid, proud and prosperous public school which he considered to the every bit as good as the much better known Gordonstoun School.

The passing years had been kind to John; although now 48 years old he was still the same weight and was almost just as healthily strong and active as when in his strenuously trained wartime prime. Some slight thinning of his hair and the first cautious, but rapidly increasing appearance of grey hairs at his temples were the only visible signs of ages stealthy progress. He was now in complete charge of organising the school's many and varied outdoor activities. With well experienced skill he still led most of the more adventurous of these outings.

The years and the stressful weight of his responsibilities on top of his much more sedentary lifestyle had taken a much heavier toll on Edmund Turner's now rather corpulent and unfit body; were eagerly turning his still abundant hair to a pure white rather than to a middle-aged grey. As, with some effort, he got himself comfortably settled in the armchair across the fireplace from John he gave a loud, self-mocking sigh, 'Oh, I wish to God I was as fit as you John.' Raising his whisky glass he smiled and gave a sincere toast, 'Here's to you, John, and to all the great unsung British heroes like you who served in the S.B.S in Western Europe during the Second World War.'

With self-effacing modestly John did not drink to himself, but with deep sincerity drank to his well-remembered S.B.S comrades who had been killed helping to restore freedom to Nazi enslaved Europe. He then asked, 'Did your brother and you manage to dig up much gen about our S.B.S exploits from out of the secret archives of the S.O.E. (Special Operations Executive) and the Admiralty?'

'Yes, we did.' Edmund pointed to an untidy heap of papers littering the small table beside his armchair, 'Those are my scrawled notes on what we found out about S.B.S activities in Western Europe.' He picked up and glanced through these papers, 'Of course my brother Harry, being a professional historian, took many more and much more fully detailed notes than I did from the mass of secret material meticulously filed away in these dusty archives.'

Over the years John had met Edmund's younger brother Harry many times. Harry, like his brother, had been a lieutenant in the Royal Navy during the latter part of the war. After the war he had studied history at Oxford and then specialised in Naval History. He had helped research and write some official histories of various Second World War naval battles. Even he, a naval historian, knew nothing about the wartime exploits of the Royal Navy's most secret unit – the S.B.S. It had been his meetings with John and hearing his un-boastful telling of one or two of the many hazardous S.B.S missions he had been involved in that had whetted Harry's historic appetite to learn much more about these most secret operations. Perhaps he would even be authorized to write an official history of the navy's most secretive, and from what little he knew of it, what surely must have been its greatest unit of specially picked, most highly trained and most outstandingly brave sailors.

After a long delay and much official discouragement, Harry had received rather reluctant permission for him – with his brother Edmund accompanying and helping him – to carry out some research in the secret archives of the S.B.S.

Harry Turner was now staying in London and continuing his research. Edmund Turner's wife Alice, had been with him in London; she was now spending some time with her seriously ill sister in Manchester. Edmund had returned to his duties in this Lakeland school two days ago. After conscientiously working long hours to catch up with the backlog of paper work awaiting him, and keen to share what he had discovered in the S.B.S. archives with the only person he knew who had firsthand experience of these secret wartime activities, he wasted no time in inviting John to his flat to discuss his findings.

Selecting one page from his bundle of scribbled notes Edmund quickly skimmed through it then smiled at John, 'As I expect you know, John every member of the S.B.S. had his own personal secret file containing full details of the specialist skills he had and of how well he had done on all the missions he had taken part in.'

John nodded, 'Yes, although we never saw these files we were all aware of them. We used to get rather bored with all the long debriefings we had to go through every time we returned to England after carrying out an S.B.S. mission. Oh, of course we understood the need for all the intensive interrogations, the gist of which ended up in our files, but nevertheless it was all rather annoying when all we really wanted was to get some decent food and drink and then grab a good, tension free night's kip.'

Holding up that one special page, Edmund said, 'These are some of the notes I made as I read your S.B.S. file, John. I was really very impressed by what I read there. All those daunting and dangerous missions you and your S.B.S. teams carried out make all the normal convoy escorting naval duties I took part in seem rather mundane, routine and un-heroic in comparison.

'Yes, John, yours is truly a most impressive record of many dangerous tasks most bravely and successfully carried out.'

John slightly nodded as if almost reluctantly forced to agree with this sincere praise while keeping a becoming modest silence.

Edmund took a sip of whisky then continued, 'I saw from your file that in between your S.B.S. activities you, like me, carried out many convoy escorting duties.' He smiled across at a silently listening John, 'But, unlike me, even in those more "normal" routine duties you underwent many drastic and dangerous experiences. Even just one of your awesome experiences was more than I experienced in all my time at sea.'

As John again nodded and sipped his whisky, but still remained modestly silent, Edmund again glanced at his notes then continued, 'I see that you were on one of the worst convoys of the entire war; one of the winter convoys to Russia round the North of Norway. That must have been really very grim.'

John once again nodded in agreement, then this time he spoke up, 'Yes it was. The fight against the terrible Arctic winter weather was often much worse, much more frightening and dangerous than the fight against German U-boats and the all too many and all too fiercely resolute Luftwaffe torpedo planes.'

It was Edmund's turn to silently and understandingly nod his head. He again glanced at his notes, 'And you twice had a ship sunk under you, didn't you, John?'

'Yes. Once by a torpedo and once by a mine.'

'And after you were torpedoed by that U-boat you, and four others, were the only survivors of your ship, weren't you?'

'Yes...yes, we were.'

Sensing that John seemed to have some reluctance to talk about this incident Edmund apologised, 'Oh, John, I hope you don't mind me asking all those questions. It's just that I find all your really quite amazing wartime experiences most interesting. I reiterate that they really do make all my wartime duties truly nothing compared to yours.'

John smiled, 'Oh, that's all right, Edmund, I don't mind answering your questions. Yes, I certainly had some truly dramatic and traumatic experiences. But it's more than twenty years since then. Thank God I've got over the strain of the psychological effects of these traumas.'

After smiling his thanks, Edmund started searching through his notes while he asked another question, 'What was the name of your ship that was torpedoed?'

With no hesitation, no need to painstakingly search his memory, John immediately replied, 'She was H.M.S Flash; a pre-war Whalehunter converted to an escort vessel. She had a mixed, but a good crew.' He paused, he sighed, 'Yes, she was a real "happy ship".'

Edmund ventured yet another question, 'And you five, the only survivors of that crew, were adrift in an open lifeboat for how long ... more than ten days, wasn't it?'

'Yes, we were exactly twelve days adrift some two hundred miles out from Newfoundland.'

'Those twelve weary, drawn out days must have been a terrible ordeal. That protracted slow drama must have been a real test of all the survivors morale fibre; a real proof of their indomitable will power. Not all that many men would have the physical and mental strength to survive that ordeal.'

Again John nodded, 'Yes, they were endless, dreary, soul and stamina sapping days right-enough; and the cold dark nights were even longer, were even more appallingly weary. We could not have gone on much longer. We were strictly self-rationed to only two hardtack ships biscuits per day from the lifeboat's emergency supplies. By the twelfth day these biscuits were almost finished. And, even worst, our supply of fresh water which had given us half a cup of water per day was also now practically finished,.' Clearly remembering that grim time he sighed and repeated, 'No, we couldn't have gone on much longer!'

He paused, then grinned, 'The American warship that appeared out of the dim dawn of our final night adrift was by far the most glorious sight I have ever seen in my entire life. Even if I was to live to be a hundred, I would never see a more sublime sight than that ship coming to our aid.'

'You must have been in poor physical shape after that terrible ordeal, John.'

'Yes, I was. We were all badly dehydrated and had lost a huge amount of weight. There was not a spare ounce of fat or flesh left on any of our famished bodies.' He grinned, 'Those twelve days were a real strict dieting, weight losing regime!'

Edmund laughed,'A rather drastic weight losing programme surely?'

Joining in the laughter, John agreed, 'Yes, it was. It's not one I could honestly recommend to anyone!'

Edmund raised his glass of whisky and once more drank a silent toast to John.

John drank not one, but two silent toasts. The first was to his four great comrades who had shared that lifeboat with him; the second was in memory of his fine shipmates who had died when H.M.S. Flash was torpedoed.

John's glass was now empty, but his mind was still full of vivid memories of that unforgettable ordeal. He smiled at Edmund, 'It wasn't only the hardtack ships biscuits that kept me alive; the watertight tin box the biscuits were kept in also played a part, a vital part, in keeping me not only alive but sane.'

With his brow furrowed in a puzzled frown Edmund asked, 'Oh, how was that?.... What was so special about that tin box?'

'It was what was written on that box – "Biscuits made by Carr's of

Carlisle". As you know, Carlisle is not far from my hometown of Keswick. Every time I saw that name "Carlisle" it keenly reminded me of my home and my mother and sister in Keswick. And from there it was an effortless leap to the top of "My mountain", Skiddaw. During some hours of those dreary long days, and during many more hours of the endless dark nights I felt I was not really in that lifeboat. It was as if I was not actually afloat on the amazingly dormant North Atlantic's ceaseless procession of steady rolling swells. I was swept away by pleasant dreams to carefree stroll around a hallucinatory Lakeland Heaven of familiar friendly hills and gentle, smooth rolling fells.'

Edmund quietly smiled with ready empathy. He again consulted his notes. 'And it was not so very long after that exhausting ordeal before you were once more on sea-going duty; were not just on "normal" convoy escorting duties, but were on that most terrible and dangerous of all convoys you've already mentioned – a winter convoy to Russia'

John quietly murmured, 'Yes, I was' He said no more.

Edmund was also thoughtfully silent for some time. He eventually asked, 'Did it take you long to get fit enough to take part in those demanding S.B.S operations again?'

'No, not too long. I was sent on some especially tough and strenuous training exercises which were designed to get me fully fit again,' – he grinned – 'or to damn well kill me in the attempt!' He sighed, 'Ah yes, I really was exceptionally fit then. Of course I was young (and perhaps foolish) then.' It was now his turn to ask a question, 'Is your brother Harry going to write an official history of the S.B.S.?'

'No, I'm afraid he's not. After what he discovered in those S.B.S archives he was very keen to write that history. He most strongly feels – and I wholeheartedly agree with him – that all those truly amazing and often most important S.B.S exploits should be better known. The outstanding bravery of all those, like you John, who took part in those operations should be now recognised, not only officially, but by a much wider public. However the "powers that be" don't want that.

'Although it's getting on for twenty five years since the end of the war the government "top brass" still insist on keeping those S.B.S activities strictly secret. Harry was most definitely refused permission to write their history or to disclose the least thing about them. He still hopes to write that history, but perhaps he'll not be given permission to do so until another twenty five years have passed.'

John said, 'I'm not surprised by that official refusal. On the last holiday Anna and I had in Holland before she died we saw for ourselves – even at that considerable length of time since the end of the war – just how strong were the feelings, how deep were the divisions between the Dutch Patriots who had resisted the Krauts and those Dutch who had collaborated with them. The release of details of some of our S.B.S. activities in the Netherlands would probably only lead to increased bitterness, to deeper divisions in already deeply divided Dutch families.

'And things were even worse in France. From personal experience I know just how irreconcilable were the divisions between the Communist Resistance Groups and the Gaullist Resistance Fighters. Most members of each of those groups were implacable enemies. Many of them seemed more interested in betraying members of rival groups to the Germans, rather than actively resisting the Boche. Some of our S.B.S duties in France entailed "eliminating" specific members of certain groups who (so we were assured) had betrayed other Frenchmen.

'Yes, Edmund, I find it quite understandable that British Government officials don't want to release details of many of our secret wartime activities in France and Holland. If full details of a number of our missions were to be made public in these countries it would be like pouring petrol on to those old, but still smouldering wartime fires.'

'Yes,' Edmund said, 'things must have been extremely difficult for everyone living in these countries during the ruthless German occupation. It is not surprising that neighbours were divided from neighbours; sons divided from fathers; and (perhaps worst of all?) brothers were – Cain and Abel like – estranged from brothers by deadly deep divisions.'

John wondered if the emphasis Edmund seemed to put on the divisions between brothers was an obliquely hinted reference to those Dutch brothers: Frans Maurik and Professor Willem Maurik? Had Edmund discovered the full details of those so very different brothers – one a brave Patriot, the other a despicable traitor? Did he now know of his part in Professors Maurik's violent death?

Watching Edmund search through his untidy bundle of papers John somehow felt increasingly sure that he was searching for his notes on those two Dutch brothers.

Although Edmund *was* looking for such notes, he was distracted from that search by something that caught his eye on another page. Lifting the page he grinned and remarked, 'Oh, John, I see that your S.B.S. code name was "Piranha 004", wasn't it?'

'Yes it was.' He laughed, 'The S.O.E. gave us such names long before James Bond's 007(licenced to kill) code became so famous.'

Edmund's laughter mingled with John's. 'But surely some of your S.B.S missions were as fantastic as any of James Bond's exploits, weren't they?'

'Aye, they were. And Sean Connery had only to pretend to fearlessly fight, ruthlessly kill, and ingeniously escape being killed. We, the Royal Navy's most expert, most voraciously deadly "Piranhas" did all that James Bond stuff for real!'

Edmund grinned and continued searching through his notes. Finding what he was looking for he lifted up some pages and immediately became engrossed in reading them.

After silently watching him for a while John smiled and asked, 'What have you got there that seems so engrossing?'

Edmund looked up. He stared at John. He did not smile. For what seemed a long, nervously hesitant time he continued staring at John.

When, in response to John's steady enquiring gaze, Edmund did speak up he did so in an un-typical nervous uncertain manner as if not sure if he should proceed or stay silent. 'I'm reading … I'm again reading all about "Operation Waterloo", John.'

This was what John had intuitively guessed. He asked, 'Are full details of my part in that operation in my S.B.S. file?'

'Yes they are.' He again hesitated then, it seemed, somewhat apprehensively said, ' But Harry and I also found some additional details about Operation Waterloo in what had been an absolutely top-secret S.O.E. file as well. That most secret information put rather a different – a tragically different – slant on that entire operation'.

There was another uncertain silence until John ended it by demanding, 'Tell me what you discovered in that top-secret S.O.E. file that puts such a "tragically different" slant on Operation Waterloo. Surely I – the only S.B.S. survivor of that operation – deserves to be told everything you know about it.'

'Yes, John, I entirely agree. You more than anyone is entitled to know what we discovered. I'm afraid, however, that you'll find this new knowledge rather distressing.' Edmund glanced at his notes then said, 'First of all John, please tell me your version of "Operation Waterloo".'

John did so. He ended by saying, 'So, once I killed that second despicable Dutch traitor, Professor Maurik, that was this vitally important operation successfully completed.' It was now his turn to hesitate; he sighed then added, 'It was a most amazing, a most regrettable coincidence that that second traitor turned out to be Anna's father.'

Edmund nodded, 'Yes, that was terribly unfortunate.' He then solemnly asked, 'How long is it since Anna died, John? ... About five years, isn't it?'

'Yes. In two months time it will be exactly five years since she died.' That simple quiet statement hid a tempest of suppressed emotions. All two clearly, all too painfully he remembered not only Anna's tragic death but all the soul-searing months before it when she bravely and almost uncomplainingly fought against the insidiously relentless, then hideously rapid progress of the cancers that triumphantly killed her.

'I'm very sorry to re-awaken such painful memories for you John, but there's one more question I must ask about Anna. Did she know that it was you who had killed her father?'

'Oh, no!.., No thank God she never knew that. Such knowledge would have been too much for her to bear. Nor did she know that her father was a terrible traitor. She was so nobly patriotic herself that she could not have coped with the awful burden of her father's treachery.'

'Yes, John, it was a real blessing that poor Anna never had to undergo any terrible mental, moral and spiritual agonies over you having had to kill her father because of his supposed treachery.'

' His supposed treachery ?.... what do you mean by that, Edmund? Surely Anna's father was undoubtedly a most despicable traitor who had been doing his utmost to help the Germans develop their atomic-bomb!'

'Yes, Edmund said, 'That's what everyone in Royal Navy Intelligence and almost everyone in the S.O.E were convinced of at the time. That's why Operation Waterloo was decided on.' He paused then reluctantly explained, ' But I'm afraid that those were not the true facts. I am really sorry to have to tell you this, John, but the actual truth is that both Professor Willem Maurik and Professor Johannes de Waal were secretly and most bravely both very great Dutch Patriots.'

John seemed stunned. 'But... but,' he stammered, 'surely, oh surely, that can't be true!' He paused, he gathered his wits, 'If they were really Patriots how could our Naval Intelligence and our S.O.E. officers in control of Dutch Operations have got it so terribly wrong?'

'Commander Richardson, the R.N. Intelligence Officer who briefed us on "Operation Waterloo", repeatedly told us that those two Dutch Professors were most vile and important traitors who had to be killed at all costs.'

'Yes, I know John. I've read his briefings in those secret files. But what Harry and I read in another – an even more secret – S.O.E. file explained how that terrible error came about. While pretending to be helping the Germans develop an atomic bomb they were actually doing everything they could to delay progress on that evil, potentially war-winning Hun weapon.' He risked a quick grin, 'I don't suppose you know too much about Nuclear Physics, do you, John? I don't pretend to understand much about that esoteric science either, but it seems that those two Dutch Professors, especially Professor Maurik, who seemingly was a brilliant nuclear physicist, persuaded the German scientists to continue to bombard uranium with *fast* neutrons as the quickest way to create an atomic weapon, while in fact he felt sure that to bombard it with *slow* neutrons was the best way to create that weapon.

'Not only did those two secret Dutch Patriots do everything to confuse and delay the Kraut boffins but they also sent what information they could get about how the German's weapon was progressing to S.O.E. Headquarters in London. Of course this vital secret information and the names of the agents who were providing it were kept absolutely top-secret. Only the Director and Deputy Director of the S.O.E. knew of and directly dealt with those two agents. Even their officers dealing with other secret operations in The Netherlands did not know that these two Dutch physicists were working for British Intelligence.

'It was this need for utmost secrecy that brought about their tragic deaths.

'Naval Intelligence had somehow been informed that those two Dutch Professors were vile traitors helping the Germans. With a minimum of consultation with the S.O.E., a S.B.S. team was quickly trained to kill these traitors in "Operation Waterloo".'

'Yes', John said, 'I remember that we in that team were pleased and quietly proud that our own Senior Service seemed to be organising this operation rather than the upstart S.O.E.!'

Edmund nodded, 'Yes, but it was that unfortunate lack of full co-operation between these two Intelligence Services that caused this fatal mistake.'

John sighed, 'Oh, Edmund, it's terrible to think that those two "traitors" I ruthless killed were actually brave Dutch Patriots... and they must have been very brave. It would take an exceptional type of courage to constantly pretend to be willingly working with the Germans while all the time they hated and despised these arrogant Krauts. They must have been well aware of the terrible fate that awaited them if the Germans ever discovered the truth about them. I'm sure they could all too vividly imagine the hideous tortures Gestapo sadists would inflict on them before the sneering executioner's bullet exploded through that boiling cauldron of unbearable pain that had once been a great scientific brain.'

'Yes,' Edmund agreed, 'they must have lived and worked under dreadful stress.' He did not say so, but he guessed that John's eloquent picture of Gestapo torture and execution accurately reflected some of his own thoughts and feelings and repressed fears on those many occasions when he too had faced the threat of such diabolical treatment.

'And there would be the additional stress of being hated and despised by the patriotic Dutchmen who knew of – or guessed of – what seemed their vile collaboration with the Krauts.' John paused. He stared steadily at Edmund, 'And I killed those two outstandingly brave Dutch heroes!'

He clearly remembered the scene at that small stone bridge where he had halted Professor Maurik and accused him of being a traitor who deserved to die. He vividly recalled – and now realised the meaning of what that Patriotic Dutchman had with hands raised in desperate pleading, been trying to tell him as he urgently gasped, "No, no, you do not understand!... I... I..."

John now thought he felt his trigger finger guiltily tremble as it had most certainly not trembled all those year ago, but had twice resolutely squeezed the trigger of his accurately aimed automatic pistol. He held up his right hand. Was that finger really trembling?... Was it – was he – trembling with guilt? Was it correct that he should feel deep guilt?

With sensitive empathy Edmund sensed John's feelings. With convincing authority he reassured him. 'Oh, John, of course it's understandable that you should feel some guilt at having killed these two Dutch Patriots, but surely you are not really responsible for those unfortunate deaths. You were resolutely doing what you had been assured was your correct duty; you were bravely obeying your most definite orders. Surely the real responsibility and the guilt – if there really is any – lies with our Intelligence Services and their often pathological reluctance to share intelligence secrets with each other.'

As John nodded his thanks and eager agreement Edmund rose to his feet, 'Give me your empty glass, John, I think another dram would not go astray!'

Once he was again comfortably settled in his armchair he lifted his glass and gave a toast, 'Here's to you John. I reiterate that you really must not let those tragic deaths get to you too much. Surely any guilt about these mistaken killings is far outweighed by the secret pride you must, fully justifiably, feel about your other S.B.S operations. Some of these dangerous missions saved many lives, didn't they?

'By destroying German V1 flying-bombs and V2 rockets in France and Holland you must have helped save hundred of lives in London. In "Operation Starlight" you helped directly save the lives of more than fifty Dutch Patriots (including that important scientist) by rescuing them after they had been captured by the Krauts. Then your many varied activities at and behind the Normandy beaches before and on D/Day must have helped save the lives of many British soldiers as they struggled ashore on that historic day.'

Once more John nodded in agreement. 'Thank you, Edmund. Yes, all you say is true .I'm confident I know myself well enough to be sure I won't let any foolish excess of unwarranted guilt build up in me. I was startled and dismayed by your sudden unexpected revelations about those Dutch Professors; thankfully however I'm sure I know a way I can to a certain extent make amends for those disastrously mistaken killings. Perhaps I'll even be able to do some positive good with this new knowledge.

'But before I explain that, Edmund, I would like to know if you found out anything in those secret files about how close the Germans got to having nuclear weapons.'

'It's quite a coincidence you should ask that, John. My brother

Harry deliberately found out quite a lot about that. As he's not allowed to write about the S.B.S., he's hoping instead (if he gets permission) to write about the frantic race between the Americans, the Germans and the Japanese to be the first nation to have nuclear weapons.'

'The Japanese?' John gasped. 'I didn't know they were in that desperate race!'

'No, very few people do. But they were... they most certainly were.' Edmund again searched through his bundle of notes. 'Ah, here we are. Two of Japan's leading nuclear physicists were in Germany working with the Huns to develop an atomic bomb. Just before the Germans surrendered they sailed in the large modern U-boat, U-234, with a secret cargo of 1,100 pounds of uranium oxide (enough to make two atomic bombs). They were heading for Japan to urgently continue work on this uranium.

'However on the 7th May, 1945 – one week after Hitler committed suicide – Grand Admiral Dönitz broadcast to all German Armed Forces ordering them to surrender to the victorious British, American and Russia Allies.

'Despite the furious protests of the Japanese, the U-boat's German captain obeyed these orders. He surrender to a American warship. Refusing to surrender, the two Japanese scientists did the "honourable" thing. They ritualistically committed hari-kari. That German uranium oxide was taken to America. No doubt it was used in the "Manhattan Project" and, with true poetic justice, helped produce the American atomic bombs which finally defeated Germany's tough, tenacious Eastern Ally, Japan.'

With fervent eagerness John said, 'Yes, thank God the Yanks did get those atomic bombs before the Krauts and the Japs. Without these decisive weapons the war against the Japs might have gone on for years longer.'

Edmund nodded in whole-hearted agreement, 'Yes, every Jap soldier and all their civilian "Home Guards" who were training to defend their Japanese homeland had sworn never to surrender, but to fight to the death. It was estimated that if the Americans had had to mount a large-scale invasion of the Japanese mainland they might have suffered over one million casualties; and the Japs could have had at least five million army and civilian casualties before being forced to surrender.'

It was now John's turn to nod his agreement, 'Yes, and I – and you too, Edmund – might well have been only two of many thousands of British life's lost if that invasion had gone ahead. And I remember a friend who had been taken prisoner by the Japs telling me that the brutal commander of the P.O.W camp had repeatedly warned them that if any American or British soldiers dared land on the sacred soil of the Japanese Homeland every Allied prisoner of war would immediately be killed in a ruthless wholesale massacre.'

Edmund again became engrossed with his notes. He refreshed his memory then said, 'There's another thing that hardly anyone knows about the Japs and atomic weapons. At dawn on the 9th August, 1945 (the very day that the second American atomic bomb was dropped on Nagasaki) the Japanese detonated their own nuclear device near a small island off the Hungnam Coast in the Sea of Japan. Containing only about five kilos of uranium, that device was tiny compared to the awesome weapon that had devastated Hiroshima and the bomb that would devastate Nagasaki later that same day.

'However it was powerful enough to vaporise not only the boat it was on, but also many of the fishing boats with their Japanese guinea-pig crews deliberately moored around it!'

Once more he glanced at his notes. 'Oh, and another thing Harry discovered was that the Japs, who years before had conquered Korea and were still occupying it, had as a matter of urgency greatly increased the amount of uranium they were mining in that country.'

John said, ' I knew nothing about all that. I did know the race to be first to get an atomic bomb had been close, but I didn't realize just how desperately close it had been.' Suddenly, unexpectedly, he grinned, 'Obviously, as the Duke of Wellington remarked about the Battle of Waterloo: "It was a damn close run thing!" And I played some small part in that race; a good part by helping rescue that Nuclear Physicist, Professor Paul Van Karson from the Germans; a tragically bad part by killing those Patriotic Nuclear Physicist, Professors Maurik and de Waal.'

Edmund repeated his reassuring statement, 'Oh John, you are not to blame for those mistaken killings. Such mistakes often happen amidst the obscuring fogs and confusions of war. Quite often what seemed for the best turns out to be for the worst; or – as the three witches in Macbeth more poetically express it: "Fair is foul, and foul is fair..."'

Continuing with that theme, John grinned as he went on to complete that quotation, 'Yes, things were often extremely confusing as we in our secretive, nocturnal, S.B.S teams had to wraith-like "hover through the fog and filthy air!"'

Edmund laughed then asked, 'What were you going to tell me about hoping to bring something positive out of those unfortunate mistaken killings?'

'Oh yes. Yes, well as you know, Edmund, practically no one in Britain except those who, like your brother Harry and you, have had access to those secret files knows about my killing of Professor Maurik. And, as far as I know, only one person in Holland knows the truth about his sudden, mysterious death. That one Dutchman is the dead Professor's brother, Frans Maurik.'

John gave Edmund full details of how he had been hidden at that Dutch farm and how well he had been looked after by Frans and his wife, Blanche He gave discreetly censored details of just how wonderfully Anna and he had got on together there. He explained why Professor Maurik sudden arrival at this farm had forced him, John, to reveal to Frans Maurik his secret knowledge of his brother's terrible treachery. He told of how, after long and tortuous discussion and agonised soul-searching, Frans had finally reconciled himself to the grim fact that his treacherous brother had to be killed. 'And,' John concluded, 'as I was the only highly trained, well experienced killer perfectly positioned to kill him, that most unpleasant, but vitally necessary task devolved on me... But now, thank God, I can at last do something, even if only in some small measure, to redeem that tragic killing.

'As you know, Edmund, we – Anna and I – used to go every summer to visit her relations in Holland. We either stayed with Anna's brother, Jan, and his wife at the family farm that was now Jan's, or with Anna's uncle and aunt, Frans and Blanche, at their retirement cottage near that farm.

'As the post-war years rapidly and happily passed, what had been all too vivid memories of wartime horrors began, mercifully, to fade. All that is except for one horrible memory that Frans had and, instead of fading, seemed to be increasingly and more painfully festering. That memory was of his brother's terrible treachery. Each year Frans confided to me – and to me alone – his continuing inability to understand, to forget, or to forgive that inexcusable treachery.

'Well, Edmund, now I can joyfully remove that false stigma of vile treachery from Frans's brother. I will take a week's holiday as soon as possible; will go to Holland; will tell Frans his brother was no traitor but was a truly great Dutch Patriot.

'Frans will be overjoyed by this news of his brother's vindication. And I am sure he will nobly forgive me and absolve me from any guilt for my having mistakenly killed his brother.'

★ ★ ★

And Frans *was* overjoyed.... was almost deliriously overjoyed! And he *did* whole-heartedly absolve John from any blame or guilt!

Standing together in the secluded corner of Frans's garden where John had revealed the truth about his brother to him, Frans fiercely grasped John's hand with both of his and repeatedly gasped, 'Oh I..I don't know how to thank you! I.. I don't know how to express my feelings!. The.... the tremendous delight, the absolute wonder I feel is inexpressible! You've lifted an enormous burden from me. The overwhelming relief I feel is like having a tooth that has been painfully and almost insistently aching for years finally removed.

'I could never reconcile myself to my brother's terrible treachery. I could have understood if he had only been a "normal" minor traitor; one of the many – the all too many – Dutch collaborators. But his having seemingly prostituted his great scientific brain to such a perverse and obscene use as to help the Krauts develop an atomic bomb was completely unforgivable. I found it agonising to think he could carry out treacherous research which might have resulted in Hitler winning the war, could have meant not only The Netherlands but all of Europe living forever under brutal Nazi tyranny.'

Once Frans grew somewhat calmer John suggested, 'Perhaps we could manage to tell your nephew, Jan, that his father was a true Dutch Patriot, without, of course giving away too much, and certainly without revealing my regrettable part in his death.'

Frans immediately agreed. So that very evening Jan and his wife, Sonja, and Frans's wife, Blanche, were told that Professor Maurik had, while pretending to work with the Krauts, actually been a secret Dutch Patriot. That other supposed traitor, Professor Johannes de Waal,

415

an only son whose parents were now dead, had no close relatives to be informed of his actual true patriotism.

Their — especially Jan's — excited interest and positive pleasure at this unexpected news was great, but, never having known that the professor had been thought to be a vile traitor, was nothing like as great as Frans's delirious pleasure had been.

Many questions were eagerly asked and were apparently openly and honestly answered. But Frans and John were careful only to give the guarded answers they had agreed on before so as to remove all risk of John's part in Professor Maurik's death being inadvertently disclosed.

Delighted to learn of his father's patriotism in Holland while be himself had been serving with the Royal Netherlands Navy in the Far East, Jan suggested that they should soon all make a pilgrimage to this hero's grave and pay their heartfelt respects to his belatedly revealed bravery.

This suggestion was greeted with unanimous acclaim; and so the following afternoon as soon as Jan and Sonja's eight year old twin daughters were released from school the four of them met up with Frans, Blanche and John and then the entire party made their way along the narrow quiet road that led to the cemetery. Their chattering progress was abruptly halted by the warning ringing of bicycle bells close behind them. Then the voices of the two youthful cyclists who cheerfully passed them announced them to be Germans — some of the younger generation who were now daring to visit a number of the countries a previous generation of Huns had brutally occupied.

As he heard that so well remembered, that so hated harsh guttural language John gave an involuntary shudder as his senses tingled a warning signal up his spine to his brain. The war was long over but its effects could still spring actively alive in nerves, blood and brain.

However a younger generation than John's reacted quite differently. The Dutch schoolgirl twins glanced at one another and, reading the same mischievous thought in the other's sparkling eyes, went into a fit of giggles then shrilly shouted after the Germans, 'Oh, Hans, give our Mother and Father their bicycles back!'

The German youths waved and continued on their way.

Encouraged by their parents unrestrained laughter, the girls went into a bout of even more hilariously uncontrolled giggles.

Eventually, with tears of mirth running down her glowing checks, their mother half-heartedly reprimanded, 'Oh, girls, that was very naughty; was not a polite thing to shout at those poor German tourists.'

Once his laughter was under control Frans explained to John, 'After the Krauts defeated then occupied our country they went on a vicious looting spree.

'They took away almost everything easily movable they could lay their thieving hands on. Many paintings; radios and binoculars; cars and motorcycles; and, perhaps the most sorely felt loss of all, many thousands of our bicycles were snatched from us.

'For our young Dutch children that shrill request they impertinently shout after visiting Krauts is something of a cheery hangover from that grim time they had been told about.'

John grinned, 'It's quite understandable that many passed on memories of the war and the German occupation should linger on amongst your school children.' He laughed, 'But at least it was pleasing to see that those young Krauts only waved and no longer raised their right hand in a stiff-armed Nazi salute!'

After having heartily laughed at the cheeky antics of the twins, Blanche had keenly listened to John's remarks. She now asked, 'Do your son and daughter take much interest in hearing about the war – about "our war" – John?'

'No, they don't. Not now. When he was a boy, William enjoyed reading – "reading" the lurid pictures mainly – in boys comics and magazines full of the exciting heroic triumphs of British Commandos against the dastardly evil Huns and the deviously inscrutable Japs. But now that he's at teacher training college his only interest seems to be in sports. I'm delighted that he's so mad keen on rock-climbing, hill-walking, skiing and camping. He hopes eventually to teach these activities.

'As for my scatter-brained teenage daughter, Elizabeth, she seems interested in nothing but pop-music. The walls of her bedroom are plastered with huge, garish posters of the Beatles and other, lesser, pop-groups.'

Blanche laughed with sympathetic understanding, 'Oh, John, I suppose that's a phase every teenage girl has to go through. The Beatles are extremely popular here in The Netherlands too.' Giving a bright loving glance at her husband who was tolerantly smiling at her, she cheerily and perhaps a touch ruefully admitted, 'As Frans will tell you, I am, even at my age, quite fond of the Beatles myself!'

Frans laughed, ' "Quite fond?"... Oh, Blanche, you know you are absolutely besotted with them! And not only with their – so you assure me – *great* music, but with their – as you again assure me they have – *great*, beautiful and charming personalities!'

All merriment and laughter faded away as they entered the cemetery. Even the twins vivacious chatter and easily triggered girlish giggles were instinctively suppressed as they slowly walked through this oppressive place of solemn silence.

The entire group gathered around the familiar grave. All read the few words carved on the unpretentious gravestone. These words announced nothing but the names and dates of birth and death of Jan's parents.

The two young girls were, understandably, the first to breach the increasingly tense solemnity before it became too unbearable. With eyes that hinted of tearful desperation, they stared up at their mother and pleaded, 'Oh , mum, can we put our flowers on grandma and grandpa's grave now, please?'

'What?... Oh, No!.... No, you must give the flowers to Uncle Frans and to your father. It is their proper right and duty to place the flowers on their brother's and their father's grave.'

Obediently, if rather reluctantly, the flowers were handed over.

Frans went first. With profound reverence he placed the neat bunch of gleaming creamy pink tulips on the grave of his brother in heartfelt tribute to his belatedly revealed most brave patriotism. After standing for some emotional, head-bowed time he stepped aside and made way for Jan.

As Jan placed his glossy blood red tulips on his parents grave he thought them a fitting tribute to his patriotic father not only from him, his only living son, but also from every Dutchman who had bravely, fought for The Netherlands during the war.

To the circle of solemn onlookers the long minutes that Jan motionlessly stood with bowed head seemed to stretch out with agonising slowness.

As if in a hypnotic trance he continued to stare at the few words on his parents gravestone. Then he gave a nervous start and made a sudden, definite decision.\

He raised his head and looked at the silent group who were staring at him with sincere and palpable sympathy. In a voice which, while unsteadied by emotion, was bright with pride, he informed them, 'I will see the stonemason tomorrow morning. I have decided that, now we know the truth about my father's wartime patriotism, there are too few words on his gravestone. Below his name, "Professor Willem Maurik," I will get the mason to engrave in big, bold, proud letters the words, "A Great, Brave, Dutch Patriot."'